The Green Mamba

Rowan MacNeill

Spruce Goose Publications

For more information about Rowan MacNeill and Spruce Goose Publications, go online at: http s://rowanmacneillstoryteller.com/

Contents

The mass of men lead lives of quiet desperation.
Henry David Thoreau

This place where you are, right now,
God has circled on a map for you.
Hafez (1325–1390)
(translated from the Persian)

Foreword

I must have been snoozing, stretched out on my hotel bed, when the hammering on the door brought me abruptly awake. There was an authoritative, almost military rhythm to it, and my first befuddled thought was: *that* is *not* housekeeping.

It sounded more like police, but the police couldn't have caught up with me so quickly; besides, I hadn't done anything illegal – at least, not here, not in Cambodia. But, who could it be? I only knew a handful of people in the country, and none of them were in Phnom Penh – and then it came back to me – in the last few days, half of those people had lost their lives. The memory caught me unawares, as if I might have momentarily forgotten all that had happened ...

The rapid staccato of knocks again.

I levered myself up and moved towards the door, then, with a guilty start, doubled back to push the little flight bag further under my bed, out of sight. Then I opened the door.

It took me a moment to recognise the two figures standing in the corridor. The one in front, the one who was doing the knocking, was a broad-built man in his early sixties, with lively eyes and iron-grey hair and a formidable moustache. The man behind him was a great bear of a man in a brown suit, slightly younger, with close-cropped hair and a square, unsmiling face.

I remembered who they were.

'Jesus Christ!' I said.

'No,' said the first man, a wide grin under his moustache. 'But almost as good, yes? *Andrew Simonovich!* So! You are pleased to see your old Russian friends?'

It seems odd to say that now, in the light of what has happened in the years since, but I actually *was* pleased to see them. Odder still, come to think of it, that one was Russian and the other a Ukrainian. Dmitry and Nikolai, two friendly faces in a strange land, very far from home.

'Yes, of course,' I managed to say as the first man, Dmitry, shook my hand in a grip that could have cracked walnuts. I stood staring at them like a fool, then, after my fingers were released, extended a hand towards Nikolai, who took it more gently and offered a smile.

Being English, of course I couldn't leave them standing in the corridor, so I stepped back to let them in. Dmitry strode past me; Nikolai ducked his head as he stepped under the door frame. I found myself glancing toward the bed, checking that the flight bag was well hidden, then I moved across to the window.

'Nice room,' said Dmitry, nodding at the décor. 'Nice hotel, I like it.'

'Yes,' I agreed. There was a silence. 'So tell me, how did you know to find me here?'

'Ha!' snorted Dmitry contemptuously, in that way only Russians can. 'How can you even ask us such a thing, Andrew Simonovich?' (I belatedly recalled the Russian habit of making a middle name from the father's first name – my father was Simon, so *Simonovich*). 'This is who we are, this is what we do, finding things out. Do you forget that we, Nikolai and I, were members of the greatest secret service in the world? Forget your Deuxième Bureau, your CIA, your MI6 – Russian Intelligence was the best of all!'

'You mean ... the KGB?' I ventured.

'Of course, KGB!' he growled, smiling broadly.

Behind him, Nikolai was muttering something in Russian.

'What's he saying?' I asked.

'He is saying something impolite about your famous British Secret Service.'

'What?'

'Nothing good.'

'Go on, tell me,' I said.

'Very well,' shrugged Dmitry, 'he is saying that if people are so impressed by a man driving down a road in an Aston Martin – then let them go and harness a dog sled team in the night, with the mercury at twenty below, and drive it through a pass in the Urals, navigating only by the stars. He says to try that, and you can call such a man ...'

'A real spy?' I offered.

'A real driver,' said Dmitry, shrugging again. 'Of course, Nikolai is only speaking from personal experience.'

'I see,' I said.

'So,' continued Dmitry, 'you ask me how we know you are here. Simple. We hear that an Englishman is brought by the British Embassy, here, to Phnom Penh, and checks in at the Sunway Hotel in the name *Richard Powell* – but then books a flight to Britain in the name of *Andrew Finch*. This is how we find you.'

'Oh,' I said and nodded. For want of something else to say, I pulled aside the net curtain and glanced out, across the road and the manicured island of grass, washed by the flat tropical sunlight. Beyond the palm trees, I could just see the little row of *tuk-tuk* taxis lined up, their drivers waiting and chatting to each other.

'So,' said Dmitry, following my gaze, 'you are here, back safe and sound. And where is our fat American friend?'

'The American?'

'Yes, the American, Bullen.'

'Ah, yes,' I said slowly. 'Bullen ...'

Bullen

One Week earlier

You know Bullen, don't you?

Big American fellow, six-two, six-three maybe, and with his belly hanging out over his belt like the gone-to-seed football player that he must have been. He is heavy-jawed, with a voice like gravel in a bucket and he has those bright, clever eyes that disappear into the creases of his face when he smiles.

Bullen is the guy laughing loudest at the end of the bar, the guy who is always ready with a grin, a joke, happy to buy you a drink.

So, you know him, right? Because I'm pretty sure that *he* knows *you*.

I say this because Bullen knows just about everybody. I never met a man who was so connected, who – no matter what you might want – always 'knew a guy' or 'knew a place'. Whether it was a complicated valve assembly that you needed in a hurry in the wilds of upcountry Ghana, or a beer at two in the morning in a dry Gulf state, Bullen knew where to go and who to ask. He was that kind of a guy, the *Hell-Yes* guy, endlessly persuasive, good-humoured, enthusiastic.

I have never entirely trusted people like that.

It was a week earlier, and there he was, as large as life, grinning at me, his meaty hand reaching forward.

'Andy Finch, right?' he said as I took the outstretched hand – and, for all he was thirty or forty pounds overweight, he had some grip on him. 'It is you, isn't it? Well, *Lordy* Lord, Andy, I declare! I did *not* expect to find you here, of all places!'

Here, by the way, being the flyblown waiting area of the little airport at Battambang in northern Cambodia – the sort of place where the departure board is a blackboard and chalk and the terminal building is basically a shed – and I certainly hadn't expected to meet Bullen here, or anyone else for that matter. I was on my way home from a consulting job in the city, waiting for my flight to Hanoi and then on back to the UK, so I was just as surprised at meeting him as he was at meeting me.

Meanwhile, Bullen was treating me like a long-lost brother, clapping me on the shoulder, telling me how I looked damned well (which I didn't), firing questions at me without waiting for answers.

'Say, though,' he said at length. 'Ain't this just the damnedest thing? I'm stood here waiting for this German fella and I'm starting to think he's a no-show. Then you turn up, just like that! And an Englishman, better still! Who needs Krauts, eh? Everyone trusts the Brits, right? You guys have that thing you do, you know,' he tipped me a conspiratorial wink, 'Stiff upper lip, *gravitas,* poker up the ass, whatever ... rest of the world don't know you as well as us Yanks, do they? It'll be perfect. You still hiring out on your day rate? What I'm saying is: can I hire you, to work for me? Starting right now, this minute. Three, four ... *five* days tops. What're you charging these days?'

I don't think, so far, that I had managed to get a word in edgeways. I was taken aback by meeting him out of the blue – the last time I'd seen him must have been a couple of years back and a few thousand miles away. Whenever I'm at a loss, I tend to say nothing – and now this unexpected offer of work. And, if I was honest, I wasn't busy, nothing on for the next couple of weeks – which to the self-employed is the worst thing; no work equals no income. I could certainly do with the money – so I hesitated, mentally adding half to my usual day rate and rounding it up. When I gave him the figure, he clapped me on the shoulder again, grinned broadly and said that was fine, *hell no,* he'd go one better, he'd put twenty-five per cent on top, and give me five days – whether the job needed that long or not. *How about that, then?*

'Plus expenses, of course,' I said, wondering if I was pushing it a bit too far.

'Sure!' he exclaimed. 'You're working for the Yanks now! But listen, there ain't going to be any expenses, because we're gonna put it all straight onto my tab – including the bar bill!' He chuckled, either pleased at how well things were working out or in anticipation of the amount of drinking we were going to do.

'So, you've got an M&E problem you need solving?' I asked.

He stared back at me, momentarily uncertain.

'M&E,' I repeated. 'You know, Mechanical and Electrical? Ventilation? Air Conditioning? Pipes and wires? Some contractual dispute you need an opinion on?'

'Oh,' he replied carefully. 'Oh, yes, I see.'

'Because that's what I do,' I said, thinking perhaps he had mistaken me for someone else. 'Mechanical services.'

'Oh, *no*, not that at all; *oh no*, this is something entirely different.'

'What?' I said.

'Oh, don't worry, you'll love it – and you can do it standing on your head.' He looked at my bemused expression. 'Think of it as a little *adventure*. You're going to thank me, I promise you.'

I was still hesitating. He laid a friendly hand on my shoulder: 'You know what they say, Andy? A *change* is as good as a rest – you should embrace the opportunity to do something different! Come on, man, say you're in!'

But then a thought occurred to me, so I said:

'Hang on though. I just — no, I'm sorry, I can't do it. I have a ticket here, booked all the way through to London. The first connection is in —'

'Get 'em to bump it for a week,' he said decisively. 'No problem!'

'I doubt that they'll do that,' I said.

'Sure they will.'

'I don't think so.'

'*Sure* they will – just go ask 'em!'

I hesitated.

'Listen, don't worry,' he said cheerfully. 'Let me do it. I know how to talk to these people. They'll do anything for you, if you ask them right – no problem. Give me your passport and the ticket.'

I imagined, when he said it, that he had been in Cambodia for a while and had maybe picked up a bit of the language, something to give him an advantage in negotiations. So I watched with interest as he elbowed his way to the front of the queue at the desk, brushing aside the locals – the Cambodians are a slim, delicate people with natural good manners. I can't imagine what they must have thought of this hulking Yankee moving amongst them muttering *Comin' through*, and '*Scuse me, ma-am, this is an emergency*'.

Then, when he got to the front, he simply announced his request loudly and in English. I caught snippets of his conversation: 'See here, now, Miss' and 'Let me tell ya, darlin'', insisting, *insisting* that it was a matter of life and death that his friend got his ticket changed. The young woman behind the desk eventually relented (what else was she going to do?) and solemnly wrote out a new ticket – I'm not sure, but I think I saw a fifty-dollar bill being passed across – and Bullen elbowed his way back, scattering the locals in his wake, grinning broadly.

'There you go, like I told you, no problem,' he said and picked up one of my suitcases.

As I walked out through the swinging door, I glanced back at the woman at the desk, and saw her scan my ticket and tear it in two before dropping it into the waste bin.

Had I known what was coming, I would have gone straight back into the dingy little departure hall, crawled through the dust and dead flies beneath the desk, pulled that ticket out of the bin, glued it together, and run onto the tarmac and clung onto the plane until it took off.

If only I had known what was coming.

The first time that I had met Bullen – indeed, despite the fulsome greetings he had given me, the only time that I had previously met him – was at a project in Qatar. They were constructing a big office complex and I had been called in to look at a problem on the operation of the chilled water system. Bullen, meanwhile, had been brought in because there was a problem with the Indian labour building the concrete frame. Some local organiser was stirring up unrest, and the result was that the workforce had downed tools during the building of the third block. Management had held meetings with the sub-contractor and the trouble-maker, talked, made some concessions, and got nowhere.

Then they had sent for Bullen.

As far as I could tell, he had attended a couple of meetings, took himself off to a side office with a phone for an hour or so, then settled down in the bar to wait. Meanwhile, I had reviewed the design calculations and technical drawings, gone and looked at the pipework and ductwork installations on site, requested some changes and organised a series of tests.

I was awaiting the results of those tests; I had no idea what he was waiting for. We drank and we talked, setting the world to rights as men will do when they have too much time on their hands. I have to say that I had liked him; he was big and boisterous and exuded a sense of optimism. He was good company.

Occasionally I went to check on the testing or went to bed. Bullen stayed in the bar.

Two days later, the Indians came back on site and the work resumed.

Bullen got up (apparently no worse for wear for all the beer and whisky he had poured down his neck), shook hands with everyone and packed his bags.

I bumped into him in the corridor of the Management office. He said he was off and away; I must have asked him a question about that and he looked me in the eye and said:

'Well, I came to do a job and she's done. The men are back on the job. See you 'round.'

And that was all anyone knew about the mysterious, short-lived labour stoppage until it was mentioned, a couple of weeks later, that the local labour organiser's daughter was in hospital with two broken legs, the result of a nasty car crash, and the man himself was staying by her side. An accident, they said.

Well, I know that whoever had done that, it certainly wasn't Bullen – he hadn't moved from the bar in all the time he'd been there. Which is not to say that he didn't 'know a guy'.

Just before Bullen had come barrelling back into my life, I had been using the time, waiting for my flight, to make one of those phone calls that you sometimes need to make when you're a little company working for a big company, even though you hate having to do it.

'Hello,' I said when my call was answered. 'Is this Reardon Contracting? Can you put me through to the Accounts Department, please?'

I waited while the switchboard connected me. I dislike making international calls from my mobile; you can almost hear the meter clicking round.

'Hi,' I said. 'This is Andrew Finch, of Andrew Finch Consulting; do you have a payment going through for us today? I can give you the invoice number.'

I did so and waited while the Accounts Clerk went onto their system.

'I'm sorry, Mr Finch,' said the voice from several thousand miles away. 'I have nothing outstanding on your account.'

'Has it been paid already, perhaps?' I said. If it had been paid in the last few days, maybe it wouldn't have shown up on my bank statement yet.

'No, Mr Finch. The last payment we made to you was ... let me see ... two months ago. When was this payment due?'

'Last week,' I said, trying to remain composed and professional.

'Well, we do have your invoice here, Mr Finch, but we haven't yet received authorisation to process it.'

'Okay,' I said. 'Then can you put me through to Peter Barclay, please.'

'Certainly. Can you hold?'

I said that I would.

And I waited.

'Peter Barclay's office,' announced a female voice.

'Yes, hello, this is Andrew Finch. May I speak to Peter, please?'

'I'm afraid Mr Barclay is on leave this week. He'll be back in on Monday. Would you like to leave a voicemail?'

'No, thank you. I have an invoice which requires his authorisation. It's already overdue, actually. Is there anyone else there who could authorise it and get a payment put through?'

'I'm sorry, sir, but that would have to be Mr Barclay.'

'Nobody else?'

'Mr Clayborne, perhaps ... but he's in meetings now, for the rest of the afternoon. And I know he's out tomorrow. But if he's not familiar with the job, he probably wouldn't want to do it anyway. I'm sorry. Would it be possible to call back on Monday?'

I said, as calmly as I could: 'Would you let Peter know that I called, please?'

'Certainly, Mr Finch. I'll send him an email him right now. Is there anything else I can help you with?'

'No, thank you.'

'Goodbye, then.'

'Goodbye.'

I cut the connection.

Damn, *damn, damn!* I bit my lip and clicked back onto my online business bank balance. Unsurprisingly, it had not magically improved since I had checked it fifteen minutes before. It was hovering close to my overdraft limit – there wouldn't be enough there to cover my salary, and that meant problems with my own outgoings.

Damn!

My cash-flow issues had been going on for weeks, starting from when a company called Broughton Mechanical had gone down, declaring bankruptcy, owing me the best part of £16,000 – and that had left a shortfall that I was having to fill … which I couldn't do and simultaneously live with late payers – like Reardon *bloody* Contracting.

I had desperately needed that payment.

'You fancy a beer?' Bullen asked, pulling up a plastic chair at one of the little two-table cafés that proliferate on the pavements in Indochina. 'This here is out of the sun. Suit you?'

'Sure,' I nodded and sat down. We dumped my bags on a third chair, and Bullen signalled to the waiter.

'Two Angkor Beers,' he said. 'And I'll have a chaser. You got any Bourbon?'

The little waiter shook his head.

'Scotch?'

'Whisky? You want whisky?'

'Uh-huh.'

'I bring whisky. Two?'

'Not for me,' I said. 'One. Bring one.'

'Okay.'

'What sort of whisky you got?' said Bullen, but the waiter was already retreating and seemed not to hear. He turned to me: 'Guess I'll just get what I'll get, then.'

'That's generally what happens in these parts,' I agreed.

Bullen sighed heavily.

'Well, there you go, you see, isn't that kind of the problem with you Brits? You put up with shit. Us Yanks, we try to change things, make 'em better.'

'Uh-huh,' I said stiffly, 'and how exactly is that working out?'

He grinned broadly. For a moment, I had been on the edge of being offended – but somehow it was impossible to be annoyed with Bullen when he grinned like that.

'Almost got me having a serious conversation there, Andy,' he said, fishing a poisonous-looking black cigar out his pocket. He hesitated, and offered one to me: 'You use these?'

'Nah,' I said.

We drank our beer in amiable quiet, watching the cheerful bustle of the street, the motorcycles, bicycles, pedestrians, donkey carts streaming past. I said, just to break the silence: 'Am I remembering right ... the last time we met up, weren't you about to get married? Or have I got you muddled you up with someone else ...?'

'Nope, you've got it right. My Thai princess. Beautiful girl, too. That'd be, oh, three years ago now. Well, yep, we got hitched, sure enough, and now she's about to be the next ex-Mrs Bullen.'

'You're divorcing?' I said 'Sorry to hear that.'

'Nuthin' to be sorry about, Andy. These things happen. I didn't realise – though, Lord knows, I should have – when I married her, I was marrying her mother too ... and her uncles and her brother and her two sisters. Them, and most of her cousins. I think that I married half a village. No wonder they were so happy-smiley when I showed up.'

'Oh,' I said, treading carefully, 'You must be disappointed.'

'I'll get over it. I always do.'

'You've been married before?'

'You know, Andy, my old Momma used to say to me, she said "Son, you find yourself the right girl, and you grab onto her and put a ring on her finger." Well, the Good Lord knows, I have found me the right girl and slipped that ring on her finger *five* goddamn times now. I reckon I must be about the world's most romantic man – *and* the guy that the jewellery business dreams about. But maybe I should have minded my Daddy more, 'cos *he* said that you should never let a woman use you any more than you use them. Perhaps my old man had more sense than I gave him credit him for.'

'Five times?' I said, incredulous that ordinary people could have been married five times.

'Yep. *Five*. And each one was the right one. That last one, my Thai princess, lovely girl, bright, considerate, and terrific in the sack. Good cook too, if you like your food spicy. Ah, well, there you go.' He paused and took a sip of his beer, before asking: 'You married yourself?'

'I was. Divorced now. Just the once.'

'Kids?'

'One daughter.'

'Still see her?'

'Yes. I see her pretty regularly.'

'That's good. Me, I got six kids, but I'm only in touch with three of them. The rest, I just send cash. Or leastways, my lawyer does. So why d'you get divorced? Get yourself a piece on the side, huh? Or just wake up one morning to discover you didn't much like each other?'

'None of the above. Money troubles,' I said.

'Money? How so?'

'She could spend the stuff faster than I could make it.'

'Hell, I know something about that! I can surely get behind that. After Wife number two, lady name of Jessica – terrific legs, gotta say – I arranged to separate my money, keep most of it out of sight.'

We sat for a moment in silence. Eventually I said:

'By the way, just a little thing ...'

'Yeah?'

'My name. It's Andrew, not *Andy*. I'm not keen on Andy.'

'What did I call you?'

'You said *Andy*.'

'I did? I'm sorry, didn't realise.'

'It doesn't matter, but I prefer Andrew.'

'Oh, sure. Not a problem. Glad you mentioned it.'

We sat for a while longer. The waiter brought Bullen his whisky, which he tossed back in one and ordered two more beers.

'So, then,' I said, 'You're going to tell me what you need me to do for you?'

'Huh?'

'This job you're employing me for. The *adventure*.'

'Well, there now, that's the thing about adventures,' he said, stretching out his bulk on the little plastic chair. 'You never know what's gonna happen next. Well I *know*, obviously, but it wouldn't be an adventure for you if I told you, kind of spoil the fun, wouldn't it now?'

He stared ruminatively out at the street for a moment, watching the tide of humanity flowing past us. For me, that's always been part of the attraction of the East, the ceaseless crowds moving busily on with their lives. I wondered if Bullen was thinking the same. I felt a trickle of sweat roll down the back of my neck. Eventually, he broke the silence.

'Will you ever look at this place?' he drawled. 'You know something? There are almost no railroads here in Cambodia. Practically none. Can you believe that? And will you look at the state of it! The pavements are breaking up, there's barely any roads worth the name, the traffic goes about any-old-how, the drainage is from the Stone Age. The country is falling to pieces! I mean – *hell*. Sixty years of French occupation and they didn't invest in this place for shit. You know what they left for their legacy?'

He paused for effect, then announced:

'Better *patisseries!* Can you credit it? I mean, you Brits stomped your way around the world, colonising and invading and stealing 'most everything that wasn't nailed down, but at least you left *something* behind you. Even us Americans usually leave behind a Coca Cola factory and a leaking oil refinery. But the *French?* A couple of churches, a post office and a better restaurant menu. *Lordy* Lord!'

He tilted his head back and took an enormous swallow of beer, then wiped his hand across his mouth. He smiled at me ruefully, then shook his head in wonderment.

'Still,' I said, 'there's nothing wrong with their beer.'

'Yep. Amen to that,' he nodded. 'I'll give them that. And you know, there's money to be made here, if you know how to go about it.'

We sat watching while a motor scooter nearly ran into a plodding bullock cart, almost right in front of us.

Bullen laughed. 'Oh, yep, *that.* Oh boy!' he said, raising his eyebrows and starting to stand up. 'I think that we are going to get on *just fine.* Now, let's see if we can't flag ourselves down one of their death-trap taxis.'

Money, if Lennon and McCartney are to be believed, can't buy you love, but it can buy you a lot of patio furniture and scatter cushions and carpets and household appliances.

And my wife – my ex-wife, as I should properly call her – bought most of it.

We had a perfectly good house on a pleasant street in Potters Bar, north of London. I was a middle manager in an engineering design consultancy, the office fifteen minutes from home. Some of our neighbours were more affluent than us, some were less so. We could afford our lifestyle. We had a daughter, Martha (Mattie, as we called her), just starting at junior school and my wife had a part-time job at a local solicitor's office.

I have no idea what changed in my wife's thinking, but the first intimation of trouble came when she remarked, quite casually, that Mrs Payne at number 26 had just had a new kitchen installed and now she had an induction hob. My wife had gone over there to admire it and decided that we ought to have one as well. I didn't give the matter much thought, merely saying that I didn't know how it would fit in our kitchen.

The next thing I knew was that she had a kitchen design company round to look; *yes*, they had said, we could have an induction hob, but *no*, it would not fit in our existing worktops. So, talking to the very helpful salesman, she had put down a deposit on a complete new kitchen, and she was expecting to see his plans in the next couple of days – did I think that we should have a breakfast bar built in?

A breakfast bar? Never mind breakfast bars; what was wrong, exactly, with the kitchen we had, and how much was all this going to cost? She was vague and cagey, only saying that (of course) we could buy a cheaper kitchen but, in the long run, we would regret skimping on quality. Besides, we could afford it, with the bit of extra money that her job was bringing in.

Thinking back, I should have drawn the line right there and then, but I was flat-out busy at work and didn't have the energy for an argument. If it would make her happy, I thought, then it was worthwhile. So I acquiesced and she went ahead with her new kitchen.

By the time it was all installed and she had changed her mind a couple of times, and we'd had a new window put in and new floor tiling and marble worktops, the bill was double any estimate that we had received. I blamed myself; if I had been keeping a closer eye on it I might have kept a grip on the costs. I said this to her, and we had a blazing row, she accusing me of being mean and small-minded and I countering that money didn't grow on trees and we had spent serious cash, just to get a damned induction hob. At which point she had burst into tears, told me that she should never have married such a miserable skinflint, and rushed off upstairs, frightening our daughter.

The kitchen argument blew over, but I felt bad about it, so when she told me that the Stapletons at number 7 were getting new teak patio furniture, I had agreed rather too readily. When I asked about cost, the figure was not as bad as I was expecting. I thought that I had got off lightly.

It turned out that she had already bought it.

The next thing was a present for me – a new lawnmower to replace the old but perfectly serviceable one that I had inherited from someone. She unveiled it in the garage, smiling broadly and saying that she knew that I had been thinking about getting a new mower for some time (I may have looked at one in passing, but I hadn't intended to buy it) and that she felt sorry for me, battling with that old rusty thing on a Saturday afternoon.

I could hardly object; it was, after all, for me.

Three or four major expenditures later, the shit hit the fan. I opened our bank statement to discover it had a serious hole in it. Another furious row.

'Your trouble,' she told me, 'is that you have no ambition. You're content to paddle along, working for someone else and earning peanuts. My father —'

She always liked to cite her father in financial discussions. To my certain knowledge her father had been never been more than a butcher with a small high-street shop. At the height of his career, he had employed a youngster to unload deliveries and help out in the back.

'My father says that nobody ever made proper money working for someone else. You have to have the courage to be your own man, to strike out on your own. And *that* —' she waved an accusatory finger at the bank statement '— just proves my point.'

So eventually, with a degree of reluctance, I set up my own little one-man consultancy and, I have to admit, I did quite well. Some of the work came from overflow referrals from my old company, some from my own contacts and some from recommendations. Our income increased.

But not as fast as her spending.

Tennis club memberships. New curtains throughout the house. A block-paved driveway. A new car to sit on the block paving.

In fairness to her, she was not selfish in her extravagance. No sooner had she acquired her new car (deposit down, monthly payments for three years, big outlay at the end) than she suggested that I, in my role as Managing Director of my own company, should have a better car than my five-year-old Ford estate.

That one I managed to head off.

I tried talking to her.

'This has to stop,' I said.

'It will,' she said.

It didn't.

Eventually, it became evident that the only work that I could do that would keep up with her expenditure were the international jobs. They paid better. Despite the fact that these jobs would take me away from home for weeks at a time, they were the Big-Ticket assignments.

And that, I suppose, was how I became someone who saw more of the inside of hotel rooms than his own home, locked in an endless spinning wheel of flights and trips and meetings and jet lag. I missed my bed, I missed my daughter and I even missed my garden (my only real hobby), which grew neglected in my absence

One day I came back from the airport to find her sitting at her new breakfast bar, a glass of wine in front of her.

'Where's Mattie?' I said.

'She's gone to stay overnight at a friend's house.'

'Oh,' I said. 'That's a pity. I was looking forward to seeing her. And you, of course.'

'Andrew,' she said, 'we need to have a talk.'

She poured me a glass of wine.

'Sounds serious,' I said, trying to make a joke of it. I do that – when something sounded serious, I try to make a joke of it.

'It is,' she said.

'Uh-huh.'

'Andrew, I have been thinking, I've decided ... that I want a divorce.'

'What?'

'A divorce.'

'I'm sorry – where did this come from? A divorce? *What?* I don't get it —'

'Andrew. You have to understand that this isn't a decision that I have come to lightly.'

'But why ever ...?'

'Andrew,' she said. 'You're never *here*.'

Bullen had booked two rooms at the Classy Hotel, by the old Colonial Buildings on the east bank of the Sangker River. Normally I would avoid any hotels with the word 'Classy' in their title, but in Indochina things

work differently; this was a fine ten-storey block, either modern or recently refurbished.

The reception area was filled with those extraordinary heavily-carved benches and seats (it would be wrong to describe such gigantic thrones merely as *chairs*) that you get in Cambodia. Elaborately ornate woodwork is one of the more striking features of the country. The walls were covered in more carvings, writhing wooden vines reaching up to the ceilings and around the huge reception desk.

While Bullen was sorting out the rooms, I meandered through the lobby and out into the swimming pool at the back. It was deserted, apart from two boys, moving about cleaning and wiping, waiting for any guests who might want to swim or sunbathe. They looked up at me hopefully as I walked out. I smiled at them and shook my head.

Back at the desk, Bullen was getting impatient with the young receptionist.

'Honey,' he was saying, 'I told you twice already, we *need* room 417. I booked 417, not 419, not 421. Room 417. *Understand?* So can you stop telling me about how difficult —'

'Sir, I am so sorry. That room is not available currently —'

'Okay, honey, I'm going to let that one go. We booked it, so we want it. And whatever you have to do to make it available, you go and do it. I am *insisting.*'

'But 417 is not our best room. We can offer you better room.'

'Honey, you're not listening ....'

'Sir, then, I will need to speak to manager.'

'You do that.'

She picked up the phone while Bullen wandered across to me. He lifted his brows in a gesture of *what can you do?*

'I made a point of booking that room. *Very* especially. That's the thing with your Oriental – when they get something wrong, they'll do anything except admit it. And all this jibber-jabber about calling the manager – it's nothing but telling a chambermaid to skedaddle over there and change the bedding. That phone call is all about not losing face.'

'What's so important about Room 417?' I asked.

'Oh, I kinda like the view from that one.'

'You like the view?' I echoed. 'You've stayed here before?'

'What, here? No, never been here before.'

'So, then, how do you know about the view?'

'You'll see,' said Bullen, distractedly. He pointed out through the back. 'What's that through there? Is that the bar?'

'I didn't see one. That's the restaurant over to the left.'

'Anyone in there?'

'I didn't notice.'

'Andy, I need you to do me a favour.'

'Sure – but the name's Andrew, remember?'

'Oh ... oh, sure, yep. Andrew, right? Anyway, what I need for you to do is to go take a good look around this ground floor, see if anyone's about.'

'Anyone? Anyone particular?'

'Yeah. Guy in his early sixties, iron-grey hair, big moustache. Russian. Probably wearing a suit but no tie. Most likely with another guy. You'll know him when you see him.'

'And if I see him? Tell him you're looking for him?'

'What? No! *Lord*, no. Don't go near him, don't say anything to him. And try not to let him see you. Look straight through him. Just come back and tell me. Check the rooftop bar as well.'

'Okay,' I said, guardedly. 'And this is all part of the adventure, right?'

'Sure is,' said Bullen.

I found his mysterious Russian at the rooftop bar. As Bullen had predicted, he was sitting with another man, a great bull of a fellow in a brown suit, both of them drinking tea and smoking.

I went back to Reception, where Bullen was ensconced in the corner.

'He didn't see you, did he?'

'No, I'm pretty sure not. I went up the stairs, so there were no lift doors opening to give me away. He had his back to me.'

'So how did you know it was him?'

'Mirror. Man in his early sixties, moustache, grey hair, with another man.'

'A mirror? You didn't approach him?'

'No.'

'Good. Nice piece of surveillance, neat and tidy. We'll make a spook of you yet, Andy.'

'Andrew,' I corrected.

'Yeah, Andrew, right.'

'So,' I said, 'who exactly is this guy?'

'Oh, you'll find out soon enough. He's an old friend of mine – or a co-worker, you might say. Anyway, listen, I got you your room. The Reception girl sorted it.'

'*My* room?' I said. '417? I thought you wanted it?'

'Nah, I wanted for *you* to have it. It's a special room.'

'Are you next door?'

'No, I'm up two floors, on the opposite side of the block.'

'Bullen,' I said, '*none* of this is making any sense. The room, this Russian guy, all the mystery ... what's going on?'

'All will be explained,' he said. 'Trust me.'

The boy took my luggage up to Room 417 and I made the usual English muddle of tipping him – searching for the appropriate value note in my wallet, failing to find it and then giving more than I intended, then feeling vaguely embarrassed about the whole thing.

Room 417 was unremarkable – a pleasant room with a bathroom, a double bed, a dressing table of the same heavy carved wood as in the lobby. The view from a neat little stone balcony was unremarkable (which made me wonder what all the fuss was about), down over a dusty street and a row of shops with corrugated iron roofs, with the tall palm trees swaying behind. I adjusted the air conditioning controls and unpacked.

Bullen had gone off to his own room, with a promise to come and collect me for pre-dinner drinks at seven and an injunction, meanwhile, to speak to no one. He had also, for reasons of his own, borrowed my passport. I wasn't happy about that but, when I remonstrated with him, he had tapped his nose and promised me that I would thank him later.

I was sitting on the end of the bed when my mobile phone rang:

'Andrew?'

'Hi,' I said.

It was my ex-wife. Was it my imagination or was her tone, whenever we spoke these days, one of mild rebuke, like a disappointed schoolteacher?

'Are you at home?' she said, without preamble.

'No,' I said, 'I'm in Cambodia, at a place called Battambang.'

'*Battambang?* Seriously?'

'Yes, really. Listen, this call will be costing you a fortune. What do you need?'

'Yes, well, alright. It's about Mattie's school fees. I dropped the invoice round to your flat a couple of days ago.'

She had decided, in view of the trauma of the divorce, that it would be in Mattie's best interests to attend a private school – hence the fees.

'I'm not there, so I haven't seen it.'

'Can you pay them from where you are?'

'Well – about that. I've got a serious cash flow problem at the moment. Can you pay them and we can settle over the next month or so?'

'Andrew, we discussed this and we agreed. Whatever happened between us, Mattie wouldn't suffer.'

'I'm not suggesting Mattie should suffer,' I said, feeling my patience stretching, 'only that you should pay them this time and I can —'

'I haven't got that kind of money lying around. Surely you —'

'No, actually I can't. And how can you say you haven't got the money?'

'Andrew, you'll just have to sort it out. We agreed all this. Anyway, as you said, this call will be expensive – I'll email you the details.'

'But —' I began.

'Bye.'

And the line went dead.

I stared at the handset, seething silently.

Fuck it. And *fuck* her.

Most of my conversations with my ex-wife these days went like that. I lay back on the bed and waited for my temper to subside.

It was still only mid-afternoon on what had been a hot and sticky day, so I put on a pair of swimming trunks, added a shirt, picked up my paperback and went downstairs to the lobby and through the swing doors to the pool. It was still deserted. The two pool boys jumped to attend me, laying dry towels on a lounger, asking if I needed anything from the bar, pointing me towards the pre-swim shower.

It was good to be in the water, swimming a length of slow crawl, then sculling on my back with the perfect azure sky above me. I watched a single cloud drifting through the blue and reflected that these were the compensations for coming to Indochina. Of course, a swimming pool in one of the best hotels was not the authentic experience of Cambodia, with its pitiful living standards, but – just for a moment – I indulged myself in the luxury that a Westerner enjoys in the East. I tried to imagine what it might be like to come and live here permanently. You could understand why the foreigners of modest means moved here and lived like lords. The landscape was green and lush, the weather spectacular. The people were good-natured, polite, smiling. Of course, to settle here, as a Westerner, was to exist in an unreal dream only made possible by the power of hard currency.

My reverie was broken a slight splash nearby. I stopped swimming and trod water, looking around. There was no one visible, just a ripple lapping across the surface. One of the pool boys was still brushing the poolside. I blinked in the sunshine.

So what had made the splash?

I got a glimpse of a shape at the far end of the pool, appearing for an instant before diving under again. Whoever it was, they were swimming lengths underwater, impressive in such a big pool.

My curiosity was piqued. I resumed my swimming, a steady breaststroke which allowed me to keep my head up and look for the mysterious swimmer. Eventually, a body broke surface at the far end, performing a creditable racing turn. There was a flash of a white costume and swim cap, pale tawny skin and black swim-goggles; and then they broke into a racing crawl stroke that cut through the water with barely a splash, the mark of a very efficient swimmer.

The figure completed two more lengths while I watched – by which time I was certain that the swimmer was a woman. Finally, she arrived at the far end of the pool, laid hands on the edge and jack-knifed out onto the side. She went to her sun-lounger, wrapped a towel around herself and picked up a mobile phone and keys and strode quickly along the poolside and out through the double doors into the hotel lobby. Looking while trying not to look, I had the impression, before she disappeared, of a slim feminine figure in a white one-piece costume – but I could see nothing of her face beneath the swimming cap and black goggles.

I wondered if she was as good-looking as her figure suggested.

I also wondered what she was doing here, using the pool – it is one of the ironies of countries like Cambodia that the last people you see in their smart hotels are Cambodians. They simply can't afford them. Most likely, she was the girlfriend (or paid companion) of some rich foreigner, a German or an American – or maybe, these days, a wealthy visiting Chinese.

I settled back into my sculling, looking up into the perfect blue sky.

Someone – I think it might have been my sister – once asked me how I truly felt about my divorce. In fact, it must have been my sister, because I can't imagine anyone else being so direct. Most people's reaction to uncomfortable news tends to follow some sort of agreed script: a pained smile, a tentative hand on the shoulder from men or, from women, a self-conscious hug perhaps, and the awkward words: 'And you? How are you ...?' and you're supposed to smile bravely in reply and say something bland: 'Me? Oh, you know ...' and you must never, ever, give vent to what you actually feel. You must follow the script and pretend.

I think that I did that to my sister ('Oh, you know, it's fine, I'm okay, it's Mattie I worry about ...') because, deep down, I didn't actually know *what* I felt. Numb, most likely, as if it was happening to someone else, someone I could monitor from a distance. I could think about this separate self, watch him going through his day, getting on a train, moving down the street, putting one foot in front of the other, one of the walking wounded. I could view this separate me making the best of things, hiding the damage, containing the self-pity burning inside, the injustice, the corrosive argument going on inside his head ('But I ... I gave her *everything* ... I went *all-in*, my affection, my trust, I made every effort ... and, in the end, she didn't even want me near her. How could I have made such a mistake; how could I have misread her – and how could somehow that I cared about be so ... cold?').

From a distance, I could watch this separate self, and approve how well he hid everything away. Because you can show people where you cut your hand, limp when you twisted your ankle, but you must never, ever, show the weight of a broken heart.

Bullen knocked on the door of my room just after seven. He was visibly excited.

'Okay, Andy,' he said, bustling into the room. '*This* is where it all gets interesting. You feeling up for it – no, don't tell me – 'course you are!'

'Andrew,' I corrected, automatically. He was making me nervous. 'So, what are we doing?'

'Doing? We're doing a bit of that old undercover secret agent stuff! Gonna be pretty cool, and *you* are going to have one hell of a story to tell your grandchildren. But we got to be quick – our Russian friends, Dmitry and Igor, are up in the rooftop bar, settling into their second drinks – I just checked on them. C'mon!'

He stepped out onto my small balcony and moved the two little plastic chairs out of the way. Outside the evening had darkened, the sudden dusk of a tropical night. He indicated the balcony next to us.

'See that?' he said.

I looked over to the right, at the little structure jutting out of the wall, a balcony identical to mine, belonging to the next room along. Beyond it, there were two more balconies and the same to my left. There were more rows of balconies above and below us.

'Uh-huh,' I said. '*And?*'

'That is why I wanted this *particular* room. That next balcony along – that's Dmitry's room. And his balcony door catch is broken – paid my guy twenty bucks to make sure it was. So, we can open it from outside – and then, we're in!'

'Okay,' I said slowly, gradually understanding his plan. 'What you're saying is, if we can get to his balcony, we can get into his room. Why, exactly, would we want to do that?'

'All will become clear, Andy, all will become clear.'

I was thinking about the wider implication of what he was suggesting.

'And how exactly,' I asked, 'are we going to get to his balcony?'

'Why, we jump, of course.'

'We *jump?*'

'*Yeah*, sure we do!'

My eye measured the gap between the two balconies. Eight, maybe ten feet. I glanced down at the ground, four storeys below; solid, unyielding stone flags.

'Bullen, don't be ridiculous, that's too far. We can't possibly jump it. We'd have to leap from the top of the ledge on this balcony – we can't get any kind of run-up. It's a leap from a standing start. We won't make it.'

'What are you talking about? *Sure* we can jump it. Why, in my time in

The Company, we'd jump a lot further if we needed to – and, from a whole lot higher up than this.'

I didn't bother saying that the height wasn't really the issue – falling four storeys was much the same as falling ten, only quicker. It was the gap itself that was bothering me or, more accurately, terrifying me. I had a horribly clear vision of myself, tumbling helplessly downward. A trickle of cold ran through my spine. Of all the hare-brained schemes I had previously come across, none had involved probable suicide.

'Well, I am not going to do it – and that's final,' I told him. 'I, for one, have no desire to have my brains splattered all over the pavement. It's beyond stupid.'

'Andy – I have to say that I am disappointed in you. Where's your sense of adventure, man? *Jeez*, this is nothing, *nothing*. I tell you what – I'll go first, and when you see how easy it is, you'll follow. Yeah?'

'It's suicide,' I said. '*You* need your bloody head examined ... or a parachute.'

'Ah, shucks. You'll see.'

He clambered up onto the top of the little wall and swayed precariously for a moment. I can picture him clearly, even now, an unsteady dark shape against the dusk sky. In that moment of heightened anxiety, I was acutely aware of every detail, the wall of the hotel, the thump of my heart, a nerve jumping somewhere in my midriff, the sound of the crickets chirping in the night. Down in the dark street below, a car with one headlight went by. The heavy night air seemed to have acquired a chill undertow.

'Bullen, for *God's sake* —' I started to say.

Suddenly, he launched himself into space. For a moment, he seemed to hang in mid-air, arms and legs pumping furiously, but falling inexorably even as he sailed forward, dropping in slow motion.

He missed.

He didn't fall completely – his chest crashed into the balcony wall, his chin level with the top and his foot landing on a little AC box bolted to the stone. It couldn't take the weight– it was ripped from its fixing and tumbled away to the paving below. As he slid down, he somehow got one arm over the edge of the wall, so that he hung there, his legs dangling in thin air.

The impact must have knocked the breath from his body – I heard an audible groan and he managed to mutter:

'*Lordy* Lord!'

He wouldn't stay like that for long, not with only one arm to hold by, not with his weight. His grip must fail.

His legs kicked uselessly in the void.

I stepped up onto the parapet and jumped.

For an agonising moment, I thought that I had misjudged my leap, that I wasn't going to make it, that my foot was going to land on Bullen's shoulder – or his head – dislodging him and sending us both spinning down to the pavement below. Then my toe touched the top of the wall and my momentum carried me forward and over, crashing down into the well of the balcony.

My fall was broken by a couple of plastic chairs, which collapsed beneath me. I won't say that it was an easy landing – you try flinging yourself into garden furniture from a height – but it could have been worse. I was winded and bruised by the impact – I rolled over and got raked on the side of the head by a chair leg.

Under normal circumstances, I might have lain there for a couple of minutes, getting my breath back, but there was no time for that. I heaved myself up, scattering seating, and lurched across to where Bullen was still hanging on.

I can't say that I had really thought about how I was going to help him; there seemed no obvious way to grab onto his body. I tried to grasp him under his arms but couldn't get any purchase.

He was still slipping downward.

I leant over as far as I dared, reaching down his back and took hold of his belt (thank God he was wearing one) and heaved as hard as I could. It's no easy matter, hauling up a couple of hundred pounds of American, and I struggled to lift him, sweating and heaving. Finally, he got his other arm over the wall, and somehow I managed to half-pull, half-drag him over the edge, until he rolled over and fell down onto the balcony floor.

Neither of us spoke for a moment – we were both shattered. I just sat there, panting in the warm air, waiting for my pounding heart to subside.

Eventually, Bullen said:

'Reckon I musta got a couple of crushed balls here, you heaving at the seat of my pants like that. *Lordy* Lord, I tell you, that hurt like a mother.'

He rubbed the affected area gingerly, frowning.

'Please don't bother to thank me, then,' I said. 'For saving your life.'

'Yeah, well, I reckon I might have slightly missed my footing there. Still, I guess I would have climbed up, in time. Anyways, it was good that you helped some – and I *knew* you could make the jump. Oh ye of little faith, huh?'

'*Jesus*, Bullen! You could have *died!* If I hadn't jumped across, you *would* have died. Christ, I could have fallen and died myself!'

'Could-a, would-a, should-a ... but you didn't, did you? And —' he gave me a roguish smile, 'You have to admit, it was kind of fun, wasn't it?'

'No, it *fucking* wasn't,' I snapped, but as soon as the words were out of my mouth I knew that I was lying. It *had* been fun, or at least it had been *something*. The moment that my foot had touched that parapet and I realised that I was going to make it – that I was going to live – an instant of enormous almost indescribable joy had passed through me, unlike anything I had felt before.

But, I wasn't going tell Bullen that.

'Oh, now, don't you go thinking I'm ungrateful,' he said. 'I reckon I might owe you a beer, right enough.'

'Oh sure,' I said.

He hauled himself to his feet, still rubbing his groin. He stood for a moment, breathing slowly, as if distracted by the pain, then seemed to shake himself.

'Anyway, let's get on with what we came for, huh?' He examined the lock on the glazed balcony doors, squinting at it in the gloom.

'Well?' I said.

'Did you bring your penknife with you, Andy?' he asked.

'*Andrew*,' I said automatically. 'And no, I didn't, as it happens. You maybe want me to nip back to my room and get it?'

He glanced over at me and grinned darkly.

'Lucky, ain't it, how I understand about your British sarcastic humour? And lucky too, seeing as how you forgot your penknife, that I remembered to bring one, huh?'

And he fished a small penknife from his pocket and pushed the blade through the gap between the two doors. There was a *click* and they swung open.

'You never said anything about a bloody penknife,' I snapped.

'You never been a Boy Scout, then?' he said innocently, grinned, and slid into the room.

I followed him through the balcony doors and into a room which was almost an exact replica of my own. Same bed, same colours, same layout – different clothes scattered about (Dmitry, I noticed, was neater than me, his things were tidily folded). A leather suitcase sat open on the little fold-out stand. A pair of reading glasses and a Russian paperback lay on the bedside table, beside a bottle of water and two packets of tablets.

'Okay,' said Bullen. His voice had dropped. 'Now we've got to be very careful. Touch nothing – I don't even want them to *suspect* that we were here. Right?'

'Okay,' I said. 'What *are* we here for, anyway?'

'Documents,' he said. 'Some very valuable documents. I don't know where he will have put them, but I'm guessing we start with the room safe.'

He stepped over to the wardrobe, ran his eye around the door slowly and pointed at something. He gestured to me.

'See there?' he said. 'Oldest trick in the book, a couple of hairs between the door and the frame! Still at it, eh, Dmitry, you old dog! We'll put those back when we're finished.'

He reached up and removed two almost invisible hairs and put them carefully to one side. Then he cautiously opened the door. The wardrobe was half-full of clothes. On the second shelf was a small green hotel safe.

'You know his combination?' I said, almost whispering.

'Don't need to,' he replied. 'People lock themselves out of hotel safes all the time, don't they? So, the management have a master key to open them.'

'And you have that?'

'Yup,' he said, peering at the safe.

'Paid your guy twenty dollars to get it for you?'

'This cost me fifty,' he whispered and grinned at me again. 'Let's see ...'

He pushed in the key and turned it. It gave with a barely audible click and he opened the door.

'*There* you are, you little darling. There. Now, if this was me, I wouldn't have put them in the safe. Too obvious. I would've hidden them somewhere about the room – or, better still, someplace outside the room altogether. But Dmitry is getting lazy in his old age. And now we have them!'

He slid out an A4 folder, about two inches thick, bound inside plastic end sheets.

I leant over his shoulder to see what it was. On the front cover, there was a mass of what appeared to be Chinese characters, with English writing beneath them. It said:

Research & Development Department
Annual Report & Summary

And below that, the name of a famous company, S—— Electronics.

'Bullen, that's not a Russian document!' I exclaimed.

'No, it's not,' he said, evenly. 'It's Korean.'

He shut the door of the safe again, inserted the borrowed key and locked it, then closed the wardrobe door softly. He picked up the two hairs and licked them, then positioned them on the frame again, exactly as they had been. He turned to me and pointed to the balcony.

'You wanna go sort out the chairs we knocked over, then shut the doors and turn the latch?' he said.

I nodded and did as he asked. He, meanwhile, was running his eye over the door to the corridor; he pointed at two small pieces of paper on the top of the door, and another at the side, jammed between the door and the frame.

'Same trick,' he murmured. 'Anyone enters the room, unsuspecting, the bits of paper fall out. Dmitry comes back, opens the door real slow; if the paper's been moved, he knows someone's been here in his room. Simple but effective.'

'I see,' I said.

'Analogue, real old-school. And see there, on the floor, the soap?'

I looked down. A bar of soap, still in its wrapping cellophane, was sitting on the floor, just touching the door.

'As Dmitry goes out, he loops a thread around the soap, pulls it until it touches the closed door. Then he pulls out the thread. Someone opens the door; soap moves and looks just like it's fallen there. A tell-tale. We'll put all these back when we go.'

He turned and grinned triumphantly at me.

'Which is ... now,' he said.

He opened the door and we went out into the corridor. I kept watch by the lift while he painstakingly replaced the tell-tales around the door, using his spit to stick the paper scraps in place, and positioned the soap using a long thread from his pocket. When he was satisfied, he clapped me on the back.

'Let's go up to my room,' he said.

'And then you'll explain all this?' I said.

'All will become clear, Andy.'

Bullen's room was a couple of floors up on the opposite side of the hotel; his view was out over the swimming pool.

'Right,' I said, trying to get some grip on the situation. I was bruised and angry and I suspected that I had pulled a muscle in my back hauling him up from the balcony. Nothing that had happened made sense and I was no longer prepared to be swept along in his chaotic wake, no matter how much he was paying me.

'Right,' he replied, dumping himself down in the one easy chair in the room. I sat on the end of the bed.

'Yes, *right*,' I said. 'Okay. So we've broken into some Russian guy's room, and stolen the contents of his safe and you've demonstrated your cleverness with bits of paper in door frames. And now I have a few questions for you – like what the *hell* are you playing at? And exactly who are you, who are you working for and what have you dragged me into —?'

'What don't you understand, Andy?' he cut in.

'Well, that document for a start. That isn't some Russian state secret thing, is it? It looks more like a commercial report.'

'Here,' he said, handing the A4 sheaf of paper to me. 'Take a look for yourself.'

I took the document and started leafing through it. There were items on the cover sheet that I hadn't noticed before; **'Controlled copy – 3 of 7'** and **'Strictly Confidential – Do Not Duplicate** '. Looking at the actual contents, there were accounts of research projects, results of experiments, even a few circuit diagrams. There were sections on 'Commercial Viability', 'Competitor Products' and 'System Lifespan'.

'What is this?' I demanded, dropping it on the bed beside me.

'It's exactly what it says on the cover. It's the Annual Report of the R&D department for S —— Electronics, probably for presentation to their Board of Directors. It's the results of tens of millions of dollars of research investment; it's a summary of where the company are going for the next five years, their technological edge in the marketplace. To a competitor, it's worth a small fortune.'

'And you – or really, *we* – we stole it!'

'It was stolen in the first place. How do you think Dmitry got it? *Of course* it's stolen. This is what's they call *Industrial Espionage*. Big companies do it to each other all the time – how else do they find out what the competition is doing? Listen, Andy,' he said, leaning forward in his chair and opening his hands in an apparent gesture of candour, 'this is how the world goes around. You know this. Don't you think that S—— aren't doing the self-same thing right now to *their* competitors? Besides, this isn't the actual research, the granular stuff. It's just the headings, pointers of what can be achieved. You can't build the products from this – but you'd be halfway there!'

'So this is nothing to do with Russia? Because I thought —'

'No, you *assumed*, because I'm American and Dmitry's Russian, that it was some sort of Cold War, Military Secrets thing? Is that right?'

I hesitated, because, to be honest, I had assumed that it was something entirely like that. Not because Bullen had said so (he had said only that it was an *Adventure*) but maybe because I had wanted it to be.

'I don't know what ... I thought ...' I mumbled.

'Well, I'm sorry, but this is commercial, this is about the money. This isn't Saving the World from Communism or anything heroic, like in the movies. Just good, old-fashioned *money*. Dmitry stole it, or bought it off someone else who stole it, and now we've stolen it!'

'We've stolen it back? To give it back to the rightful ...?' I asked hopefully.

'No, not ... exactly,' drawled Bullen.

'I see,' I said, not really seeing at all. 'Then this is illegal.'

'Sort of,' he replied. 'It depends. Anyways, you asked *who* I am. Well, just so you know, I'm what they call a *Contractor*. I get things done – a middleman in arrangements like these. I'm the guy who reaches into certain delicate situations that other people don't want to involve themselves in.'

I stared at him. I didn't know what to think. I had never actually stolen anything before, let alone industrial secrets. All this was a million miles away from my normal world, the humdrum world of design and testing and design and commissioning and pressure readings.

'So,' said Bullen, standing up, 'I promised you something exciting, and I reckon I'm delivering. Now then, all this jumping and climbing and breaking-in and stuff has got me somewhat sweaty, so I'm going to grab a shower and change my shirt. So, on to the next part of the plan. I'll come and collect you from your room in – what? – twenty minutes. That okay with you?'

'Yes, sure,' I said. Then I repeated: 'The next part of the plan? What's the next part of the plan?'

'Why, we go get ourselves that beer that I owe you,' he said, grinning.

It was nearer to half an hour before Bullen presented himself at my door, hair damp and neatly combed, sporting an untucked Hawaiian shirt of truly hideous design over a pair of chinos and brown leather shoes. He had one of those plastic flight bags over his shoulder.

I ran my eye up and down him – it was the sort of get-up that positively screamed 'American'.

'What?' he said.

'Are you wearing that shirt for a bet or something?'

'No, Andy – I'm sorry, *Andrew* – but sometimes you gotta dress to impress. This here,' he tapped his broad front, 'is my *drinking* shirt.'

So you can be sick down the front without anyone noticing, I thought darkly, but refrained from saying it. Instead, I said:

'Bullen, listen. You've got your documents – surely now is the time to get going? Before your Russians discovers they're missing? This isn't the moment to be drinking. We need to make our escape!'

'Andy,' he sighed, as if instructing a recalcitrant teenager, 'I accept that you are new to this. If we run now, we just advertise that we took it. We stay put. We brass it out. You watch carefully now, and you'll see how it all works out. C'mon – there's a beer up on that rooftop bar with my name on it!'

'Isn't that where Dmitry was —'

'No more arguing. This now is the fun part! C'mon.'

We went up in the lift. Bullen slid a large manila envelope out of his flight bag and passed it over to me.

'You hang onto this until I say so. Keep it out of sight, okay?' he said.

I felt the weight of it. 'Is this the document? *For Christ's sake*, Bullen! Why the hell are we bringing it with us?'

But he simply shook his head and put his forefinger to his lips. 'Keep it out of sight,' he repeated.

The lift door slid open and we stepped out. Outside the air-conditioned interior, the night air was warm and soft, scented by something that was ineffably Eastern – the heavy vegetation, cooking fires, diesel fumes, sandalwood, something indefinable.

The rooftop bar was a wide area overlooking the city below. There were neat tables, mostly empty, a brightly coloured bar area, a wooden trellis with light bulbs strung around it, potted plants.

'There's Dmitry and Igor,' said Bullen, pointing out two men sitting at one of the tables. 'Let's go and say hello.'

'*What?*' I said, in a stage whisper. 'What? You're going to speak to him? You're out of your mind!'

'Just follow my lead, Andy. Don't panic. Sit one table away. And don't say or do *anything* until I signal you.'

He strode out ahead, and I forced myself to follow, wondering what this new insanity was. As he approached them, the two seated men turned to look, obviously recognising him. They stood as he got to the table.

'Bullen!' said the older man, the one with the grey moustache. 'You keep us waiting – so we started drinking without you!'

'Dmitry Spiridonovich,' said Bullen. 'How are you?'

They shook hands, smiling.

'Igor,' said Bullen, acknowledging the other man, the big man in the brown suit. Close up, he looked even more massive than I had realised. Beneath the close-cropped grey hair his face was unreadable. He, too, shook hands with Bullen.

'Who is your friend?' asked Dmitry, glancing across at me. I was trying hard remain calm, selecting a nearby table and sitting down.

'Andrew Finch,' said Bullen.

'He does not join us?'

'After we have got our business out of the way, maybe.'

'Very good. He is – what? – your Assistant? He does not look like ... how do you Americans say it? ... muscle.'

'Ex-British army,' lied Bullen, without so much as missing a beat. I kept my face neutral. 'Don't worry about Mr Finch there. He can take care of himself.'

A waiter came over and Dmitry waved a finger around the table – same again – then called across to me: 'Mr Finch, may I buy you a drink?'

'A beer,' I replied. He nodded at the waiter.

I sat quietly, watching the three men, wondering what was going to happen next. I took the opportunity to look at Dmitry properly. I had guessed he was in his mid-sixties, his face lined but well-preserved, awareness evident in the grey eyes, the iron-grey hair receding but neatly cut, a decisive mouth beneath a luxuriant moustache. Not a man, I thought, to be taken lightly.

They obviously knew each other well; there was a guarded warmth between them. Bullen sat grinning, looking relaxed, a slightly absurd figure in his riotous shirt. He lit a cigar and waved it in the air as he talked.

'So, Bullen,' said Dmitry at length. 'You have?'

'Of course.' He unzipped his flight bag and let the other man inspect the contents. 'Choose one, any one,' he said and Dmitry dipped his hand in and took out what looked like a stack of banknotes. He handed it to the man called Igor. I could see that they were American hundred-dollar bills. Igor counted them with the edge of his thumb and nodded.

'Check another one,' offered Bullen.

'There is not need,' said Dmitry. 'You think I do not trust you?'

'I think that you don't trust anyone.'

At this, the old Russian let out a bellow of laughter, slapped Bullen on the shoulder and lifted his beer. He chinked it with the American, and said: '*Za vstrechu!*' Then he turned to me:

'Your health, Mr Finch!'

I raised my beer bottle in return.

'And now, Dmitry,' said Bullen. 'You have your side of the bargain?'

'Up here? No, but now we have seen the colour of your cash – my friend will bring.'

He spoke rapidly in Russian to Igor, who nodded, and took his room key from him and got up.

As he passed my table he gave me a glowering glance which was half-warning and half-curiosity. Doubtless thinking that I didn't look much like a bodyguard.

I couldn't help but agree.

Ten minutes passed. Bullen and Dmitry exchanged pleasantries, jokes, complaints, cheerful insults. I watched them sparring and reminiscing about mutual acquaintances.

Eventually, Igor reappeared, looking even less affable than before. He spoke to his boss in a torrent of furious Russian and, as he talked, Dmitry's face grew concerned, then darker, then outright thunderous. The two Russians barked at each other – the older man slammed his fist down on the table, upsetting the glasses and bottles, Igor spread his arms in an angry appeal to heaven itself.

Bullen sat and watched in innocent incomprehension – although you didn't need subtitles to see that something was seriously wrong. Finally, he said:

'Problem here, Dmitry Spiridonovich? Something the matter?'

'The *matter*! What are you talking about? Of course is something the matter – *big* problem here.'

'So, you have the document or not?'

'No. God be damned, no. There is a thief come —' For a moment his command of English deserted him and he spat out '*Yob tvoyu mat*'.

'Then – so, is our deal off, huh?'

'What?' snapped Dmitry.

'The deal – is it off? You haven't got the document? That's a pity. So, we have another drink and call it a day ...?'

'*Yebat!* No, of course not – it must – no, give me time to think!'

'Perhaps my friend here can help you.' He pivoted around to me. 'Andy, you got that thing with you ...?'

'Sure,' I said, getting up and taking the half-dozen steps to the table. I laid the thick manila envelope down in front of Dmitry.

He glared up at me in incomprehension, then tore open the envelope. The document spilled out onto the table.

The two Russians stared at it in a mixture of horror and amazement. Then Dmitry pointed his finger at me, a finger that physically shook with anger, and for a ghastly second I thought that he was going to tell Igor to do something brutal. His face was black with anger.

'You!' he snarled, then the finger went around and pointed at Bullen.

'This is you, Bullen. You are *fuck* ...'

And Bullen started to laugh.

'You and you – you *stole* this –'

'Your money's right here, Dmitry,' said Bullen, his shoulders shaking up and down with laughter.

'You American bastard!' shouted Dmitry, then he started to laugh too,

Igor too, and then we were all laughing (mostly, in my case, from relief), laughing like idiots.

'Your face,' mumbled Bullen, barely able to speak.

The little Cambodian waiter had been watching the pantomime in dumb terror. Doubtless he had feared that it was going to develop into violence, and the look on his face was a sight to see. Between gales of laughter, Dmitry beckoned to him, indicating the mess of spilled drinks on the table; he made a *clear this* gesture, then called for more drinks. The man darted forward and gathered up the debris, then came back with a cloth and cleaned the table. Four more beers materialised as if by magic, then four glasses of whisky.

'Hah,' said Dmitry, 'American bastard! This is why nobody trusts Yankees.'

'It was worth it, just to see your expression,' guffawed Bullen, tears starting to roll down his face.

'You know, I was ready to say this man to kill both of you. *Both of you!* My God, Bullen, next time my friend, next time you pull shit like that, I kill you for sure!'

'Not if I kill you first.'

'Hah! You say!' Dmitry turned across to me. 'Andrew Finch – now you sit down with us, here, here, sit! You know, I have tried to kill this American bastard two times —'

'Three times, Dmitry, *three* times.'

'Yes, you are right – three – and each time he survives —'

'And I have only tried to kill him the one time. I was *that* close —'

'Pah! *Not* so close!'

'But your friend, not so lucky ...'

'He was a fool – but I, I am protected by St Basil! You see, I wear the – what do you say this? – medal.' He indicated a chain around his neck.

'Medallion,' I said.

'More drinks!' cried Bullen, waving toward the little Cambodian waiter.

'So now, Andrew Finch,' said Dmitry, turning his attention on me. 'Tell me something about yourself; what is your father's name?'

'My father?'

'Yes, your father! You have a father, no? You are really English? Not like this Yankee criminal here! So, his name?'

'Simon,' I said.

'Good, then, so you are *Andrew Simonovich!* Tell me, what was it feel like, when you were almost murdered tonight?'

'Tonight?'

'Yes, yes. Here, now. By the terrible, angry Russians.'

'Very bad,' I said, trying to catch their jokey attitude. 'I am very relieved.'

'*Relieved* – what is this word? What does this mean?'

'Happy.'

'Good, then I am happy that *you*, the England man, are happy. We drink to your happy!'

And we did.

I've never been a big drinker. A couple of beers with colleagues on the way home from work, two or three glasses of wine at a party, the occasional Scotch at home if we had company. I have never had the craving for alcohol that some people have.

But, if I was a rank and unpractised amateur, the other three men at that table were Olympic standard. They could pour what a friend of mine used to call the *electric soup* down their throats like no one I had ever seen before. Their capacity was enormous – and I foolishly tried, if not to keep pace with them, to at least stay in the field.

Which, obviously, was going to end badly.

But it was very agreeable sitting out in the warm night air, the first drinks giving me a pleasant buzz. I remember thinking what an extraordinary turn of events this was – here was I, as ordinary a fellow as you could meet, rubbing shoulders, socialising, with these amazing characters. By complete accident, I had stumbled into another world, a world of Industrial Espionage and spies and bodyguards and adventures and secrets. They might be grey-haired, but there was no doubt that they were still formidable, *neck-or-nothing* men. If only my ex-wife – who had always thought me a dull sort of fellow – could see me now!

I felt a warm glow with the thought.

At some point, Dmitry, Igor and I went and looked down over the edge of the roof, at the little balconies all jutting out from the front wall of the hotel. Bullen must have gone for a toilet break.

I could see that the Russians were impressed when I described how we had leapt across the gap.

'You made that jump, just to make a joke on us?' said the Russian in some disbelief.

'Yes,' I admitted.

'Of course, I have seen men do more stupid things than even this, for a joke,' said Dmitry. 'And you both did it?'

'Well, I didn't want to, but Bullen went first ... and he fell, so I had to try and help him.'

'He fell? You rescued him?'

'Yes.'

Dmitry translated for Igor's benefit and the big man said something in Russian.

'There was a time,' said Dmitry, almost wistfully, 'when Bullen might have made such a jump. Ten, fifteen years ago, perhaps. He was lucky that you were there, I think.'

'Well, perhaps,' I said.

Igor said something else in low bass rumble. I looked inquisitively at Dmitry for translation.

'He says: "We all get older – only some men don't realise it."' He paused. 'Ah, here is Bullen now.'

As the glasses of Scotch stacked up in front of me, I used the old tactic of pouring them all into one glass and excusing myself for a comfort break, muttering 'I'll take this one with me', then pouring the contents down the toilet pan. But there are only so many times that one can pull that trick – and soon the evening took on a fuzzy focus. I started to wonder when I could excuse myself altogether and slide out to bed.

Dmitry and Bullen, however, were in fine form, and Igor (even though he said very little) matched them drink for drink. None of them seemed to show any effects from the amount they consumed.

While I still had some of my wits about me, I listened and gradually understood more about them. Bullen, apparently, had once been a CIA field officer, while Dmitry was Russian Security Services, GRU or maybe even KGB. They had encountered each other during their service, as enemies or rivals, and several of these encounters had been hostile – or near-fatal – which they seemed to find inordinately funny and delighted in regaling me with details of their escapades.

Both Dmitry and Bullen had now retired from their respective Governments' service, and were using their skills in the private sector ('And making *damned* much more money in this way,' declared Dmitry). They operated in their shadowy circle, go-to people for extra-legal dealing, occasionally rivals, no longer enemies.

I remember my attention starting to wander as they spoke, and I remember making some careful observations (that stage of drunkenness when you have to remind yourself to speak slowly), and I remember laughing hysterically at something or other, and I remember picking my way back from the toilet at one point when my legs seemed to belong to someone else and lurching against the chairs.

What I don't remember is passing out.

When I woke, I was aware of a momentous throbbing pain in my skull, as if someone had slid a tangle of barbed wire in there while I slept, and a filthy dry taste in my mouth. I opened my eyes and shut them again as the light from the window seared the back of my head. My stomach ached.

I lay still for a moment, trying to find a part of my body that didn't actually hurt. I assessed my situation; I was in bed and undressed. I couldn't recall how that had happened. Very slowly, I turned my head to one side (the barbed wire now had a heavy steel ball in the middle of it, rolling around inside my skull) and opened my eyes again.

I was not in my room.

I let out a low groan – even that was painful – and a deep voice said: 'Hello!'

I croaked something, and a figure came into view. It was the Russian giant, Igor, clad in trousers and a white vest, and he was standing, polishing a leather shoe. I squinted at this and realised it was one of my shoes.

He walked around to the side of the bed and looked down at me.

'*Khorohshiy?*' he asked.

'What?' I said, in incomprehension.

'Good?' he asked.

'No,' I said. I dragged something up from the depths of my brain. '*Nyet.*'

He smiled in a not-unfriendly way.

I continued to lie there, too delicate to consider moving. On the opposite side of the room, my clothes were placed on a chair, neatly folded. Igor continued to polish my shoe assiduously – the thought *soldier* randomly passed through my mind – and I wondered if I was actually going to die. Maybe that would be for the best.

Eventually, Igor finished polishing my shoes, inspected them closely and put them on the floor. He nodded at me and said: 'Come'.

'No,' I said. 'I can't.'

'Yes. Come. *Breakfast.*'

When I eventually stumbled into the ground-floor dining room, flanked by Igor, Dmitry was sitting on his own at a table for four, looking fresh, happy and relaxed. He smiled under his moustache and stood to greet me.

'*Good* morning, Andrei Simonovich,' he offered brightly, shaking my hand.

'Is it?' I said. My sight was blurry in one eye. The display fish tank on one wall was disgustingly colourful; something about the motion of the fish made my stomach queasy. I sat down.

'You sleep well, I hope?'

'Tell me, I … I don't remember going to bed – and I seemed to have spent the night in Igor's room. I don't recall what happened, not exactly anyway …'

'What happened? Nothing unusual. We drank a little, we think you were perhaps unwell, you fell asleep. We tried to wake you, but it was not possible. Our friend here picked you up and put you to bed in his room, so that he could care for you if you are ill in the night – it's possible, if you are sick, you can – how do you say it? – choke? I have seen this happen. But I see you now, you are good. You will have some breakfast?'

'No,' I said.

Dmitry smiled at me encouragingly – my kindly Russian uncle.

'He was *cleaning my shoes*,' I said, irrelevantly.

'Of course,' replied Dmitry. 'He is old soldier. It is his habit. He is very good at this.'

'I see,' I said.

'What will you eat?'

'Nothing,' I said.

'Have you bad stomach? Bad head?'

'Very bad.'

'I understand. Now, you listen to Doctor Dmitry. I have some tablets in my room, we will bring them, they clear your head. But first you must go to bathroom and drink two glasses of salt water, warm; this will be for your stomach.'

'I'll be sick!' I protested.

'Naturally,' he said calmly. 'This is Russian cure, to clear your stomach. Then no more alcohol goes in your blood, empty stomach, my tablets for your head, you will feel better. Then a little vodka, then some potatoes or rice. I promise you, you feel better.'

'Oh God,' I said.

'You want to feel better?'

'I think that I want to die.'

'Yes,' he said. He called the waitress and ordered two big glasses of warm water, into which he emptied the contents of two salt cellars.

'My friend will carry them for you – I will be here when you get back.'

Anything would be better than this, I thought, as I lurched to my feet.

When I got back, feeling both terrible and slightly better, Dmitry was sitting waiting for me. He pushed three red tablets across the white table cloth, and gave me a fierce nod. There were also three shot glasses on the table.

'What are these?'

'Vodka, of course. Whisky for night, vodka for the morning.'

'No,' I said.

'But yes,' he said. 'And take the tablets.'

I swallowed them with some coffee.

'Now, *za zdorovie*,' he said, raising his glass. 'To health!'

I complied automatically.

On my left, Igor was speaking urgently in Russian. Dmitry was nodding, agreeing with him. When the big man had finished, Dmitry poured me some coffee and folded his hands in front of him.

'He wants to tell you something,' he said, 'But his English is not good, so he has asked me to translate.'

'Very well,' I said.

'Firstly, he wants you to know that his name is not *Igor* and he is not Russian.'

'It's not? And he's not Russian?'

'No. Igor is from some stupid American film, I think. His name is *Nikolai*, and he is originally from the Ukraine. For myself, I do not think this is something to be proud of, but he wants you to know it.'

'I see,' I said.

'He likes you, and wants you to know this also.'

'He does?'

'Yes. But – don't worry. Not in a sex way. Nikolai is a grandfather, with a very long-time wife, still very beautiful. He is a family man, very big for his family.'

'Good,' I said, groggily.

'Yes. Now, there is the important part. Nikolai says you are obviously not a bodyguard. In fact, it is very simple to see that you do not belong in this world at all.'

'This world?' I asked.

'Yes, *this* world, our world!' he said, encompassing the dining room with his hand. 'This world of secrets and deals, of old spies, muscle, stolen documents ... *my* world, Nikolai's world, Bullen's world. But, this is not your place. He thinks that you wandered in from outside. He thinks that you are ordinary guy, nice guy. Not like us. So, he has some advice for you.'

'Not to spend an evening drinking with Russians?' I ventured.

'No!' growled Dmitry. 'You are welcome to drink with us anytime! No, Nikolai's advice is this: *Go home*, Andrei Simonovich. Go home to England to your nice wife and nice children. This man, this American, Bullen – he is a dangerous man. Like you say in English, he is the "Accident Waiting to Happen." People around him, sometimes they get killed. Keep away from him. Go back to your nice normal life.'

'I don't have a wife anymore,' I said.

'We know,' replied Dmitry. 'You talked about her last night.'

'I did?' I said.

'Go and find yourself a wife – not so difficult. Look at you, nice guy, intelligent, not so bad-looking. You will catch the wife – no problem.'

'Thank you,' I said, wondering if *not so bad-looking* was a compliment or not.

'Good. *Now*, I give you *my* advice.'

'Right,' I said.

'Nikolai is correct. You do not belong in this world. We only meet yesterday, you played a very good joke on me and I enjoyed this joke. We drink together, so now you are a little-bit my friend.'

'Yes. That's good to hear —'

'If you were my *big* friend, an old friend, or if you were my son, or my young brother, do you know what I would do?'

'No,' I said.

'I would tell Nikolai here to pick you up, by force if needs – he is very strong – pick you up and put you in taxi, right now, and go to the airport. I would give him some money and tell him to buy you ticket on the next plane to England. Then I would tell him to sit with you in the airport, not letting you go, then to put you on this plane and wait until it goes in the air. Then come back to me and tell me that you are safely on your way home. You understand?'

'I see,' I said.

'Of course, you are only *a little bit* my friend, so I do not do this. I will only give you this very good advice: Go home, stay far away from this man Bullen – live a long, ordinary life in England.'

He sat back in his chair and glared at me.

'There!' he said. 'I have done my best, my young friend, and so has Nikolai. One day, you will thank us for this! Now, it is up to you.'

The waiter arrived, bearing a plate of steaming white rice. I looked at it unenthusiastically.

Nikolai glanced across at me. He made a scooping gesture with his hand.

'Eat,' he said.

Having tried his room, the rooftop bar and the swimming pool, I finally found Bullen in the hotel's 'Business Centre', which was nothing more than a couple of desks with antiquated computers, a printer-scanner and an internet connection.

'Hi,' I said.

'Hi,' he said. 'You okay?'

'Not entirely,' I said.

'No, you didn't look too good last night. Something you ate, you reckon?'

'Maybe,' I said, noncommittally. I was starting to feel a little better – Dmitry's pills, whatever they were, were having an effect. Bullen himself, I couldn't help noticing, looked as bright and fresh as an overweight daisy.

'What are you doing in here?' I asked.

'I've been scanning the document we acquired last night, then emailing it to myself. There's a courier coming here, in an hour or so, to take it to the Client – but I figured that an insurance copy would be sensible, just in case, you know?'

'Okay,' I said.

'Say, Andy, you ever been on the Bamboo Train?'

'The Bamboo Train? No, never even heard of it.'

'I guess that it's kinda the main tourist attraction in these parts, that and the cave where all the bats fly out at sunset. You've got to do it while you're here. It's a real rustic thing, half a dozen people on a bamboo platform, wheels taken from old tanks, little motorbike engine to drive it along, no brakes. During the Cambodian Civil War, the first carriage was a minesweeper – they let people ride on that one for free. Nowadays it's just a single platform thing, for tourists. And there are no mines anymore. You fancy a run on it?'

'Sounds dreadful,' I said.

'Yep, but *fun*. And you can't come to Battambang and *not* ride it.'

'I'm not so sure.'

'C'mon! I'll spring for the ticket. Pick you up in a couple of hours from your room?'

'Nah, Bullen, I don't think so —'

'I'm not taking 'no' for an answer!'

He was always a hard man to refuse.

The Bamboo Train, in the event, turned out to be not as scary as Bullen had painted it, but a great deal less comfortable. To call it 'basic' would be to put it too highly; a wooden pallet, a motor, a set of ancient rail lines waving through the low jungle, and zero suspension. Every time the little steel wheels hit a gap in the rails (and there were a lot), there was a solid jolt that went through my spine and rattled my fillings.

Bullen made the journey sitting behind me, and when we got off at the end he was grinning from ear to ear.

'Wasn't that something, huh? Like a roller-coaster without the safety features! I tell you, that's so *real* that it almost hurts!'

'What do you mean, almost? I think I dislodged two discs.'

'*Arhhh*,' he said, swatting an imaginary fly in the air. 'You're exaggerating. Few bumps along the way – adds to the excitement!'

We walked back to where our transport was waiting in the car park, one of those white Toyota people carriers with little curtains at the windows that they use for moving tourists around in Indochina. The driver, a wizened Cambodian in a white shirt, scurried across to open the sliding door for us. We climbed in and set off, lurching along the potholed track. Unlike the Bamboo Train, the people carrier had soft suspension, so had a tendency to wallow on the broken roads.

I sat staring out of the window at the heavy jungle – this must be about the most fertile country in the world, greenery wherever you looked – at the barefoot kids playing and laughing in the streets, the scattered platform houses which were little more than lashed-together bamboo, the bullocks in the fields, the occasional patches of cultivation, the strings of higgledy-piggledy power lines overhead.

After about twenty minutes, I started to notice that we weren't arriving back in the city; we seemed to be out in the country. I turned to Bullen.

'This is the scenic route back to the hotel?' I asked idly.

'We ain't going back to the hotel.'

'We're not?'

'Nope. We're on our way to the Mekong Riverside Resort – which is, by the way, just about the best damn hotel in this part of the world – to meet some people. This is where you get to do the exhilarating part, the part I hired you for —'

'*Whoa there!*' I snapped, suddenly serious. 'Just hold on a minute! What are you talking about? The exhilarating part? The part you're *paying me* for? We've done all that, jumping around hotel balconies like a couple of deranged cat-burglars and nearly getting ourselves killed in the process. Not to mention annoying ex-KGB men and their giant bodyguards, which – *let me tell you* – could have gone either way —'

'What? Messing about with old Dmitry and Igor? You're joking, right? You think I wanted to hire you for *that?* That was just a bit of fun ... a bit of comedy on our way to the serious stuff. That was the *hors d'oeuvres* before we get to the main course! Hell, I promised you an *adventure*, not just a bit of fooling around.'

'Okay, right,' I said. 'That's enough, Bullen! Stop the damn car!'

'You upset about something, Andy?'

'Oh, you think I might be, huh? What about my luggage, for a start?

Where the hell is my luggage?'

'Oh, you don't have to concern yourself about that,' replied Bullen with a little smug smile, folding his hands across his belly. 'I've taken care of it. It's all packed up neatly and in the back.'

'When did that happen?'

'While we were on the Bamboo Train – I sent the driver back to the hotel to collect it. Got the Hotel Manager to pack it all up.'

'How *dare* you!' I snapped.

'Oh, excuse me!' said Bullen, in a good approximation of affronted innocence. '*Excuse me* for making sure you have your toothbrush and clean underwear with you! *Pardon me* for bringing along your socks and your razor!'

'Who said I was coming with you anyway? Where the hell are we even going?'

'Okay, Andy, *okay!*' said Bullen, holding his hands up like someone appealing for calm. 'Let me just say this, while you're gettin' so all high and mighty, I seem to remember that, yesterday morning at the airport, I offered you work, paying twenty-five per cent on top of your normal rate, which *you accepted*. Am I right, or was that a dream I had? And, what is more, I said three days, four tops, but that I would guarantee you five days' money. *Five* days! Now, I was never really hot on math at school – more of a track and field sort of guy, to be honest – but if we began yesterday morning, I figure this is now the start of day 2.'

He paused and took a deep breath.

'You know what?' he continued 'Driver! *Driver!* Stop the car. Stop, right here.'

We pulled to a halt. Bullen reached over and slid open the door and climbed out; he gestured me to follow him.

We stood on the little road, and he gazed around him. It was a hot day, the sky a deep blue, the sun beating down on us. The road itself was barely more than a rutted gravel track, hardly wide enough for two vehicles to pass. Either side of us, the grass grew shoulder-high, swaying in the slight breeze.

Bullen stood staring at nothing, into the distance, his jaw moving reflectively, like a man chewing on a big decision.

'It's okay, it's okay,' he said finally. 'Maybe it's my fault. Maybe you're not cut out for this stuff. If you're going to welsh on me – okay, fine. I've got to say I'm disappointed ... I mean, a deal's a deal. I didn't think you, of all people, would let me down, but ... okay. We can drive on to the next village or something, drop you and your luggage off. I'm sure that you can find someone to drive you back to the hotel or the airport, then you can catch a flight back to wherever you want. Yep, that's what we'll do.'

I listened to him, unwilling to commit. I hesitated. Absurdly, I felt bad, as if I was letting him down in some way.

'Bullen,' I said, at length. 'I'm *sorry*. I mean ... I don't know. I don't even know what I'm doing here.'

'You don't know what you're doing here?' he echoed. 'You don't? Oh, well, that's easy – I think I can help you out there. I can tell you *exactly* what you're doing here. You're here because you're fed up with the life you're living right now, you're pissed at your ex-wife because she's squeezing your balls for money which she's frittering away, you're tired of anonymous hotel rooms and tedious meetings and being the hamster spinning in the wheel and getting nowhere. And you can see a long, long road ahead of you of the same nothings and the same shit and this – *this*, Andrew, is a little taste of something that makes the blood fizz in your veins again.'

'What?' I said. 'Who the hell told you that?'

'Why, Andy, *you did*. You told us last night. You were maybe a bit drunk, but I reckon you were telling the truth. *In vino veritas*, you know? Like, you're the definition of a man leading the life of quiet desperation. So, I kind of thought I was helping you out a little.'

'I see,' I said, nonplussed. The thing was, he was completely right. I had no idea that I'd said all those things, but they sounded like the truth.

'Andy,' he went on. 'I'm not going to tell you what to do. It's up to you. You decide. But, my old daddy used to say something – there comes a time in a man's life when he's gotta *do* – or he's gotta *don't*. For you, I guess that time is right now. And yeah, you can pull out, just say the word, and they can chisel it on your gravestone one day: *Here lies the mortal remains of Andy Finch – a guy who might have done ... but didn't*. So, you in or out? What do you say?'

I stood wavering – I could go back to my ordinary life of calculations and technical drawings and alimony payments and empty hotel rooms – *the life of quiet desperation* – or I could follow through with this strange journey I was being offered. For five days. It's not, I reflected, the things that you do that you regret in this life, it's the things you don't.

I don't know, I should have felt the world tilting below me, the ground slipping under my feet, but I didn't. I should have, but I didn't.

'Bugger it,' I said. 'Okay, I'm in.'

Bullen clapped me on the shoulder.

'Good man,' he said, and we climbed back in the car.

The Green
Mamba

The Mekong Riverside Resort was, as Bullen had promised, something special, a simply stunning location. Set on the banks of the Mekong, the place was a complex of modern two-storey glass and white-rendered buildings, spread out across manicured gardens. Every block of four apartments had its own infinity pool where one could swim in the clear water and gaze out over the river.

Near the gate and surrounded by flower beds, there was a little Reception building with one of those ornately steep Khmer roofs. We were greeted by an extremely pretty young woman dressed in a pale blue Cambodian *Sampot Hol* outfit; she spoke perfect English and scanned our passports and conducted our check-in with charm and effortless efficiency. She told us if there was anything she could do to help us enjoy our stay, we had only to ask, or phone '0' from our rooms for assistance. She then summoned a couple of young men to escort us to our chalets and carry our luggage.

Bullen strolled alongside me down the gravel path. He leaned over as we walked and said in a loud, conspiratorial whisper:

'See that little honey at Reception? There's something *she* could definitely do to help me enjoy my stay here. Chalet 8, darlin'! Chalet 8! Reckon I should call her over later?'

'No,' I said, looking straight ahead. 'She wouldn't come.'

'Andy, *buddy*, you really gotta lighten up. I'm joking. Thing about an adventure, you've got to enjoy it as it rolls along, y'know? And appreciate the view.'

'The view?' I said.

'Yes, the view. Look at that there – the Mekong River! Amazing, ain't it?'

The sun was starting to lower, setting a soft red haze over the meandering water, where we could glimpse it between the trees. This truly was a little lush bit of Paradise dropped to Earth.

'It really is beautiful,' I acknowledged.

'Yep,' said Bullen. 'And all of this for about the same price as a Howard Johnson in downtown Detroit.'

Earlier that afternoon, during the drive over, Bullen had surprised me by rummaging in his shoulder bag and producing two British passports and handing them to me.

I flicked the first one open; it was my own passport, returned. Then, I opened the pages of the second passport – which, amazingly, was also my own passport.

'You made a copy of my passport?' I said.

'Nope, not a copy. Take a closer look.'

'Okay,' I said, suspiciously. I opened the first passport and riffled through it. The stamps of my travels were scattered through the pages, the countries I had visited on business – everything seemed in order until I got to what I always think of as the 'title page' with the photo and details. There, beside my photograph, was a new surname, '*Powell*' and below it, '*Richard John*' and a completely different place and date of birth.

I stared at it blankly for a second, trying to absorb what this meant.

'This ...' I said, 'this is a ... fake passport.'

'Uh-huh,' replied Bullen.

I checked the second passport. It was my own – unaltered.

'How did you get this?' I said, waving the fake in my hand.

'I used a fair amount of money,' Bullen said evenly. 'Not that difficult to do, if you know the right people. Mind you, much cheaper here than in Europe or the States. I guess it would pass most tests, shy of the forensics people at the FBI or something like that. Certainly good enough for what I have in mind.'

'This is a fake,' I repeated. 'I mean ... this is *illegal*.'

'Yep, of course. But you're not going to use it in the UK or to gain entry to the States or anything. In fact, you can throw it away in a couple of days.'

'What do I need it for?' I asked.

'Honest truth? To protect your identity – I'm doing you a favour. Just shows how well I'm taking care of you, huh? For the next part of your *adventure*.'

'Which is what?'

'*Lordy*, there you go again! Do I really have to keep telling you that anticipation is half the fun —'

'Bullen, I swear to God, this time I'm not going into anything blind. I'll walk away before I do that again.'

'Nah, don't worry. When we get to the hotel, I'll explain it all to you, I promise. Over a cold beer or something. And I tell you, it is *so* easy. You'll be fine. You won't have to do anything or say anything.'

'It doesn't involve jumping off balconies —'

'Andy, I guarantee that there is absolutely no jumping involved – or running or anything.'

'And you'll explain it all? Tonight?'

'Full briefing and every question answered.'

He stared at me.

'Yep,' he said. Then he smiled, so that the little folds of his skin obscured his eyes. 'When you check in at the resort, be sure to use your *new* passport. And make sure you don't let anyone see your other one.'

He tapped an admonitory finger on the cover of the little red passport, and then stretched out in his seat, pulled his hat down over his face and snoozed.

The focal point of the hotel complex was the restaurant, which was an open-sided block set above the level of the surrounding garden, a sort of roofed-in dining platform, with views out over the river. I met Bullen there just after seven, ordered a couple of beers and went down the wide staircase to tables laid out in the grassed area near the water. There, we could talk privately. A waiter brought down the drinks.

Bullen took a long pull at his beer, made a contented sigh like a man who has exactly what he needs, and cut the end of one of his black cheroots.

'First beer of the day,' he said, 'always the best one. Get the travel dust out of your throat.'

'Uh-huh,' I said, noncommittally, waiting for his explanation to begin.

'Andy, I told you I was a Contractor. I wonder; do you even know what a Contractor is?'

In my own line of business, I knew full well what a Contractor was, so I said:

'A Contractor is someone who undertakes a Contract, who signs up to deliver something for a price ...'

'True. It's slightly different in ... what I do, I suppose – but it's kind of the same. I mean, a *Contractor* does certain things for a *Client*. They provide a cut-off between the Client and the actual work being done, they deal with *risk*, they provide expertise, specialist knowledge. The Contractor makes a profit in return for providing the Client with certainty of outcome, protects him from the hazards ... stuff like that.'

'Are we talking about your line of work or mine?'

'Both, I reckon.' Bullen broke off to light his cigar. 'You see, say you're a Client, and you want something done – something that maybe you don't have the skill for, something that you don't necessarily want to be associated with. So you go to a Contractor – like me – and you pay them to make it happen.'

'Like what?'

'Well, for example, say you are the US State Department and a particular person is impeding what you want done; an oil exploration project, or a transport route ... anything really. And you've tried to solve your problem with negotiation, or with money, whatever, and finally you reach the end of your tether. And you *really* need this thing to happen. So, you decide that you want this person, the guy impeding you, out of the way. But you don't want to get your hands dirty, and you don't want a reporter from *The New York Times* or *The Washington Post* to be able to even *suggest* that you had a hand in it. Then ... you come to someone like me and I deal with it.'

I looked at him.

'When you say "out of the way", you mean – like, *kill* people?'

'Yup. Sometimes not, but if it comes to that ...'

'*You* kill people?'

'Nah, no, no,' he said, taking a long pull on his cigar. 'I don't *kill* anybody. That's the point. It's like I said, a cut-off. I find guys who can do it, do it properly and cleanly, then I set it up.'

'So you *arrange* to kill people? You're serious? Like ... assassination?'

'The point is, when the problem is resolved, the fellow at the State Department is interviewed by the reporters, *CNN* or *The Times*, whatever, and they ask: "Did the government kill that guy?", they can honestly say "No, we did not" and when the reporter asks: "Did the US government pay someone to kill that guy?" they can still honestly say "Absolutely not". That's how it works.'

I looked at him in horror. Bullen leant back in his chair with an air of satisfaction and took another gulp of his beer.

'That's appalling,' I said. 'You hire *assassins! Actual* assassins. Jesus

Christ, Bullen, what *kind* of man are you?'

'The kind of man who lives in the real world, Andy. You don't think this sort of thing goes on all the time? Well, think again.'

I knew, of course, that things such as he had described did take place – I wasn't naïve. But I had never actually met anyone involved in it – and, insofar as I thought about it at all, I imagined that the people involved would be ... *different* somehow, sinister, remote. I couldn't picture their world and mine intersecting. And yet here was Bullen, telling me that he was one of those shadowy people.

He was staring at me. He went on:

'And don't you be givin' me that morality horseshit, fella, because people get killed all the time, and you know it.'

'Yes, but —'

'There is no *but* about it. All over the world, people are deliberately killing each other, right now, this very minute. Why, I'll bet, while we've been having this conversation, thirty or forty people have been killed by their fellow man.'

'In wars, you mean? You're talking about armed conflicts? Well, but that's different —'

'There's *no* difference! Dead is dead. No difference at all. Tell me, Andy, what exactly is the difference between some Arkansas boy unloading bombs from a B-52 at thirty thousand feet and killing a coupla' hundred people and an assassin picking out one targeted guy? I'll tell you – coupla' hundred people who ain't dead!'

'It's barbaric. It's murder, and you know that as well as I do.'

'Oh, sure, but that's how the world goes round. When George W. Bush wanted Saddam gone in Iraq, he did the honourable thing and declared war. And killed maybe two hundred thousand people! Instead of a single assassination! Just one. Maybe a dozen or so other guys might have needed to be got rid of as well, but *Lordy* Lord! – look at the damage in doing it the so-called "honourable" way!'

I stared at him; I was sure that he was wrong but I struggled to put together my argument.

'Cat got your tongue, Andy?' he said. He smiled conspiratorially. 'Besides, we Americans have a long and honourable tradition of assassination. Did you know that out of just forty-four US Presidents, four have been assassinated and two more have been wounded. That's almost ten per cent.

Plus another *thirty-odd* attempts.'

He took a drag at his cigar.

'It's the real world. You may not want to see it, but it's there.'

'Of course, I *know* it happens. Doesn't mean you need to be part of it, though, does it?' I said.

'If not me, then someone else will.'

I shrugged, still unwilling to accept his argument.

'And so, what has this got to do with why we're here?' I said.

Bullen swallowed the last of his beer and waved up to the waiter standing at the edge of the dining platform. He signalled with two fingers, mouthing 'two beers'. The man nodded and disappeared from sight.

'Well, you will be pleased to hear,' he began, 'that this does *not* involve setting up a killing. Not at all. But it's going to *look* like we are.'

'You're going have to do better than that,' I said darkly.

'Sure. We are going to set up a *fake* assassination.'

'What, here, at the hotel?'

'Oh, no, no! We're just meeting them here.'

'A fake assassin?'

'Of course not! A *real* assassin.'

'That's ridiculous,' I snorted. 'Why do you need a real guy for a fake killing?'

'Because *they* won't know that!'

'So you're going to lie to a professional killer?'

'Why not? Does it offend your sense of morality? Lying, I mean?'

'Bloody *hellfire*, Bullen! You are actually planning to mess around with an actual killer!'

'Dmitry is an *actual* killer, or was, before he retired. They're just people, like you and me.'

'Like *you*, maybe. Not like me. I've never killed anybody – never even thought of it. So no, they are *not* like me. And you certainly don't mess around with them!'

'What do you think a paid assassin does, Andy? How do you think they live their lives? Somebody's rude to them in the line in the supermarket, they kill 'em on the spot? They shoot the waiter who spills their drink? These people aren't psychos, you know? They are usually very careful types, quiet, unassuming – and they don't hurt the people that they ain't paid to hurt.'

'But, you are going to try to trick them, yes?'

'I am going to engineer a situation where they will be in a particular place at a particular time.'

'Because?'

'Because my Client wants them there, because he needs to question them, and he thinks that this will be the best way to arrange it.'

'Bullen, you are going to have to start at the beginning, because right now nothing you are saying makes any sense.'

'Okay,' he said. 'Look, here comes the beer.'

'The first thing you need to understand,' began Bullen, taking a sip of his second drink, 'is that Cambodia – this place, here – is basically a basket case. You might call it a complete shambles, but I wouldn't rate it as high as that. It ranks as number 160 out of 180 countries for corruption. The International Community feels bad about Cambodia because of, I don't know, the French occupation and the Vietnam War and the carpet bombing and the Pol Pot regime and the genocide and the Killing Fields and so on and so on. So every year, the international donor community sit down and say to each other, 'What are we going to do about Cambodia?' And every year they stump up about a billion dollars and hand it over and it disappears like water into sand. It's more or less *all* stolen.'

'Oh,' I said. 'I had no idea it was that bad.'

'Oh, yep, it certainly is. Thing is, there are resources here: agriculture, rubber, textile industries, some oil and gas. So it doesn't have to be like this – except that the corruption is so endemic that very little of the value gets properly exploited, or gets reinvested or benefits the people.'

'Uh-huh,' I said.

'Okay. Now, you're asking, what has this got to do with you and me? Well, there was a Minister in the government here who was promoting a big infrastructure scheme, with lots of international investment. The project was huge, with potential to do something to open up the country, maybe do some good – but, six weeks ago, he got assassinated. Shot getting out of a car in Phnom Penh.'

'Oh, I see. Jesus,' I said.

'Yup.'

'And the assassin was our guy, the one we're meeting?'

'No. Nobody knows who the gunman was – and, in a sense, it doesn't actually matter. What *does* matter is who hired them, who *wanted it done*. And that is what we are going to be instrumental in finding out. Because, what we *do* know is that the person we are meeting here tomorrow was approached to do the killing; they were the first choice, so to speak, but they turned down the job. Don't ask me why, and it's not important. But *they* do know who approached them – and that is what we're interested in.'

'So, you are going to ask them?' I said.

'If only it were that simple. Thing is, with these people, the professional hit-guys, they don't kiss and tell. That's part of what you pay for – to keep their mouths shut. So straight-out asking them isn't going to cut it.'

'Really? Seriously?' I interjected sarcastically. 'They have – like, an Assassin's Code or something? Or is it more like guidelines?'

'That's a line from *Pirates of the Caribbean*, isn't it?' he snapped, and he wasn't smiling. 'Quit fooling around, Andy, we are dealing with serious shit here.'

'Okay then,' I said. 'How are we going to get them to tell us who approached them, if they won't do it voluntarily?' I asked.

'We aren't. We can't. What we *are* going to do is to hire them for an assassination. A *fake* assassination – like I said before. But at a particular place and a particular time – and, because these are very serious people, they will go there in advance, look around, check out the location. And that's where my Client's people will grab them – and then they will *have* to talk.'

'Like ... an ambush?'

'Exactly like an ambush,' said Bullen. He picked another of his poisonous black cigars out of the packet, cut the end and lit it.

'But ...,' I said, slowly, 'but ... what if they smell a rat? You say these are professional people, careful people. They won't just walk into a trap.'

'There you have it! And that is our job – *your part*, specifically. We have to *convince* them that the set-up is real. In this world, sincerity is everything – if you can fake that, you've got it made. And money comes into it, too. They are going to want an upfront payment and we are going to give it to them.'

'An upfront payment? And where do we get that from?' I asked.

'I've got it with me.'

'How much?'

'A *lot*. They don't work cheap. That's another thing. In this country, killing people is no big deal – happens all the time. But, you know what the favourite method of killing around here is? It's really crude.'

'No idea,' I said.

'Two guys on a motorbike. They wait until the target is out in the open air, crossing the street, at a public meeting or something. Then the guy on the back of the motorbike lobs a hand grenade into the crowd and they drive off. Boom! You get the target and a dozen bystanders as well. It's basic but effective – and *real cheap*. And, the following day, the police will probably find two bodies in a back alley somewhere, the guys on the motorbike, with a couple of bullets in them. Dead end for anyone investigating who really did it.'

'God Almighty! This is getting worse!' I said.

'Yeah, really crude and really cheap. But the good people, the ones who act surgically, they're expensive.'

'And the person we're meeting tomorrow – they're good?'

'Oh, yes. Very good indeed.'

'Who is it?'

'Someone called the Green Mamba.'

After dinner, I strolled down to the long stretch of lawn fronting the Mekong. I perched on a rail fence that marked the edge of the cultivated area and watched the waters rolling past. Somewhere in the distance, a lone narrowboat with a thatched roof at its stern was working its steady way south, the pilot barely a dot against the shimmering light reflected off the water.

There is always something peculiarly pleasing about slow-moving water, something reflective and calm – which was exactly what I was needing right then. I had listened carefully to Bullen's explanations and my part in his scheme, which was basically to play the role of the Client, the instigator who was putting up the money, and to greet someone – this so-called *Green Mamba* – then to sit mostly silent and nod while Bullen did the negotiation. He had given me a little story to tell, should it be needed. It sounded simple and I would even be acting, according to Bullen, on the side of the angels. But – I found myself balking at the idea of meeting an actual assassin. Whichever way I considered it, the prospect of looking a professional killer in the eye, especially one that we were trying to trick, made my blood run cold.

I could, of course, walk away right now, refuse to have any more to do with his scheme – I still had that choice. But something else made me want to stay and see it through.

It wasn't just Bullen's money that I wanted – though, God knows, I needed that. Without his cash, I was going to default at the bank and that was a whole new level of misery. I needed the money.

But more than the question of payment, there was the idea of *not chickening out*, of showing courage, of knowing that I hadn't run away.

I could remember, back when I was a kid, how a boy called Hudson had taken to picking on me at school. I must have been about nine. He liked to come up behind and punch me in the back, or lunge his fist at my face, jeering at me. *'Finch the Flinch!'* he'd shout. He was a heavy-set boy and I was, I had to admit, frightened of him and he seemed to delight in making my life miserable. I took to avoiding him whenever I could, in the playground, in the corridor. I would even stay an extra twenty minutes after school to be sure not to meet him on the way home.

It went on for months, and those months felt like years, because everything goes so slowly when you are young and unhappy. It got so that I didn't even want to go to school, I was so scared of him.

Then, one day, in the playground, things came to a crisis. Hudson was pushing me and I was trying to get away from him, and one of my own friends used his phrase, *'Finch the flinch'* and joined in.

My feelings boiled over inside me.

I lashed out at Hudson – something I had never dared to do before. Then I hit him again and I went at him, nine-year-old arms pistoning out in front of me. I advanced on him as he fell back. Then I was suddenly in the midst of a crowd of boys, chanting 'Fight! *Fight!*' and he was backing away from me. I doubt if I even hit him more than three or four times, but that wasn't the point – *he* was retreating from me. Eventually, a teacher broke us up and we were both punished for fighting.

That didn't matter – he never bothered me again.

Sometimes you need to move towards what frightens you.

I mused about all the things that people – men generally – say about each other: 'The good man to have at your back' or 'The right man when the chips are down'. Childish rubbish, of course, but these ideas are ingrained. I'd come this far; I didn't want to think of myself as the guy who had bottled it when it came to the crunch.

Bullen, I told myself, did this kind of thing all the time without batting an eyelid. Perhaps, he was simply braver than me. Especially as he had assured me that it was only a matter of a couple of hours sitting at a table, then another evening at this beautiful hotel and the following morning, the hotel car to the airport and a flight home via Hanoi.

A good man to have at your back – I realised then that I was going to have to do it, if only to prove something to myself.

I finally stood up and attempted to clear my head of my worries. Then I walked back to the apartment and took myself off to bed.

But, before I settled down, there was one more thing that was troubling me. I've never really been comfortable with deception – I don't do *lying*. Not in business, not in my personal life. I've always preferred the truth to fabrications; it's simpler and easier. And you gain people's trust that way. Some folks can lie without missing a beat, but not me. And Bullen, to whom lies were almost second nature, probably hadn't even considered this – he just assumed that everyone was as casual with the truth as he was.

And what we were going to do tomorrow was all about deception.

That night, I hardly slept at all.

The Mekong Riverside Resort provides a splendid selection of dishes for their guests' breakfast, served in the elevated dining area. I met Bullen there just before eight o'clock and discovered that I could eat none of it. My stomach was a solid lump; panic had locked up my digestion.

Rattan screens were rolled down on the sunny side of the dining platform, shielding the diners from the low morning sun. Bullen seemed his normal bumptious self, tucking into toast and omelettes and tropical fruit and coffee. I sipped at a cup of black coffee and waved away everything else.

Bullen ran through the bones of the arrangements again, the story he was planning to spin. I asked a few desultory questions to show interest. Eventually, he said:

'Something wrong this morning, Andy? You don't look so great.'

It was surprising that the obvious explanation didn't occur to him, that I was simply scared. I don't think men like Bullen imagine people being scared of what he thought of as routine.

'Don't I? Well, maybe I picked up a bit of a bug of some sort.'

'Ah, now don't you say that – we need you on top form today, when our guests arrive. Your most charming – and *British*. Not too reserved, but not too friendly – just somewhere in the middle, like Prince Charles or something.'

'You want me to fiddle with my cufflinks?'

'Excuse me?'

'That's what he does when he's nervous, fiddles with his cufflinks.'

'Does he? Really? I had no idea. Say there, you're not nervous, are you?'

'A little,' I said.

'Nuthin' to be worried about,' he said, and gave me one of his *Aw-Shucks* grins – which did nothing at all to reassure me.

We sat in silence for a moment then I excused myself, saying I was going to take a turn around the grounds, maybe get in a swim.

'Sure, sure, you relax some. I'll come over to get you when they arrive.'

'Fine,' I said and tried to arrange my features into something like a smile. 'See you later.'

Bullen knocked on the door of my apartment a few minutes before eleven and I followed him down the stairs and across to the elevated dining area.

The day was already hot and the air heavy; I could feel perspiration start to stick my shirt to my back. There was scarcely a cloud in the sky.

We went up the steps to the restaurant; I was struggling to put one foot in front of the other. I could feel a nerve was jumping just below my neck. A sudden thought occurred to me and I whispered to Bullen:

'Are you armed?'

He turned to me and frowned. 'Of course not.'

There were three people in the dining area, two men and a woman. They had taken a table in the far corner. The woman was standing, the two men were sitting.

The first man was about my own age, mid-thirties, dressed in denim jeans and a loose white shirt. He looked European, and had deep-set eyes under dark straight brows, sculpted cheekbones and a narrow mouth. He had the broad shoulders and narrow waist of someone who worked out regularly. He got up to greet us and, even in that simple movement, he exuded animal vitality.

The Green Mamba. I hadn't expected him to be a European.

The second man was Cambodian. I should have guessed him to be in his late fifties, grey-haired, the beginning of a paunch, a smiling face, gentle eyes. He raised himself from his chair carefully, and stepped forward to Bullen, his hand extended. He said something in Khmer, which I didn't understand.

The first man, the European, spoke:

'Good morning, Mr Bullen. I am Edi Sarachi, and this gentleman is Banh Sar.' His English was good but accented. I guessed Eastern Europe, Bulgarian or maybe Romanian.

'Pleased to meet you,' said Bullen, shaking hands with both men. 'Let me introduce you to our Client.'

'Mr Powell, of course, good to see you,' said the man who had called himself Edi Sarachi. He leant out a muscular hand toward me; his grip was hard, just a touch too tight.

'Mr Sarachi,' I said, acknowledging him. I turned to the older man. 'Mr Sar,' I said, shaking the outstretched hand.

Edi Sarachi smiled politely.

'Mr Powell,' he said gently. 'You should know that in Cambodia the family name comes first, like in Chinese.'

'I see,' I said, cursing myself for my stupidity. I had known that, of course. But the moment was lost in Banh Sar saying something in his own language, accompanied by his cheerful laughter.

'Mr Powell, Banh Sar says that he would be honoured if you would use his first name, *Sar*,' offered Sarachi.

'Oh, good,' I said. To cover my embarrassment, I reached forward and shook the older man's hand again. 'Good morning, Sar,' I said. 'My name is Richard.'

'*Rish-aard*,' intoned Banh Sar, smiling broadly.

'And,' said Sarachi, turning to the woman who had been standing quietly watching us, 'This is Banh Chanlina.'

Bullen and I duly shook hands with her. She smiled demurely, ducking her head.

Formalities completed, we sat down, all except the woman. Mentally, I was trying to work out the relationships between the three. If Banh was the surname, then the older Cambodian, Banh Sar, and the woman, Banh Chanlina, also probably Cambodian, were related. Man and wife? I took a quick sideways look at her. She was dressed in a modest white blouse and a calf-length royal blue skirt with a patterned hem. I would have guessed her age at about thirty. Too young to be his wife, more likely his daughter. Maybe she was the Green Mamba's girlfriend? I turned my attention back to the two men.

'Gentlemen,' began Sarachi. 'Shall we begin? You have told us in your phone call that your Client, Mr Powell here, needs a certain matter dealt with. Well, we are now here to hear the details. So would you care to provide?'

'Sure,' said Bullen, lighting up one of his black cigars. 'As I told you when we spoke, Mr Powell has business interests in this region. He has some long-established trading relationships and transport links throughout Indochina —'

'These business interests – they are narcotics trading, yes?'

'Our Client,' replied Bullen evenly, nodding slightly across to me, 'has a diverse portfolio of investment in machinery, agricultural products, transport, construction. His involvement is primarily financial, logistics, business facilitation. He has no hands-on participation in any of these transactions.' Bullen paused for emphasis. 'So, no, he does not trade in drugs.'

'I see,' said Sarachi, lighting a cigarette.

'Moreover,' added Bullen, 'our Client has no criminal record or active involvement in illegal activities.'

'Yes,' said Sarachi. 'We wondered about this and have made some discreet – very discreet, of course – enquiries, to check his *bona fides*. Nobody we have contacted has heard of Mr Richard Powell; not only does he have no criminal record, he has no *'name'* at all in the region. We found this very difficult to understand ...'

There was a pause. Even I could guess that this was Sarachi, very gently, calling our bluff; of course 'Richard Powell' had no visible presence in Indochina, because he didn't exist. Bullen appeared to be momentarily at a loss – I sensed that the situation was about to get away from us, so, with my heart in my mouth, I interjected:

'Mr Sarachi —'

'Please, *Edi*.'

'Edi, then ... I'm gratified that you've taken the time to make enquiries about me – it shows that you are serious people – but let me say, I am even more gratified that you drew a blank. I have made it my business to remain one or two steps removed from any direct involvement with these commercial transactions. Even my agents have *agents*, if you know what I mean? If I had wanted a public persona, I'd have one, but I don't. I would have been seriously disappointed if you had been able to connect my name with ... anything.'

There was a moment's silence as Sarachi considered this, then he said:

'And yet, you are here today.'

I couldn't tell if that was a statement or a question so I didn't reply. Instead Bullen took over:

'You specifically requested that you got the opportunity to meet our Client, so he agreed to come , mostly upon my assurance that the Green Mamba's reputation for total discretion is justified. We are assuming that you are as professional as your reputation suggests?'

'We are,' said Sarachi.

Just then the woman, Banh Chanlina, interrupted.

'Tea, coffee?' she asked.

I hadn't notice that there were cups and saucers laid out on the adjacent table. The question seemed to be addressed to Bullen and myself, so I asked for tea and he coffee, she nodded and poured and carried the cups over, then did the same for Sarachi and the man that I now thought to be her father. She poured a cup for herself, brought it over and took a seat at the end of the table.

Bullen was speaking again, detailing the 'subject that was to be elim-inated', a Thai criminal 'boss' commonly known as Jackie Sam – some complicated story about his liking for Jackie Chan, who was a huge star in this part of world. His real name was Thanathorn Vejjajiva and I had, with some difficulty, memorised the name in case I had to say it. Bullen outlined how this man was encroaching on my (completely fictitious) business operation, and how his removal had become necessary.

Sarachi cut in from time to time to translate what was being said for the benefit of the older man, who nodded vigorously and even smiled at us. The woman remained silent and gave no indication as to whether she understood or not.

I sat and listened, my face neutral.

While they talked, I found myself reflecting that anticipation can often be worse than the event itself. Now I was actually sitting opposite these people, some of my fear seemed to have evaporated. A curious fatalism was creeping over me.

I found myself observing Sarachi. He certainly looked the part of the ruthless killer, with his dark good looks and watchful eyes. But I also remembered Bullen's comment about real killers being *careful types, quiet, unassuming*. Maybe that was what the old Cambodian was, an assistant or decoy. You might pass him in a crowd without a second glance. He looked harmless, even benign.

Bullen was getting to the significant bit, the part about exactly where the kill was to take place. Jackie Sam was a difficult man to get close to, he explained; he was cautious and well protected. And, moreover, his death should be public, a message to others who might try to emulate him. There was a selected location, and this was very important.

Everyone leant in closer as Bullen described how a relative of the target, an uncle, had died recently and wanted their ashes, after cremation, scattered in the Mekong. Accordingly, a party of family and friends would be bringing them to the Khone Phapheng Falls in southern Laos, a natural beauty spot just over the border. It was not unusual in Thailand, he said, to make up such a 'Funeral Party', part holiday and part memorial journey, and the mourners would all dress in white, the traditional colour of mourning in Thailand. In eight days' time, Jackie Sam and his family would be at the Falls, in the open. And *that* was where he was to be killed.

Bullen had spread a map and an aerial view of the Khone Phapheng Falls Park on the table; the two men were bent over examining it, discussing it in rapid Khmer. At length, Edi Sarachi looked up and said:

'You have made your requirements clear. Would you allow us a moment to consult amongst ourselves, in private – if this is an operation we would be prepared to carry out ... and also to give you an idea of fee?'

Bullen looked at me, making a show of asking my permission; I nodded.

'Fine, sure,' he said. 'We can go down to the gardens by the river. Call us when you're ready.'

'Thank you. But, before you go,' said Sarachi, 'one question which we need to ask. Richard, why do you want this man Jackie Sam killed?'

'I thought we'd explained that already,' put in Bullen with a slight frown. 'There are clashes of business interests —'

'We understand all that,' said Sarachi, cutting across him. 'But we would particularly like to hear it from Mr Powell – from Richard here – directly. Your motivation is important to us.'

Bullen was about to say something but I raised my hand to stop him.

'There is, yes, Edi, something else – not just business,' I said. 'Let me tell you about it – and it's not only financial.'

I cleared my throat carefully before I continued:

'Some months ago, one of my subsidiaries, a financing company, invested money into a new business, RSK Logistics, with my authorisation. As you know, there are a lot of shipping companies operating around the Gulf of Thailand, into the South China Sea, even into the Sea of Java. They serve the ports of Thailand, Vietnam, Singapore, Jakarta, sometimes around to China. But most of the shipping is large-scale, docking in deep-water harbours. They can't use the smaller, shallower ports; I saw this as a gap in the market. This new venture was initially two container ships which could service the shallow-water harbours. We started with two, with a view to expansion.'

I smiled dryly and went on.

'It was a sensible business venture, and I had modest hopes for it. Unfortunately, this man Jackie Sam has a stake in another company doing the same, or similar, thing. Obviously, they perceived us as rivals to their business. Eight weeks ago, the shipping office of RSK Logistics was visited by two men representing Jackie Sam, who warned our General Manager that he was crossing a line, treading on toes, and should cease operations.'

'And?' asked Sarachi.

'Well, obviously we didn't stop. We carried on. And then someone visited the house of one of our captains when he was home on leave.' I took a deep breath. 'They killed our captain, and his dog, and his wife. And when his two children – a boy and a girl – came home from school, they murdered them as well.'

I looked around the little group, and put my hands on the table.

'And then,' I said, 'I asked Bullen to find us a professional to deal with Jackie Sam. So you see, it's business, but it's personal as well. There ... the other part of the story. We'll wait for you in the garden.'

Bullen and I rose to our feet. They politely stood up as well and the two Cambodians bowed slightly.

We walked down the staircase from the restaurant; when I was sure we were out of earshot, I turned to Bullen, trying to contain my elation.

'That went well, didn't it?' I said. 'I mean, you think they swallowed the bait? It seemed like they did.'

'Andy,' said Bullen, very evenly, 'Calm down. We haven't landed them yet.'

'Yes, but it went okay, huh? Don't you think?'

'Perhaps,' he said, smiling grimly. 'But, did you notice something? They *knew your name*. And I have *never* given them your name, only ever referred to you as 'The Client'. Which shows that they must have sneaked a look at your passport in the hotel records, last night, then made their checks. *Lordy*, Lord. Oh yes, these people are good, *real* professional.'

'Oh,' I said, suddenly reminded of the horrible risk we were running. 'But, they were checking my fake passport, weren't they? Just as well we had that.'

'Yeah. And now you're going to thank me?'

'Yes,' I nodded.

'But, you did your part good, Andy. I gotta say that, just the right mix of warm and cool. You did the story well too – even I was starting to believe you. I reckon you began to enjoy yourself, right?'

Now that the worst was over, I had to admit that I had enjoyed it, just a little. But I wasn't going to tell him that, so I said:

'To tell the truth, I was trying to work out how the three of them fitted together. Is the old guy's the woman's father? And, is she Sarachi's girlfriend or something? I was watching Sarachi mostly, trying to guess what he was thinking as you were talking. God, though, doesn't he look the dangerous type; I thought you said that killers didn't look like killers – but he does.'

Bullen suddenly paused and looked serious.

'That's what you were thinking, eh, Andy?'

'Uh-huh.'

'Well, thank *fuck* you didn't say any of it. My God, you could have screwed the whole thing. You haven't a clue, have you?'

'What?' I said, startled and nettled in equal measure.

'I didn't tell you the set-up? I'm sure I said last night.'

'Bullen – believe me, I'd have remembered.'

'Well, you're wrong. The two men, they're *both* the monkey. The organ-grinder is the woman. *She's* the one we're after – *she's* the Green Mamba.'

I followed him down to the chairs in the garden and sat down. I was shaken by what he had told me – and how close I had come to saying something stupid and blowing our story out of the water. But more than that, I was thinking of something else, something worse – he *hadn't* told me the set-up (I would have remembered; if there was one thing I could rely on myself for, it was grasp of details and I would *never* have forgotten a detail like that) – and it was his careless oversight that had endangered us. It reminded me – as if a reminder were needed – that we were dealing with very dangerous people and the man in whom I was placing my trust was by no means infallible.

Ten minutes later, Sarachi came down the long staircase and asked us to re-join them in the restaurant. We followed him back and resumed our seats. Banh Chanlina, who I was seeing in a new light, topped up our cups with fresh tea and coffee, then quietly took her place at the end of the table.

'We have considered your proposal,' said Edi Sarachi.

'Yes?' said Bullen.

'It is difficult.'

'In what way?'

'Normally, a Client will ask for a particular person to be dealt with. We can then study them and make the best arrangement. You are specifying where and when you want it to happen. It limits our ... opportunities.'

'Okay,' said Bullen, his face betraying nothing.

'This location – there are no high buildings – or any buildings at all. Long-range shooting is therefore impossible. There might be crowds of people around. These are problems, you see?'

Bullen said nothing.

'In such a situation, the best method may be close work. A direct approach to the target, strike, move away quickly, before anyone realises what has happened.'

'A gun or a knife?'

'A knife, for speed and silence.'

'You would need to have surveyed the area very carefully beforehand,' said Bullen. His face was completely neutral as he dropped his hook into the conversation.

Sarachi translated this for the old Cambodian, who said something in reply. Sarachi grinned, a smile that didn't touch his eyes: 'Sar says that we *always* survey the ground very carefully.'

'Of course,' said Bullen.

'Such an operation ... would be very exposed, potentially dangerous. Our price must reflect this.'

'I'm sure.'

Sarachi took a piece of paper from his pocket and handed it to Bullen who unfolded and read it.

'*Wow!*' he said.

'I said it would be expensive,' offered Sarachi.

Bullen passed the piece of paper across to me. I took it and scanned it. Written on it, in pencil, was an extraordinary figure.

I decided, on a sudden inspiration, to act up to my part. We could, of course, agree to any number, because it was never going to be paid – but, I reasoned, if we were too casual about the money, it might arouse suspicions. I frowned, allowing my eyes to roll around the noughts, and handed it back to Sarachi. I turned to Bullen.

'That is too much,' I said. 'This number is unrealistic.'

'But you want your target eliminated? You must be prepared to pay —'

'I am prepared,' I cut in, 'to pay the correct price. I assume that this is simply your opening offer.'

'Do you have your own price in mind?'

I, of course, had absolutely no idea of a figure, so I glanced across at Bullen. He picked up Sarachi's piece of paper, scored out his number and wrote his own underneath. He handed it to me – another amazing sum. However, I knew my role in this bit of theatre. I nodded and he passed it to Sarachi.

Sarachi grinned when he read it, and showed it to the two Cambodians. Banh Chanlina's eyes narrowed and her father simply shrugged.

'This number is not possible,' said Sarachi shortly. 'Do you think that this is a market stall where you can barter down some peasant trader?'

'No, of course not.'

'If you want it done cheaper, there are others who could do it ... for less.'

'If we wanted others to do it,' replied Bullen calmly, 'then we would be talking to them, not you.'

'Our numbers are very far apart,' said Sarachi.

'Yep,' said Bullen. There was a very long pause. 'Naturally.'

The two men stared at each other for a moment. I waited, aware that that the mood had changed, that this was starting to go wrong.

Then Bullen began to smile, and Sarachi's mouth gave an involuntary twitch. On either side, bluffs had been called and they both recognised it.

'Of course,' said Sarachi smoothly, 'this is just the start of a negotiation. Naturally we are far apart. We must discuss this further and find common ground. I'm sure it is possible, with goodwill ...'

'Edi, I think that we shall be able to do business together,' said Bullen.

'One moment, please,' said Sarachi.

There was a hurried conversation, in Khmer, between the three visitors. Without understanding what was being said, it seemed something was being suggested by Banh Chanlina; her father agreed with her but Sarachi opposed it. Gradually, a consensus was reached. Sarachi turned to us and said:

'Gentlemen ... obviously we must negotiate further – and understand your requirement better. So, now we invite you to come to our home for a day or two, as our guests. Transport will be arranged – it is about three hours away, and we can promise to make you very comfortable there. We should be proud to show you Khmer hospitality. It is the tradition of the country here – so we insist, and you cannot refuse.'

Even Bullen was momentarily surprised by this suggestion – he hesitated before he said:

'That is a very kind, but I'm not sure ... Richard has engagements, meetings already arranged. He's a busy man, as you will appreciate.'

'We understand. But, surely his agents will be able to manage matters ... for a couple of days? And you need to get this matter – which is no trivial matter – concluded, yes?'

'Why can't we conclude it now?' asked Bullen. 'Here, today? We are all gathered now, so let's agree it.'

'If you were selling us a bag of rice,' replied Sarachi, 'then we could do it in a minute. But this is not a bag of rice, is it? This is a very special thing, a *dangerous* thing ... an *expensive* thing. It should not be hurried. Of course, if you prefer, you could take your proposition to others, and we will conclude here and part as friends.'

I was listening to this with a sinking heart, although I was trying desperately to keep my face impassive. I had thought that we were home and dry. If it hadn't been for the infuriating Oriental habit of haggling over every damn thing – then we would have been.

And, as to this new suggestion, honestly, I could have wept. I knew what Bullen would want; he'd agree to anything to get his devious little scheme to work. Well, I, for one, wasn't going anywhere as their bloody house guest, and Bullen would just have to go whistle – and if he didn't stump up all the money, I would have to live with it. I was out of this, just as soon as the meeting broke up —

Bullen was talking again:

'You will have to give a little time to see if Mr Powell's schedule can be rearranged. Can you give us an hour?'

'Of course,' said Sarachi.

I could feel their eyes on us as we made our way out of the restaurant.

Back in my room, I closed the door and then carefully slid the glass screen shut on the balcony. I turned furiously on Bullen:

'They smell a rat!' I exclaimed. 'It's obvious!'

'Well, they don't trust us, I'll give you that – and we don't trust them either. We anticipated that. But, let me tell you Andy, they *are* on the hook —'

'Damn *right* we don't trust them! And there is absolutely no way I am going to be involved in some assassins' house party. So help me God, I'll swim in blood first! *This* is the end of the line. You said a couple of hours of sitting and nodding and saying nothing much – well, I've done that! No further! You can carry on, on your own – though if you want my advice, you'll do no such thing. Anyway, what do you even need me for?'

'You know, Andy, I half-expected you would say something like this —'

'You did, did you?' I rasped.

'And I knew you might need to think about it, quietly and calmly —'

'I don't need to think about it. I'm not getting involved. I'm *out*.'

'Andy —'

'Out! I can spell it for you if you need it made any clearer! Out! Just give me my money and I'll make my goodbyes and be on my way – and you can do whatever the hell you like.'

'*Andy*, Andy, Andy. I *really* need you to think about this. From both sides. Firstly – think of the opportunity we have here. To go to her house! We wouldn't even need to go through with this whole Khone Phapheng Falls nonsense. When we get there, we can just call my Client and tell them where she *lives*. Nobody else has ever known that. *Secondly* – if we refuse the invitation, the whole thing falls apart. You know, these Orientals are very hot on their hospitality; they get offended when you turn them down – then, no deal, no payment. For you *or* me.'

'Hang on a second!' I said. 'My money wasn't conditional on their accepting the plan. I don't remember that being mentioned!'

'Andy ... you, your *refusal*, could cause the whole deal to collapse, just as it was going so well. You can hardly expect the Client to pay for that, can you?'

'I did my part!'

'So far, yes, but we ain't over the line, are we? And, thirdly, let me remind you of something. You're right – they don't trust us. And maybe, *just maybe*, yes, they smell a rat. And if we flat-out refuse them, perhaps they're gonna turn nasty.'

'*What?*' I said, something in my innards going cold.

'What do you think they're going to do if they even begin to imagine we were setting them up?'

'What on earth could they do? Here, at the hotel? They can't touch us here.'

'You think that, huh? You're ready to bet on that? Bet your life? Because, let me remind you – these people are killers. If only *half* of what they say about this Green Mamba woman is true, she could fillet out your spine and hand it to you while you're still wondering if there's someone standing behind you! I am *not* joking! You talk about how you'll swim in blood – well, maybe, that's exactly what you'll do!'

That gave me pause. I knew I was clutching at straws when I said:

'I thought you said that meeting them wasn't dangerous.'

'I *may* have exaggerated a little – to keep your confidence up. You know how it is —'

'No, Bullen, I don't know how it is. Not with professional murderers. This is all new to me ...'

'I understand that, Andy. So, I'll give you one more good reason why you should play along ...'

'Which is?' I demanded.

'Twenty-five thousand dollars. Twenty-five thousand! Never mind any five day's fee. I'm sweetening the pot. A straight twenty-five grand. It's *that* important to me. And, you know, it's the safest thing to do anyway. C'mon,

Andy, we can pull this off. Let's live a little. *The adventure* rolls on!'

I hesitated. I won't say that the money didn't tempt me – and I was caught between a rock and a hard place. And while I wasn't convinced by Bullen's retribution scenario – I wouldn't have bet against it, either.

'*C'mon*, Andy, you know it's the right thing to do!'

Actually, I knew that it probably wasn't. But I was weakening.

'Damn it, Bullen!' I growled.

'Easiest money you'll make in your life. Twenty-five thousand. Say that you're in!'

'Jesus!'

It was the wrong thing to do.

But I did it anyway.

Bullen made the arrangements. Sarachi would send a driver to pick us up that evening; in the meantime, we should pack our suitcases and enjoy the afternoon, have an early dinner. I took a swim in the pool by my block, thinking it might calm me a little (it didn't). We agreed to meet up for drinks at five, as the heat of the day was starting to cool.

I got there first, on the lawn down below the restaurant, selected a table and sat down. I distracted myself watching a lizard climbing on the bark of one of the trees nearby, hoping to catch some unwary insect.

Bullen arrived ten minutes later.

'Hi,' I said.

'Hi yourself,' he said, settling himself into the plastic chair. 'You all packed?'

'Yes,' I said. 'All ready to go.'

'Good,' he said and then lapsed into an uncharacteristic quiet.

I continued to watch my lizard.

Bullen seemed uncomfortable, shifting in his seat. Eventually, he broke the silence: 'What you thinking about?'

I looked round at him. Introspective questions weren't his style.

'Oh, this and that,' I said. 'Watching the little reptile on that tree – he's hunting for insects or grubs or something.'

'Where?'

I pointed it out; 'There.'

In truth, I had been more or less day-dreaming, thinking about my little flat back in Potters Bar. It was about a mile from my old house, easy reach for my daughter visiting. She liked to refer to it as 'Dad's Monk's Cell,' because I kept it so neat and tidy – she had probably heard my wife (my ex-wife) call it that. I used half the sitting room as an office: a desk, a computer, a filing cabinet, a bookshelf with reference books and stuff. I dislike clutter, so the place was almost Spartan in its orderliness.

Despite being there for two years, I hadn't got around to putting any pictures on the walls, nor adding any other personal touches. On the rare occasions when I invited someone there – usually a woman who I had met through one of the dating websites – they always remarked upon it. 'This could only be a man's apartment,' they would say, 'not a scatter cushion in sight.' I would smile and nod and promise to get some as soon as the shops opened.

It was hardly an inviting or homely place. And I missed my garden.

And it also seemed a terribly long way from the meandering banks of Mekong River and palm trees and climbing lizards – and cold-blooded assassins.

'Andrew,' said Bullen, abruptly breaking into my musings. 'You ever done a parachute jump?'

'Good God, no,' I replied. 'Why on earth would anyone want to do something like that?'

'Oh, I don't know,' he remarked, cutting the end of one of his black cheroots. I had the impression he was in an uncharacteristic pensive mood. 'I did it in Basic Training. Got pretty good at it. I remember the first jump I did without a fixed line – you know, where your parachute cord doesn't get pulled automatically when you leave the 'plane – and there I was, fifteen thousand feet up in the air, just me and the sunshine, and I remember thinking to myself, "Bullen, right now, you got a big choice and maybe half a minute to make it. Pull the ripcord or don't. Up to you." It was a … one of those *moments*, you know.'

'Surely there's no choice,' I interjected. 'You either pull the ripcord or you die.'

'Well, now, that there – that's the choice.'

'I would have said that anyone who thought he had a choice at that moment was borderline crazy.'

'Yup, probably.' He paused to light his cigar, drawing the smoke into his lungs. He inspected the glowing tip, then said:

'You know when … something happens? Something nearby? How you can feel something?'

'What do you mean, "when something happens"?'

'Oh, anything, I mean, like an accident, a crash on the highway, something significant, you know? A bad thing … or a good thing.'

'What are you getting at?' I asked.

'A car crash – or someone has a heart attack in the street. You know? I tell you what – you know that town in France, Reims?'

'I've heard of it, yes.'

'Yup. Well, there's a room there, ordinary, shabby little room, maps on the wall, table and chairs. It's above a school now, but they've preserved the actual room. It's where they signed the surrender at the end of the Second World War, the war in Europe anyway. The Nazi generals, Jodl and so on, and the Brits and the Americans and the French. Anyway, this ordinary little room, eighty million people dead, and they sit down and they end it. Something *happened*. And even now, you walk into that room, and you can *feel* it … like a wind passing by you. Something important happened in that room.'

'Uh-huh,' I murmured.

'Or a hospital room where someone just died … or where two people fell in love… or a wreck on the highway where people slow down to look. You know? They can feel that wind passing them by – something *important* happened here. And don't you want to know what it was, how it felt, what they thought? What I'm trying to get at … I don't know, maybe you want to be a part of it, to say this was *me*, *I* made it happen, I'm not just a passer-by. To stir that wind, you know?'

'Okay,' I said, not really seeing at all.

'And the parachute jump … the plane flies on, leaves you alone in the sky with your choice.'

'There is no choice,' I said flatly.

'No, you're probably right, there's no choice – leastways, I never made anything but that one choice.' He paused and puffed at his cheroot. 'I ain't done a parachute jump in something like twenty years, but I still dream about it, sometimes. In my dream – you don't mind me talking about this, do you?'

'No,' I said.

'In my dream, I sometimes make the other choice, so – sure enough – I know that I'm gonna die up there, fifteen thousand feet up, flying high in the sky, alone in the sunshine.'

'Surely you don't die up in the sky, you die on the ground when you hit it.'

Bullen was looking into the distance and didn't seem to have heard me.

'When you make that choice,' he said, talking mostly to himself, 'You die up there, in the sun. That wind is rushing past you. And ... and I think it would be, you know, *alright*.'

He fell silent, lost in his thoughts.

'Bullen?' I said.

He stared out over the river.

'Bullen?'

'Oh – yeah. Sorry, Andy, miles away.'

'You okay?'

'What? Yes, yes, well, it's just a stupid dream, you know?'

'Right,' I said.

'Say, you think we could get a drink here? Can you see the waiter?'

It was nearly dark when the car and driver arrived; we had finished dinner and returned to our respective rooms. Bullen knocked on my door and I opened it. The driver was standing behind him, a middle-aged Cambodian who insisted on carrying my suitcase to the inevitable white Toyota people carrier. He had no English to speak of – when I had asked him how long the journey would be, he smiled and shrugged apologetically.

We set off immediately.

Bullen was tense, which made me feel tense as well. The car turned left out of the hotel complex, then right through the little town, then right again. We drove along a long unmade road for a while, turned onto what seemed to be barely more than a track, then crossed a narrow bridge and made several more turns.

Bullen stared out the window.

'What's the matter?' I said.

'We've driven in a circle,' he said, tightly.

'How do you know?' I said. 'What, you can navigate by the stars or something?'

'No, but I can spot the North Star. And we've gone around the compass, twice.'

'What's that mean?' I asked.

'It means that they don't want us to know where we're going.'

'Oh,' I said. 'Oh, shit ... should we ... tell him to stop the car?'

'No. It means that they're being very careful.'

'I see,' I said, and settled back into my seat, all my misgivings flooding back.

Eventually, we seemed to be driving in one direction. As usual in Cambodia, the road was rutted and bumpy – we wallowed around horribly in the back – but the progress was good. Looking out of the window, I couldn't see anything. Occasionally we passed a few isolated houses or a crude temple, but mostly there was nothing under the crescent moon but dark fields and jungle.

We pulled up after about an hour. The driver got out, said something incomprehensible and opened the back and started to unload our luggage. Bullen and I alighted.

We were on a gravel road, apparently in the middle of nowhere. There was a small Buddhist shrine at the edge of a field and nothing else to be seen. No houses, no street lights, no shops.

'Where are we?' demanded Bullen. The driver was carefully placing our suitcases beside the shine. He shook his head.

'What are you doing?' said Bullen. 'What the hell's going on?'

'I don't like this,' I said.

'Me neither,' he grunted. He walked across to the driver and stood in his path. 'What are you doing? Where are we?'

The man stared at him blankly. When he tried to step around Bullen, the American cut him off. Finally, he looked at his mobile phone and pointed at the shrine.

'You, here,' he said. 'You go here.'

'What?' snapped Bullen.

'Here. This you go. You.'

He slid past Bullen and made to get back into the Toyota. Bullen pulled at the open door.

'No,' he said forcibly.

The little Cambodian started the engine and rolled the car forward, Bullen hanging onto the door. Then he revved the engine noisily and picked up speed, forcing him to release his grip.

The tail lights disappeared into the darkness.

'God Almighty, Bullen,' I said. 'What are we supposed to do now?'

'We sit tight, I guess.'

'What? In the middle of the bloody night, in the middle of nowhere.'

'Hang on a minute, Andrew. Listen, will you!'

Bullen stood stock still in the middle of the road, listening. I strained at the surrounding silence. Crickets and the croaking of frogs.

'You hear anything?' he said.

'No.'

'Me neither.'

'And?'

'This is a break point.'

'What's a break point?'

'A stop in the journey. They're checking to see if we have arranged to be followed.'

'And did we? Arrange to be followed?'

'Of course not!'

'That's a pity,' I said, darkly.

'Okay, so we sit tight.'

'Shouldn't we start walking?'

'Where to, Andy? We don't know where we are. We wait for them to come to us.'

'Or to murder us,' I ventured.

'If they wanted us dead, they would have done it already. No, this is just them being really cautious. It's a good sign, I think.'

I sat down on the stone slab of the little shrine, and flipped out my phone, to see if I could get anything with the GPS, but I had no signal coverage. After a moment, Bullen eased himself down beside me and lit one of his nasty black cigars. He said:

'So, partner, here we are, lost in the dark in the wilds of South East Asia. At least we had ourselves a good dinner and a couple of drinks, pleasant temperature out – so, couldn't be finer, huh?'

I knew better than to say what I was really feeling, so I simply said:

'Nope, as long as we don't get attacked by snakes', and carried on listening to the grasshoppers chattering into the night.

There was a pause, so I said:

'Anyway, talking of snakes, now we are definitely alone, I need to ask you a question.'

'Sure.'

'This woman, Banh Chanlina – *Green Mamba* – why do they call her that?'

'It's kind of her nickname. Like *The Jackal*.'

'So why *The Green Mamba*?'

'Because she does close work, knives, razors. Not so much rifles and guns. She's supposed to be really fast ... I mean, like rattlesnake fast. She walks past you in the street, you don't even see her hands move.'

'And she's killed a lot of people?'

'Maybe. Certainly a few. Folks like her don't exactly advertise, you know? But, yes, I've heard of a good few – eight, perhaps ten. But you can never be sure.'

'How?'

'How does she kill 'em? Definitely one walk-by, a Macau gangster, just took him out as she passed. They say she didn't even get his blood on her. Because when she wants to be, she's just an ordinary woman in a crowd, nothing to notice. A young mother or a factory girl on her way home.'

'And they *say*,' continued Bullen, 'that she did two Cosa Nostra guys in Las Vegas. Made men as well, tough cookies. They were at a party, very fancy, very lush, with pretty little waitresses in frilly black dresses and aprons, you know? And one of those waitresses was an Asian girl – and anyway, both these guys are found in the ladies' restroom, one with his throat cut and the other stabbed through the heart. And rumour has it that the waitress was the Green Mamba. Or so they say.'

'Good God,' I said.

'And, there was a Russian businessman in a hotel room in Bangkok. He sends out for a little professional female company to help pass the night, you know? The guy has two bodyguards on duty in the corridor and they let the girl into the room, checked her over for any weapons, then let her out after an hour. And then they find their guy dead, killed by asphyxiation with a hand towel. Later, they discover the real prostitute, scared shitless, tied up in a cleaners' cupboard. Story is that the Green Mamba let the

Russian have his money's worth before she did him. That takes some brass balls.'

'And this is the woman who served us tea today? Jesus!'

'Even stone-cold killers are able to serve tea, Andy. They're just people like the rest of us. And in this fucked-up country? They reckon that the Cambodians killed about two million of their people during Pol Pot's time, so murder isn't exactly unusual here.'

We sat for a moment in silence, then I said:

'Explain to me about the story. What was that in aid of?'

'The story?'

'The story about the ship's captain. That you wanted me to tell them?'

'Oh, that, yes. Well, that's the thing, see, Andy. You know, there are really two types of professionals out there. There are some who kill, I guess, just about anyone at all, so long as you pay 'em. And there are others who want to believe that they only doing *the bad guys*, the guys who really deserve it. Maybe it's something to do with their consciences, how they sleep at night, I don't know. Fortunately for them, there's no shortage of bad guys out there who deserve to get iced. Anyway, just in case this Banh Chanlina is one of the latter, I gave you the story to tell them.'

'God,' I said. 'So you thought it up.'

'Oh no,' he said. 'It's a true story. Just happened to someone else.'

He broke off. A set of headlights was approaching.

'You guys need a lift?' said the man in the driving seat.

It was Edi Sarachi, grinning at us laconically with his elbow through his open window. Another man, a bearded Cambodian with badly pitted skin, sat in the passenger seat beside him.

'Surely do,' said Bullen. 'Our ride kinda fizzled out on us.'

Sarachi laughed, a short cackle that reminded me of dry wood snapping.

'Jump in the back then,' he replied. 'Ak here will get your bags.' He said something to the Cambodian, who got out and went round to the shrine.

The vehicle was the standard people carrier. I worked the handle on the rear sliding door and glanced momentarily at Bullen. He nodded imperceptibly; I climbed in.

'Just one quick thing,' said Sarachi, leaning over the back of his seat. 'Here is where I'm going to ask you to hand over your cell phones. You understand, of course?'

'You don't trust us, then?' grunted Bullen.

'Mr Bullen, I do trust you – exactly the same amount as you trust us.' He gave the same sharp cackle. 'But people like the Mamba stay alive by not taking unnecessary risks. You're professionals; you know how this works.'

'Sure,' said Bullen, and took out his phone.

'Best to switch them off, save your battery.'

'Uh-huh,' said Bullen. He gestured to me to hand mine over too. I wasn't happy – those phones were our only link to the outside world – but I didn't see what else to do.

Having finished collecting the suitcases, the man called Ak came round to the open door. Sarachi reached over and handed him two little grey metal boxes and a reel of tape and a pen. Ak slid the back off Bullen's phone, pulled out his SIM card and placed the card and phone into one of the boxes. He then taped around the box crossways and lengthways. He handed the box to Bullen, with the pen.

'If you could sign on the tape,' said Sarachi. 'Don't want you to think that we would tamper or pry into your cell.'

'Okay,' said Bullen, scribbling his name on the top and bottom of the taped box. Meanwhile, Ak was taking my phone apart in the same way, extracting the SIM and repeating the taping-up process. He handed me the box to sign (at the last moment, I remembered to write 'Richard Powell'). I passed it back.

'Thank you, gentlemen. Just a precaution, you know,' said Sarachi. Ak was sliding the door shut. He got back into the front passenger seat and we set off down the rutted road.

'You guys being waiting long?' said Sarachi over his shoulder.

'Ten, fifteen minutes,' said Bullen.

'Oh, not too bad. I had meant to be here to meet the other car, but I got held up.'

'Lucky it wasn't raining,' remarked Bullen.

'Rainy season's all but gone,' said Sarachi absently.

He drove for a while in silence then, half turning toward me, said conversationally:

'Is this your first time in Cambodia, Richard?'

I hardly had a second to think what the correct answer might be, then decided that the truth was probably best.

'No,' I said.

'That so? Seen much of the country? On your previous visits?'

'Some,' I offered, trying to be noncommittal. 'Battambang ... and the capital, you know. Not much of the countryside.'

'You should try to get to Siem Reap. The temples there are really spectacular.'

'I can imagine,' I said, in a tone which didn't encourage further chat. We relapsed into silence, bumping along the road. Bullen and I exchanged looks; mine a furious question, and his an answering half-shrug: *just go with it.*

I glanced at my watch. It had turned eleven.

'We got far to go?' I asked Sarachi.

'Couple of hours, maybe. Got to take it steady on these roads.'

'Quite,' I said.

'Open a window if you want to smoke.'

'No, that's okay,' I said, and glared pointedly at Bullen.

Nobody spoke for the rest of the journey. Despite the lurching ride, I'm pretty sure that Bullen nodded off.

We arrived slightly before two o'clock. I had the impression, in the darkness, of an open set of metal gates set in a high stone wall. The car went down a short length of driveway and pulled up outside a neat single-storey structure.

Ak jumped out and gathered up our bags. Sarachi climbed out and stood at the side of the car

'We've put you gentlemen in the Guest House, to give you a little privacy,' he said. 'There are all the usual facilities there. The meals will be served in the main house. Water here is okay to drink if you want to, but there's bottled water in there as well. I'll do you the tour of the place in the morning. Breakfast at nine? Give you a chance to catch up on sleep.'

'Fine,' said Bullen.

'You should find everything you need in your rooms.'

'Fine,' said Bullen again.

'Well, I'll say goodnight. Main house is over there, by the way.' He gestured further round the driveway.

'Fine,' said Bullen, for the third time.

'Goodnight,' I said, and followed Ak into the wooden bungalow. Whether from the long drive or the lateness of the hour or the strain of the day, I was dead beat, ready for my bed.

It had occurred to me that, despite their apparent hospitality, we were now, to all intents and purposes, their prisoners.

But I could worry about that in the morning.

When I awoke, it was just before seven. I sat up and took a long drink of the bottled water and took a look around the room.

The previous night, I hadn't bothered to do more than clean my teeth and lay my head upon the pillow; I'd paid no attention to my surroundings. The room in which I found myself was the size of a decent hotel room with a polished wood floor. It had been tastefully decorated in natural wood and pale grey; everything looked clean and new. There was a comfortable double bed, a slat-fronted wardrobe, a good-quality table. Underneath the big window, there were a couple of easy chairs.

I showered in the little bathroom, unpacked my suitcase and laid out my clothes, dressed and wandered out into the corridor, and then through the outer door and into the morning air.

And found myself, of all places, in the most beautiful garden.

There was a wide lawn between flower beds of glorious colour, backed by tall trees. In the middle distance, surrounded by ferns, there was a pond, almost a lake, with a fountain playing in the middle. I strolled onto grass that still had the morning dew on it – I had the foolish notion of slipping off my shoes and walking barefoot, although I didn't – and saw that the lawn divided further on, with more banks of flowers.

'Good morning!'

I twisted my head to locate the owner of the voice; a woman was getting to her feet away to my left. She had evidently been working on the flower beds. She was dressed in a man's shirt, stained baggy trousers, a pair of wooden clogs and a frayed straw sunhat. She held her gardening trowel in one hand. Below the shadow of the hat, I could see that she was smiling broadly, presumably at me.

'Good morning,' I called back.

'Do you like our garden?' she said.

'Yes,' I said. 'It's extraordinary.'

'It is, isn't it? The result of much hard work, but all worthwhile.'

I must confess that, in that first moment, I didn't recognise her. Then the penny dropped – in my defence, I should say that she had been dressed quite differently at our previous meeting, and the only words I had heard her utter were 'Tea' and 'Coffee'. The woman approaching me seemed to be almost a different person, relaxed, friendly – and not in the least demure – and she was speaking fluent English with, perhaps, the slightest trace of an American accent.

'I'm sure,' I said.

'Indeed,' she said. She stopped a few feet from me and produced a clean white rag from her pocket and wiped it over her face. She had obviously been perspiring in the sunshine. 'I love this garden – it's almost entirely my own work, you know, mine and my two boys.'

'Your boys?' I said, thinking she was referring to children.

'I have a couple of local boys who work on it with me. Everything grows so quickly here. Keeping it under control is half the work.'

'I see,' I replied, for want of anything better to say.

'Are you a gardener yourself, Mr Powell?'

I had to take a second to think – would the fictitious Richard Powell be a gardener? Some instinct made me opt for the truth.

'I used to be. I live in an apartment now. I don't have a garden.'

'You don't? That's a great shame. I take so much pleasure from my garden. Edi has his gymnasium, where he loves to work out and I have my garden.'

'His gymnasium?'

'It's over on the other side of the house, by the swimming pool. We built it for him – he has strange complicated machines and weights and exercise bicycles in there. He can spend hours, working out, honing his muscles. Sometimes I catch him, *surreptitiously* – is that the right word in English? – looking at himself in mirrors. So very vain. Do you work out yourself, Mr Powell?'

'Me? Oh, no.' I said. Without thinking, my hand slid over my flat stomach. I shrugged. 'Never saw the need.'

She smiled.

'You Europeans all seem so large compared to us little Orientals. Especially men like your friend Bullen.'

'I think that we can safely assume that Bullen doesn't spend a lot of time working out.'

She laughed out loud at that, an open laugh that showed her teeth.

'No,' she agreed. 'Come, let me show you our garden.' And with that, she looped her arm into mine (she seemed, from my small experience of Cambodian women, remarkably forward) and took me off on a tour. We strolled along the flower beds, with her pointing out various species which were new to me; displays of what she said that the French call 'Rose porcelain', a bright red flower that looked halfway between a dahlia and a large strawberry ('They use that to treat anaemia,' she said in passing), banks of riotously deep-pink Siam tulips, the vibrant green of the *Cryptocoryne* ferns surrounding the pond. She pointed out the clumps of carnivorous *Nepenthes kampotiana*, mottled red and green which, to my eye, looked almost obscene in their shape.

'And these,' she said, as we paused in front of a display of pale pink and yellow flowers, delicate blooms with three spreading petals. 'You must surely know what these are, yes?'

I had to admit that I didn't. She laughed again.

'They are the *Rumdul* flower. You must know them! They are the national flower of Cambodia; the scientific name is *Mitrella mesnyi*. Beautiful, are they not?'

'Absolutely,' I agreed.

'Do you miss your garden?'

'Oh, yes, but it was never as special as this – it was a very ordinary English garden.'

'You know, of course, that most of what you call "a very English garden" originally came from China. Your plants are not English at all; camellias, hydrangeas, magnolias, even buddleia and hollyhock.' She glanced up at me as she spoke. 'We have some magnolias and buddleia here. Come, let me show you.'

Our walk through the garden was interrupted by the appearance of a lean young man in work clothes and a red baseball cap so faded from the sun that it was almost pink. She broke off and switched into rapid Khmer. As she spoke, she pointed from time to time around the flower beds, apparently giving him a list of tasks. He trotted off and she turned back to me.

'That is one of my boys. Dara – we call him Da. He is one of my co-workers, my boys.'

'I see,' I said.

'Do you know the time? I haven't got my watch with me ... and I lose track working out here.'

I glanced at my wrist; 'it's a quarter to nine.'

'Then you must be ready for your breakfast. I ate earlier; forgive me for keeping you from it.'

'Not at all; I was enjoying the tour.'

'Oh, dear,' she said suddenly, frowning. 'Now, if I was a proper hostess I should shower and change and join you for breakfast – but I have some more work to do out here. And then I would have to change back into my work clothes again. Would you be offended if I came to breakfast like this? It is not exactly gracious ...'

'No, not at all,' I said.

'You are very polite. We will sit out on the veranda – Sita would be much affronted if I came into the house in my gardening clothes.'

'Fine,' I said.

'Then, I will see you there in ten minutes. The house is over that way. Sita does not speak English, by the way – but she will smile a lot. Remember to always smile back, and you will be in her good books.'

'I will. And Sita is ...?'

'She is our old housekeeper. She rules over the kitchen and the house with a bar of iron.'

'A rod of iron,' I corrected, like a pedant, and instantly wished I hadn't.

'Oh, yes, a *rod* of iron. Thank you. You must always tell me if I make a mistake. A rod of iron. Anyway, Sita is ... well, sometimes, I think that all of us here work for her.'

'I will make a special effort to smile,' I promised, and turned to go.

'Oh, and Mr Powell?'

'Yes?'

She had turned around and was looking up at me very directly. For a moment, I could see her face unobscured by the tattered straw hat.

'I forgot to say – welcome to The House Above the Jungle. I'm so pleased that you agreed to come.'

'I am very pleased to be here.'

And, improbable as it sounds, in that moment I almost was.

I strolled along in the general direction she had indicated, musing on our strange encounter. It was, I reflected, the first conversation that I had ever had with a professional assassin, and it was nothing like I would have imagined – putting aside, of course, the fact that I never expected to have met such a person in the first place.

It had given me a chance to size her up – and it occurred to me that it had also given her a chance to size me up. Had I said anything that I should worry about? No, I decided, I had been only neutral and polite. How much trouble could a man get himself into discussing gardens?

Not, I imagined, very much.

Then I thought about the way that she had, uninvited, slid her arm into mine. It was odd behaviour – but the proximity would have allowed her to gauge my mood, to detect whether I was anxious or not.

Not, then, as odd as it had seemed.

I recalled her neat hand resting on my forearm – was that her knife hand? Were those the same fingers that wrapped themselves around a blade, just before plunging it into some poor soul's jugular?

Gardener or not, it was a pretty scary thought.

And her face ... what had I been able to see in her face? There was a narrow shape to it, not as rounded as most Cambodian women. But no, that wasn't it. That wasn't what I had noticed.

Her eyes – she had shrewd eyes. She saw things.

Whatever else she was, or wasn't, she was no fool.

I found the main house fifty or so yards further on, a splendidly complex wooden structure, set up on long timber columns. The roof was steeply pitched with carved fascia boards and the wood was very red, a deep orange-red. The ground floor was mostly open, and there was a fine timber staircase leading upwards to a great veranda, surrounded by an ornate balustrade.

There didn't seem to be anything happening on the ground floor, so I walked up the staircase to the deck of the veranda, which was deserted. There was a table and a set of heavy chairs.

'Hello,' I called out.

A small grey-haired woman appeared from the interior, bowed, and said something incomprehensible in Khmer. I remembered to smile excessively.

'Breakfast?' I said, hopefully.

She smiled back, said something else that I didn't understand, then pointed first to the interior and then to the table on the veranda. I guessed that she was offering me a choice of whether to eat inside or out. I indicated the veranda table, she nodded, twittered some more, pulled out a chair for me and then disappeared, still talking.

I sat down.

Bullen joined me ten minutes later. He seemed in a serious mood.

'I knocked for you,' he said, 'but you'd already gone. Where you been?'

'I woke early, so I got up and had a tour round the garden. It's amazing, isn't it?'

He grunted something vague, by which I gathered that he didn't care much about horticulture.

'Chanlina showed me around,' I said. That caught his interest.

'That so? What did she talk about?'

'What do you think? Gardens, carnivorous plants, Siam tulips, the national flower of Cambodia – which, I'm told, is something called the *Rumdul*. Stuff like that.'

'The *Rumdul*, huh? That figures,' he commented. 'Nothing else?'

'No,' I replied easily, enjoying his slight discomfort. 'We didn't get as far as cuttings and compost and fertiliser.'

'Hmmm,' he said.

'You and I,' I said, leaning forward, 'have some things to talk about.'

His eyes slid left and right. We were alone on the veranda, but there were sounds of activity from the interior.

'Not here,' he said.

The housekeeper, Sita, emerged with a pot of coffee just as Chanlina, still in her gardening clothes, appeared at the top of the stairs.

With Bullen there, Chanlina was more reserved that she had been earlier. I got the impression that she was wary of him – and he of her. I made various conversational sallies, mostly about gardens, which I guessed was safe ground. Just to annoy Bullen, I asked Chanlina about which fertiliser she preferred to use ('Here in the countryside,' she laughed, 'there is only one option – animal dung!').

In due course, Sarachi appeared – I resisted the mischievous urge to ask him if he had been in his gym – and he suggested that we convene to continue yesterday's discussions about money.

'Fine,' said Bullen.

'Then, I am going to let you do that without me,' I said, 'and let my colleague here earn his fee.' I thought it wiser to sit out any discussion that might expose my ignorance.

'Sure,' said Bullen, easily. 'I have all the stuff I need. No need for you to involve yourself in the details.'

'Can you give me a couple of hours, then?' said Sarachi. 'I have some things I need to do this morning.'

'Okay by me,' said Bullen.

Breakfast over, Bullen and I strolled off, ostensibly to look at the garden but really to confer. We found a quiet spot around the back of the pond where we were sure we couldn't be overheard and settled ourselves on a couple of benches.

'Okay, now, Andy,' he began, but I cut him off abruptly.

'Not *okay*, now, Bullen,' I snapped, glaring at him. 'So bloody much, then, for your idea of simply allowing ourselves to be brought here and ... giving your Client a call and telling him where these people live! *Eh?* Have you got any idea – any idea at all – where we are?'

'Well, nope,' he said slowly.

'That's a pity, then,' I said, 'seeing as how we've handed over our phones! And you didn't anticipate that? Just their little precautions, eh? Didn't see that one coming, did you?'

'You're right, maybe I should have thought of it. Anyway, listen, the thing now ... is not to panic. The plan is still working. I'll do my negotiation with Sarachi and —'

'Yes,' I said sarcastically, 'so, that's Plan A that we're back to ... Plan B having got buggered up by something that you possibly-per-haps-maybe-*should* have thought of. Have you got a Plan C? I assume that you have some kind of tracking device concealed in the sole of your shoe or in your luggage, or maybe injected under your skin or something like that —'

'Andy, you've been watching way too many movies. That stuff doesn't happen in real life.'

'No, in real life there are — you know something? In movies, the hero isn't so bloody stupid that he trots along willingly into the villain's lair! Tell me at least that you told your Client that we were going to the Green

Mamba's house? You did do that?'

'Yup, I did,' said Bullen.

'So, how is he going to find us?'

'What?'

'If we don't surface again – if they decide to hold us here – how is your Client going to come and get us?'

'They aren't,' said Bullen flatly. 'They won't. Andy, you don't seem to understand the relationship between guys like us and the people who are paying us. The way it works, they don't come and rescue you. If you deliver on your deal, then you get your money - happy days. But, if you *don't* deliver, if you get into trouble, then – *adios amigo* – they never even heard of you; it's not their problem.'

'So ... we're on our own?' I said, incredulous, something fluttering in my gut. 'There is no back-up plan?'

'Nope.'

'Jesus *Christ!*'

'Andy, you're panicking —'

'You think so, huh?'

'Andy – we just gotta stick to the plan. I do the deal with Sarachi, we get out of here, you go home with your cash. Simple. Panic's not going to help. So you just play your part, remain calm, and everything will work out.'

'I wish I shared your confidence, because there's another thing that I wanted to mention. I was speaking to Chanlina this morning and I came away with one very distinct impression.'

'Which was?'

'These people, her especially, they are not *stupid*. In fact, they're pretty smart. And they *are* going to see through us.'

'No, they are not,' said Bullen firmly. 'They are *not* going to see through us, and I'll tell you why. Sure, they're clever; they wouldn't have lasted this long if they weren't. But there's a factor here that you are missing.'

'Which is?' I demanded.

'Greed,' said Bullen. 'All human beings are greedy, including Sarachi and Chanlina and her father. I know about people like them and I tell you this: they want the money and they want to believe that they are going to get it. They actually *want* to believe in this plan, because they want the pay-off. Their greed is doing half our work for us.'

I wasn't convinced, but whether Bullen was right or not was never tested. Because, just before noon, something happened that changed everything.

Bullen reminded me that I needed to hide my original passport and anything, in fact, that had my real name on it. 'Sarachi is quite capable of searching our rooms – in fact, in his place, I definitely would – and you *do not* want them discovering you ain't who you say you are,' he told me. For once, I agreed with him.

There was no point in using any of the obvious places – under the mattress or beneath the drawers in the wardrobe. Bullen assured me that wouldn't fool a professional for a moment. I ran my eye around the room, and even out into the corridor, searching for a possible nook or cranny. I looked to see if there was a gap at ceiling level between the roof and the wall, but the place was properly built; there was nothing. Finally, I had an idea.

'How about the shower tray?' I said.

'What about it?' he asked.

'There has to be a U-bend underneath it – and there must be access for maintenance.'

'Andy, I don't even know what a U-bend is.'

'Never mind,' I said and went into my bathroom and got down on my knees. There was a step up to the shower itself and, sure enough, there was a removable panel at the side, held in place by a couple of little screws with plastic caps.

'You got a screwdriver?' said Bullen, looking over my shoulder.

'No,' I said, 'but you've got your little penknife on you?'

'Okay, let me get at it.'

I stood up and let him hunker down with his penknife. He put the blade into the screw-head and tried to turn it.

'It's tight,' he grunted, forcing at it, and promptly crumpled the edge of the knife.

'Oh, for God's sake,' I said in exasperation. 'Get out of the way. Give it to me.'

I knelt down, turned the knife over to use the blunt edge in the slot, eased it clockwise to loosen the screw, then unscrewed it anti-clockwise. I did the same to the others and then lifted the panel off.

Lying flat on the floor, I peered inside the void. As expected, there was dust and wood shavings and a couple of cobwebs, but whoever had built the shower had cut a good-sized hole out of the floor. I reached in – there was a cavity I could get my hand into.

'Hang on a minute,' said Bullen and left the room. A moment later, he returned with a half-full plastic flight bag.

'What's this?' I asked.

'Working capital,' he said. 'Never you mind what. Think that you can hide it down there?'

'Yep. Put my passport and credit cards into the bag.'

He did so and handed me the bag. I dropped it into the cavity.

'There,' I said, 'even if they remove the panel, they won't be able to see it.'

'That's great,' he said. He stared into the gap. 'What part is the U-bend?'

'Never you mind what,' I said and started to replace the panel.

I had already seen two aspects of Chanlina: the self-effacing and demure Oriental serving tea at our meeting in the hotel and, by contrast, the cheerful gardener in her straw hat and old clothes proudly showing me around her flower beds. That morning, I was to observe a third, entirely different side.

I was never sure whether or not this was something that I was supposed to see; I can only say that I chanced upon it by accident.

I was wandering through the garden, having abandoned Bullen and taking a few moments for myself, when I heard strange sounds nearby, like someone clattering sticks together, interspersed with grunts and the occasional laugh or high-pitched giggle. Intrigued, I threaded my way between the hedges and found myself in a little enclosed space where the most extraordinary display was taking place.

It was Chanlina and Ak - and they appeared to be engaged in sparring with what looked like curved sticks. They each had two, one in either hand, maybe a metre long and about as thick as a heavy broom handle, and they were dancing around the space, occasionally darting forward and attempting to hit their opponent around the head or the body. Each sally would be blocked – that was the noise I'd heard. I noticed that they held the sticks about a third of the way along, and they could both spin their weapons in their hands, the better to block an attack.

Ak was barefooted and bare-chested, dressed only in a pair of long shorts. His wiry body, impressively muscled, was sheened with sweat and his face was a picture of concentration as he weaved about, trying to strike Chanlina. She, in turn, was also barefoot and was wearing what looked like black harem pants below a sort of wrap-over scarf that was tied to cover her top but left her midriff exposed. She had her back to me.

I heard her say something to Ak, some sort of instruction, and he took a step back, panting, then surged forward, his sticks rotating as he went in, trying to break her guard. What impressed me was the shocking speed with which he moved, almost flying into the attack. My eye could hardly follow his whirling sticks, the *clack-clack-clack* as they smacked against her defence.

Chanlina, responding, seemed to have springs on her heels, shifting her weight left and right, reacting to his attacks so quickly that her own sticks were a blur of motion. She fell back, then seemed to move past him, coming around in a circle.

She spotted me and, without a pause in her sparring, nodded and smiled across the little space. She said something in Khmer to Ak, and looked to change gear, moving from defence to attack and drove forward.

I had thought that Ak was fast but he was nothing compared to Chanlina. Her sticks were like two windmills – no, that's wrong, they were more like propeller blades, spinning in her hands and I realised that she had only been toying with Ak previously. He was quite unable to do more than fall back in front of her onslaught and she grasped her advantage and twisted around inside his guard, knocked one stick clean out of his hand then somehow tripped him and put him flat on his back.

Chanlina laughed lightly and leant down to lift him to his feet, saying something to him that I couldn't understand but sounded encouraging.

As she straightened up, she turned her attention to me.

'Mr Powell, would you like to try?' she asked, then spun her sticks up into the air and casually caught them.

'Me?' I said. 'God, no, I wouldn't last two seconds against either of you.'

'Maybe we'd go easy on you. The important thing is not to think too much, just let your body move as you need it to. *Please,* come on, give it a try!'

I picked up one of the fallen sticks and hefted it in my hand. Up close, I realised it was carefully carved, with a small metal guard. It had a nice balance, which allowed them to spin so easily.

'This is a samurai sword, isn't it – or at least, a practice version.'

'No, this is a *Dha* sword, Mr Powell, an ancient Khmer weapon. Maybe the Japanese copied their *katana* sword from us. We have the real ones over here – which, of course, we would never use for practice.'

'When *would* you use the real ones?'

She thought for a moment. 'Probably never,' she said ruefully, 'they're not very practical, not in the real world. You couldn't walk around carrying one. But Ak wanted me to teach him a couple of moves. So I'm having a few sparring sessions with him. He's getting better.'

She paused, regarding me, and I couldn't read her expression at all. Then she reached down and picked up the two real swords and unsheathed them.

'These are deadly things,' she said softly, weighing them in her grasp. 'Beautiful but deadly. And there is something about death – the closeness of death, the possibility of it, that is always strangely beautiful ... don't you think?'

Then she suddenly knelt on one knee and crossed the swords in front of her, resting their tips on the ground, staring straight at me. It was at once both darkly elegant and menacing.

I felt the cool breath of fear on my neck.

'I've never thought about it,' I said quickly. Chanlina stood up and smiled again, then carefully re-sheathed the swords and laid them back on the grass.

'So,' she said, 'one sword or two?'

'Well, just one then.'

'Very well,' she said and passed me a wooden practice sword.

'Wouldn't I be better ... maybe ... sparring with Ak?'

'No,' she replied, moving her fingers in a gesture of dismissal. 'Ak does not have the *control*, not yet.'

I stood like a fencer, my arm extended. She copied me, although I suspected it wasn't the correct stance. She tapped the tip of my sword with her own.

'You are ready?' she asked.

I nodded.

She came at me and I parried, trying to keep her at a distance. I aimed a cut at her shoulder, which she blocked almost without looking at it. I switched my attack and went at her but she swept her sword upwards and came in under my guard. I expected to feel her sword touch me, but instead I managed to fend her off with my free hand and tried to use my weight to push her backwards, but she twisted away then came at me from the front.

I blocked and blocked and blocked again, and I realised that she was really going very easy on me - so I tried an attack again, slashing left and right and she had to duck to protect her head. I drove forward, pressing my advantage, hacking at her so she had to defend her torso, then suddenly I saw a glint of something serious in her eye and her blade whirled past me and I lost sight of it as it spun past my shoulder, my chest, in front of my eyes and almost parting my hair. She allowed me one last lunge, then I felt a light, controlled slap of her blade on the side of my neck.

Chanlina stepped back, bowed slowly and said: 'And now, Mr Powell, you're dead.'

I stood, panting hard.

'Of course,' I said between gasps. 'Well, thank you for making my death so painless.'

'You are our guest here – it is the least we could do.' Then she grinned, a girl again, and the serious glint was gone. 'Please – I did not hurt you, did I?'

'Only my pride,' I said.

'But, you did very well ... and I believe that most men would have been too frightened to even try. So, I think your pride is undamaged.' She bowed again, lower this time.

The first intimation that anything unusual was going on was when Sarachi appeared and told Bullen that they would have to postpone their discussions. He seemed distracted – his usual smug composure had deserted him. Then, later on, I spotted two strangers up on the veranda of the main house, an older man and a younger one, both locals. An unfamiliar vehicle, a small pick-up with scuffed paintwork, was parked in the driveway.

'What do you think's going on?' I asked Bullen.

'Search me,' he said. 'They've got visitors, that's plain to see. I don't think that it's got anything to do with us, though. They'll tell us if they want us to know.'

The next thing that happened was that the grey-haired housekeeper, Sita, appeared with a tray of food, followed by the young man I had seen earlier in the garden, Da, similarly laden. She laid out the plates on a table near the big pond; this was our lunch. With elaborate sign language, she indicated that we should come and eat there.

We were evidently not being allowed into the house.

While we ate, Bullen kept glancing around, as if he might somehow deduce what was happening, but nobody came near us.

'What do you think ...?' he asked me.

'I have no idea,' I said, wondering the same thing.

'Me neither,' he muttered. He was nervous.

'Probably best if we keep out of the way,' I said. 'Don't you think?'

'Not sure – I don't like it. I don't like not knowing ...'

Lunch finished, he smoked one of his cigars. He was skittish and seemed to want some displacement activity.

'We could go find their pool, maybe have a swim?' I suggested, for something to do.

He didn't reply.

We waited.

Eventually he stood up.

'That's it,' he said, with finality. 'I'm gonna go up to the house and find out what going on.'

'Shouldn't we stay here, out of their way, and let them get on with it?'

'Hmmm,' he said, standing up. 'Well, they can always tell me to get lost.'

With that, he strode off up the lawn. I stayed where I was and waited.

I watched the butterflies fluttering across the flower beds. It was hot in the sun; I was wondering about going back to my room to fetch a hat. Maybe get my paperback and sit and read, though I was hardly in the mood for reading. Bullen's nerves had unsettled me – not that I wasn't unsettled enough already.

Half an hour later, Bullen came back. He was smiling broadly.

'Andy,' he said, sitting himself down beside me. 'I think we just got the chance to get this thing, our arrangement here, moving.'

'How?' I said.

'We can do something that puts Chanlina and Sarachi and old Bahn Sar seriously into our debt.'

'Oh yes?' I said.

'And for these people, the Orientals, being in debt to someone is heavier shit than it is in the West.'

'Okay,' I said cautiously. 'And how exactly are we going to get them into our debt?'

'Because of what's happened this morning.'

'Oh, for Christ's sake, just tell me what's going on.'

'Okay, the big excitement, then. Well, it seems that the grandson of one of the local landowners, an old guy called Nuon, was kidnapped last night. And Nuon and his son, the boy's father – they were the two strangers we saw up on the veranda earlier – have come to Chanlina for help.'

'Why have they come to her?' I said. 'Shouldn't they have gone to the police?'

'You know, Andy,' said Bullen patiently, 'this is why you need to understand more about how things work in this country. It's difficult for a foreigner to properly grasp the level of corruption here. Folks don't really trust the police – and especially not in a case like this.'

'Go on,' I said, struggling to follow.

'Well, it seems that the guy who kidnapped old Nuon's grandson is the brother-in-law of the local Chief of Police. So, there's no point going to the cops for help.'

'What? You're joking? The Chief of Police's brother-in-law is a criminal, a kidnapper?'

'Yup.'

'Oh.'

'So, how things work here is ... that people don't simply go to the police when they need something sorted out. The police only act for whoever is bribing them – it really is *that* corrupt – so they go to the local *Big Man*, the person who has the power to act, for help.'

'You know, Bullen,' I said in exasperation, 'I sometimes think you are wasted in your business. You should have been a politician; anytime you explain anything, I wind up knowing less than when you began. Are you saying that the *Big Man* is, in this case, Banh Chanlina?'

'Yep, apparently so. And they've agreed to help.'

'Why?'

'It's kind of the *quid pro quo* in these parts. They shield her, keep strangers away from her and she protects them – like with, say, the Mafia, you know? You ever see that scene at the beginning of *The Godfather*?'

'What?'

'*The Godfather* – when they go to Marlon Brando for justice. You re-member?'

'*The Godfather?* What the hell are you on about?'

'Listen – take my word for it, okay? They come to her for help.'

'Okay,' I said, thinking this over. 'So ... how does that affect us?'

'Well, the kidnapper, a guy called Khem Lundy —'

'The Police Chief's brother-in-law, yes?'

'Yes, well, he's sent a demand to Nuon for cash, to return the boy.'

'How much?'

'Don't know. A lot. Probably all that old Nuon has – and a bit more. Anyway, Khem's got a place, about fifteen miles from here, where he's holding the boy. But he has men with him, most likely armed, maybe five or six of them. Say six.'

'Go on,' I said, horribly aware of what was coming.

'So, Chanlina has agreed to help. To go and rescue the boy. And count-ing up, Chanlina and Sarachi and their two guys, Ak and the other one —'

'Da, the lad I met in the garden this morning?'

'Uh-huh. Plus the boy's father. That's only five.'

'What about Banh Sar?'

'Too old. Full of arthritis. No use.'

'And?'

'So I said we would help. You and me,' he grinned.

'*What!* You are fucking kidding, aren't you?'

'No, I'm not. Listen, seriously, Andy, this is a terrific opportunity. We go in with them on this, and they *owe us* – like I was trying to explain to you. You want all this finished and to get gone? Well, we help them, they can't refuse to work with us, can they? Think of the kudos we gain! It's heaven-sent! You can see that, can't you?'

'I can see that you're out of your tiny mind!' I snapped. 'Go storming into some house against five – no, sorry, *six* – armed men to rescue some kid? You seem to be forgetting who I am! I don't know one end of a gun from the other ... Jesus! I mean, I'm sorry about the kid and everything, but I would be absolutely useless —'

'I appreciate that, Andy, and I've explained that to Sarachi and Chanlina. They believe that you're more like an accountant, a business man; you won't have to go in. Probably just stay with the cars and make sure they're ready to go. But you're able-bodied and fit – and we haven't got enough people.'

'No. Absolutely bloody not! You'd be better off taking the old house-keeper than me!'

'You can't back out now. It wouldn't look good – for either of us.'

'What do you mean – *back out*? You volunteer me for this hare-brained scheme and now, somehow, it's my fault. That's bloody absurd – and I won't do it.'

Bullen sighed heavily and put his palms on his knees in a gesture of resignation. He paused and glanced disappointedly at me, like a man who has all his worst fears confirmed.

'Well, if that's the way you feel, Andy ... I reckon you had better come up to the main house and say it yourself. It would be better coming from you, I think, to tell them that you've turned chicken-shit on us.'

I drove the second car, a big Nissan estate. Bullen and Sarachi travelled with me. Chanlina was up ahead in the lead car, with Ak driving and the child's father and the young gardener called Da.

I had gone up to the main house to break the news, genuinely intending to say straight out that the idea of my going on their rescue mission was ridiculous. I didn't do that kind of thing; I would be no use to them.

But, when I walked into the room where they were all grouped around the table, studying a Google Maps printout of the house, the boy's father had rushed across to me and started babbling in Khmer. I couldn't un-derstand a word of it, but his expression, a mix of misery and terror and utter gratitude, made his meaning clear enough. Chanlina translated for me: 'He is thanking you from the bottom of his heart', and so I hesitated and then I found myself looking at the map as well, getting caught up in the discussions. I caught a little questioning glance from Bullen who was standing across from me. I shrugged back.

They had, sensibly, already taken on board the fact that I was unused to violent action and had assigned me the role of staying with the vehicles, parked half a mile from the house, while they did the dangerous stuff.

And yet ... despite my misgivings, there was something in the atmosphere around the table, a feeling of suppressed excitement combined with quiet competence, the cool determination that exuded from Chanlina and Sarachi and even from Bullen, the sense that they were doing something risky but also necessary and right – so that, somehow, I actually *wanted* to be involved.

Or at least, I didn't want to be left out.

Sarachi and Chanlina led the planning, with an occasional interjection from Banh Sar, who wasn't coming along himself but knew the area. Now and then, Bullen put in advice (all those years of CIA training had to count for something), the child's father simply absorbed it all, seemingly on the verge of breaking down altogether. The two other Cambodians, Ak and Da, watched and listened and said nothing at all.

It was decided to go in at dusk. The kidnappers would be expecting a night attack (insofar as they were expecting anything) and Chanlina's father speculated that they would have been getting bored during the day, and were liable to have been drinking.

That seemed sensible to me.

Eventually, the moment came to distribute weapons. There, I drew the line. I was as likely as not to blow my foot off with a gun as to hit something useful, so I flatly refused to take one. The rest of them helped themselves from an assortment of automatics and revolvers and other weapons that appeared from somewhere; I recall Ak picking up a light machine gun and Bullen taking a modern-looking automatic, while Sarachi selected a pump shotgun.

Then it was time to go.

Everyone was subdued as we went down to the cars, until Bullen spotted something on the cargo floor of the estate car, the one that I was to drive. I leaned in to look. It was a furled black umbrella with a curved handle.

'An English umbrella, Andy,' he grinned. 'You'll feel right at home.'

Sarachi glanced over at it: 'I think that's probably made in China,' he said.

'We'll be okay if it rains then,' I said. It was the best joke I could think of.

To maintain the chance of surprise, we coasted the vehicles, engines off, for the last couple of hundred yards along the rutted track. Da had scouted ahead of us, to see if they had put a look-out on the road. When he had established that they hadn't, he waved us in.

I let the car roll to a halt without using the brakes. Sarachi made the 'O' gesture with his fingers – *good* – then eased his door open. Bullen, moving with a silence that I would not have thought him capable of, did the same. I followed suit and we gathered up by the lead car.

I was to stay put here. The rest of the group split into two and moved off down the road, then at a signal from Chanlina, they disappeared into the fields on either side of the road.

The plan was that I should wait here, doing nothing, until I heard noises from the house. Then, I was to turn the cars round so they would be pointing in the right direction for a quick getaway. I checked the lead car to make sure that the keys were in the ignition.

There was nothing for me to do but to stand in the dusk, peering into the distance, wondering how close they were to the house, what sort of a reception they were going to get. The sky was darkening, there were big slate-grey clouds gathering over to the west. I felt a warm breeze on my face.

I thought, idiotically, about all those movie clichés: 'It's the waiting that's the hardest part.' Well, I was content to wait. I was feeling, genuinely, that curious empathy that soldiers must feel with their comrades, just before battle, excited, but – all the same – I was happier to be back here.

I couldn't help it – it's at times like these that my darkest thoughts race off on their own. I was thinking what would happen if Bullen got hurt – or worse still, killed? Would I be able to call a stop to the whole thing – all bets are off? Would Sarachi and Chanlina want to continue with the whole nonsensical charade? Could I pull out without arousing suspicion? Or, for that matter, what if Sarachi himself got hurt – or even Chanlina? They had seemed so confident of the success of their rescue, but what if their confidence was misplaced?

Still, they knew what they were doing. I should actually be more concerned about the boy's father – presumably he was just as much an amateur as I was.

Or, I realised guiltily, I should be worried about the boy himself.

Then I thought – what I would do if it was my own daughter who had been kidnapped? Would I be brave enough to creep into the dusk with a gun in my hand?

My musing was interrupted by the faint sound of gunfire, the muffled bangs that must be pistol fire, a series of distant thuds, followed by the heavier boom that was probably the shotgun. It had begun. I stood straining my eyes, staring out into the half-light, but there was nothing to see.

Shit! I was standing about when I needed to get on with turning the cars round. If things went badly, our little team might come running down the road at any moment, expecting me to have done my part. I climbed into the Nissan, started it and reversed, half turning, then changing gear into forward and hauled it round.

And got stuck.

I tried reverse, and spun the wheels. Cursing, I got out and saw that the offside tyre was on loose gravel and had no grip. I flung my weight against the bonnet, trying to push the car back, tried again, but it was too heavy. I looked around in a panic ... what could I do? Maybe I could use the other car to shift it, push it or pull it, but the damn thing was jammed halfway across the road. What to do?

What to do? *Hellfire!*

Think, damn it, Finch, *think!*

I made myself stop for a second. I needed to get something under the spinning wheel. I ran around the car looking for something, anything that I could use. *Nothing*, so I went to the other car, looked in the front, in the back – finally I popped the boot and there, there was a little heap of discarded overalls. I snatched them up and took them and stuffed them under the tyre.

I jumped back into the driving seat, took a breath, selected second and eased the clutch.

And moved.

Carefully now, I completed the manoeuvre and finally got the car positioned in the middle of the road and pointing in the right direction. Thank Christ, I muttered to myself.

Okay, now for the second car. I got out of the driving seat.

Just then another idea suddenly struck me.

My God, I thought.

It occurred to me that I was here with two cars, the keys of both of them in my hands. I had the means to run, to get away from Bullen and his damn-fool schemes, to escape from professional murderers and their sinister henchmen. I had money in my pocket – not much, but enough. I could drive one car away, disable the second somehow (a couple of flat tyres?) That would give me a good head-start on anyone coming after me. I didn't actually know where I was and I had no passport or credit card, but if I just drove straight and I could get to the authorities, the British Embassy, whatever, surely someone would help me?

But , on the other hand, I thought of the responsibility to the people I would be leaving behind. Even Bullen would have a hard time explaining how his Client had deserted him. Sarachi would take a very dim view of it and would, quite probably, take it out on him. And what about Chanlina?

Also, more to the immediate point, what about right now? I imagined them rushing down the road pursued by the kidnappers, exchanging gun-fire like something out of the Wild West, only to find that their getaway plan was stymied. For all their optimism and cool confidence, it might all still go wrong at the house.

And I would be the one who had dropped them in the shit. That felt ugly —

That was when a man appeared through a gap in the foliage – and not somebody I recognised.

I honestly thought my heart stopped for a moment. The man was in his twenties, definitely a local, in a tee-shirt and jeans, short but powerfully built. He had a livid gash on his left temple and blood was dripping down his face. He was panting and glaring around himself furiously. He had obviously escaped from the house.

He wiped a hand across his forehead, spreading blood across his hairline.

That was when I noticed the long carving knife in his other hand.

I could see him reviewing the cars, me, and his thoughts were as plain as day. Here was his getaway route and the only thing standing between escape and him – was me.

He shouted something and I realised that I was still holding the keys of the Nissan. I stuffed them into my pocket as I retreated . His face took on a look of dark cunning. He waved the knife in the air and shouted again, his meaning clear. I skirted around the car, keeping my distance. Then he lunged and I gave ground, and it struck me forcibly that I had absolutely no defence against a desperate man with a knife.

I was at the back of the car and he came at me fast but I managed to flip up the back door of the estate and his momentum carried him into it and he fell ...

I reached into the boot and snatched up the stupid furled umbrella.

He was up on his feet like a cat, angry now – I wouldn't care to describe my own emotions at that moment – and came at me again. I held the umbrella out in front of me like a fencer, waiting for him to come into range, then I lashed out and caught him a good whack on his forearm. It might have hurt him but it wasn't going to stop him and he rushed at me again, getting past my guard and I had a glimpse of the knife flashing inches from my eyes and I got a hand to his chest and managed to shove him back while he was off-balance. I scrambled away, panting hard, and we faced each other again, with him maybe a little wary now.

I had a moment to size him up. He was breathing heavily, weaving – that gash on his head, however he'd got it, had to be slowing him down. I had a height and weight advantage, but he had the deadly weapon. The umbrella, I realised, was more or less useless.

I pushed forward, slashing wildly left and right. He fell back, surprised I think, and caught the tip of the umbrella on his shoulder, then he grabbed at it but I snatched it away, and then he lunged at me again and somehow I deflected the knife, and we closed and he was trying to reverse the knife and I punched him hard in the stomach and we both fell and I rolled away, wincing as I imagined the blade slicing into me – but it didn't – and I regained my feet unscathed.

We faced each other again. The blood from his gash was getting in his eye and he reached to wipe it away and I —

I played my one advantage.

I reversed the umbrella and reached forward desperately, trying to avoid the long blade as I hooked the umbrella handle behind his ankle and yanked hard.

He went down.

I laboured at his head with the umbrella and he grabbed the handle and pulled and I lost my grip on it – I saw it flying off as he hurled it away into the field.

He glared at me in triumph and, very slowly, clambered to his feet. He crouched, waving the knife in front of him. I fell back, out of ideas.

Something flashed past me, a glint of metal, and he halted suddenly in mid-stride and glanced down at his chest. There was a something solid growing out of it and I stared in incomprehension – then I heard a slight rushing sound in the air, a glimpse of spinning metal, and this time he was knocked back and there was a second object, clearly a throwing knife, sticking in the base of his neck – and his legs buckled and he fell forward.

I glanced behind me, back towards the house, and there was Chanlina running down the road in the dusk and then I understood what had just happened.

'Richard!' she shouted as I sank down heavily to my knees.

'An umbrella!' guffawed Bullen. 'You took him on with a fucking umbrella! Only a Brit could do that! Ha! That's brilliant.'

We were sitting on the lawn outside The House Above the Jungle, Bullen, Chanlina, Edi Sarachi, Banh Sar and myself, drinking beer and discussing our evening's adventures. Ak and Da were sitting a little way from us, also drinking. In contrast to their opaque manner before we had set out, they were chattering and giggling away to each other like excited schoolboys.

Bullen and Sarachi were in fine form, exchanging comments and slapping each other on the back. I was quietly elated myself, probably the relief of having survived my little battle (who said that there was no better sound in the world than the sound of the bullet that's just missed you?) and Banh Sar was chuckling away, occasionally laughing outright or exclaiming with widened eyes at some particular bit of the story.

The boy and his father had been dropped off on our way back, a poignant and tearful reunion and a (frankly embarrassing) outpouring of emotion from their family. They had been overwhelming in their gratitude towards everyone – except to Chanlina herself, to whom they had been immensely respectful and had kissed her hands like she was some sort of living saint.

Which, in their eyes, I suppose she was.

Sarachi and Bullen were getting steadily merrier, with old Banh Sar not far behind. The housekeeper, Sita, regarding us with an amused indulgence, kept up a steady supply of beer and titbits.

Mindful of what had happened the last time I had spent an evening drinking with Bullen (could that be only two nights back?) I was watching my own consumption carefully.

From what I could gather from the stories being told, the raid on the kidnappers' house had gone off without a hitch. Sarachi and Bullen had surprised two of them sitting outside smoking and they had fled immediately into the fields behind the house, abandoning their weapons; Chanlina and Ak had broken through a window into the room where the other four were sitting, (the boy was left upstairs on his own – 'Amateurs,' sneered Bullen) and had shot two of them. One had run next door, straight into Sarachi's shotgun and one had been winged and had escaped – the man I had encountered up the road.

Chanlina had described my fight, including the use of the umbrella, and it was adjudged the highlight of the whole event (which, personally, I thought was laying it on a bit thick).

I found myself looking around me at the assembled group. Apart from Bullen – who, in all candour, I couldn't really describe as more than an acquaintance – I hadn't even met these people until a couple of days ago. How strange then, I thought, to feel a glow of affinity to them, to feel comfortable, almost happy in their company.

Bullen, meanwhile, had reached that stage of cheerful inebriation when everyone was his friend, leaning back in his chair, waving his cheroot around as he expounded on some point or the other, laughing uproariously at every second remark. Then he said:

'Say, Edi, I know just what tonight needs. I'm in the mood for ... a little female company. Man has a bit of tension, a bit of action to set the pulses going, then a coupla' beers and good fellowship and a chance to shoot the breeze, and to top it off – well, you know what I'm talking about! One or two of your pretty little yellow ladies. Any chance of that around these parts?

Sarachi seemed to exchange a subtle glance with Chanlina – I might have imagined it but I thought I saw her giving him the slightest of nods.

'Well, I'm sure that can be arranged,' Sarachi said.

'Of course, I wouldn't like to drive these roads at night with a few beers on board. Maybe we can get one of the boys to run us someplace?'

'There's no need for that. I can make a call, and the women will come to us. I am sure for such honoured guests as yourself, they will provide immediately.'

'That'd be swell,' said Bullen, chinking bottles with Sarachi.

'I will call Madame Tioulong,' said Sarachi, pulling a mobile phone from his pocket and pressing a couple of buttons.

'Got her on speed dial, huh?' cackled Bullen, with an expression of mock surprise.

Sarachi smiled, a thin smile that didn't touch his eyes.

'It's not the first time she and her girls have been here,' he said.

Bullen grinned back at him, like an unruly dog who had just heard the biscuit tin being opened.

It must have been at some point during the evening, maybe while we were waiting for Madame Tioulong and her 'girls' to turn up, or maybe before, I can't exactly remember, that I had a quiet moment alone with Bullen. He grasped me by the shoulder and put his head close, in a confidential way. He seemed a little drunk.

'Andy,' he said, 'I gotta tell you something.'

'What? Don't take an umbrella to a gunfight again?'

'No, no, not that. You did good … real good today… but it's not that. It's our pal Edi Sarachi.'

'What about him?'

'I mean, today, up in that house. Ak and the other one, Da … they were fine. Chanlina, well, what a woman …! Brave as all anything, I'm telling you. Even the kid's dad was okay, you know? But Sarachi – I don't know. Like, if you ever get into that situation yourself – well, keep him in front of you, that's all I'm saying. He's a guy who's always going to go in second.'

'I'm not expecting to get into that kind of a situation,' I said.

'No, no, sure, yes, you're right. I'm just saying … with him, watch your back, 'cos he ain't going to. You get a feeling about these people, you know? The ones you can rely on and the ones you can't. And he's never going to go through the door first. Just that. A little warning, in case. That's all.'

He stood gazing at me for a moment, so I nodded.

'I'll bear that in mind,' I said.

'People like Sarachi, you know, I seen 'em before. They're like the flotsam and jetsam of Euro-trash – they get around somehow – and he's washed up here.'

'I thought you liked him?'

'I can drink with him, laugh with him, do business with him. Doesn't mean I like him.'

Chanlina had, wisely, slipped away by the time Madame Tioulong and her 'girls' arrived.

First came the Madame herself, a stooping old witch of a woman with dyed hair and thick make-up, dressed in an unlikely get-up of black watered silk. She gave herself great airs, carrying a sun-parasol (even though, by then, it was full dark). Following her were six women of various ages, wearing what were probably communal dresses and shoes. Two were very young and plain with sulky expressions, and these were assigned to Ak and Da, who immediately disappeared off with them. The remaining four, who I guessed were Madame's regular girls, stood in a little quartet in front of us, preening themselves and smiling suggestively, with their hands either posed on their hips or running through their hair.

Bullen chose the tallest one, a handsome woman (I guessed) in her early forties. She smiled in feigned delight at being preferred and immediately linked arms with the American. Old Banh Sar chose a dumpy girl with pock-marked skin who, at least, looked friendly.

Sarachi turned to me questioningly, gesturing towards the remaining two women. Ever the correct host.

'Oh, you carry on,' I told him. 'Your choice.'

He laid his hand on the chest of the woman on the left, one with dyed red hair and a snub nose. She grinned cheerfully.

'You guys go on,' I said. 'Don't wait for me.'

They set off across lawn and up the big wooden staircase, the men rumbling in low voices and the girls twittering and swinging their bottoms provocatively.

When they were out of sight, Madame Tioulong sat down on one of the chairs and gazed from me to the last woman. The girl herself straightened her back and bent forward slightly at the waist, allowing her hair to fall forward in a practiced pantomime of sex appeal, staring at me with her lips slightly open.

'You not like?' said the old harridan. She took a packet of cigarettes out of her handbag and screwed one into an ivory holder. 'Nice girl?'

'I'm sure,' I said.

'You have light, please?' she asked, leaning towards me.

Bullen had left a disposable lighter on the table, so I used it to light her cigarette. Getting close to her, I was hit by a solid miasma of cheap scent and stale tobacco.

'Thank you,' she said, dragging smoke deep into her lungs. She paused significantly and said again: 'You not like?'

'Yes, of course. But no, thank you.'

'No thank you? You not like?'

'I don't want to,' I said. I smiled encouragingly at the girl who was now biting her lower lip and fluttering her eyelids, unaware of what we were saying.

'I see,' said Madame Tioulong without expression. 'You are sure?'

'Yes.'

The old woman spoke a few words to the girl, whose face changed immediately from seductive to disinterested. She frowned once at me and set off up the big staircase into the house.

'I send to the big American. He can have two.'

'Good,' I agreed.

'And you? What is for you? I can make call to someone, he bring a boy for you?'

'What? Good God, no! I mean, no thank you. No boy.'

'So,' she said, her black eyes watching me, 'no boy, no girl, for you. Nothing?'

'No, nothing, thank you. I have my beer.' To cover the moment, I picked up a bottle from the table and took a gulp.

She continued to stare and it occurred to me that perhaps she intended to sit there for the rest of the evening. That, I felt, would be awkward.

We sat in silence for a solid couple of minutes, while she smoked her cigarette. Insects buzzed around the lights set in the lawn. Eventually, she relented.

'I wait in the car,' she said.

'Will you? Oh, fine, if you want to ... well, good evening to you. Thank you.'

'So,' she said, rising. She paused. 'You ... you are American?'

'No,' I said. Further clarification seemed to be needed. 'British,' I added.

'Yes,' she said as if that explained it, and stumped off back to the drive-way.

Alone at last, I thought. I breathed a sigh of relief and relaxed back in my chair.

I was neither surprised nor offended at the idea of importing ladies of easy virtue for Bullen's entertainment – I'd seen it before often enough, especially around the big construction jobs.

I remembered discovering, on one of the first major projects that I had worked on, that two of the women who ran the site canteen spent the hours in between the ten o'clock break and lunch taking turns providing various paid services for the pipe fitters and welders. When I mentioned this to the Project Director, he took the news calmly, only remarking that he 'hoped they remembered to wash their bloody hands before they make my bacon sandwich'.

I found myself smiling at the memory of his moral concerns – strictly limited to his bacon sandwich.

I was still smiling when Chanlina strolled back about ten minutes later. I had finished my beer and was thinking of taking myself off to bed.

She paused beside my chair and looked at me questioningly.

'You were smiling,' she said.

'Just remembering something absurd,' I said.

'You were enjoying yourself? Is that the right English phrase? In Khmer, we say that you can enjoy your children, or enjoy your dinner, or the sunshine. Only the English can enjoy themselves.'

'Yes,' I agreed. There was a pause. I was reminding myself that this strange woman, this *assassin*, had physically saved my life only a few hours ago and I hadn't found a moment to properly thank her. I was searching for the right words when she spoke again.

'All alone?' she said.

'Yes.'

'Madame Tioulong did not bring a girl for you?'

'No, she brought a girl.'

'And she was not suitable?'

'Oh, no, she was fine,' I said. 'It's just that, well, I ... I don't really indulge myself in that sort of thing.'

'You were embarrassed? The famous British reserve?'

'Maybe, a little. But the whole thing is, well, so *artificial*, so forced. And Madame Tioulong herself ...' I trailed off.

'Madame Tioulong is a little strange, isn't she? Creepy?'

'Grotesque, I would say.'

Chanlina laughed, sitting down on the chair next to me.

'Yes, that is the word in English. Grotesque. But she tried her best, yes?'

'Oh, absolutely. She even offered to send for a boy.'

Chanlina laughed again and clapped her hands together in delight.

'Oh, excellent! I should have liked to have seen your face when she did that.'

'I was very polite,' I said, and passed my hand over my face, wiping away all expression. 'You see: the perfect gentleman.'

'Of course,' she said, still laughing.

We looked at each other.

'Your command of English is extremely good,' I remarked casually.

'Oh, you are very kind. Sometimes I think my sentence construction is a little ... too formal. I have not the mastery of your idiom.'

'How did you learn?'

'Oh,' she said lightly, 'here and there. And watching American movies.'

'I thought that I detected a slight accent.'

'An American accent?'

'Uh-huh.'

'Oh, then I shall have to be more careful.'

'Or watch British movies instead.'

'Yes, maybe,' she said and smiled again.

There was a pause.

'Where,' I asked, 'did you go off to – while Madame Tioulong and her troop arrived?'

'Oh, I went down to the other end of the garden. We planted night-scented stock there, two years ago. It has a wonderful perfume at this time of the evening.'

'I see.'

'Come, Richard, let me take you down there so you can see for yourself.'

We stood up and strolled along the lawn. She put her arm into mine and gently leant into me.

'Everything grows here,' she said happily, gesturing at her flower beds and the tall shrubs behind. She paused and kicked off her shoes, so that she could walk barefoot. 'I'm sorry, but sometimes it's good to feel the grass under your toes.'

'I know what you mean. Sometimes I would like to do that as well —'

'Then why don't you? Come, you can take your shoes off now. The grass is soft and quite dry, you know ...'

I hesitated and then reached down and undid my laces, slid off my shoes and socks.

'There,' she said, 'that is better, is it not?'

I agreed it was.

We reached the stock-filled beds.

'You can't see it in the lamplight, but these are all pink and white and, at the back, there are the violent ones ...'

'Violet,' I said automatically.

'Violet? Oh yes, of course.' She smiled, showing her small white teeth.

'I like that,' I joked. 'A garden full of pink and white and *violent* blooms.'

She paused and looked up at me.

'You know, Richard, I feel very bad that the others are off celebrating their adventure with Madame Tioulong's ladies, and you are stuck here with me, discussing flowers. I think that I am failing in my duty as a proper hostess.'

'Oh, not at all,' I said. 'I would much rather be here with you.'

'Indeed,' she said, smiling to herself. 'So, you disapprove of our lax habits here? Does it offend your moral sense, perhaps?'

'Oh, no,' I hastened to reply. 'It's not that at all. It's just not – those women, I mean – something that I am not used to doing. Anyway, I have a wife —'

'An ex-wife,' she corrected.

'Yes, well, an ex-wife. And if other people want to use those ... *services*, then fine by me ... I mean ...'

'Maybe we Buddhists are more open about these things, about our bodies, than Christians are?'

'Maybe,' I said. 'I've never thought about it.'

'You mustn't judge us, you know,' she said and smiled.

'I try not to judge anybody.'

She turned away.

'Ah!' she exclaimed in a dismayed tone, as if arriving at some decision.

'It is no good. I think strongly I am failing as a correct hostess; simple good manners dictate that tonight you should not go alone to a cold bed, not after the bravery with your umbrella!'

'The umbrella was irrelevant and ridiculous,' I said.

She moved in closer to me, so that I could smell the perfume in her hair. I could also feel the twin pressures of her breasts on my chest.

'I shall remedy this shortfall in hospitality myself,' she said. 'It is the least that I can do.'

'Oh, that's not necessary,' I started to say but she cut me off with a finger on my lips.

'I will have no argument! Anyway, must I remind you – I saved your life today, did I not? Two good throws in a poor light, not bad, even though I say it myself. I was pleased with my accuracy. Were you not pleased?'

'Very much so,' I said.

'Very well, then. You owe me your life. So, for tonight at least, I have command of you. No, no arguments, Richard, please, I have decided. The matter is settled.'

How could one possibly refuse a lady?

I forgot that she was a killer. I forgot that, barely five hours before, I had seen her put two knives into the body of a living human being. It was easy to forget – there was no mark of Cain on her splendid, pale-golden skin.

She was a responsive lover, at ease within her own body, active and affectionate by turns. Sometimes she spoke to me in English, sometimes she was lost within herself and murmured in Khmer, sitting rocking on my lap with the white moonlight streaming through in a gap in the curtains.

I don't pretend to understand women – and any man who tells you that he does is either a fool or a liar – and I certainly didn't understand Chanlina. She was a child in my arms, then she was a vixen, selfish and imperious; she was quick and eager, then she was slow and open and generous. She was a mixture of the warm and the ferocious.

I don't understand women, and I especially didn't understand her; not that night nor in the days that came after.

The next morning, I rose even earlier than I had the previous day. Leaving Chanlina sleeping, her face in repose, her black hair spread on the pillow, I pulled on my shirt and trousers and slipped outside.

There was dew on the grass – the day having not yet warmed – and I walked across the lawn feeling the cool dampness on the soles of my feet. It was not something that I had ever done before yesterday – and I resolved, if I managed to get through this, to walk barefoot on wet grass more often.

Having the garden to myself – except for the insects buzzing around the flowers and the birds singing high above – made me reflective, thinking about the past few days. How could someone like me, equipped only with a hole in his bank balance and a dull sense of disappointment, have arrived here? Leaping between hotel balconies, getting drunk with Russian spies, rescuing kidnapped children, grappling hand-to-hand with desperate men ... and strolling in a flourishing Cambodian garden.

And, to top it all, spending the night with an assassin.

The feel of the grass brought a sense of perspective; surely this couldn't be real, surely it was just a dream, like one of those ketamine fantasies that you read about? Had someone slipped the red pill into my drink along the way? I imagined telling my ex-wife about it: *You'll never ever believe what happened to me in Cambodia.* Which was true – she would never believe it.

One thing I had to admit to myself. Despite my misgivings, Bullen had been right; at some unlikely level, part of me was actually enjoying the adventure.

My reverie was broken by a figure walking towards me. Chanlina.

'Good morning, Richard,' she said brightly. 'I didn't hear you get up. Are you admiring our garden again?'

I saw her eyes flick down to my bare feet and she smiled fleetingly.

'Good morning,' I said, 'yes, I was.'

I wondered awkwardly if I should maybe kiss her – did a night together entitle me to that? Or would it be considered, here in Cambodia, too forward?

I hesitated and the moment passed.

'Will you come and have some breakfast?' she asked.

She bent and plucked a flower from one of the beds, something red with a long stem, and carefully slid it into her hair.

'Good?' she asked, and smiled again.

We ate on the balcony of the big house, looking out over the gardens. The old housekeeper, Sita, appeared with coffee and croissants and fruit and set the table for us.

'Where are the others?' I asked.

There was a short exchange between Chanlina and Sita, at which they both laughed.

'What?' I said, wanting to be in on the joke.

'Sita says that Madame Tioulong and her ladies left just after three; then the men carried on drinking until five, at which point they staggered to their beds.' She checked her watch. 'Two and a half hours ago. Sita says that, when they had gone, she came and cleaned up. She doesn't expect to see them for a good long while. Possibly lunchtime.'

'Has Sita been up all night then?' I asked.

'She hardly sleeps. She has – what is the English word? – insomnia? Perhaps she might nap a little during the day.'

'I see. So we have the place to ourselves?'

'Yes. Maybe Ak and Da will drag themselves out of bed at some point; but, after their good work yesterday, I won't object if they sleep. They risked their lives with us; they deserve a little relaxation.'

'Uh-huh.'

We ate in companionable silence for a while. I wondered if I might broach a subject that was bothering me. More fool me; me and my big mouth.

'There was something I had meant to ask you,' I began.

She was halfway through a croissant – rather than speaking, she nodded at me to continue.

'Well, it's just this ... I'm not sure how to put it. You see, this place, you yourself, your garden ... it isn't at all what I had been expecting.'

'What you had been expecting?' she echoed, frowning a little. 'And, so, tell me, what *were* you expecting, Mr Powell?'

'If I may be direct ...?'

'Of course.'

'Given your, err, profession, I wasn't expecting a garden, a beautiful home, your involvement in the community. I imagined something *differ-*

ent. Something … worldlier, harsher … colder.'

'Something colder, or someone?'

I hesitated.

'Very well. *Someone*, then.'

She smiled.

'What makes you think that I am *not* a cold person?'

It was my turn to smile: 'Because I've met you.'

'I don't think that you understand me at all, Mister Powell. Do you have any idea *why* I do what I do?'

'*Mister* Powell? Why the sudden formality?'

'Because we are talking business – *my* business,' she said, and repeated her question. 'So, do you know why I do what I do?'

'I don't know. For the money?'

'For the money, yes, of course. It is certainly not for some strange desire to murder people.'

'I never imagined it was. But you have … eliminated people, haven't you?'

'Eliminated? The nice euphemism, yes? Let us say "killed" instead; let there be no dishonesty between us. And, it almost sounds as if you find the idea unpalatable – and yet – and yet, it is you who has come here, to ask me to kill someone for you, isn't it?'

I knew I was skating on thin ice. I said:

'Well, if there was another way to deal with my problem, I would have used it.'

'So you say,' she said and there was something in her tone that set off a small alarm, as if I had offended her. 'But, let us go back to the question – why exactly I do what I do, which is to kill people? Yes, for money, of course, but that is not the whole story.'

'Then tell me the whole story.'

She sat looking at me, without speaking, for what felt like a long time. She wasn't smiling any more – indeed, her expression was almost antagonistic. I might have imagined that she was appraising me, wrestling with some perplexing question. I wondered, too late, had I overstepped the mark? I held her level gaze as best I could, remembering that this was an extremely dangerous woman.

Eventually, she said:

'Mr Powell, you are a strange man. So, you say that I am not what you were expecting? Very well, then, I tell that you are not what I was expecting, either.'

'Really?' I said. I felt a cold shiver go down my spine. Something had changed between us, and I was not sure what it meant. 'In what way?'

She stood up abruptly.

'You have finished your coffee?' she said. 'Good. Then you will come with me.'

'Why? Where are we going?'

'You shall see. We will take a car.'

Of course, I could have flat-out refused. I had stupidly said a crass thing and I had lost her confidence and she had now made some decision that I didn't understand – so why would I risk going anywhere with her? For all her behaviour last night, for all her talk about gardens and night-scented stock and flowers, she was a professional murderer – and if I hadn't quite believed it before, I did now. I had seen it with my own eyes.

On the other hand, if I didn't go with her ... I had no doubt that she could deal with me just as easily here as elsewhere.

I stood up and followed her down the ornate wooden staircase.

Without speaking, she drove out through the big iron gates and turned and followed the road for what felt like a couple of miles. We turned left, and then left again and drove a little further, past a small ribbon of simple stilt houses, a village, and on up a hill until we came to a little hardstanding area, between three single-storey brick buildings with metal roofs. These didn't look like houses. She pulled up, unbuckled her seat belt, and opened her door.

'We're here,' she said.

'Where?' I asked.

'You are going to meet someone. Come on.'

I stepped slowly from the car and looked around me. The area seemed tidy, almost formal. There was a flat field of cut grass over to the right of the brick buildings.

A Cambodian woman appeared from around the side of one of the buildings, dressed in a skirt and blouse. She looked to be in her mid-thirties – and something about her that was familiar, although I was sure I had never seen her before. Smiling, she greeted Chanlina and came over to where we were standing. The two women embraced warmly, speaking to each other in Khmer.

Chanlina turned to me, her arm still around the other woman.

'Mr Powell ... Richard. I would like you to meet my big sister.'

'Your sister?' I said. No wonder she looked familiar.

'Mr Powell,' said the sister, now turning her smile on me. Her English was heavily accented. 'Welcome. We do not know you coming. But we very happy to see you.'

She held out her hand, which I shook.

'Thank you,' she said. 'Please, now come!'

Mystified, I followed her around the corner of the building, Chanlina walking behind. We went in through a metal door, down a painted cinderblock corridor. She opened a door to her left. She paused and indicated that I should go in first.

I don't know what I was expecting to see, but it certainly wasn't a room full of children seated at rows of neat wooden desks. Another Cambodian woman was standing at the front by a blackboard, evidently the teacher. Seeing us, she gestured for the children to rise.

The children – maybe thirty-five of them – stood up as one. I guessed the average age at about eleven.

The teacher beckoned for me to join her at the front of the class, so I did. Then she pointed at the children and raised her hand as if conducting an orchestra.

'Good morning!' chanted the children. The woman lowered her hand and they all sat down, with a great clattering and scraping of chairs. She turned to me, raising her eyebrows.

'Oh,' I said and looked at thirty-five pairs of eyes, all of whom were looking at me as if I was from another planet. 'Oh, yes. Good morning, children.'

They beamed back at me and a couple of them giggled.

Chanlina's sister came to the front of the classroom, still smiling.

'Thank you,' she said. She exchanged a few words with the teacher, then turned to back to me and said: 'Come, please.'

The children's eyes followed us as we walked back to the door, where Chanlina was waiting. Just as we went out, some devilment made me half-turn and wave to the kids.

'Goodbye!' I called out. They replied in an excited shout, saying I don't know what – obviously that part hadn't been rehearsed.

I closed the door behind me.

Chanlina's sister beckoned Chanlina and me down the corridor and into a small, tidy office with a desk and chairs. She indicated that I sit, and offered me coffee. Not wishing to cause trouble, while also not wishing to refuse, I accepted. She went out and Chanlina and I were momentarily left alone.

'What on earth is this place?' I asked. 'Why did you bring me? I mean, it's nice to see a school and the children and everything, but I don't understand why you wanted to show me ...'

'Mr Powell,' she said. 'You must wait.'

Her sister returned with the coffee and sat down behind her desk. She frowned in concentration as she offered me a short description, in broken English, about the school, the catchment area, the teachers' wages, about the number of classes and the curriculum and when the school was established. Every so often, she stumbled over a word and turned to her sister for help in translation.

I listened politely and sipped at my coffee. When she had finished, I felt I should offer some questions;

'So, you are the Head Teacher?'

Chanlina supplied the word for her in Khmer. The sister nodded and smiled self-deprecatingly.

'And the funding comes from the government?'

Again, Chanlina helped out. Her sister seemed better at speaking English than in understanding it; the word 'funding' was well beyond her vocabulary.

'No, no money from government.' She smiled again, then added: 'We are private money school.'

'The children's family pay then?'

At this, both sisters laughed lightly. The woman behind the desk gave up on her English and addressed her reply directly to Chanlina in her own language.

'She says, no, these children are from poor families. They cannot pay.'

Her sister, gaining confidence, was speaking again in Khmer.

'She asks if you have seen the clinic in the village?'

'What clinic?'

'I have not shown you that yet. I will explain to her.'

The sisters spoke again, then Chanlina said something and her sister stood up and said carefully:

'Mr Powell, thank you for come to our school. It was our presh ...'

'Pleasure,' cut in Chanlina.

'*Pleasure* to show you what we here do.'

'Well, thank you for showing me,' I said, being as cordial as I could.

We filed out of the little office and Chanlina led the way back to the car. The two women embraced again, then I shook hands with the sister and she thanked me and I thanked her and she bowed and thanked me again and I bowed back and then Chanlina rescued me by opening the car door.

The sister (whose name I had not actually learnt) waved us off as we set off onto the little rutted road.

We had driven for a mile or so when she pulled the car over and killed the engine. She turned to me with something like a challenge in her eyes.

'Okay,' I began, 'that was great – but ... why did you take me there?'

'We went to meet my sister and to visit her school, of course. Was it not interesting for you?'

'Of course. It's just that I wasn't expecting to visit a school —'

'Ah, Mr Powell!' she said, exasperated. 'There is *so much* that you do not expect, isn't there? You don't expect to visit a school, you don't expect to find a pleasant house and gardens, and you don't expect a woman like me to be the assassin that you try to hire. I am trying to imagine what you *did* expect. Did you think that we lived in some dirty shack at the back of a factory, oiling our guns and counting our money and forgetting to wash? Drinking and smoking underneath a grimy light bulb?'

'Well, no, of course not! I'm not stupid —'

'And you cannot understand why I show you a school!'

'Yes ... I mean, no. I thought that you were angry for some reason —'

'And you don't realise that the school is the answer to the question?'

'What?'

'The question! Our question!'

I stared at her blankly.

'The question,' she said. 'I do what I do – for the money – and what do I *use* the money for?'

'The school?'

'Yes. The school!' She crowed at me in genuine delight. 'The school! *My* school, that is run by my big sister, the teacher.'

'You pay for the school!' I said.

'Yes!' she cried, clapping her hands together.

'And the clinic? Your sister mentioned a clinic.'

'Yes, the school and the clinic! Both! Of course, I have a fine house, and a fine garden, but these things are not so expensive in Cambodia. So *this*, this is what I do with my money.'

'I don't understand. You pay for the ... but doesn't the government here pay for schools and hospitals?'

'Oh, Richard, you know little of our country! Yes, the government is *supposed* to pay for schools and hospitals, and they do, sometimes. They get very big donations from the international community for it. But often the money does not come, because it is stolen by some government official. Yes, really! You look so shocked, as if such a thing were impossible. This is *Cambodia*, Richard! You know what happens here? Teachers don't get paid, so they demand money from the children who come to the schools, for lessons, and they sell off the books. Doctors and nurses in the hospitals don't get paid, so they steal the drugs and sell them on the black market. Yes, really! But not in *my* school! Here, the teachers get paid well and work hard. And I know that I can trust the Headmistress, because she is my own beloved sister.'

'And they don't steal the drugs from your clinic?'

'No,' she said, 'because, they are properly and regularly paid. And besides,' she smiled conspiratorially, maybe even with a hint of pride, 'who would dare to steal from the Green Mamba?'

We drove back in silence, until we passed her Health Clinic. She pulled into the side of the road so I could see it for myself; a utilitarian group of low buildings with cinderblock walls and metal roofs – unfussy, neat and functional. Chanlina briefly described the staffing and patient arrangements, and suggested that I might like to visit it, but not today because she didn't like to disturb their routine without warning. I agreed. We drove on.

I was struggling to put my thoughts in some kind of order, stacking the contradictions up; she was a paid assassin who gave away a lot of her money to help the local people, genuinely concerned for others in her country. But – *none-the-less* – someone who murdered for money. It was all so far out of my experience, it was beyond comprehension. And yet ...

Yet ...

Why had she chosen to show all this, her philanthropy, to me? Why me?

I had no great illusion about my attractiveness to women. I remembered

Dmitry's rather thin assessment on my prospects of getting a new wife: '*nice guy, intelligent, not so bad-looking*', hardly a ringing endorsement. My own self-image was of Mr Average, a man never going to set the world on fire, the normal guy, reliable, honest, slightly dull. Exciting things never happened to people like me. But they *were* happening. And I wasn't entirely sure whether I liked it or not.

I sneaked a sideways glance at Chanlina and she glanced back at me and smiled. I didn't know what I should say to her so I said nothing.

We drove in through the gates of the house and pulled up on the drive. She switched off the engine and half-turned.

'Here we are,' she said. 'I don't know about you, but I'm starting to feel the heat.'

'Yes,' I said. The sun had warmed; I looked at my watch – just short of eleven o'clock.

'Do you like to swim?' she asked lightly.

'You have a pool?'

'Oh yes.'

We got out of the car and she led me across the lawn, away from the house itself, until we came to a gap in the tall hedge, which opened into a passage between two walls of greenery, then to a large open space, all surrounded by hedges, in the middle of which was a long rectangular pool with white tiles. The surface of the water was perfectly still, without even the trace of a ripple on it, shining with sunlight.

It was the most inviting swimming pool that I had ever set eyes on.

'This is our pool,' she said, smiling. 'Do you like it?'

'Yes,' I said.

'Would you like to swim in it?'

'Of course,' I said.

On the far side of the pool there was a little wooden cabin, made of the same red timber as the house.

'I'll go fetch some towels,' she said, indicating the cabin. 'I think that my costume is in there.'

'I'll go and get my swimming shorts from the guest house,' I said.

'No need,' she said. 'There's probably something in there for you.'

She trotted around the pool and disappeared inside.

I stood waiting; a trickle of sweat ran down my forehead and I wiped it away.

She emerged from the hut carrying a little pile of dark grey towels and dropped them by the pool edge.

'Sorry,' she said and smiled lightly. 'No costumes.' She started to unbutton her blouse.

'No costumes?' I repeated.

'No.'

'Then, what are we going to use ...?' I said.

Chanlina had kicked off her shoes and was undoing her trousers. She slid out of them, and started to take off her bra.

'Nothing,' she said. She raised her eyebrows in mock alarm, and gestured at the high hedge surrounding the pool area. 'Look around you – nobody can see us here.'

'But ...' I said.

'But ... what?' she smiled mischievously at me and pulled off her pants. She stood still for a moment, naked, staring at me. 'Oh ... shocking, yes? Under her clothes a woman is nude. Who could have imagined it?'

She stepped to the edge of the pool, called '*Come on*, Richard!' over her shoulder and executed a perfect standing dive into the water and disappeared under the surface. I was left gaping.

Half-reluctantly, I disrobed, dropping my clothes onto the grass, and followed her in.

The shock of the cool water was both alarming and wonderful at the same time. I swam a few strokes underwater then came up for breath. Paddling on the surface, I looked around for Chanlina but she wasn't in sight. I reached down with my foot, feeling for the bottom, but couldn't touch it. This was obviously the deep part, so I struck out in a slow crawl for the opposite end of the pool.

When I reached it, I extended my leg again to touch the bottom but, to my surprise, my foot didn't reach it. Just then, I felt something grab me around the ankles and give a sharp tug and I was pulled under in a wave of bubbles. Water went up my nose and I was dragged lower until my knee bumped the tiling on the bottom. A pale golden shape shot past me and I kicked upwards for the surface.

I felt air on my face and there was Chanlina waiting for me, her hair slicked back from her forehead. She was laughing.

'You see, Richard,' she said, 'In *my* swimming pool – as in life itself – there *is* no shallow end. There is only room for those who want to swim –

and everyone else can stand on the side and watch.'

'Yes,' I said, and she suddenly jack-knifed below the surface again. I looked down into the water for her – she was below me and I felt her torso slide between my legs (a surprising, but not unpleasant sensation) and was lifted bodily up in the water as she surfaced. I was tipped backwards and went underwater again only to feel her hands under my shoulders, pulling me back up into the sunshine.

'Oh, Richard,' she laughed, 'There, again I save your life!'

'Thank you, but —' I spluttered out some water. 'Yes, thank you, but I can swim perfectly well, you know —'

'Yes, yes, of course.' She trod water, looking almost penitent for a second. Then her face split into a playful grin and she pushed a wave at me and shot away backwards. 'C'mon … catch me if you can!'

I gave chase, determined to grab her but I might as well have tried to lay my hands on a sunbeam. Every time she was near my grasp, she would dart like a fish and move, sometimes away, sometimes going right underneath me (her ability to dive down was amazing). At one point she was lying, apparently prone, on the bottom of the pool; I gulped air and dived down to catch her but she shot off as I reached her, then suddenly turned and came up beneath me so fast that I was almost thrown into the air.

Eventually, we tired, and lay sculling on the surface. We regarded each other like two silly teenagers, and she said:

'So, Englishman, you admit defeat?'

'Only out of politeness to my hostess; of course, I will.'

'Nonsense,' she laughed. 'My Oriental victory over your lazy Western physique is absolute.' And with that, she kicked her legs, shot to the edge, laid her hands on it and seemed to vault out of water in one motion. I had a glimpse of her splendid wet shoulders and back (swimmer's shoulders, I thought) and her firm buttocks as she trotted along the poolside and picked up a towel. I got out more sedately, and wrapped myself in another towel.

We sat down, side by side, on the grass.

'That was good, yes?' she asked.

'That was great,' I agreed. 'Fun.'

'Yes,' she said and looked away at the pool, then at me, and then at the pool again. With her hair slicked back, she looked very young, strangely innocent, like a teenage girl, almost shy now she was out of the water.

'The water is your kingdom,' I said. The moment I said it, I realised how gauche I must sound, so I added: 'You are a terrific swimmer.'

'Thank you,' she said, and ducked her head politely. Once again, I was struck by the contradictions in her – yesterday, she had killed a man, right in front of me; today she played in the pool like a girl without a care in the world. In between, she had shown me her philanthropy, her serious side.

'What are you thinking?' she asked me suddenly.

I realised that I was staring at her.

'Nothing,' I said.

'No,' she said slowly. 'Not nothing ... *something*.' She carefully placed the tip of her index finger in the middle of my forehead and twisted it back and forth, miming a drilling action. 'Something is going on, in here. I think ... you are judging us.'

'I was not,' I protested.

'I think you were, judging me.'

'No,' I said.

'You were, Mr Powell. You come here with your cold northern eyes and you look at us here in our poor broken Cambodia and you judge us. You ask yourself: why is this place not like England or France or America? What is wrong with these stupid little yellow people that they cannot organise themselves, cannot build their roads, cannot treat their sick, cannot teach their children?'

'I was absolutely *not* thinking that!' I expostulated.

'It is no matter. Of course, you would think that. You say to yourself, even now, who is this strange woman who murders people so she can swim in her pool and build her school?'

'Very well,' I replied, turning towards her, determined to challenge her. Perhaps I was allowing the sun to get to me or perhaps I had been disarmed by her playfulness in the pool. I suddenly decided to speak of the unspeakable. 'Have it your own way, then! Who is this strange woman with her good works and her terrible profession, a profession of murder? How does she square her circle, satisfy her conscience? Is she a good woman? Is she a bad woman?'

She met my gaze and held it.

'I am only an ordinary woman, good and bad together. Sometimes I am selfish and unkind, like everyone else, sometimes I try a little harder and do some small good thing. I set myself standards and I fall short of them. Like everyone else.'

'I think,' I said (God alone knew what idiocy had got into me), 'that cold-blooded murder does not qualify as "selfish and unkind". I think it is a very grave thing that you do. Do you admit that, if not to me, then to yourself?'

'A very grave thing,' she repeated softly, staring into space, as if turning the words around in her head. 'You do not understand us, do you, Richard Powell? You think that we are just like you but with better sunshine and heavier rain. But we are not like you; this country is not like your country.'

'Killing is killing, in every country.'

'Killing ...?' she murmured. 'Killing? Like slaughtering a pig, a sheep? Like an American GI running up a beach in your World War Two, shooting his machine gun at German boys whose names he doesn't even know? That is killing, too, no?'

'That's in a war ... it's different.'

'Is it so different? The action of the soldier, and the result, is the same.'

I paused, thinking how Bullen had used almost the same argument for what he did.

'Let me,' she said carefully, 'tell you a story. Would you like to hear a story?'

'What's it about?'

'It is about Cambodia.'

'Okay, then. Tell me a story.'

'It was a long time ago,' she began. 'I was only a girl, fourteen or so. It was just after the time of the Khmer Rouge. The Vietnamese had invaded Cambodia, driving out Pol Pot and his armies. The official version is that they all fled to Thailand – but some did and some did not. There were Khmer soldiers separated from their units all over the country, desperate, dangerous men, well-armed, men for whom killing had become a way of life. They were like outlaws. They took whatever they wanted and moved on.

'Three of them came to our village, here, *this* village. There were two Cambodians and one other, I don't know, maybe from Laos. They said that they had been sent from the Government, to take charge. They called our village Headman to them, told him that they were taking over and from now on everyone was to do as they said. When he asked them which Government had sent them, whether it was the "Khmer-in-exile" Government or "People's Republic of Kampuchea", they grew angry and beat him very,

very badly. He almost died.

'The three men moved into the big house on the hill and took two of the village women to cook and clean for them. They went around collecting money, confiscating livestock, taking anything they wanted to take. One man objected when they took his cattle, three cows maybe, and they beat him. Another man, a man who had a herd of goats on the meadow by the river, he stood up to the interlopers, shouting at one of them, the one called Ieng, saying we would not tolerate them, that they had no right to be there, that he was not frightened of them. The soldier called Ieng waited for the farmer to finish, then he took out a pistol and shot him in the head. He said: "Let that be a lesson to everyone", and walked away.'

'Couldn't you send for help?' I interjected.

'In those days, there was no help. There were no police, no Government, no law. We were in chaos. No, nobody was going to help us.'

She paused for a moment, then continued:

'The three men stayed. For a week or so, we thought they would move on, but evidently they had decided that they liked it here. Then, one day, they came into the village and chose one of the village girls – they told her parents that they must bring her up to the house on the hill that evening, and that they would "entertain" her. There was much confusion and distress at that, but when the evening came, the girl did not go. Her parents kept her in their house and her father stood guard all night. Nothing happened, but in the morning two of the men came into the village, to the girl's house, and they dragged out the father and beat him with sticks until he was crawling on the floor, covered in blood, then they beat the mother as well, then they beat the girl. Then they set fire to their house and stood and watched it burn.

'They went around the village and chose another girl, and told her parents to bring her to the house that night. And, that time, the girl went.

'They gave her a meal and then two of them raped her.

'Nothing more happened, for week or so, then they came into the village again. This time they chose my sister, my big sister, the one you met today. My father was very angry and scared (at that time, my mother was no longer with us, but that is another story), and said she could not go, but he knew what would happen if she did not. She said that she would go although she was terrified, but he refused. He said, then we must all run away. It was a terrible day.

'Then, I said that I would go instead.

'My father became very angry and shouted at me, but I was – how do you say in English? – *resolute?* I said that I was not frightened (although, truly, I was very frightened) and, even though I was younger than my sister, I was stronger. In the end, they could not stop me. As the sun went down, I put on my sister's dress and hid a small, sharp knife in my sleeve and walked up the hill.

'When I got to the big house, one of the men came out. He said: "You are a different girl", and I told him my sister had the women's time and I had come in her place. I was very meek and looked at the ground when I spoke. He took me inside and the other man was there, the one called Ieng. They sat me down at the table between them, and one of the two older women who cooked for them gave us some food (she would not look directly at me), but I was very nervous and could hardly eat. I tried to smile at the men, tried to be a good actress playing my part. They drank beer and smoked and made jokes and were almost friendly towards me, then they tossed a coin and first man took me into the back room and shut the door.

'I took off all my clothes while he watched, keeping my dress nearby, and I lay down on the bed, waiting for him. I reminded myself that I was an actress playing a role, and when he pushed his man's part up into me, I feigned enjoyment and moved with him and purred in pleasure, and he said: "You are a good one, you, maybe you want to stay with us here in the big house", and I said: "It would depend on whether you are kind to me" and he said: "Oh, we can be very kind to you", and I smiled and moved faster and cried out a little, and then I felt him spasm and the hot wetness and I stroked his face as he relaxed and I said: "Please, let us sleep a while", and he nodded and closed his eyes. When he was breathing regularly, I reached out for my sharp knife, then I rolled on top of him, straddling his shoulders, put a pillow over his face and slit his jugular.

'He fought me, but I was strong and held on and a huge amount of blood spurted out from his neck, more than I expected, then gradually he became weaker and stopped moving. I waited a long time, to be sure, then I got off the bed. I rearranged the sheets and pillows – I remember that I was very calm, a strange and terrible calm – then I went to the door, still naked, and I opened it and I went to find the other man, who was sitting reading a magazine and drinking beer and I said: "Mister Boss, there is something wrong with your friend, he has coughed up blood, come quickly", and he got up and went into the room and I followed him and, as he bent over the man in the bed, I jumped onto his back and stabbed him in the neck.

'At least, that was my intention, but he was too quick. I missed and only cut him and he flung himself backwards and I tried to hang on, still stabbing at his shoulder, then he threw me off and I crashed onto the floor. The knife was embedded in his shoulder and he was coming for me, bleeding but still very strong and very dreadful. I scrambled to my feet and darted out of his reach. He was trying pull out the knife but he couldn't get his hand to it and I retreated around the room, thinking that he was certain to kill me. I saw a water jug on the dresser so I flung it at him and I was lucky, it hit him on the side of his head and he staggered. I jumped across the bed and leapt onto his back again, grabbing for the knife but it slipped from my hand – I was slippery with blood myself – and he was roaring and I hung on like a cat and beat at his head and he slammed me against the wall but I hung on, then he drove his elbow into my ribs, very hard, again and again, but I hung on and he hurled himself backwards into the wall again, against a mirror that shattered and cut me badly. I slid off and found myself on the floor, amidst the broken glass, and he kicked out at me and his foot caught me in the temple and I felt my vision start to go grey and I made myself be strong because I knew that if I allowed myself to stop for even a moment, he would definitely kill me and I saw a shard of the broken mirror sticking in my forearm, a big piece, so I pulled it out and as he came at me again I jumped up and stuck it into his eye.

'He went down screaming – but I couldn't hesitate. I saw the knife on the floor so I snatched it up and attacked him with it. This time, I found his jugular – just like I had with his friend – and it went in. He lashed out at me and I went backwards over the bed and cracked my skull on the floor … and when I sat up, I could see him reeling around the room, blinded, and he must have pulled out the knife but the blood was gushing down his shirt.

'I kept my distance from him and watched him die.

'When it was over, I lay there, dazed and bleeding from a lot of places and my ribs were agony and my head was throbbing. Then one of the women who cooked for them came in and helped me to get up. She asked me if I could walk, but I couldn't, and so she picked me up and carried me into another room and laid me on the bed. I think that she must have sent the other woman for my father, so I lay on the bed, and she sat beside me. I was weeping with the pain and she washed my cuts and soothed me.

'After a while, there was a heavy footstep coming into the house. I realised that it was the third soldier coming back. I mewed with fear; I was in no condition to defend myself. I heard him shouting and moving around, and then the cooking woman called out: "In here! We are in here!" and I thought: "Oh God! She has betrayed me, she is giving me up to him to save herself!" and the door was flung open and the third man was standing there in the doorway and then ... and then, there came the loudest noise that I think I had ever heard, like a cannon in my ear and flash of flame in the darkness, again and again, and I realised that it was the cooking woman who was firing from beside me, she must have found one of their guns because she had a big revolver in her hand, firing into the doorway, and I saw the man fall and then she got up and walked to the doorway and stood over the him and she fired again and again until the hammer snapped down on an empty cylinder.

'After that, I think that I must have fainted, from relief or from shock. Anyway, the next thing I was aware of was my father leaning over me, saying "Chanlina, Chanlina" and I knew it was going to be alright.'

She turned to me with a strange look in her eyes, determined, almost angry, almost proud.

'So, you see, Mr Richard Powell, when you speak to me of the morality, I know something of what I am talking about. Those three renegade soldiers, they deserved to die. I do not regret it. I lay in the bed in that house on the hill for a month, my cuts and bruises and my broken ribs healing, attended by my sister and the cooking woman, and when I came back into the village, the people looked at me as if I were a stranger, from another world. But I tell you this, Englishman, I *know* about killing, I know the value of life in Cambodia. I know of what I speak. And I will also say that I have *never* killed a good man.'

She glanced downwards, and the anger seemed to seep out of her.

'Now, you can judge me, if you want to.'

'I don't want to,' I said.

'Indeed,' she said. She stood up and dropped her towel from around her torso and slipped into her clothes. 'I must leave you – I have things to do. If you go up to the House, Sita will provide you with some lunch. She loves to feed people. I think that you will treat her food with great respect, now that you know her secret.'

'Her secret?' I asked.

'Yes, of course. Sita is the cooking woman who fired the revolver.'

With that, she walked away and disappeared between the walls of greenery.

I don't know what happened to the afternoon; as Chanlina had suggested, I went over to the house and had something to eat (now seeing Sita in a new light, imagining her gunning down the third soldier), then I went back to the guest house and lay down on my bed for just ten minutes. When I woke, it was early evening, and Bullen was hammering at my door, calling 'Hey, fella, you in there?'

I got up, feeling groggy, and he came tumbling in.

'You not hear me? I was knocking for an age,' he said.

'Sorry,' I said, rubbing my eyes. 'I was catching a quick snooze.'

'Uh-huh,' he said.

'Anyway, where have you been?' I said. 'You must have been having a pretty long lie-in yourself. I thought that drink didn't affect you much.'

'The drink? Nope, doesn't usually get me – anyway, it was mostly beer; old man Banh brought out some local-brewed poison late on, but that didn't get to me. I *can* tell you what it was, though.'

He looked at me expectantly, willing me to ask.

'Okay, go on,' I said wearily.

'Well, you know that you didn't take up on the offered entertainment?'

'The young women, you mean?'

'Yup, the Ladies of the Night. When you turned yours down, she got sent up to me. Kinda like a tag-team thing, two taking it in turns, know what I mean?'

'Spare me the ugly details, Bullen.'

'Oh, *Lordy* Lord, and there were indeed some ugly details – and some pretty fine ones too! The tall one, I didn't actually get her name, we communicated mostly in sign language —'

'I can imagine.'

'Lithesome as a cat, for a big woman – and the one you passed on? *Whoa!* I am telling you, you missed out there. If we get a second round of that, you make sure you go for her, not a doubt. Anyways, when I was getting buckled down with the pair of 'em, in wanders Edi and I says to him: "Edi, this may all be a bit much for a man of my advancing years", and he disappears off and brings me back a couple of white pills, says "Try these".'

'Viagra?'

'Nope. I've done that before - who hasn't? These pills were something else. I tell you, fifteen minutes after I took 'em, I could've *pole-vaulted* my way around that room! Know what I'm saying? Huh?'

'Ugly details, Bullen – spare me.'

'Oh, sure. Anyway, super-charger applied, yes siree Bob, and when the girls had gone and we'd had a couple more drinks, I put my head on that pillow. And wow! Haven't slept that good in months. Woke up about an hour ago, grabbed a coffee and come over to see where my old buddy was.'

'Well,' I said, 'here I am.'

'And what did you get up to, then, while we were all tripping the horizontal Light-Fantastic?'

'Me?' I said. 'Nothing much.'

'Say, wait a minute. *Just* a minute. You were missing ... and Chanlina wasn't around much. You two didn't ...?'

'No, of course not.'

'You and Chanlina ... you're saying you didn't ...?'

'We didn't.'

'Oh fella, don't you ever try getting a job that involves lying, 'cos you ain't good at it! You did, didn't you? My God, you *are* a sly dog! There's us romping with the second-hand ones, and you slide off and sleep with the Lady of the House! You are *one* dark horse!'

'And you're well wide of the mark —'

'Don't try to kid a kidder! Hell, you're colouring as I look at you! Anyway, come on, take a little walk with me.' He gestured around the room and cupped a hand to his ear in a gesture that said – *this room may be bugged* – and beckoned me to follow him.

We went outside.

In the garden, the night was folding itself over the tree-tops, in that way that it does in that part of the world, inky-blue above us but light at the horizon. A couple of bats were whirling around above the pond, hunting the evening insects.

'Let's walk,' said Bullen.

We strolled across the grass, silent for a moment. I was thinking my own thoughts about the events of the day and the previous evening, so I said to Bullen:

'You know, your Clients ...?'

'What about them?' said Bullen, without slowing his pace.

'You know what you said about them wanting to get information from her, from Chanlina?' I was just beginning to appreciate the full implications of Bullen's plan.

'Yup,' said Bullen. 'What of it?'

'They won't, you know ... *torture* her to get it? Will they?'

Bullen stopped and turned to me.

'You know something, Andy? This isn't like the movies.'

'Sorry?' I said, missing his implication.

'They're gonna grab her, take her someplace, and they're gonna ask her some questions, you know? And she isn't going to want to tell them, sort of professional courtesy for someone like her; but she *is* going to understand her situation pretty damn quickly. And she knows that ... if they torture her ... *if*, I said ... then she will eventually tell them everything. She knows the business. She's not dumb. She will know that there's no way she won't talk in the end, so she'll talk, more or less immediately. Save everyone a lot of trouble. So, no, they won't have to torture her. That's how professionals work – as I said, not like in the movies.'

'And then they'll let her go?'

'Oh sure. Why wouldn't they? She hasn't done anything to them, has she? She turned the kill-contract down.'

'Good,' I said.

'Say! You've gone spooney on her, haven't you? Pretty face – and damn me, I knew it! You *did* go to bed with her, didn't you?'

'No,' I said, lying because it was none of his business. 'But this morning, while you were sleeping off your fun, she took me to see what she does with her money.'

'And what is she doing with it? Building a big shrine to Our Lord Buddha?'

'No. Better than that. She pays for a school and a medical clinic. Her sister runs the school, classrooms, desks, kids, the whole thing —'

'What, so now you think that she's Mother Theresa or something?' he said, in a tone that I didn't particularly care for.

'No, but —'

'Andy, you ever heard of Pablo Escobar, the Cocaine King?'

'Yes, of course.' I paused. 'Is there a relevance to this?'

'Yes, there is. The relevance is that Escobar made *huge* amounts of money supplying coke into the States, *billions* – and he used some of it for projects to help the ordinary people in Columbia, sports facilities, housing, water supply and so forth. And they loved him for it. Saw him as a kind of Robin Hood figure, the great benefactor. Good move on his part, clever. And Chanlina's doing the same kind of thing, right? Makes sense – but that doesn't make her any sort of a saint, though. Just good business practice; the folks round here will look up to her, protect her from outsiders – well, you saw it with the kidnapping yesterday, how they came to her for help.'

I shrugged. I didn't like his casual dismissal of her philanthropy, but I wasn't interested in arguing about it.

'But,' he continued, 'if you and she are getting a mite closer ... I don't know, but taking you to visit her pet projects seems like *something*, I reckon ... maybe that can help us move it on a bit with my negotiations with Edi. Can't hurt, anyway, can it? You think you can put a bit of pressure on her?'

'Maybe,' I said, non-committal. 'And what's holding up your negotiation anyway? We've been here two days – how hard can it be to arrive at a price, for God's sake?'

'From what I can understand,' said Bullen carefully, glancing up at me from a lowered brow (and maybe even thinking that his little pet Englishman was becoming a mite uppity), 'Edi Sarachi has a guy called Noy, a contact in Laos, and he's getting him to scout out the Khone Phapheng Falls and the surroundings. And I still think that he's trying to check out the target, the Thai guy. And you.'

'Well, he's not going to get far with checking out Richard Powell, given that he doesn't actually exist.'

Bullen snorted with impatience at me and said: 'Well, *obviously not*, Andy, obviously not. But the Thai guy, Jackie Sam, is real and a member of his family has just died – natural causes, don't worry – so that should check out.'

'And if Edi still won't agree to the deal?'

Bullen stopped walking. He seemed to be distracted by something he was thinking about, chewing it over.

'I said,' I repeated heavily, 'what if Edi —'

'I *heard* what you said, fella.'

I looked at him. Just for a moment, I was reminded that Bullen, for all his bonhomie and booming good-fellowship, was not actually my friend. I hardly knew him, not properly, and I had that slight feeling of the ground moving beneath my feet. Here we were, in a precarious situation, and he was only my ally to the extent that it suited him – and it gave me a little queasy sensation to be reminded of it.

'There is something though, Andy,' he said, at length. He seemed to have recovered his good humour.

'Which is?'

Bullen paused, staring into the distance, before he spoke:

'Maybe a Plan B. This afternoon, when I woke up, I was looking through my bag to find some clean clothes, and deep down in the bottom I found something. Something I'd forgotten all about ...'

He was staring at me like a magician about to pull a rabbit from out of a hat.

'Go on,' I said.

'A cell phone!'

'You found your cell phone?'

'No, not *my* cell phone – well, no, obviously it is *my* cell phone, but an old one, a spare. I kept it because I didn't trust these new-fangled smartphones, and I thought it would be good to have a back-up, one that I could actually work, you know?'

'What is it?'

'It's a cell, like I said —'

'I mean, what type? What make?'

'Uh ... it's an HTC.'

'Okay. Good phones. Has it got GPS on it?'

'No, I don't think so ... I'm pretty sure not. It's a very old model.'

'Has it got a SIM card? And a live account?'

'Well, I never took anything out of it ... and I never cancelled any accounts. Forgot all about it, I guess. So, yes, probably. There is a problem with it, though.'

'Which is?'

'It hasn't been used in a while ... years probably ... and the battery's completely dead. Flatter than a pancake in Kansas. Now, what I need – do you have a charger with you?'

I thought about that for a moment.

'Not one that's going to work with an HTC. My charger is for an iPhone.'

'Can we, like, adapt it? Figure some way to make it fit? You're a techie, ain't you?'

'Well, no, it's not that simple.'

'You got some tools with you though, huh?'

'Bullen, I'm a design engineer, not a mechanic. I've got my Swiss Army knife with me, and that's all.'

He glared at me with a mixture of disappointment and reproach, like a man who's been told his second-favourite hunting hound has been run over.

'Sorry,' I said, shrugging. 'That's just the way it is.'

There was a pause. To fill the gap, I asked him what, had he got the cell working, he would have done with it.

'Not sure,' he said slowly. 'Switch it on ... maybe figure out where we are.'

'It's not got GPS.'

'No ... but they can locate it from the phone towers, can't they? So I can maybe call the Client ... and they can do, like, a triangulation thing?'

'Here in Cambodia? Perhaps,' I said, 'if the technology works like that here. If there are enough towers nearby. If they can get the phone company to cooperate with them – but it doesn't matter, because you say the phone's dead.'

'Yeah,' he said doubtfully. 'That's a real crying shame. If it could be made to work ...'

'What?'

'Well, I could have called my Client, and he could have set up some kind of a tactical strike team. Small-scale stuff – he would need just enough men to come in and deal with Chanlina and her dad and Edi and the two boys. With the element of surprise, and you and me on the inside giving them the dispositions, I reckon six good men would do it easy. They could scoop up Chanlina, ask her their questions, whatever, and give us a ride to the nearest airport.'

'You mean, like a commando raid?' I said, aghast.

'Yes. Have to be very slick getting here because, as you said, the local population would be apt to forewarn her. But in the middle of the night ... fast attack ... every chance of success.'

'Shooting? They'd come in shooting?'

'A little, maybe.'

'And if they accidentally shot Chanlina in the process?'

'Just have to make good and sure they take her alive.'

He looked at me, smiling, then laughed.

'Andy, you should see your face! Don't worry. I've been around this kinda thing most of my life. You keep your head down, you'd be fine.'

I stared at him. It wasn't me that I was thinking about. A thought struck me:

'But isn't that illegal, I mean ... armed men in a foreign country? International relations? There would be issues – diplomatic issues. And the Americans ... they don't just barge into sovereign territory and shoot people, do they?'

'Well actually, the *Americans* do. How about when they went into Pakistan to get Bin Laden, for example?'

'Yes, but —'

'Anyway, who said our Client was the United States?'

That stopped me dead in my tracks.

'Aren't they?' I said. 'I had assumed that ...'

'Just because I'm American, you thought I was working for Uncle Sam? No, Andy, I work for whoever pays me, that's what the free market is all about.'

'So,' I said slowly, 'who exactly *are* we working for?'

'The Chinese.'

'*What?* We're working for the fucking *Chinese!* Jesus *Christ!*'

'Why not? We're not acting against US interests. Why not work for the Chinks? They pay well, cash on the nail. The guy who's set this up, he's a top man, Chinese Military Intelligence, good reputation.'

'Chinese Military Intelligence! *Jesus!*' I said, still horrified at the revelation. 'Who is he?'

'You really want me to tell you?'

'Of course I do,' I snapped

'Okay. It's a guy call Zhou, Colonel Zhou. Solid guy, been around for years.'

'I've got to tell you, Bullen, I am not happy about working for the

Chinese.'

'Andy, I ain't happy about a whole heap of things, but I don't go round bitchin' about them, though.'

'You know, I think it's about time that you explained to me *precisely* what we're doing here. You know, in detail.'

'How come you're suddenly so interested? Because you've gone soft on Chanlina, because you found out she has a school and a bit of a clinic?'

'No,' I said. 'Because, you know, this began with me just having to sit in a meeting and nod and say nothing. And now, you are contemplating ... a full-scale raid with guns and shooting and stuff like that. And that seems to me to be moving the goalposts, I think, by about a mile.'

Bullen stood still in the garden, staring at the fading light at the horizon. To the south, there were the big slate-grey clouds starting to stack up in the sky, their edges tipped pink with the setting sun.

'Look at that,' he said, gesturing at the clouds. 'Reckon we'll get rain soon. Serious rain.' He stood immobile a moment, then he fished his pack of cigars out of his breast pocket, selected one, bit the end and lit it.

'Okay, Andy, I'll lay it out for you.'

'Andy – you know what's the best thing we Yanks ever invented?'

I was becoming used to his oblique way of explaining things by now, so I said that I didn't, but hazarded some vague guesses: the Otis Lift Brake? The Windows Operating System? The Ford Mustang?

'Nope,' he said. 'Not even close. *Coca Cola*. Simple as that. Now, people say there's a secret formula that makes it special but, truth be told, the rival companies worked out that shit fifty years ago. It's not the formula or the ingredients. It's *the idea*. Coca Cola is not just a flavoured sugary drink. Coke is America in a bottle. It's Elvis Presley and James Dean and the moon landings and kids in convertibles and pretty girls with great tits and perfect white teeth and rock 'n roll and Saturday night and the good life. And some little guy in Africa or Venezuela or any other shit-hole country – he can't have all that stuff, the American dream, the good life, whatever, but he *can* have a Coke and, just like that, he's drinking the drink of champions, the same soda as the masters of the universe, and he can have a glimpse of the dream.

'It's the perfect example of soft power,' he went on. 'But China, see, hasn't got that. It may be the workshop of the world, it may be the second biggest economy and coming up fast, it may own most of the US's sovereign debt and Government bonds, it may be catching up in terms of living standards and technology, building roads and factories and bridges and power stations like crazy – but it doesn't have the soft power of America. Its influence doesn't stretch out beyond its borders like the USA. But it really wants that. It wants the respect, the place at the table. It wants the world to ask: "*What does China think?*" Just like nowadays they say: *What does the USA think?* It believes that the next century will be the Chinese century, like this last century has been the American century.'

I didn't say anything. This wasn't news to me.

'So what does China do? It spreads out. It spends money outside China, across the world. It gets itself involved in things, something called the "Belt and Roads Project", a sort of Chinese Marshall Plan. It invests in other countries, builds infrastructure, industry, facilities. Initially in Asia, but gradually getting further afield, Africa, Australia, South America, even Europe.

'And the rest of the world is barely waking up to this,' he continued. 'They think that this is an American world, and it still is. So far. But that's changing and it's changing fast. The Chinese have big ideas.

'And *one* of those ideas was to open up Cambodia and Laos and Vietnam. You've seen yourself, there's nothing here, no decent infrastructure, hardly any roads or railways. But there are plenty of natural resources: farming land, minerals, oil, gold and diamonds up north. And then some bright spark in Beijing comes up with another big idea – there is a natural road which could, or might, be used – *the Mekong River*. Runs all the way through Vietnam, Cambodia, Laos. If that was navigable, if you could move ships up it, transport materials, it's an artery right through South East Asia.'

'But,' I interjected, 'the Mekong meanders all over the place – and it runs shallow and wide. There are major rapids on it ... You couldn't take shipping up it, not big stuff. To change that would be a huge project, immense.'

'Exactly. You said it: *Immense*. That doesn't matter, because the Chinese think in exactly those terms. They think big. Just like the good old US of A used to do. Just because it's difficult, doesn't mean they can't do it. But the first step is always political. They get themselves a local man, a Cambodian Government Minister and they persuade him to get involved, to buy in

– hell, I don't know, probably they bribe him – and he starts to promote the scheme, lay the political foundations, persuade the Government, and begins to put together a pilot scheme, a small section of the river at first. The Chinese manage him closely; he effectively becomes their puppet, their mouthpiece. But then, out of the blue, someone assassinates him, like I already told you. Somebody who does *not* want Chinese involvement, who doesn't want the Chinese taking a slice of control in the region.

'So now, the Chinese Government need to find out who did that. They don't care who actually pulled the trigger, but they need to know who ordered this Minister killed. They need to know who their opponent is – because, right now, they're blind. However, what they *do* know is that the first approach was to the *Green Mamba*, to Chanlina and Edi. So they need Chanlina to tell them who came and asked her to do the hit. And to do that, they need to isolate her and arrest her. And *that* is where I come in, because Colonel Zhou came to me to organise it, because they've got to be careful how they tread now, politically, you understand? So Zhou and I dream up our scheme, to get Chanlina some place out in the open, where they can lift her. And Zhou wants it done in Laos because ... I don't know, maybe the Chinese can more easily bribe people, the law there, to look the other way, I'm not sure. But Edi and Chanlina and her old man, they're cautious, they hesitate, maybe they smell a rat and so they say that they want to meet my *Principal*, the guy calling the shots and then, lucky old you, I asked *you* to help me. And here we are.'

He looked at me like some sort of overgrown schoolboy who has just given the correct answer to a maths question. He grinned and said:

'Well, what do you think?'

I took a breath. What did I think? Good God, laid out like that – clear and simple – what *did* I think?

'What I think is that we've been here too long,' I said. 'I think that your plan has got stuck someplace.'

'You know, Andy, you remember you signed up for five days —'

'*Fuck* five days, Bullen! I'm not talking about that. We have been here – wherever the hell *here* is, which we don't even know – almost three days, and if they were going to take the bait, they would have done it by now. And, every hour we stay here increases the risk that they'll see through us. Because, you know damn well, if they knew what we were *really* doing here, they would kill us, no question. And they are not stupid, not stupid at all.'

Bullen stared at me. I went on:

'So *this* is what I think. I think that tomorrow morning, first thing, you go see your good pal Edi Sarachi and you tell him we are *leaving*. Time is up. Tell him to either agree to your concocted little scheme – or else forget about it. But either way, we're leaving.'

'I don't think that I can do that, Andy,' said Bullen quietly.

For once, his ebullience had deserted him. It crossed my mind that he was himself answering to a third party, this man Colonel Zhou, and failure might have ugly consequences for him. He added: 'What if Edi refuses to be pushed? What if he says *no*?'

'Then, he says no,' I replied flatly. 'Maybe he's going to say that any- way. Maybe he's hesitating because something smells off to him – and he wouldn't be wrong there, would he? It doesn't matter anyway. Tomorrow, you go and tell him.'

Bullen hesitated.

'I don't think that I can do that, Andy,' he repeated.

'Then *I* will,' I said.

'You can't.'

'I can – and I will. As far as they know, I'm the instigator in all this, aren't I? The guy who calls the shots? So, what I say, goes. If I say the deal is off, then it's off.'

'You can't do that.'

'You just watch me, Bullen. You can't stop me – or at least, you might try, but how are you going to explain to Sarachi and Chanlina that your *Principal* isn't around suddenly, huh? So, yes I can.'

He stared at me.

'Tomorrow morning, understand?' I said.

He said nothing. He was still staring at me when I turned and walked away.

Generally speaking, I'm a pretty accommodating sort of fellow – prob- ably a bit too accommodating if I'm honest. So I don't know where I had found the resolve to stand up to Bullen so directly. Maybe I was just sick of being the pawn in someone else's game. Or, maybe, I was just now realising that following Bullen's lead wasn't working out all that well.

And probably all this talk of midnight raids and commandos (and Chi- nese commandos, at that) had shaken me and finally tipped me over the edge.

None-the-less, I was surprised at myself – my sudden burst of boldness. The truth was, despite Bullen's insidious suggestion that Chanlina and I were getting close, that I was still healthily scared of her – and Edi Sarachi too, for that matter. As far as I was concerned, the sooner we were out of there the better. It wasn't even the prospect of the money, or losing it – by now I would simply be happy to leave with my skin intact.

I walked back to the guest house and into my room; it was only when I got there that I realised that I was breathing hard. *Steady son*, I thought, you can't afford to let yourself panic ; you need to keep your wits about you.

I looked at my watch. Dinner time. Okay then, I told myself, nothing's wrong, behave normally.

I wandered outside and crossed the lawn to the main house and went up the outside staircase to the wooden balcony.

Edi Sarachi was sitting at the big table, smoking and sipping a beer. He looked up when I approached.

'Richard,' he said in greeting. 'Is Bullen not with you?'

'No,' I said shortly. 'Chanlina not about?'

'No – she had to go into the village on some business. You'll have to make do with me this evening.'

'Oh, sure, fine,' I said, drawing up a chair. He pushed a bottle of beer across to me and tossed over the opener.

I was surprised to realise that I was both relieved and disappointed that Chanlina wasn't there – I was having what you might call 'mixed feelings'. On the one hand, I was uneasy around her – on the other, I was excited at the prospect of seeing her.

'So,' I said to Sarachi while I was opening the beer, trying for casual conversation, 'you've lived here in Cambodia for long?'

'Seven or eight years. I go back home every year.'

'Where's home?'

'Albania. I have an apartment on the coast, a town called Durrës. You may have heard of it – it has a huge Roman amphitheatre, quite famous.'

'Is that where you're from originally, Durrës?'

'No, from Tirana, the capital. You ever been to Albania?'

'No, I'm afraid not.'

Sarachi laughed dryly.

'Nobody has been to Albania,' he said. 'That's because there is nothing there. Nobody goes there, nobody has ever heard of it. That's why it's easy to leave.'

'I see,' I said, unsure how to respond.

'There's going to be big weather this evening,' he said. 'See those clouds stacking up from the south? It's going to rain like hell.'

'I thought that the monsoon season was over.'

'It is, but you still get the odd isolated downpour at the tail end. When I first came here, I couldn't get used to the weather. The locals talk about the hot and cold seasons – for me, it's always damned hot. And the rain tends to come in sudden storms, torrential, but usually no more than an hour or so. Weird. After the hot season, the wet season is almost a relief.'

Sita appeared from inside the house. She looked at the two of us and said something to Sarachi.

'She is asking if Bullen is coming for his dinner?' he said.

'Tell her that I don't know. Maybe.'

He spoke to her in Khmer and she shrugged and went back inside.

'So,' I said, conversationally, 'what brought you here originally? To Cambodia, I mean.'

He shifted in his chair uncomfortably.

'Opportunity, I suppose. And there are a lot of similarities between Albania and Cambodia, you know? Two countries completely screwed up by stupid people who got sold a bunch of ideas by some philosopher – *hah!* Do you know what *philosophers* actually are? Let me tell you. Philosophers are guys who give advice to people who are happier than they are.'

I smiled dutifully but I couldn't think how to respond to that. We continued with our desultory conversation, this and that, nothing at all. It occurred to me that, unlike Chanlina and her father, I didn't really care for Edi Sarachi.

Just then, Sita came out with my meal.

As I was finishing my dinner, a chicken *amok* and rice, Bullen appeared. He nodded curtly at me, shook hands with Sarachi with rather more warmth and helped himself to a beer. He sat for a while in silence, smoking one of his poisonous cigars; he was evidently annoyed with me.

'You want to eat something?' asked Edi Sarachi as he finished his own food.

Bullen drew in a breath.

'Maybe. What have ya got? Ham and eggs over easy? New York strip?'

Sarachi laughed mirthlessly, his dry cackle: 'Almost certainly not. I shall call Sita.'

He shouted something in Khmer and the housekeeper emerged from the interior of the house and exchanged a few words with him. I, of course, couldn't understand what they were saying, but I got the gist; Sita wasn't pleased at being asked to provide dinner for latecomers to her table. She stumped back inside.

'And?' said Bullen.

'She'll get you something,' said Sarachi. 'Probably.'

Bullen grunted.

'I really don't know why we keep her on,' remarked Sarachi casually. 'It's not like her food is anything special.'

'Uh huh,' said Bullen.

'I think I might be able to guess,' I said, thinking about what Chanlina had told me about Sita and the revolver. I wondered if she'd ever told Sarachi about that.

'What, the warmth of her personality?' said Bullen.

'A bit more than that,' I said, rising from the table. 'I'll leave you both to your meal. Going to get an early night, maybe read in my room a while.'

I headed back to the Guest House.

That night, it rained. Well, I say rained, but that seems too small a word for what erupted from the sky. I've seen heavy rain in different parts of the world, but nothing compares to a full tropical downpour in Indochina. It starts with a few thudding, heavy drops, then the heavens open and it's as if someone has turned on a thousand fire-hoses up above, a solid curtain of water that hits the ground and immediately floods, so that the water splashes up knee-high. There is no question of running through the torrent – you can't see more than a couple of yards in front of you anyway – and you would be soaked to the skin in seconds.

I had been reading my paperback when the deluge started and I heard the sudden drumming on the roof, so I poked my nose out of my room and opened the door to the outside. I stood on the little veranda and watched the deluge, the trees bending under the weight of water, the gutters over-flowing, a concrete wall of water at the edge of the roof, the smell of the rushing air, the sudden rivers forming on the lawn in front of me.

It's odd, but I've always loved the rain.

The following morning, I woke early. The rain had stopped and the birds were singing. I could see sunlight streaming in through a gap in my curtains. I was feeling good; today was the day when everything would be resolved. Bullen would state our position and, one way or the other, we would leave – I had a moment's concern that he might try to duck out of it, but I felt confident. Either he would do it or I would myself. Tomorrow I would think about this and sit back and laugh.

I got up. I was minded to take an early stroll in the rain-soaked garden; everything, I thought, would be fresh and sparkling. I cleaned my teeth and dressed, remembering to put on closed shoes against the sodden grass, then slipped out of my room, down the corridor to the outside door.

I put my hand on the door handle and turned it. It rotated, but the door didn't open. I tried again. It was, for the first time I could recall, locked.

I looked around; there was only one door to the exterior – why was it locked? I had a sudden sense of unease, that something was wrong, something I didn't understand. Then, I caught a hint of movement outside, so I pressed my face to the glass and saw Ak on the little veranda. He must have seen me at the same time and he came over to stand outside the door.

He didn't look overly friendly; in fact, his pock-marked face was scowling and he made a gesture with his hand that said, unmistakably, *Get back.* He repeated it: *Get back from the door.*

I shrugged and spread my hands wide, the universal expression of *I don't understand.* I pointed at the door handle and the lock and he shook his head vigorously. He made his *Get back* gesture again.

It was only then that I realised that he had a light machine gun slung around his shoulders. I retreated away, down the corridor.

I went back into my room and slumped down on the bed, the full impact of what was happening sinking in. We were blown! Somehow, our flimsy ridiculous little story had been discovered and now our hosts had become our captors. We were no longer guests – we were prisoners.

God damn it! I buried my face in my hands. I don't think that I actually wept or beat my breast, but it was a close-run thing. I could have banged my head on the wall in anger and frustration. Our position, I was realising, was suddenly desperate. We'd left our hotel with some random driver, been dropped off in the middle of bloody nowhere, in the middle of the night, to be taken to God knows where; nobody knew we were here – we didn't even know ourselves. And anyone who might come looking for us (and who *exactly* would that be? The British consulate? The police?) would find no trail to follow. We were lost in the wilds of a lawless country – and our bodies might easily be dumped in a swamp somewhere and never be found.

In a sense, a part of me was not surprised – some quiet small voice inside had been expecting this all along ... a voice of reason that I had wilfully ignored. I had wandered, like a complete fool, into a situation I didn't understand. As the Russians had told me in the Battambang hotel, 'This is not your world'. I hadn't the first idea what I was doing ... I had been lucky to get this far. Give me a problem that I understood, a tricky pump calculation, an air flow arrangement, whatever, and I knew what to do. *How,* in the name of the good Christ, had I imagined I would be able to survive in this shadowy fog of spies and plots and assassins?

I suppose that I may have sat there cursing myself and my stupidity for a good fifteen minutes, knuckling my forehead and damning my own idiocy. Then, slowly, some calmer part of my mind starting to make itself heard. Yes, the situation was dreadful, but I wasn't dead yet. *Do what you always do, Finch,* said the voice, *find out what is going on and try to work a way out.*

I got up and washed my reddened face in the little bathroom sink, spending a brief moment glaring at the face in the mirror and growling '*Fucking idiot!*' at my reflection. Then I went back into the corridor, checking that Ak was still standing guard at the outside door, knocked hard on Bullen's door and entered without waiting for him to answer. He was in bed.

'Andy,' he mumbled, pulling himself awake. 'What ...?'

'I would say "Good morning" but it isn't,' I said harshly. 'It looks like we're in big trouble.'

'What?'

'We're locked in – and there's a man with a gun guarding the door. We're prisoners. Something's happened. Something's changed. Our friends are not our friends anymore.'

'Locked in? What?' He started to sit up in bed, rubbing sleep from his eyes.

'Yep. With a guard at the door.'

'Oh shit,' he groaned. '*Oh Lordy!*'

'Bullen,' I said, 'is there something you need to tell me?'

'What are you talking about? Oh ...,' he said. He sat up on his bed and took a sip of water from the bottle on the side table. He fumbled for his packet of cigars.

'You know something about this, don't you?' I said, the niggling doubt growing in my mind.

'Well, Andy, there may be something ...'

'Go on.'

'You see, what with you laying down the law last night, all high and mighty, and everything with Edi going so slowly ...'

'Yes?'

'Say, can you see my lighter? I musta left it someplace —'

'*Fuck* your lighter!' I snapped. I suddenly thought about the possibility of listening bugs in the room so I dragged Bullen into the little bathroom and turned on the shower to create some background noise. 'What are you telling me?'

'Well, what with everything, you know – listen, it's probably nothing ... but, you remember I was talking about that HTC phone I found?'

'Yes,' I growled.

'I asked Edi Sarachi whether he had a charger.'

'You did what?' I said. It was all I could do not to shout.

'Not for a phone! Jesus, I'm not *stupid*. I said it was for an electric razor. And he said, sure, okay, and he got out a box of old charger cables, you know, like everyone has, and so I selected one that would fit, and he said okay and gave it to me —'

'Show me!' I snapped.

'Oh, sure, it's here somewhere.' He went out and scrabbled around his bedside table and produced a black wire with a plug on the end. When he came back into the bathroom I snatched it off him and examined the connector.

'Bullen! Look at this! Just look at it, will you?'

'What? It's a connector!'

'It's a mini-USB connector. A *USB* connector! There are no razors in the world that use these. This is a data connector. These are used for fucking phones – *never* razors! You have, as good as, told him that you have a mobile phone here. So, he knows that you're lying to him.'

'How was I to know?'

That gave me pause. I said, in as carefully a controlled voice as I could manage: 'You might just have asked me. Or better still, not gone looking for a charger at all.'

'I'm sorry,' he said.

'Did you use it?'

'Uh, yes, I called the Client last night.'

'And?'

'He didn't answer – I left a message.'

'So, all this shit and no actual result, eh? And if they're bugging the room, then Sarachi will have heard you.'

'Andy, I can only say sorry so many times.'

'Sorry! Jesus wept!' I growled. '*How* could you have been so fucking stupid? They had their suspicions before – they weren't quick to take the bait, were they? – but now! Of all the bloody stupid tricks! We aren't going to be able to talk ourselves out of this, are we? *Fuck me, Bullen!*' I was almost shouting now, I was so furious. 'You are beyond belief! You stupid, ignorant, bull-headed twat! My God, you've probably gone and got us both killed!'

'Well, I think that you're maybe exaggerating a bit there —'

'Exaggerating! *Exaggerating?* How dare you!'

'Andy —' he started, in a placatory tone.

'No! Don't you "*Andy*" me, you dull fucker! I don't even want to look at you. In fact, I should murder you myself!'

And I stormed out.

Satisfactory as it was to stride manfully out of the room, Bullen and I were still in this mess together; we would have to work out some strategy. So I wasn't particularly bothered when he shuffled into my room ten minutes later, looked suitably contrite – an effect somewhat spoiled by his wearing the appalling garment that he called his 'drinking shirt'.

'Listen, Andrew,' he started, but I cut him off.

'I see you got dressed with your eyes shut,' I said.

'Uh? Oh, this,' he said, glancing down at his front. 'Only clean shirt I got left.'

'Yes,' I said.

Oddly, I was feeling a little calmer myself. The worst had occurred. What I had been dreading all along was happening – there was nothing more to worry about. The only thing was to work out what to do next.

'I've been thinking,' I said. I beckoned him into my own bathroom and turned on the shower to muffle our conversation. 'There are only two ways we get out of this.'

'Go on,' he replied carefully.

'We can either do it with violence, or with talking. That's it.'

'I see. Well, what's the violent version then?'

I explained my thinking, that there was only one guard, Ak. He was armed and dangerous. But, there were *two* of us. The door to the outside was locked, but our rooms had windows made of glass and glass was, of course, breakable. Our rooms were on opposite sides of the building, so, if we both broke through our windows at the same time, Ak could only approach one of us with his gun. The other man – I suggested that it should be Bullen, with his more useful skills and experience – should then come at Ak from behind and overpower him.

'Okay,' said Bullen slowly. 'Say it happens like to say – you crash out of your window and Ak goes to you ... what's to stop him simply shooting you, then turning and shooting me?'

'If they wanted us dead,' I said 'they could have killed us already. So, it's reasonable to assume that they want us alive, at least for the moment. I reckon that he is going to hesitate before he pulls the trigger – maybe only for seconds, but enough for you to get to him. You're twice his size, you should be able to deal with him easily.'

'Right then ... just say, maybe, your plan works and we overpower Ak. What then?'

'Then, we have a weapon. You know how to use it, so we make for the cars, steal one – I assume you can hotwire one if the keys aren't in.'

'And then drive away?'

'Yep. Then drive away.'

'You know, Andy, we used to have a joke in the Company. The joke was:

"I've heard of suicide missions that had a better chance of survival than this."'

'Good joke,' I said.

'Yeah, they used it in some movie one time. And it applies especially here.'

He stared at me meaningfully.

'You're not really serious about this plan, are you?' he said.

'No, I'm not,' I admitted.

'You don't think that it's going to work, do you?'

'No, I don't.'

'Didn't think so. I've done some damn-fool things in my time but I gotta tell you I ain't doing that.'

'Okay,' I said. 'In that case, that only leaves talking our way out.'

'Uh-huh,' replied Bullen. 'Lucky, then, that you've got an "in" with your girlfriend.'

'Chanlina's not my girlfriend – and anyway, I wouldn't put too much faith there. It would be better if you can think up some good reason for charging and using a phone you're not supposed to have. Something convincing.'

'I could say that I needed to make an urgent phone call. That's half-true at least. What do you think?'

'I think that you need a better story.'

The morning passed uneventfully, broken only by Sita arriving with a tray of breakfast, consisting of *congee* rice pudding, coffee and bread rolls. Ak stood behind her with his weapon levelled as she unlocked the door and slid the tray onto the floor.

'I need to see Chanlina,' I called out, keeping back from the door. 'Chanlina! Or Edi Sarachi! Tell them I need to speak to them.' Neither Sita nor Ak acknowledged me, or even gave me a glance. Sita locked the door again and walked back to the main house, leaving Ak on guard.

Bullen regarded the breakfast tray with disfavour. 'Fuckin' *congee*. Never could stand the stuff. You can have my share.'

'I don't much care for it either,' I said, as we sat down to eat.

There was no air conditioning in the little guest house, so it became hotter and hotter as the day wore on. I sat on my bed and looked out of my

window at the view of the garden. Da took over from Ak on guard duty –
I tapped on the glass to get his attention, but he ignored me.

Mostly, I just sweltered and fretted and perspired.

Later on, Bullen came into my room.

'You know something Andy,' he said, by way of opening, 'this isn't the
tightest spot I ever been in.'

'Oh no?' I noticed that the material of his hideous shirt was damp with
sweat.

'I ever tell you 'bout the time I was here, in Cambodia, with the crocodiles?'

'Crocodiles?'

'Yep. I never told you?'

'No,' I said. "Go on, you'd better tell me.'

'Well, I'd been in Siem Reap on a job, a bit of business, you know? It was
a – well, doesn't matter now what it was, but we fell out with some real
nasty people. Thought I'd shaken them off, I was on my way out, but they
caught up with me and my guy —'

'Your guy?'

'Kind of my assistant-cum-translator-cum-driver guy. Local man. Good
guy, name of Phea, very useful. Anyway, they got us outside the hotel, must
have been waiting for us – one minute I'm standing in the sunshine, next
minute, crash! I'm in the bag. Phea too.'

'Like we are now?' I said, but he pretended not to hear me and carried
on:

'So they used something, chloroform maybe, and I am dead to the world,
Lord knows how long. Next thing I know is I'm waking up in a cage made
of chicken wire, half-submerged in cold water.'

'A *cage*?'

'Yes, me and Phea both. Big old cage, ten, twelve feet square, maybe seven
feet deep. I mean, this is nothing flash, this is real crude, bits of rough plank,
chicken wire tied together. There's wooden piling around us, so I figure
out we must be in one of those floating villages on the big lake here, Tonle
Sap.'

'A floating village?' I interjected.

'Yep. You never seen them? They lash a load of empty barrels together,
cover them in planks, live there on the fishing from the lake and whatever,
freshwater pearls, bit of tourism I guess. Build small huts on top, make up

little communities.'

'No, I've never seen them.'

'Well, that's not important. I'm taking in my situation, making *an assessment* of the opportunities and risks, so to speak, keeping still and biding my time. And that's when I realise that Phea and I are not exactly alone in the cage.'

He looked at me, expecting some reaction.

'Go on,' I said.

'On the other side of the cage, lying half in the water, same as we were, are two enormous crocodiles.'

'*Crocodiles?* You're joking!'

'Afraid not. There they are, two prehistoric monsters, huge. I mean, *Lordy* Lord, that's about the worst waking up I ever done in my life. Can you imagine it? I thought my heart was going to stop. I was watching the nearest one, and it was watching me, not moving a muscle.'

'Jesus,' I said. 'What did you do?'

'Do? Well, I managed to stay silent for a start, perfectly still, you know, thinking that *just maybe* they are as frightened of us as we are of them.'

'Were they? Frightened of you?'

'Hell, no! They were just wondering which bit to bite off first. So, I collected my wits and started to run my hands over the chicken wire, searching for a gap, or a weak spot, anything. And I was looking at the top of the cage, the lid if you like, but it was a criss-cross of planks and mesh. I was trying to calculate if I could maybe get up and climb out of there before one of the bastards got me. But whoever had put us into that cage had thought of that, because I could see a sort of hinged cover that had been chained shut, with a padlock on it. I thought to myself, Bullen, buddy, *this is it*, this is the day you are going to meet your Maker.'

He was staring at me, wide-eyed, gripped by his memory.

'So,' I said, 'what did you do?'

'Do? Well, there wasn't a whole lot I *could* do. The CIA trains you for lots of things, believe you me, but I don't think that there is anything covering crocodile wrestling. And these horrors were *big*, six, seven feet, maybe more. So I'm wracking my brains for everything I knew about crocodiles which, I can tell you, wasn't much. I had no illusions I could fight them off with my bare hands, my pockets were empty, not even a bunch of keys, nothing!'

'And?' I said.

'So I used about the only thing I could think of.'

'Which was?'

'Phea was starting to stir, coming to. I couldn't trust him not to panic when he regained consciousness and saw the situation. Then, he'd maybe upset them, make 'em attack. It wasn't a risk I could take. He was lying beside me, bit further down the cage. So, I made a decision.'

'Which was?'

'Well, looking back, I don't know if I'm proud of what happened next – or ashamed. But, there seemed to me only one way out, so I took it.'

He paused, whether for dramatic effect or because he was overcome with emotion I couldn't tell, then he said:

'I drew my leg back, about as far as I could, and I kicked Phea hard in the back of the head, real hard. Reckon I knocked him cold, then I grabbed him – he was only a little guy – and shoved him across that cage, right at those fuckers. He landed on top of one and then all hell broke loose! They reared up and went for him, tearing at —'

He stopped abruptly, lost in memory. When he resumed, it was in a cold, quiet voice:

'I never seen anything like it. It was carnage, pure carnage, blood and gore everywhere. They ripped at him, like he was a rag doll. The worst thing was ...'

'Was what?'

'I think that he might have regained consciousness at one point, leastways his eyes opened and I thought he looked at me, perhaps only for a second or two. Perhaps I'm wrong, but I believe that he knew what I'd done ... maybe it's just my imagination, maybe he knew nothing. It was very fast, the rending and tearing – he came to pieces in those terrible jaws, he must have been dead inside a minute. Inside two minutes, you wouldn't have recognised what was left as a human being. The crocs were swallowing hunks of meat – because that was what he was then, hunks of meat. I mean, *Jesus* ...'

He shook his head, then seemed to regain himself.

'So you see, Andy, I reckon if the Good Lord had wanted to take me ... well, that was the day he would have done it, no doubt. But He didn't. And sure, I felt sorry about Phea, I truly did, but mostly I blame whoever had put us into that cage. We were both, in a sense, dead men, the moment they shut the lid. Except that I ... I found a way to survive – I stepped ahead of death that day.'

'What happened next?' I said.

'The crocs had fed; when they're full, they go into a kind of digestive stupor. They went quiet. So I just lay there, in all the blood and gore, then I called out. I said that I had one hundred thousand dollars for anyone who let me out of that cage – I repeated it over and over, until finally a couple of guys came and released me. One of them spoke a bit of English – I told them I had the money in my hotel safe, they had to take me back to Siem Reap, and they could have it. They got me cleaned up somehow, then we took a boat back up the lake, then we went to the hotel. I opened up the safe, but they were real stupid because I had some money in that safe – not a hundred thousand, but some – but what I actually had was a .38 calibre revolver and I pulled it out while they were standing there, their tongues hanging out with greed.'

'And then?'

'What do you think? I ain't going to talk about it. Cost me eight grand to the hotel manager to clean the mess up, but he did and I got on the next flight out.'

He stared at me, daring me to say something.

'I have a question,' I said, at length.

'Yep?'

'Where did the crocodiles come from? I mean, that's like something from a bad movie, a cage of crocodiles, just waiting ...'

'Nah, the crocodiles weren't especially for us. Believe it or not, they are part of the economy of those floating villages. They catch the crocs when they're little, or steal the eggs, then they feed 'em and watch them grow, and then they slaughter them and sell their skins. Where do you think all the crocodile skin handbags and shoes come from? Crocodile farming.'

'That's a hell of a story,' I said.

'Yeah, well,' he sighed. 'Like I said, Andy, this isn't the tightest spot I ever been in. I reckon we'll get out of this one, somehow ... Okay, I'm going to slide off now, stand by the little window in my room and have a smoke. See you later.'

He walked out and, as I watched him leave, I had one thought uppermost in my mind: it *was* one hell of a story, but the man who had paid for whatever Bullen had done wasn't Bullen – it was Phea, his assistant-cum-translator-cum-driver. The other guy.

And, in *this* story, I was the other guy.

I had no idea why Bullen had thought to tell me his appalling story –
maybe he had intended to reassure me, or maybe to impress me; whatever
the reason, it had brought an idea into my head that had not really occurred
before. Up to that point, I had thought of us a pair, almost a team. We
would get through this, succeeding or failing, together. We had started it
together and, for good or bad, we would finish together.

You may think me dull, or sentimental or slow-witted, but I had assumed
– on the basis of no evidence at all – that Bullen and I were looking out
for each other. We were, if not actual friends, then at least partners. That
afternoon, sitting in my room in the guest house staring out at the green
of the garden, I suddenly thought that only one of us might get out of this
with our skin intact. And I realised with horrible clarity that Bullen would
not hesitate to leave me behind if that was what he had to do.

On the basis of that, I would be a fool not to be ready to do the same.

The afternoon turned into early evening; Da tapped at my window,
gesturing at me to move to the corridor. He was saying something that I
couldn't understand, but I gathered that he wanted Bullen there as well. I
called out to Bullen to come out of his room, which he did, and we both
stood in the corridor. Da waved his hand at us, urging us backward as he
unlocked the door – still keeping his gun levelled on us – and Sita appeared,
carrying a tray of food that she put on the floor just inside. She also dropped
half a dozen plastic bottles of water on the threshold.

'Edi Sarachi,' I called out. 'Chanlina! Fetch Chanlina! We want to speak
to them!'

'Yeah,' shouted Bullen, 'tell Edi and Chanlina to come here. Explain
what's going on! Hey! You hear me? Edi or Chanlina!'

But neither Sita nor Da acknowledged us, and Sita locked the door again
without even glancing in our direction.

Bullen picked up the tray, sniffed at the noodles and stew and said: 'No
beer, huh?'

He turned to me.

'Well,' he said, 'at least they're not starving us to death. Your place or
mine?'

I shrugged.
We ate in my room.

Bullen and I chatted for a while after we had eaten, small talk about countries we had visited, people we had known, where one got the best food and drink, trivia. Neither of us mentioned our present predicament; there was nothing to say. After a while, we ran out of conversation and he went back to his room for a shower. Outside, the light had gone. I looked out of my window; in the gloom, I could see that Ak had taken over the sentry duty from Da. I made a desultory attempt to read my paperback, but the print swam in front of my eyes and I abandoned it.

With nothing to do and nothing happening, feeling thoroughly depressed and anxious and with a dull headache, I went to bed. I lay for a long time staring up at the ceiling fan, watching it rotating slowly above my head, and kept asking myself the same question: did my night with Chanlina mean anything? And why had she shown me the school and the clinic? Was there something – a tiny spark, *anything* – between us? I had no illusions about my appeal to the opposite sex; women were not in the habit of falling in love with me.

And, more to the immediate point, would her feelings for me have any bearing on our predicament? If it came to it, would she save me?

I slept badly, if at all.

The following morning, both Ak and Da were on hand for the breakfast delivery; they were evidently changing shifts. As before, we called out our demands to see Sarachi or Chanlina, and once again we were flatly ignored.

Bullen and I ate in silence. Some of his bravado seemed to have deserted him during the night – he seemed distracted, which was understandable. I didn't feel exactly buoyant myself. His one remark to me was to ask me if I thought something might happen today, and I couldn't answer him. I had no more idea than he had.

But, late in the morning, with the day starting to get really hot, something did happen. Ak tapped on my window and summoned me into the corridor. There, standing by the door, he asked me a question through the glass:

'You,' he said, 'you swim?' He made an exaggerated dumb-play of a breast-stroke and pointed at me.

At first I thought he was asking me if I could swim or not, then I realised that he was asking if I wanted *to go* for a swim. Yes, I nodded vigorously, *yes*, anything to get outside. He mimed something that I took to mean swimming trunks, so I fetched them from my suitcase.

By now, Bullen was behind me in the corridor.

'What's going on?' he demanded.

'No idea,' I replied, truthfully. 'I seem to be being invited to go for a swim.'

'Make sure that they don't try to drown you.'

'I will,' I said. 'You want to come?'

'God, no,' he said. 'Anyway, they're inviting you, not me.'

'Uh-huh.'

'Well, find out what you can, will you? See how long they're planning on keepin' us here.'

'I will. If I can.'

Ak gestured us backwards, then he unlocked the door and opened it. Keeping his gun trained on Bullen, he indicated that I should step out.

I walked out into the garden and stood a distance away while he locked up again.

I walked ahead of Ak as we made our way across the garden, although he didn't seem particularly alert, hefting his gun casually at his hip. Maybe he thought that I wasn't much of a threat. +

I made my way between the high trimmed hedges to the open area around the pool. It was deserted. There were a few leaves that had blown into the water. Ak gestured to me to stop and to stand aside, while he picked up a long-handled net and walked around the pool.

'No, no, no,' he muttered to himself, then I saw what was bothering him. Not the leaves; there was a dead snake floating on the surface. It was a formidable creature, perhaps five feet long, and it had evidently slid into the pool at some point, mistaking it for fresh water. The chlorine must have killed it.

Ak struggled to collect the body, finally scooping it up in his net. He lifted it out of the water – the handle of the net bent under the weight – and dumped it onto the grass. Then he fished out the floating leaves and cleared the surface.

As he was doing so, the snake suddenly twitched and gave a convulsion that lifted its whole body clear of the grass. The horrible thing writhed violently, twisting and turning, and for one awful moment I thought it was heading back towards the water, then it moved with surprising speed across the grass and disappeared into one of the hedges.

Ak turned and said something to me and laughed. He pointed to the little timber changing room, evidently suggesting that I use it.

When I emerged in my swimming trunks, carrying a clean towel from the stacks I had found within, he was gone. I had been left alone.

I took a long hard look around – the snake had made me nervous – then slipped into the pool. The feeling of the water closing around me was glorious, refreshing and cool. I allowed myself to sink below the surface, then came up again and did a couple of lengths of backstroke, a length of slow crawl, then floated on my back, sculling, gazing at the cloudless blue sky. The sun was glinting in my eyes, so I closed them and hung almost motionless in the water, enjoying the sensation of weightlessness.

If I could just stay here, I thought, with the sun on my shoulders and the cool water beneath me ...

My reverie was disturbed by the slightest vibration in the water – I started, thinking about the snake. I let my legs sink down until I was vertical and could look around myself. A shape was moving under the surface of the water, something I could tell was another swimmer.

It was Chanlina.

I hung in the water while she completed two fast lengths of the pool, only coming up for air on the turns, then she swam across to me.

'Hello, Englishman,' she said, treading water. Her expression was neutral, opaque, almost curious.

'Hi,' I said.

'The water is fine, yes? On such a warm day, I like very much to swim.'

'Yes, me too.'

'And it is good for you to be outside, in the open,' she said. It was neither a question nor a statement.

'Yes.'

She hung in the water for a long moment and I had the feeling that she was assessing me, examining my face, as if making some decision.

'Come,' she said, and struck out for the edge in an effortless crawl. She jack-knifed herself out of the water and sat on the poolside, dangling her legs in the pool. She was wearing a white one-piece swim suit which accentuated her broad swimmer's shoulders and she ran her hands through her wet hair, pushing it back behind her ears. I followed her, laying my palms on the edge and hauling myself out of water. I sat myself beside her and waited for her to say something.

She was staring at the sunlight dancing on the rippling surface.

'Chanlina —' I started to say, but she silenced me with a finger on my lips.

'Don't speak, Englishman,' she said. 'I don't want ... because, I don't want you to say something, to *lie* to me ... so, say nothing.'

I remained beside her in silence.

'I need to know ...' she said, frowning, and then stopped herself. 'I want to understand – but ... maybe better *not* to ask.'

I watched her, still saying nothing.

'I wonder, Englishman, are you trying to betray us? I ... I hope not. I really do,' she said, and suddenly ducked her face to mine and kissed me on the forehead, very lightly and quickly. She rose to her feet and I almost spoke, but her raised finger stopped me.

'When you have finished your swim and have changed, go up to the main house, to the balcony. Sita will bring you lunch.'

I nodded.

'And *stay* there,' she said with sudden emphasis. It was a clear instruction. She turned and walked out through the gap in the hedges.

I continued swimming and sculling and floating for perhaps another twenty minutes, more confused than ever. What had she meant? Obviously, treachery was in the air – and she wasn't far wrong, was she? – and I was implicated. But she had said *I hope not*. That must have meant something. I felt myself churning with mixed emotions, anxious but strangely calm at the same time. And anger at Bullen – stupid, fucking Bullen, dragging me into his absurd schemes and wild plans, and getting caught over a charging lead.

Who was it who had said: 'In the end, it's the hope that kills you'? I couldn't remember, but I could feel it now; the dread foreboding with a dim sliver of hope.

I left the pool and changed into my clothes, then made my way back to the big house. The garden looked magnificent, more vibrant than ever after the downpour. Every plant seemed to be blooming, every colour more vivid.

There was absolutely nobody around; I thought about going back to the guest house and speaking to Bullen, telling him what had happened, but that wasn't what she had told me to do. I ascended the redwood staircase to the balcony and sat down at the table. I must have sat there for no more than two minutes when Sita came out and placed a jug of iced water and a glass on the table, then disappeared inside the house again. She had obviously been expecting me.

Ten minutes later, she brought me a dish of pork and rice in a pepper and tomato sauce. I thanked her and smiled and she ducked her head and smiled back. I ate in solitude, occasionally glancing down into the garden to see what, if anything, was happening. The birds were wheeling around in the trees, butterflies, a little lizard was climbing one of the branches, but there was no other activity.

Sita appeared again, just as I had finished the pork, with a bowl of prepared mango slices. She picked up my empty dish.

'Thank you,' I said, pointing at the dish. 'That was very good.'

She smiled again and said something in Khmer.

I ate the mango and she brought a pot of coffee and poured a cup, then disappeared back into the house. I sipped at the coffee and watched the wildlife in the garden below me.

It was warm in the sunshine; God knows how, but after a while I must have dozed.

When I awoke, the sun had lowered in the sky. I checked my watch – just after four o'clock. I blinked and forced myself fully awake, feeling sluggish and disorientated. Someone, presumably Sita, had come while I was asleep and cleared the table, all except the jug of water and a glass. I helped myself and drank.

Christ knows how I had managed to sleep for three hours – probably the tension of the last few days had taken it out of me. I felt vaguely guilty for deserting Bullen for so long – he must be wondering what had happened to me.

There was still no one around – the big garden below me was deserted. I called into the house for Sita, but she must have gone off somewhere, out of earshot. I stood up stiffly, flexing my muscles and went down the stairs from the veranda to the lawns.

I went first to the swimming pool, half-expecting to find Chanlina there, but it was empty. On my way, I noticed that the big iron gates were open – I could see down the little road as far as the bend. Then I made my way back to the Guest-House.

To my surprise, there was no one standing guard there, and the outer door was open. Odd, I thought, wondering what had changed. I walked inside.

'Bullen,' I called out, 'I'm back.'

No response.

I wandered into my room, where everything was exactly as I'd left it. It was then that I had a premonition that something was terribly wrong.

'Bullen!' I called, again without reply.

I went into the corridor and tapped on his door, which was ajar. When there was no response, I pushed the door open and went in.

What I saw in the room will stay with me for the rest of my life.

Bullen was sitting on a chair in the middle of the room, motionless. The bed had been shoved against the wall, to give an area of space. He was facing slightly away from me and I could see that his hands had been tied around the back of the chair and his head was lolling back. There was something dark and wet spilled onto the polished wooden floor.

'Bullen?' I said.

I walked around the chair, keeping my distance, until I faced him. His eyes were open and staring half-up into the ceiling, and the front of his absurd shirt was stained, discoloured with the blood that had spilled from a great gash across the side of his throat. He'd had an artery cut – the blood had spurted a yard across the room. And, even to my untrained eye, it was obvious that he was dead.

'Bullen?' I said again, stupidly, half in shock, even though I knew that he was never going to answer.

'Oh, Good *God*,' I muttered, still circling him. I felt my foot slipping in the blood on the floor.

I wondered how long he had been dead, and had the idea of reaching out to see if he was still warm, but I couldn't make myself touch him. *What difference would it make?* I thought.

I don't think that I had even seen a dead body before these last couple of days, and now I had seen two, both murdered.

I sat down on the edge of the bed, still staring at the ghastly shape tied to the chair. It didn't seem possible that he could be dead. I hadn't known him well – I wasn't sure that I even liked him much, but he had seemed so solid, like some great craggy rock of a man, arrogant, bullish, enduring.

And this simple action, a blade across his throat, had reduced him to a sack of inanimate bones and meat, a fat carcass tied to a chair.

I think that it was that thought that finally made me weep; I put my head in my hands and sobbed like a child. I wept for him and I wept for myself, because now I was completely on my own, lost in a strange land, without a clue where to go or what to do next. *This*, I thought, is where the stupid bloody adventure ends, sitting in a little room with a corpse and the dawning realisation of how ridiculous it was, how ridiculous *I* was.

Jesus, what must have I been *thinking*?

My train of thought was broken when I sensed that somebody had entered the room and was standing watching me. I looked up: Edi Sarachi.

'I didn't think anyone would weep for the old Yankee,' he said. There was a hostility in his voice that I hadn't heard before.

I stared at him.

'You killed him,' I said flatly.

'We questioned him. He was planning to betray us. Traitors die.'

'How was he betraying you?'

'Oh, who knows? Some scheme or other. Who can know the devious mind of a man like him? Maybe I should ask you the same questions that we asked him.'

I shuddered inwardly; *God help me*.

'So, you just killed him?'

'*We* killed him.'

'Who – you or Chanlina? Or the old man?'

'Does it matter? We told him that he should tell us the truth, or he would die. And he told us part of it ... but not enough.'

My mind was racing – had Bullen implicated me? What had he said before he died – was I *safe*? Or, was I next?

'What will you do ... with the body?' I said.

'Oh, don't worry about that. There are plenty of places around here, in the countryside, where he'll never be found. You know something? Out in the jungle, there are wild pigs. Those bastards will eat *anything*, crack up the bones, chew them up, don't leave a trace. This'll be a feast for them. Plenty of meat.'

'No chance of a decent burial, then?'

'No,' said Sarachi. 'You don't bury liars and traitors – you dump them. He got what he deserved.'

There was a silence in the room. I wiped my hands across my face.

'You know,' said Sarachi, 'if it was up to me, you would be joining him. But Chanlina wants you kept alive. Until we work out what to do with you.'

'Oh yes?'

'Yes. Some Cambodian idea of hospitality or something – like I said, I wouldn't have such scruples. As far as I'm concerned, whatever it is, you are in it with him. Chanlina is not so certain. So, we will see.'

'And, what? You just going to keep me locked up in here while you work it out.'

'No, Richard,' he smiled mirthlessly, 'we don't intend to keep you locked up at all. Why should we? You can come and go as you please.'

'I could just walk off?'

'Where to, Englishman? Where could you go? Without transport, you won't get far. The people around here, the locals, you know that they worship Chanlina. So you walk down the road, any road, and we will know where you are. Or, if you prefer, you could try hacking your way through the jungle – in which case you wouldn't get very far, and – between the snakes and the spiders and the heat and thirst – you'd probably be dead within a day.'

We stared at each other. I tried to gauge his thinking – and decided that he was simply indifferent, one way or another. He shrugged his shoulders and made to leave, then paused at the door.

'The boys will come and clear this up,' he said casually, indicating the awful thing in the chair. 'Why don't you come up to the house later, for dinner? Say about seven? Or I can have it sent here?'

'I'll come to the house,' I said, without thinking.

'Good,' he said. 'Who knows – maybe you are the innocent in all this. In which case, you're still our guest.'

And with that, he left.

I looked again at the dreadful body of Bullen, still staring sightlessly up at the ceiling, and went out.

Chanlina didn't appear at dinner. Sita served Sarachi and Banh Sar and myself, and we engaged in the most bizarre and stilted conversation I think I've ever had, constrained on my part, but apparently careless on Sarachi's. The old man was talking about football, of all things, and the Albanian translated bits for my benefit. It was weirdly disorientating to be discussing the merits of European football teams, Liverpool and Barcelona and Bayern Munich, sitting in a garden in Indochina with the pall of Bullen's death hanging over me.

I made my excuses and left early.

The following morning, after a night during which I barely slept, I got up very early and showered and went out into the garden. There was mist hanging in the trees, dampness dripping from the leaves. The sun, still low in a pale sky, hadn't yet warmed the day.

The two Cambodian men, Ak and Da, were working on one of the flower beds, trimming the bushes. In dire need of some kind of human contact, I wandered across and started to make the sort of small talk, half in signs and half in grunts, that you make with people with whom you share no language. I was admiring one of the plants with Da, a flower whose name I was sure that Chanlina had told me, and he was showing me something when Ak came over and spoke sharply, evidently telling him not to talk to me. Da broke off and turned his back.

Well, I thought, *that's that*. When even the hired help shuns you, you know you're in real trouble.

I meandered about, past the pond, watching the little fish in the shallow water and a big toad crouching under some leaves. I walked past the tall trimmed hedges and visited the swimming pool, which was deserted. The surface of the water was as flat as glass.

I headed for the house, thinking to get some breakfast, then I noticed that the big iron gates were wide open. Sarachi had said that I was free to go anywhere I liked ('Where could you go?') and the notion came to me to test the idea. Without hurrying, I walked towards the gates and paused for a moment in the shadow of the wall. Nothing happened; nobody came to stop me. There was no sound except the morning birds singing in the trees. I nodded to myself and stepped out through the gateway.

The road – more like a track of rutted gravel – stretched out in front of me. On either side the vegetation grew tall, as high as my head, except for the strip immediately adjacent to the walls which had been roughly cleared. I strolled down the road, waiting for some reaction.

Suddenly, I was outside.

Ten yards, twenty yards, thirty ... all the time I was expecting some shout of alarm, but nothing came. There wasn't another person in sight – so, with an air of affected carelessness, I sauntered down the track. I kept glancing over my shoulder, back towards the gates, anticipating something ...

Nothing.

I had gone maybe a hundred yards when the track started to bend round to the right. On either side of me, the foliage was dense, almost impenetrable – I could understand what Sarachi meant when he'd said that I wouldn't get far trying to cut my way through it. I carried on around the curve, occasionally glancing back. The gates were out of sight now. I stopped and looked around me, savouring the sensation of being alone and unobserved.

What would happen if I just kept walking? I tried to recall what I had seen on the occasions when I had left the house before, how far it was to any settlement, where exactly the roads divided – but I hadn't paid much attention. I had no clue of the local geography. But, if I just kept walking ... maybe meet up with a passing local in a vehicle, offer him a fistful of cash to take me further? Sarachi had said that the local people were loyal to Chanlina, but would they resist serious money? I had my wallet with a couple of hundred dollars in it – a fortune by Cambodian standards.

Could I simply get away? Was it worth the risk? I was sorely tempted to try it. What did I have to lose, anyway?

I must have been walking for a good half-hour before I saw anyone. The jungle had thinned out and there were fields to either side of the road. I had seen a couple of water buffalo wallowing in some wet ground, but without any sign of anyone attending to them.

The man I spotted was walking across a field. He was dressed in a baggy shirt and trousers and a straw coolie hat; I noticed that he had worn leather sandals on his feet. I called over to him and waved, then I hopped over the small drainage ditch and went over to where he stood watching me.

'Hello,' I said. He nodded but said nothing.

'I'm wondering if you could help me,' I continued. His flat gaze conveyed total disinterest; obviously, he didn't understand a word I was saying. To engage his attention, I took out my wallet and showed him some money.

His eyes went from my face to the money and back to my face. He shrugged. I mimed driving a car, making ridiculous revving noises, then showed him the money again. I pulled out a couple of notes and offered them to him but he didn't take them.

Then he shook his head, with a look that seemed to imply either indifference or disappointment. Then he started to walk away.

I followed him for fifty yards or so, repeating my driving mime, and waving money (feeling oddly like the worst kind of Western tourist). Eventually, he turned back to me and snapped something and, although the words were lost on me, his meaning wasn't. I backed away.

I gave up on him.

Back on the road, I walked for maybe another hour. A woman on a little motorbike passed me but, when I tried to wave her down, she swerved around me and continued on her way. Finally, I came to a small settlement. There were three stilt houses, with a kind of pigsty underneath with four piglets. There were a couple of cows munching grass in a field behind.

'Hello?' I shouted.

A boy appeared from somewhere and regarded me with what I was pretty sure was mild dread. I went through my driving pantomime again, smiling and offering money, but he kept his distance. Then I mimed a phone call and pointed to him. I held a twenty-dollar bill out, but he didn't move and, when I moved towards him, he retreated.

A middle-aged woman emerged from one of the houses, and started to chatter in Khmer. She darted across to the boy and wrapped a protective arm around him and pulled him away. I tried both my mimes on her, again without any effect. Suddenly she snatched up a rake and began to shout at me. A man appeared from the first floor, climbing down the bamboo ladder, took one look at me and joined in the shouting, gesturing at me to go.

I gave up on them too.

I walked on, heading vaguely south. By now, I was starting to get hungry and thirsty, so I stopped by a little stream and drank water that I scooped up in my cupped hands. I cursed myself for not waiting for breakfast before I set out, but it had been a spur-of-the-moment decision; I hadn't thought ahead.

It was maybe an hour later when I saw two men bent over and working in a flooded field, up to their ankles in water. They straightened up when they heard me waving at them, but didn't respond to my gesturing them to come to me, to come to the road. They simply stared in a manner that was disturbingly bovine. There was nothing for it – I would have to go to them.

I had the sense to take off my shoes and socks, then clambered over a little wire fence. Immediately I got into the field, I sank down to my calves, soaking my trousers. I cursed inwardly but tried to keep smiling away as I waded across. When I got close enough, I did my two pantomimes again, the car and the phone, grinning broadly (and, I hoped, reassuringly) and showed them the cash. They looked at each other and – for a moment – I thought they were tempted, but then they seemed to confer, and the taller one shook his head. I added more cash to my hand, which apparently upset them. The tall one pointed angrily back across the field, back towards the road. He said something in a harsh voice, and when I shrugged my incomprehension, he repeated it louder and pointed again.

I retreated.

I must have walked another two miles without encountering anyone, then, hot, hungry and weary, I sat down in the shade of a tree by the roadside and rested. I hadn't intended to sleep, but suddenly I woke to the sound of an approaching truck. I jumped up and waved, positioning myself in the middle of the road to force the driver to stop, but he wasn't slowing – I had to jump out of the way as he shot past, allowing me a glimpse of a man and his wife in the front, staring fixedly ahead. I landed badly and grazed my elbow on the gravel.

I plodded on for what seemed like hours, seeing nobody, until I heard another engine coming towards me. I wondered if this was the truck coming back, and then a car came in view. This time, the driver *was* slowing and he gradually came to a halt beside me.

It was Edi Sarachi.

'Need a lift?' he said, his arm leaning out of the window.

I looked around for something to use as a weapon and picked up a short stick that I hefted between my hands.

'Don't be ridiculous,' he said calmly, glancing at it. 'If I wanted to hurt you, I would have done it already.'

I stared at him.

'I told you,' he said, 'that the locals wouldn't help you. They know that you're with us – so they wouldn't dare, even for your dollars. And you'll get nowhere walking along here. There's a town up that way,' he pointed forward, along the road, 'about thirty kilometres or so. They might help you, but you'll never get that far.'

'So, how did you know where to find me?' I said.

'Oh, we always knew where you were. The villagers have been calling it in. Now stop being stupid and get in. We'll go back and you can get a beer and a shower – put some iodine on that graze – and get cleaned up in time for dinner.'

I stood for a moment, undecided. Then I opened the car door and climbed in.

Finch

We drove back without speaking much. Sarachi pointed out a couple of local shrines as we passed them. He didn't mention my own situation or anything about Bullen and I didn't raise the subject.

We went back in through the big gates and he drove me round to the guest house and pulled up. I climbed out.

'I'll send one of the boys over with something for that graze on your elbow,' he said casually, as I was passing his side of the car. 'Oh, and before I forget – we never found the phone.'

'The phone?'

'Bullen's cell phone. Did you see it?'

'No,' I said. 'I never saw it. Maybe he threw it away.'

At least that was truthful.

He stared at me, and I had the distinct feeling that he was assessing me.

'Okay,' he said. 'See you at dinner then.' He dropped the car into gear and pulled away.

Chanlina didn't appear at the meal and I didn't ask where she was. Sarachi chatted about this and that, talking mostly about his gymnasium, and I feigned interest. 'I'll show you tomorrow, if you want a workout yourself,' he offered. I grunted noncommittally.

I sat and had a beer with him, then said I'd have an early night. The sky was starting to darken as I wandered back through the garden to the guest house.

The door to Bullen's room was open so I went in. Whoever had cleaned up the room had done a good job – there wasn't a trace of blood anywhere and the furniture had all been put back where it belonged (I noticed that the upright chair was missing). I stood there, thinking about him and his strange crocodile story, spooling back over our meeting in the departure shed at Battambang airport, the absurd jump from the balcony, his 'adventure', his recklessness. I remembered his talking about parachute jumping, the weird dream he'd told me about dying up in the sky, and how that would been *alright*. Well, for him it had all ended here, in a nondescript room in up-country Cambodia. Maybe, he would have thought that was *alright*. I'd never know.

I realised that I didn't even know enough about him to be able to notify anyone – his ex-wives, his children – of his death; he had passed through my life without my really knowing anything about him at all.

Poor, foolish, careless Bullen, I thought.

I walked out and back into my own room, full of dark thoughts about my own situation. Was I in terrible trouble? Where was our ridiculous plan going now? Well, nowhere, obviously. I was going to be lucky to get out of here with a whole skin.

And that was when I heard the muffled sound of a cell phone ringing.

In the years since, I have sometimes wondered what would have happened if I hadn't answered that call. In fact, it was probably wrong of me to have answered it – it definitely wasn't for me. But the habit of responding to a ringing phone is too ingrained – and nobody else was going to pick it up.

Firstly, I had to find the damned thing. The noise seemed to be coming from my bed, so I lifted the pillows, then the duvet. Nothing. I lifted the mattress and looked under that – still nothing. I looked under the bed, without result. It had to be somewhere, so I tipped the mattress right off its base, and noticed a little rip in the underside. I felt the material around the rip and sure enough, the sound was coming from there, so I slid my hand inside and felt something plastic and smooth. I pulled out the phone.

I pressed the green symbol for 'answer' and put it to my ear.

'Hello?' said a voice. Male, with an accent, difficult to place. Eastern certainly – Japanese? Not Cambodian. Maybe Chinese?

'Yes,' I said.

There was a long pause.

'Bullen?' said the voice tentatively. I resisted the idiotic urge to say that Bullen wasn't here right now, sorry, may I take a message, and instead I just said: 'No'.

'Who is this?' said the voice. 'Where is Bullen?'

'Bullen ...' I started, and hesitated. What to tell them? Presumably this was the Client, Colonel Zhou, or maybe one of his people who spoke English. And what I said next was dangerous and significant. Should I tell him the truth? Could I lie, or sustain a lie?

'Yes?' said the voice.

'Bullen — is dead.'

There was a pause. Someone was speaking in the background.

'Is that true?' said the voice.

'Yes. I saw his body. He's gone.'

'I ... understand.'

Another long pause. There wasn't going to be any expression of regret.

'I assume you are his Assistant?'

That was an interesting way of describing it. His stooge, more likely.

'His Assistant?' I said.

'He told us that he had an Englishman working with him. You are the Englishman?'

'Yes.'

'How did he die?'

'They executed him. He asked for a phone charger cable, so they realised he had an illicit phone, and then they questioned him.'

'Did he talk?'

'I don't know,' I said. 'I wasn't there.'

Another pause.

'The plan must continue. You must bring the target to the rendezvous point.'

'I don't see how that will be possible,' I said, struck by the absurdity of the suggestion. I felt a small kernel of anger rising within me. 'They are very suspicious of me.'

'That is your problem.'

'What?' I retorted, my voice cracking. 'What are you *talking about*? I'm going to be bloody lucky not to wind up bloody *dead* as well! Jesus, I'm already on thin ice. You're mad if you seriously imagine that I can make these people do anything —'

'Please do not give us your excuses. We want the target to come to the Khone Phapheng Falls; the arrangements are in place. We have contracted this with Mr Bullen and, in his absence, we will hold you responsible, Mr Powell. We have paid, and we will not be happy if you let us down. There would be consequences.'

I think that my heart must have missed a beat. They *knew my name* or, at least, the alias that Bullen had set up for me. I was thinking furiously: could they trace me from that? Did they have a photograph? Could they get one from the Mekong Riverside hotel? Trace it back to Battambang? I didn't know but it seemed horribly possible. This was Chinese Military Intelligence. They would have their methods.

'Did you hear me, Mr Powell? We will not be happy.'

'No,' I said. 'Well, it may not be possible. I don't know how I will be able to persuade them —'

'Then it is up to you to find a way. We are working on an alternative plan, but we would prefer not to use it. There might be … repercussions.'

'What alternative plan?' I asked.

'Mr Powell, do you know your current location? A map position? Bullen said he did not – have you been able to find it out?'

'No.'

'We have been working on triangulating your position from the cell phone signal. It has been difficult; record keeping here in Cambodia is poor and the towers are badly positioned. But we have had some success. We have your location within about 600 square kilometres. We are surveying and checking, and will try to use aerial photography. We should be able to be certain within forty-eight hours. However, for obvious reasons, we don't want to make an extraction there if we can avoid it. But we will if we have to. If you fail us.'

'I see,' I said.

'If you fail us,' he repeated ominously.

'I see,' I said again.

'Call us when you have arranged the situation,' said the voice. 'Goodbye Mr Powell.'

And the line went dead.

I don't know how long I sat staring at the face of that cell phone.

This was something I hadn't anticipated. I thought I was in enough trouble already, right here, right now – being confined to the guest house had been a dreadful blow, Bullen's execution was utterly devastating, and God alone knew what they might do to me next … I suspected that it was only Chanlina's good graces that were keeping me alive … safe from the *wild pigs* (horrible thought) that Sarachi had mentioned … but *this*, this Chinese intervention, was a new disaster. I had never imagined that they would still expect me to continue with Bullen's absurd little scheme – and I knew that I had exactly zero chance of persuading Edi and Chanlina to buy it. It was laughable.

But it was worse than that. The damned cell phone had changed every-thing. If the Chinese could triangulate the signal – and it sounded like they already had – they were coming, just like Bullen had said they might, a sudden raid, armed men storming the wall and fighting their way into The

House Above the Jungle. What chance would Chanlina and Sarachi have against them? Well, none at all. Ak and Da might help, but that was four defenders (Chanlina's father would be pressed into service, so five) but they would be no match for professionals arriving in force.

And I would be in the middle of it, unless I could get out before they came.

And I had already discovered that I couldn't.

I was sitting staring into space, fighting off despair when a thought occurred to me —

A white one-piece swimming costume!

And I remembered ...

A woman in the white one-piece swimsuit! With the desperation of a drowning man, I clung onto the idea, a tiny shred of hope.

How could I have missed it? What with everything that was going on, I suppose, but I was *so* stupid ...

I stood up and wandered outside, into the darkened garden. Somewhere, on the edge on the breeze, I could just detect the fragrance of Chanlina's night-scented stock. I almost smiled.

I had one card to play, and I would play it in the morning.

Just before eight, I went up the big redwood staircase to the veranda. Sita came out of the house, looked at me, and fetched coffee and croissants. Without a word, she put them on the table and retreated inside. I ate alone and in silence, contemplating my next move.

And, amazingly, I realised that I was no longer frightened.

'Sita!' I called out, then again, loud enough for her to have heard it inside the house. Eventually she reappeared from the interior. She stared at me coldly and said something in Khmer.

'Chanlina!' I said, speaking very clearly. 'I need to speak to Chanlina. Now, at once. Please, can you fetch Chanlina?'

She looked at me for a long moment, then nodded and went back inside.

It took a few minutes for Chanlina to appear. She came out onto the veranda and looked at me questioningly.

She was wearing a pale blue cotton dress, something like a sarong, and even in my fearful state, I registered how lovely she was, her hair up in a coil around her head, neat gold earrings in her small ears, her oriental eyes so dark in her oval face.

'You wanted to see me?' she said.

'Yes.'

'And?'

I hesitated over my words.

'Do you have one of your knives with you?'

'My knives?' she echoed.

'Yes.'

'Do I need one?' she asked and smiled at me.

'Yes,' I said. 'Then we must go into your garden and talk.'

'We can talk up here.'

'Yes, but I want to sit in your garden – in a beautiful place, the most beautiful place, the absolute best place – and then we can talk.'

'You are being very ... mysterious.'

'Perhaps,' I said.

'So, if you like, I will fetch a knife,' she said.

While waiting for her, I was in a fever of impatience. Some foolish whim made me want to go and sit in a beautiful spot ... because, if this conversation went badly, I wanted to be somewhere wonderful at the end.

She returned, and motioned for me to follow her down the stairs. We crossed the lawn and she led me beyond the pond, to a bench between the flower beds, almost out of sight of the house.

'This place,' she said, 'the view from just *here* ... like a little fragment of heaven. The garden in bloom ... is it this that you wanted?'

'Exactly,' I said, and sat down on the bench. She sat beside me, but I turned so I was facing away from her. I put my finger on my windpipe. 'Now, take your knife, and hold it *here*, as if you were about to cut my throat.'

'What?' she said sharply.

'As if you were about to cut my throat – just like you did with Bullen.'

'I did *not* cut Bullen's throat,' she snapped.

'You didn't?'

'No. Edi did – we were asking him questions, and I think he would have told us more, but then he hesitated ... and Edi suddenly cut his throat. I did not want that to happen.'

'Oh,' I said, and something else niggled at the back of my mind, some tiny clue that I couldn't grasp.

'So, no, I did not kill your friend.' She relaxed a little, I thought, and went on: 'And besides, if I wanted to cut your throat, I would not cut there. That is your – what is the word? Your windpipe? But that would not kill you. I would hold my knife to the side, *here*, where the artery is.'

'So hold your knife there,' I said.

'What nonsense is this, Englishman?' she said, annoyed now. 'What stupid game are you playing? All this talk about cutting throats and killing and special places in my garden! Have you gone quite mad?'

'No,' I said. 'For the first time in a long time, I am thinking clearly. I am not playing a game, Banh Chanlina, this is very serious, because now I am going to speak and I am going to tell you the absolute truth and, if ... if you do not believe me ... then you will cut my throat at once. And it will all be finished. So I wanted this to be here, the loveliest place in your lovely garden, because if I am going to die, then here is a good place.'

'You are mad, Richard,' she said softly. 'I will not do this.'

'I *want* you to do it. You will understand.'

'Why?' she demanded.

'Because I don't want to be frightened any more. *Do it!*'

I waited until I felt the cold knife on the side of my neck, felt her hand tremble a little, and I began:

'My name,' I said, 'is not Richard Powell. My name is Andrew Finch. I am not an important international businessman with dealings in Indochina. I am a Mechanical Engineering Consultant, a design engineer, and I live in an ordinary apartment in the ordinary town of Potters Bar, in England. I am not rich; I am quite poor because I pay my ex-wife a lot of money and my business has had difficulties recently. I have a daughter. I met Bullen, whom I already knew slightly, in an airport in Battambang, and he offered me very good money to assist him for a few days. He offered me money and he offered me an adventure, and I accepted because I needed the money and ... and ... I wanted an adventure, because my life is ... dreary and unhappy. I think that I needed some excitement, to feel like I was alive again. In this, I was very stupid. And gradually he explained his plan to me, how he wanted to fool you and Edi Sarachi and your father, so that you would believe him and believe in a scheme that he had devised. And now, this game has gone too far – and now I have been very afraid and I don't know what to do, and I do not want to betray you ... and —'

I felt the cold pressure on my neck release and Chanlina said, very softly: 'I know.'

For a moment, I didn't grasp what she had said.

'*You know*?' I gasped, unable to believe my ears.

'Yes, I know. Most of it, anyway.'

'*You* ... you were the woman in the swimming pool in the hotel in Battambang – with the swimming hat and the goggles, weren't you?'

'Yes,' she said, and I felt her hand on my shoulder, turning me back to face her. 'In fact, I watched you when you met Bullen in the airport. You never saw me, a little Cambodian woman in cheap street clothes, just a face in the crowd. We were following Bullen, seeing what he was doing, and he found you. Then we went to your hotel – *The Classy Hotel*, right? – and I checked in, and when we saw you go in the pool, I went for a swim too, to take a closer look at you.'

'I don't believe it,' I said. 'It's not possible!'

'Of course it is possible, Englishman. What shall I call you now? Not Richard, I think?'

'Andrew.'

'Yes, Andrew, okay. But yes, it is very possible. Do you think that I have survived across the years by being foolish and unguarded? When the American approached us, we knew that there was something wrong. What he was proposing was strange, unlikely. Just a small suspicion, no more, but we were very careful. We are *always* very careful. We started to follow him, first at the airport, then at the hotel. There was that business with the Russians that we did not understand – what was that? I was outside, on the other side of the street, watching from the shadows, when Bullen tried to make the stupid jump between the balconies. *Oh my God!* I thought he was going to die – and then when you jumped as well! I thought you must also fall. But you jumped and you saved him.'

'I was terrified when I did it,' I said, starting to feel a weight lifting off my shoulders.

She laughed at me, right in my face, a proper open happy laugh.

'You were terrified? And now, you tell me you are afraid, here, today. Oh, the quiet Englishman! Always *so* frightened. But I – I do not believe it! Firstly, you make the jump that your friend could not make ... to save him. That looked brave to me! Then, when we went to get the boy, you fight off a desperate man – with an umbrella! I think that is what a brave man would do – a coward would have run away. And now, you tell me to put a knife to your neck, to kill you if I think you are lying to me – this is not the action of a man without courage.'

'Well,' I said, starting to feel embarrassed. 'I can promise you that I *was* afraid —'

'Hah!' she snorted.

I paused, struck by a sudden thought.

'But if I *had* lied to you ... would you ... have killed me?'

She smiled, a slow secret smile, full of mischief.

'Maybe,' she said.

'Wait, I need to tell you more.'

'Go on,' she said, still smiling. 'But, this time, I will not hold the knife at your neck.'

I ignored that and continued:

'I am not this businessman, this Richard Powell – and there never was a Richard Powell – which is why you could not discover anything about him – he was a myth, he never existed. The plan was simply to persuade you to go to the Khone Phapheng Falls on a certain date. Bullen's Client, his *real* Client, wanted you – and maybe Edi as well – to be there, out in the open, to trap you and kidnap you.'

'But, why does he want to kidnap me?' she asked.

'Because you have information that he wants.'

'What information?'

'Well, what Bullen told me was that, some months ago, somebody came to you about the killing of a certain Cambodian Government Minister but, for reasons of your own, you turned them down. But the man was killed anyway, by someone else.'

'Yes, I remember this,' she said. 'I read that he had been assassinated. It is unfortunate. He, the politician, was not a bad man, from what I could understand.'

'Maybe not so good as you think. According to Bullen, he was in the pay of the Chinese, being bribed by them to promote a big civil engineering scheme on the Mekong River.'

'Yes?' she said, perplexed. 'But ... I did not kill him. So why do they want me?'

'Because *you know* who approached you in the first place! That's what the Chinese want to find out, the name of the people who wanted him dead. And presumably you know who it was.'

'Yes, I do. So does Edi.'

We looked at each other.

'So,' she said, looking at me meaningfully, 'all of this deception is to discover the names of the people who wanted the Minister dead?'

'Yes.'

'Who was paying Bullen? The Cambodian Government?'

'No, the Chinese. Military Intelligence. A man called Colonel Zhou.'

'Oh!' she gasped, and her hand went to her mouth.

'You know of him?'

She nodded.

'If you go to the Falls, you will fall into their hands – so you must not go to the Falls. But there's more – Bullen's phone ...'

'So,' she said calmly, 'there really was a phone? Edi was right.'

'Yes – and they, the Chinese I mean, they called it last night. It was hidden in my room – Bullen must have put it there.' I found myself rushing my words. 'I answered it and I spoke to this Colonel Zhou, or one of his people. He wants me to persuade you to go to the Khone Phapheng Falls. He stated that he considers that it is my responsibility to continue Bullen's plan —'

'Then you are doing a very bad job.'

'Yes, of course. Because I don't want you to fall into his hands.'

'You don't? And why should you care?'

'Because —' I started to say then stopped myself. 'Because ... I care about you.'

There was a pause and I felt her gaze on me.

'Do you, Andrew Finch?'

I swallowed hard.

'Yes, I do.'

'Oh,' she said.

'But there's something else. The Chinese, Colonel Zhou and his people, they've used the phone signal to work out where we are, where we are now. Not exactly, but they're searching an area. They are going to find you – and if I don't persuade you to go to the Falls, they're coming for you *here*, to The House Above the Jungle.'

'Is that possible?'

'Yes,' I said. 'It's very possible. They will be here in a day, maybe two.'

'Here?' she asked, almost absently, as if she was absorbing what I had said.

'Yes, here.'

'I see,' she said, 'We cannot go to the Falls, because it is a trap, but if we stay here, then the Chinese will come for us. So what can we do? Run away?'

'Yes, you can run away, very far away. But there is one other possibility I've thought of ... this man Zhou wants to know who tried to hire you to kill this Cambodian Minister, right? Why not simply call him – use Bullen's damned cell phone and call him up, and just tell him the name? Then he has what he wants – and so there is no reason for him to come after you!'

'Yes,' she said and her expression was unreadable. I was struck, not for the first time, by how utterly inscrutable an Oriental could be.

'No,' she said at length. 'Because, Andrew Finch, there is something here that you do not know. Telling Zhou the name of the man who tried to order this killing will not make him go away.'

'Why ever not?' I blurted.

'Because he knows already.'

I stared at her.

'The man who approached us to assassinate the Cambodian Minister — was Colonel Zhou himself.'

'You think that Bullen knew that?' asked Edi Sarachi. He was lolling in his chair and looking at me with a mixture of scepticism and interest.

We were sitting around the table on the veranda of the main house, Chanlina, Sarachi, old Bahn Sar and myself. Chanlina had called everyone together and made me repeat what I had told her, in detail, and we had got to the part about Zhou being the instigator of the original assassination.

'I have no idea,' I said, truthfully.

'He might have done, and not wanted to tell you,' Sarachi said. 'In case it frightened you off. That's the thing about this business – everybody lies all the time. You wouldn't understand this, of course. Or maybe Zhou lied to him.'

'Does it really matter?' I said.

'Probably not,' he said.

'What matters,' said Chanlina, a little frown creasing her forehead, 'is what it means.'

'Yes,' I said.

'What about this suggestion that the Chinese can find us here? How realistic is that?' asked Sarachi. 'You're the technical guy – can they do that?'

'Oh yes,' I said. 'You measure the signal strengths on three masts and you can get a position on the transmitting device. That's all a cell phone is, in practical terms, a transmitter and receiver, a glorified walkie-talkie.'

'But,' said Sarachi, suddenly leaning forward, 'you said that they had a fix within 600 kilometres. That might be anywhere! That could cover the whole of the country.'

'No,' I replied, 'what I *said*, what he *told* me, was that they have the location within 600 *square* kilometres. Completely different thing. 600 square kilometres is an area of ...' – I did the mental arithmetic – '... an area a bit less than 25 kilometres by 25 kilometres. It's not a big area. How many large houses are there within 25 kilometres of here? They'll be studying maps, maybe do an aerial survey. You know this area better than me, but I didn't see many places like this locally.'

Chanlina was translating all this for her father. He grunted something and nodded at me.

'My father says that they will find us.'

'Yes,' I said, 'I think that they will.'

'And when they come ...' said Chanlina, gazing into the gardens below.

'When they come, they will try to kill us,' said Sarachi flatly. 'They don't need to question Chanlina, or me, because they know the answer already. This mission is not to ask a question, it never was. This mission is to silence us because we know something that Zhou cannot allow to be known.'

'*Who*, exactly ...' I said slowly, 'is Zhou hiding this information from?'

'We don't know.'

'Maybe we do,' I said. 'If what Bullen told me was true, or even partly true, then this Cambodian Minister was working *for* the Chinese, promoting their big investment scheme. So why would Zhou want him dead? Why would the Chinese Government want to kill a man who was working for them?'

'They wouldn't,' said Sarachi.

'So maybe, Zhou wasn't acting for the Chinese Government when he set up the assassination. Maybe that is who he is hiding the facts from! His own people!'

'You think that he's acting on his own?'

'Could be,' I said. 'You just said it, everybody lies all the time. Maybe he has his own little scheme going ... and maybe this Cambodian guy got in the way, or maybe he was going to expose something Zhou was doing. Zhou is covering his tracks.'

They were staring at me.

'Look,' I said. 'I really don't know. How can I know any of this? I could be wrong. It just fits the facts, that's all. The real question – the *only* question – is what are you going to do?'

'We can't go to the Falls, and we cannot stay here,' said Sarachi.

'So you're saying we should run?' asked Chanlina. 'What if we stand and fight?'

'Against the Chinese?' countered Sarachi. 'Arriving in force, well-armed, professionals? You, me, the two boys, your old father? The Englishman, who has never used a gun in his life?'

'Sita would fight,' snapped Chanlina.

'Sita!' said Sarachi. 'You're joking, aren't you?'

I think that Chanlina would have replied to him but Bahn Sar suddenly started speaking. I couldn't understand him but he seemed animated, chopping at the air with his hands. Chanlina's frown deepened as she listened.

I leant across to Sarachi. 'What is he saying?' I asked.

'He is saying that we already live in the shadows. But now we are under the gaze ... the eye of the Dragon itself, China. When the Dragon looks at you, you cannot stand still. You *must* move. This man, this Colonel Zhou who has tried to play a trick on us, is very dangerous and soon he will know where we live.' Sarachi paused. 'He says that a mouse cannot live on the lip of the Dragon.'

Now Chanlina was responding, speaking in Khmer. Her voice was low but forceful.

Banh Sar was watching me as his daughter spoke, his eyes never leaving mine. I nodded respectfully toward him, acknowledging his words. This seemed to be the correct thing to do; he gave me a stiff little nod in return. One forgets sometimes that, in the East, elders are held in higher esteem than in the West – Banh Sar might appear to be just a jolly old man, but his opinion mattered.

Chanlina had stopped speaking and turned to me:

'My father talks about the mouse, who cannot dance upon the lip of the Dragon. Of course, this is true, but I have reminded him that *we* are not mice —'

'No,' agreed Sarachi, cutting across her, 'no, of course not. You are the Mamba and there are people who fear you, and with good reason. But you cannot hope to defeat the Chinese if they come here —'

'Yes, I am the Green Mamba, and *I will not run*. Nor will I allow this man, this Colonel Zhou, to invade our home. Even if we ran – which we will not – he would not know that, and he would send his soldiers anyway. They would ransack the whole area searching for us, the school, the hospital, the village, this house ... even my garden. That cannot be allowed to happen.'

Personally, much as I liked her garden, I wouldn't have thought it a major factor. Then Chanlina was speaking again:

'But for now, we have one advantage over him; we know what he is planning to do. We will never have a better opportunity than this. And this time, we are choosing the battlefield – next time he will have the benefit of surprise.'

It took a moment for the full implication of what she was saying to sink in. There was a silence, during which Banh Sar reached across and touched his daughter on the shoulder, a simple fatherly gesture. I found myself speaking:

'You mean – go to him? Go to Zhou?'

'Yes.'

'Where?'

'Where we want him to be, at the Khone Phapheng Falls. Where he will not be expecting us to fight.'

'I see.'

'What are you thinking Chanlina?' asked Sarachi.

'That the Englishman must telephone this Colonel Zhou; tell him we are coming. He must convince Zhou that he has persuaded us to go through with the plan. Then we go to the Falls with everything we have. You, me, Ak and Da, my father, fully armed. Five of us.'

'You're forgetting about Noy, my guy in Laos.'

'Will he be prepared to stand by us?'

'He'll do whatever you want – if you pay him enough.'

'Then pay him.'

Sarachi abruptly switched language and said something to Chanlina in Khmer. I couldn't follow, of course, but when she glanced over at me, I understood the meaning.

She turned back to Sarachi and shook her head.

'You will stay here, Englishman,' she said, 'with Sita. When we come back, we will take you to an airport and you can go home.'

Then I distinctly heard a voice saying: 'No, I'm coming with you,' and it was only after the voice had finished speaking that I realised that it was me.

The first part of their plan was simple. I was to call Zhou on Bullen's mobile phone and tell him that I had succeeded in persuading Chanlina to take the contract, and that she and Sarachi would go to the Falls.

Having decided to do that, I was ready to go and speak to them immediately, but Chanlina stopped me.

'If you call straight away,' she said, 'they will not believe you. It will all seem to have been too quick, too easy; better to wait – call this afternoon. Make it appear that we were difficult to convince.'

'And … say that you only did it by agreeing to pay more money,' said Sarachi. 'The Chinese understand the idea of a hard bargain – they will accept that.'

'You must sound angry, too,' added Chanlina. 'Like … it was very hard to persuade us. And, another thing – we will go early!' She counted off the days, on her fingers. 'Bullen said that the plan was for eight days from when we met you at the hotel. Today is five days – we will go *tomorrow*, leaving here tonight. That will not give them much time to prepare. They will object, but you must say that it was the best that you could do. They must take it or leave it.'

I waited until two o'clock – the heat of the day was heavy in the air – and went back to my room in the guest house. Sarachi came with me, to listen in; I wondered if he didn't entirely trust me. I had put the phone back in its hiding place inside my mattress so, with Sarachi watching, I turned the mattress over to fish it out again.

'When we're finished, I'll take that,' he said. He definitely didn't trust me.

'Sure,' I said.

I checked that the phone had enough charge, and sat down on the edge of the bed. Sarachi sat close enough to be able to listen in to both sides of the conversation. I keyed the number. It rang.

'Yes, hello,' said the voice at the other end.

'Who is this?' I said.

'Is that Mr Powell?'

'Uh-huh.'

'Good afternoon.'

'Yes. Listen, I have news for you.'

'What is it?'

'I have succeeded. I have persuaded them to take the contract.'

'That is good. How did you manage this?'

'It was very difficult. I had to offer them additional money. It was necessary, because they were very suspicious —'

'Additional money?' said the voice at the end of the telephone, a note of annoyance creeping in.

'Listen,' I snapped back. 'This was very *hard*. They don't trust me. You remember what happened to Bullen, don't you? I was risking everything —'

'How much money?' said the voice.

I gave him a figure, and there was a pause.

'It does not matter. I assume that you promised to pay after the contract was completed?'

'Part up front, part afterwards. I had to use our own money. I will be recompensed? Can you assure me of that?'

'You will be recompensed in full, but after we have the Cambodian woman.'

'Good. Because I've been risking everything here ... You have no idea of the position I'm in —'

'Yes, yes,' said the voice, without any vestige of sympathy. 'When are they coming to view the location?'

'Tomorrow,' I said.

'Tomorrow! No. That is too *early* – you must delay them. We will not be able to assemble —'

'No,' I cut in. 'It's tomorrow. No discussion. It was all I could do to get them to agree to the contract, I can't change that.'

'But you must. Tomorrow is not acceptable —'

'No,' I said again, acting up my part for all I was worth. 'There is no discussion. Tomorrow. Take it or leave it, it's up to you. Say so now ... it's tomorrow or nothing. What do you want to do?'

There was a hurried exchange away from the phone on the end – I could hear raised voices speaking in what, I suspected, was Mandarin Chinese. The voice came back on and said:

'Mr Powell —'

'Yes?' I said shortly.

'We are very unhappy about —'

'I'm sorry, is that relevant to me? Please do not ask me to change the day. What do you expect me to say to them ...? "You must delay your scouting of the location because the trap that I am sending you into will not be ready?" You think that will work? It is tomorrow – or nothing.'

More heated words in the background, and the voice came back on:

'Very well. Tomorrow, Two o'clock in the afternoon. And, Mr Powell ...'

'Yes?'

'You will be there yourself.'

'No,' I said. 'Why should I?'

'You will make sure you are there. That is not a request. You *absolutely* will be there, with the targets. Also, we will have your money.'

'I have to tell you that I was not planning on —'

'Goodbye, Mr Powell. I look forward to meeting you tomorrow.'

And the phone went dead. I stood for a moment, then handed it across to the Albanian. He was staring at me.

'You did well,' he said. He smiled narrowly. 'They've bought it.'

'I thought so,' I said. He walked out.

I was feeling pleased with myself as I walked back out into the garden. I had made the call to Colonel Zhou (or one of Zhou's people – I realised that the voice had never identified himself) and I had kept my wits about me and not panicked or made a mess of it. I thought that, for an amateur, I had made a pretty good fist of it – and, best of all, I could see an end in sight.

I was wilfully ignoring the fact that the encounter with Colonel Zhou was going to be dangerous – but I had faith in Chanlina and Sarachi, who seemed confident that they could handle it.

The afternoon was still hot and clammy; my shirt was damp on my back. Maybe a cold beer would be in order.

It was quiet. Sarachi had disappeared off somewhere. There was nobody about on the big veranda, nor in the garden itself. I walked through the gap between the hedges surrounding the pool and found Chanlina in the water, swimming idly on her back, cooling herself after the heat of the day. She was wearing her white swimsuit. She waved when she saw me, so I went to the side of the pool and knelt down.

'How did you get on?' she asked, treading water.

'Very well,' I said. I told her about the telephone conversation, my account of persuading them to take the contract, the pressure to change the date, my resistance to it; I concluded by saying that I thought they'd been convinced.

'You really think they believed you?' she asked, her face serious.

'I think so.'

She paused a moment, still treading water, then her expression brightened.

'Come in and swim, then, Englishman. It is refreshing on such a warm day to swim.'

I considered it for a moment – it was tempting. Why not?

'Okay,' I said, 'I'll go and get my trunks.'

Chanlina snorted dismissively.

'Always the same with you English. Tell me – because I have never met another Englishman, not properly anyway – are you all so prudish?'

'I wouldn't say that it was *prudish*, exactly, to wear swimming gear to swim.'

She laughed at me, and said: 'There is nobody here except us. Take your clothes off and get in.'

'Well ...' I said, hesitating.

She snorted again, and sank below the surface for a moment. I could see her doing something underwater, and when she came back up again, she threw the white swimsuit out onto the grass.

'There!' she said cheerfully. 'You see how simple it is. Now, you do the same – I promise that I will not watch you, because you are so *prudish*.'

I smiled at that – I was not used to people who were so casual about nudity – and shed my clothes and dived in.

I came up behind her. She swam beside me, laughing, then ducked under the water and surfaced on the other side.

'There,' she said, 'not so difficult, was it?'

'No ...' I said. 'Tell me, because I have never met another Cambodian woman, not to speak to anyway – are you all so eager to take your clothes off?'

She made a pantomime expression as if thinking deeply, and shook her head. 'No, not all Cambodians are like me. Of course, most do not have a private swimming pool. And, you should remember, that I am not *entirely* Cambodian.'

'I'm sorry?' I said but she had already ducked under the water again – really, the woman was like a bloody fish.

'*What* did you just say?' I repeated when she broke surface. She sculled on her back for a moment then replied:

'Well, I have a Cambodian passport. I was born here ... but I also have an American one.'

'An American passport?' I said, surprised.

'Oh yes,' she smiled at me, a little smile of triumph. 'It can be useful when I travel. It depends where I am going ... in some places it is better to be a Cambodian, sometimes better to be a citizen of the USA.'

'How did you get an American passport? Is it kosher ... I mean, is it a real one?'

'Of course. There would be no point having a fake, would there? And, as to *how*, well, my grandfather *was* American. He was a soldier, serving in Vietnam during the American War ... what you Westerners like to call the Vietnam War.' She was treading water now, and she had become serious. 'My grandmother was his lover in those days ... when she was young and very beautiful. She was Vietnamese, not Cambodian. But in the confusion at the end, they were parted. He was sent back to the US with his unit. When the South fell, she ran; anybody like her, with an American child, was in grave danger from the Northerners, so she came over the border into Cambodia. Her daughter, my mother, was brought up here – and lived in this region, a simple village girl. She married my father here. But in the times of the Khmer Rouge, a woman who was half-American ... well, it was a terrible time. They took her away – we never found out where.' She hesitated, and a shadow went across her face. 'I believe that she was killed. Just another one of the millions who died in Cambodia at the hands of the Khmer Rouge, some for being able to speak English, some for knowing how to read and write, even some for just wearing glasses – anything. And my mother, being part-American ... it was enough in those days.'

She stopped abruptly and I realised that she was silently crying, the tears slowly running down her cheeks and mixing with the water of the pool. I reached out for her and she came into my arms, and I cradled her.

'Shall we get out?' she said quietly.

We moved over to the side of the pool and climbed out. She draped a towel around herself and offered me one. We sat on the grass in the sun and I wrapped my arms around her. She seemed to gather herself and leant into me.

'You don't have to talk about it,' I murmured.

'No. It was a long time ago – and anyway, you asked a reasonable question. I *want* to tell you ... when my mother – *our* mother – was taken, and my father lied to save us, my sister and me. We were barely more than babies, and he said that he and my mother had no children. Another woman in the village took us and told the Khmer that we were her children. So they went away ... although they might have taken my father too, for marrying a half-foreigner. He was lucky.

'Later, after the Khmer time, after the thing that happened with the three Khmer soldiers that I told you about before, my grandfather, the American, he came to trace his daughter, and he found out what had happened. He offered to my father that he would take my sister and me to his home in Chicago. He was trying to do the best thing for us, even though he was an old man then, with a family of his own in the States. He arranged all the papers, demonstrated our heritage, arranged US citizenship. So we went and lived in Chicago for two years.'

'Oh,' I said, the penny dropping in my brain. 'So, that's why you have the American accent ...!'

'Yes. You remarked upon it. We learnt to speak English. For me, it came easier than for my sister. But we weren't happy there. It was never our home; America was nothing to us. And our grandfather was not a rich man – life there was not so easy. It was not exactly the American dream. I missed my own people, and so did my sister.'

She paused, then said simply.

'We missed our father, our family, our village. So we came home.'

'My God,' I said. 'I had no idea that you had been through so much.'

She shrugged.

'Why should you? You came here and you saw what you expected to see. You were told about an assassin, a woman who was a machine for killing; why should you think that there was any more to her than that? But there is always a human being inside, a woman who was once a child, a girl, with memories and hopes and fears and dreams. Besides ... my story is not so unusual here. Everyone in Cambodia has similar stories to tell, about a brother, a father, an uncle, a sister, a mother, lost in the Khmer Rouge time, the Civil War, the Vietnamese invasion. Have you been to our Tuol Sleng Genocide Museum in Phnom Penh? Seen the glass cases full of human skulls? The burial pits, the little brick cells, the torture rooms?'

She looked at me, unblinking.

'Truly, Englishman, you have come to the most dangerous place on Earth, a place where life is worth ...', she snapped her fingers dismissively, '... nothing at all. To kill here is – *nothing*. That is what I meant when I said that you cannot judge us, cannot judge *me*. This is a different world to your rich, safe country. We have got better, yes, slowly, inch by inch, but not so long ago, Cambodia was truly a hell on earth.

'And if I,' she continued, a vehemence creeping into her voice, 'by eliminating a few men who deserved to die anyway, can make things even a *little* bit better for a maybe a hundred people with my school and my clinic – then it was worthwhile, and my conscience is strong enough to deal with it. If I am very lucky, I will survive and, one day soon, leave all this behind me. I shall miss my garden and my House Above the Jungle and this wonderful pool with no shallow end – but I will take myself away from this life while I still can.'

'Really?' I said. 'You're planning on leaving?'

She smiled at me knowingly.

'One day, Andrew Finch, one day. I shall take my US passport and go to America and live the life of a nobody, somewhere like Florida, in the sunshine. Maybe I shall become the funny little Chinese woman in a dry-cleaning shop in some quiet town. You think I could do that?'

'I think that you could do much more than that,' I said.

'Maybe I don't want to,' she said, and smiled again.

She burrowed her head into my shoulder, while I held her. Her mood seemed to have lightened. It was very fine to sit with her on the lawn, in the warmth of the evening; just for a moment, everything seemed right. For once in my life, I was in the right place at the right time.

We set off for the Khone Phapheng Falls directly after dinner, in the dark, taking two cars. Chanlina and her father and Da went in the first car, Ak and Sarachi and I in the second. We had a journey of over two hundred miles in front of us, driving in the pitch dark on roads barely worth the name.

I snoozed in the back seat, as best as I could with the erratic surface of the road. Ak drove, peering into the dark at the tail lights of the car in front.

I remember that at one point, with the car bouncing along, I had a short conversation with Sarachi. I think that I must have mentioned the Cambodian politician whose killing had started off this whole thing. I spoke about the scheme to make the Mekong navigable.

'You actually believe that?' said Sarachi.

'Why? Don't you?' I said.

'I never believe anything that comes from an intelligence service, neither the Chinese or anyone else's. Everybody lies, all the time. It *could* be true, or not. It could be a complete fabrication – the reason for his execution could be something entirely different.'

'Really?' I said, realising how naïve I had been to accept the story at face value.

'There is one thing you learn in this business. Distrust everything and anyone. Assume the worst of everyone; that way you don't get disappointed – or taken advantage of.' He paused. 'Or killed.'

I considered this for a moment.

'That must make life very difficult,' I said.

'You get used to it,' he said. In the darkness, I could just about see him give a resigned shrug of his shoulders. 'It's how you survive.'

We lapsed into silence. More for something to say than anything, I asked: 'And we're meeting your contact at the border?'

'My contact?'

'Your contact in Laos,' I said.

'Oh, Noy, you mean? No, we're meeting him at the Falls.'

'Who is he?'

'Noy? Just some guy, you know. He comes in useful, from time to time.

You pay him, he does what you want, no questions asked.'

'You trust him? I mean, to stand up with us, when we meet the Chinese?'

'Do I trust him?' murmured Sarachi and paused. He smiled his mirthless smile. 'More than I trust you, Englishman.'

There seemed no answer to that.

I snoozed again.

I woke when we got to the border into Laos. There was a surprisingly ornate customs building, with a steeply sloping tiled roof, set beside the road. The lights from the windows illuminated the ground around it. There were no other vehicles there.

A bored official came out and inspected the cars. He stuck his head inside each one and checked how many passengers there were. Chanlina's father got out and spoke to him briefly. A small wad of cash, US dollars, was passed across.

We were waved through without further comment.

I must have slept again. When I opened my eyes, there was a greyish light in the eastern sky and we were parking up. I checked my watch – it was a little after six o'clock.

'We're here,' said Sarachi.

We had parked the cars a long way from the river; normally, visitors are ferried by motorised rickshaws (the ubiquitous Eastern *tuk-tuks*) along the narrow trail between the car park and the entrance gate. It was far too early for that – we would have to walk.

There was a man waiting for us there, a muscular Laotian in a tee-shirt and faded black jeans. He went through an elaborate fist-bumping ritual with Edi Sarachi, who introduced him as Noy, his man here in Laos. I would have guessed his age at late twenties; he had a slight cast in one eye. The newcomer insisted on enthusiastically shaking hands with everyone, grinning broadly. He chattered away in broken English, then fell in with Sarachi.

Ak and Da loaded the weapons and other equipment into two canvas bags and we set off, moving quietly past the rows of closed tourist shops. When we got to the gate of the park and the ticket office (closed at this hour), we simply by-passed it and climbed over the fence. The two younger men assisted old Banh Sar over. I noticed the respectful way that they did it, without any fuss, a tiny reminder of the difference between the East and the West.

We had the place to ourselves as we walked along the track, a path of beaten earth between trees and low scrub. The sun was up on the horizon, casting long shadows in front of us. As we got closer to the river, we could hear the water tumbling and roaring before we could actually see it.

The Khone Phapheng Falls are not vertical walls of water in the way of, say, a Niagara or Angel Falls. Rather, they are a stretch of the rushing river with numerous changes in level, spread over five or six miles, broken up by massive rock formations like small islands around which the white torrents rush. Some of the drops are small – five or ten feet; some are huge – fifty or even sixty feet. There are great foaming races interspersed with oily, brown, swirling pools created by the back-eddies.

There is a strange attraction to these epic displays of nature, the racing water, the crashing falls, the spray rising up into the morning air. I felt myself drawn to the edge, like a man looking over the side of a cliff, half in appreciation, half in ghoulish awe. To go into *that* water, I thought, that's certain death – drowned or dashed against the rocks.

There was a viewing area, a large wooden platform with a stout timber handrail, overlooking the furious torrent. I paused and stared down.

'Englishman!' called Chanlina. 'Come on! Keep up.'

I looked at her questioningly. She smiled back at me, but for the first time I thought I saw a slight anxiety in her face. I felt a shadow of uneasiness go through me – she and Sarachi had been so confident that this encounter would go their way; that tiny show of concern was enough to send a shiver down my spine. They were the ones who knew what they were doing; I was relying on them.

We carried on along the riverside. After a while, Chanlina paused and went into a little huddle with her father and Sarachi. I stood with Ak and Da and the newcomer, Noy, keeping a discreet distance back. They seemed to be debating this particular spot which, to my untrained eye, looked the same as almost everywhere else on the path. Sarachi was pointing at the approach from the east, Banh Sar was indicating the gaps between the trees, the low bushes away from the river. Eventually, they seemed to agree to disagree and continued up the path.

Half a mile further on, Chanlina's father stopped. His face split in a wide grin and he was speaking quickly. He pointed at the ground with both hands. *Here*, he seemed to be saying, *this is it*. His daughter stood beside him, looking up and down the path. Again, the significance was lost on me.

We were amongst a sparse glade of spreading trees, with bushes perhaps fifty yards over to the south of us. There was a big fallen trunk nearby. What worried me was that the fence to the river there was almost completely gone, barely a couple of posts and some thin rails which had collapsed. A fence wire had been strung across, but it was sagging almost to the ground. I edged across to it. There were tussocks of grass on the bank, which sloped down vertiginously. Twenty feet below us, the water raced white; downriver there were a couple of craggy boulders, the size of small houses, which divided the flow into twin torrents.

Sarachi walked past me.

'What? What are we talking about?' I asked him.

'*Here*,' he said. 'This is the place, the killing ground. See how the trees provide cover, the open ground behind us leaves anyone approaching exposed, without protection. Someone in those bushes can command the whole space. This is the right place.'

They spent the next twenty minutes walking around, selecting positions, looking at angles. Ak was assembling a heavy rifle from components in the canvas bags. There was much serious discussion. Weapons were distributed.

I went over to Sarachi, who was debating some detail with Chanlina's father. I glanced at the firearms nervously.

'Do you think that it will come to shooting?' I remarked. The phrase 'killing ground' preyed on my mind.

He looked around himself absently.

'*They* think that we are walking into their trap. Instead, they are coming into ours,' he said. His tone was grim, business-like. He paused to light a cigarette. 'Will there be shooting? Your guess is as good as mine, Englishman.'

I stared at him wordlessly.

'There are two ways this can go,' he said, almost conversationally. 'The Chinese come down that path over there, we surprise them by being prepared for them, armed. They realise we have the tactical advantage, we talk, see if we can find some kind of accommodation, an arrangement where everyone's satisfied. Nobody has to get hurt.'

I nodded. 'And the other way?'

'They come down the path and, despite our advantage, they start shoot-ing – in which case, they will come off worse. Unless, that is, they've brought an army with them. Which is unlikely. That's why the ground is important; Banh Sar and the two boys have good cover, we can get to cover quickly, they're pinned down out in the open.'

He looked at me.

'There's a Smith & Wesson .38 in the bag for you,' he said.

'I'm not sure that I want ...'

'It's no use for long range, but close up it's a good weapon. You want me to load it for you?'

'I've never shot anything before,' I said simply.

He shrugged and said: 'If it comes to it, a man with a gun who doesn't know how to use it is better off than a man without a gun. You should take it. I'll load it for you.'

'Okay,' I said.

'Now, we have only to wait.'

'Wait for them to arrive?'

'No,' he said. He glanced at his watch. 'For the cafés by the entrance to open. *Breakfast!* Are you not hungry, Englishman?'

Colonel Zhou had said two o'clock, which gave us plenty of time. Chan-lina and Sarachi had wanted to be early, to be in position first; but now we were here, there was nothing to do but wait. We went and got some breakfast, then wandered casually about the park for an hour or so. I think that Ak and Da found somewhere out of the way to go and have a nap – they had, after all, driven through the night. Chanlina asked if I wanted to do the same, but I said that I had got some sleep in the car.

I was too nervous to sleep. Besides, I had something else in mind.

Old Bahn Sar sat himself down on one of the benches, folded his arms and nodded off, a picture of elderly innocence. Chanlina and I walked up to the middle of the park and back, then I left her and went over to the trees where we had decided to position ourselves. I got out my Swiss Army knife and began cutting lengths of vine.

Chanlina wandered over.

'What are you doing?' she asked.

'Oh, I'm making a tree swing for you.'

She laughed: 'Are you mad, Englishman?' and left me to it.

I carried on, cutting away, grubbing under some of the surface roots, bending down several branches and tying them off. I wedged some wood off-cuts carefully in place. Sarachi paused, watching me work.

'A tree house, maybe? You're making a tree house?'

I smiled. 'A tree swing.'

'What?'

'Like, you know, a swing in a tree.'

'Seriously?'

'I like to make things. It passes the time.'

He wandered away. Later, Bahn Sar came over and grinned and nodded, doubtless thinking that the sun had finally got to me.

At a few minutes past twelve, we moved back into our positions, where the track snaked through the trees. Chanlina, Sarachi and I were together near the path, while Da and Ak and Banh Sar were further away, half-concealed and spread out in the bushes. Noy was standing a little way back, behind us.

We waited.

I can still picture it now, the sunlight dappling through the surrounding trees, the heavy heat of the late morning, the occasional tourist passing by, the sound of the birds high overhead. That, and the dull booming of the rushing river beside us, the smell of the dry sandy earth and scrub grass.

I could almost feel the adrenalin coursing through me, a feeling of unreality.

Da, with his young man's eyesight, spotted the Chinese first. It was barely half-past twelve; evidently, Colonel Zhou and his team had had the same idea as us, arriving early. They were maybe three hundred yards away, coming down the riverside path in the open. I counted four Chinese men, flanked by two police officers. With their white shoulder cross-belts against their blue uniforms, they were easily recognisable.

'So we were right,' murmured Chanlina. 'They *do* have the local law in their pocket.'

We watched them approaching.

'Get your weapons ready,' said Sarachi, loosening his gun in the holster under his jacket. The others followed suit. I was holding the Smith & Wesson in my trouser pocket, my finger wrapped safely outside the trigger guard as I had been shown to do.

Two hundred yards ... a hundred and fifty ...

'Steady, everyone,' said Chanlina. Ak, half hidden in the bushes, went down on one knee, the rifle loosely held, pointing at the ground.

The Chinese spotted us and seemed to pick up their pace. I swallowed hard, barely breathing.

They were within a hundred yards, then less. Their leader, a man in his forties with greying hair, dressed in a white shirt and dark trousers, was giving some instruction. The group seemed to spread out, widening their approach. I could see one of them reaching under his armpit for what I guessed was a gun.

I glanced towards the others, Ak and Da and Chanlina's father. They had their weapons out, turned toward the Chinese group. I pulled out my revolver and held it loosely by my side. I noticed Chanlina and Sarachi were both holding automatics.

Chanlina cleared her throat, about to call out to the Chinese, but she never got the chance —

The man called Noy moved suddenly, shifting himself in one smooth action behind Chanlina , his arm around her neck and his gun pressed into the side of her head.

I froze, staring at him in surprise. He shifted his grip slightly, dragging Chanlina backwards, pulling her off-balance.

He caught my eye and scowled.

'Drop gun!' he snapped, and then he shouted to the others, telling them to do the same. Ak and Da looked at Banh Sar; the old man hesitated for a second, nodded, then let go of his weapon. They followed suit. Chanlina dropped the gun she was holding. I let go of my Smith & Wesson, which landed on the side of my foot.

An idiotic thought went through my head – a statement of the blindingly obvious – Noy, Sarachi's 'guy in Laos' was betraying us. We had been set up. I distinctly remembered Sarachi saying the words – *if you pay him*.

Seeing us disarmed, Noy allowed himself a triumphant grin. He pulled Chanlina back again, so that she half-stumbled. A distraction.

Out of corner of my eye, I saw Sarachi suddenly stooping, reaching down for his gun. But Noy had seen it too, and he spun around and his arm moved.

Noy fired while Sarachi was still straightening up. The abrupt boom of the shot, close to, was shocking and Sarachi was flung backwards and went down.

There was a moment of stunned silence. Sarachi, I could see, wasn't moving.

'Colonel!' Noy called out to the Chinese. I gathered that the older man leading them must be Colonel Zhou himself. 'Here we are! They have dropped their guns. Come on in.'

One of the Chinese was speaking quickly to Zhou. They advanced into the wooded area, their guns now out and levelled, two aiming at us, the others on Ak and Da and Chanlina's father. They gestured *hands up* and came towards where Noy was holding Chanlina.

The leader was speaking, saying something in Chinese. The man to his side translated and said: 'We shall take her now.'

'Just a moment,' said Noy, and he used one hand to slip into her blouse, down towards her side. He brought his hand out and I saw that he was holding one of Chanlina's throwing knives. He nodded to the Colonel, smiling.

Colonel Zhou said something and smiled. The translator looked at Noy and said: 'The Colonel says that you have drawn the Mamba's venom.'

'Yes,' said Noy.

Now, I thought.

I took half a step sideways, like someone carelessly rebalancing themselves. Nobody was watching as I glanced down at the ground, where I had a short stick wedged under a tree root. I gave it a casual kick, nothing really, a man shifting his weight, and the stick slipped out from under the root, releasing the vine attached to it.

And it all worked better than I could have ever hoped.

Unsecured, the vines slithered away and the tree limbs, the ones that I had pulled down and secured under tension, shot violently upwards in a great *swoosh* of wood and leaves, a sudden explosion of foliage and branches. A moment of confusion and one of the branches hit Noy in the back of the shoulder, a hard thump – and that was all Chanlina needed.

I knew that Chanlina was fast, but I never realised she was *that* fast.

One moment she was being held by Noy, her head pulled back, the gun pointing at her temple. Then in a blur of motion she slipped downwards, out of his grasp, a knife seeming to appear magically in her hand (a *second* knife, I realised) and she was straightening her legs and turning in one fluid action. The Laotian seemed transfixed by the speed of the woman in front of him; he didn't even flinch as the blade rose upwards. Then there was a three-inch gash in the side of the neck – I hadn't even seen her stab him – and the blood came spouting out, an arc of red, and his knees were buckling as she spun away —

Looking back, I don't think that Noy had any chance at all. When a person can move that fast – well, it simply didn't seem possible. She had struck so quickly, uncoiling her body and slicing him – it was like watching an animal strike, a lethal snake —

A *Mamba* ...

I doubt if it had even been three seconds since she had started moving and she was flying away from him (I don't believe that his blood had even touched her) and coming —

Towards *me* ...

I was transfixed and I sensed – rather than saw – her move behind my back and suddenly the blade, bright and wet with Noy's blood, was at my own neck, her arm was locked around my shoulders and I felt myself pulled backwards.

In front of me, all four Chinese guns were pointed at us. The two policemen (who, I registered, were unarmed) were standing still, looking frankly bewildered. This, their expressions made clear, was *not* what was supposed to happen. Over to one side, Sarachi's body was twitching on the ground in some sort of post-mortem convulsion.

My mouth was full of the tang of pennies, the electric taste of fear.

'Get back!' Chanlina shouted, the first sound she had uttered since Noy had grabbed her. 'Get back or I'll cut the Englishman the same way!'

Looking at those unwavering guns, I wasn't entirely convinced that concern for me was going to stop them. I could feel the edge of the blade across my windpipe, Noy's blood dripping down my shirt.

'Get back!' she shouted again.

The Chinese were hesitating – I was wondering if one of them was thinking of chancing a shot. Chanlina, half-a-head shorter than me, was well covered by my body.

She was retreating backwards; I could hear the rushing water behind us. The four guns were moving slightly, gradually advancing.

'Keep back!' she shouted again, and the two outermost Chinese were spreading sideways, outflanking her. She stepped back again, and I felt the sagging fence wire under one heel.

'I'm warning you,' she snapped at the men and jerked my neck back.

'Chanlina,' I said. 'For Christ's sake —'

'Shut *up*,' she said. I could feel the blade pressing into my neck.

The Chinese were glancing at one another. Perhaps they were thinking of rushing her but were wary of getting too close to the sloping bank and the torrent of white water twenty feet below.

'Chanlina,' I gasped, 'we're at the edge, for God's sake —'

In that moment, did she stumble? The knife suddenly flashed across my vision, and her grip on my shoulders slackened and I felt the ground slide away beneath us, we were on the slope, both slipping, and she let go of me and went backwards as I fell forward onto my face. I was still slithering down – *Jesus!* – and I grabbed at a tussock of grass and felt it come away in my hand, then my feet were in fresh air and I was falling and I grabbed at a useless little clump of grass – which somehow held. I clawed into the ground with the fingers of my other hand and scrambled with my knees on the slope.

And stopped moving.

I took a moment to catch a breath. Chanlina was gone, disappeared over the edge. My own position was still fearfully precarious – I felt as if a light breeze would push me off. I grabbed at another clump of grass.

There was no immediate rush to rescue me.

'Help me, you fuckers!' I bellowed. At that instant, it occurred to me that it might be very convenient for Colonel Zhou if the Englishman also went into the rushing river.

'Damn it!' I shouted. '*Help me!*'

And then they were scrambling forward, edging over the pointless fence wire, three men cautiously linking together as they reached down and gripped my wrist.

I was hauled back up until I could lie on the level ground. Then, trembling, I managed to get up to a kneeling position and was violently sick on the grass.

If I was expecting sympathy from the Chinese – or even common courtesy – I was to be sadly disappointed. As soon as I was fit to sit upright, Colonel Zhou hunkered down next to me, berating me in Mandarin. Apart from the fact that I couldn't understand a word he was saying (the interpreter didn't bother to translate), I could gather his meaning: he was furious.

My hands were still shaking as the policemen knelt and snapped a pair of handcuffs around my wrists. I badly wanted some water, but my requests were ignored. One of the policemen pulled me to my feet.

I had a moment to glance around the little glade. In the confusion, Banh Sar and Ak and Da had melted away into the bushes. Two of the Chinese were staring down into the white torrent, cautiously peering over the edge, presumably looking for Chanlina's body. One man was collecting up weapons, while another was examining the two dead bodies.

I was marched unceremoniously through the park, half-supported by one of the policemen. The few tourists stopped and stared at us as we went past. We bustled through the ticket office, down the track to where a dark grey police van was parked and I was bundled into the back.

The van lurched violently as we set off.

As I sat on the bench seat, with one of the officers sitting opposite me watchfully, I had the absurd and irrelevant thought: *Well, that makes four.* Barely a week ago, I had never even seen a dead body; now I had seen four, and three of them killed right in front of me. And that was not even to count Chanlina herself, lost into the rushing waters of the Mekong.

Chanlina! I felt something constricting in my chest. Chanlina was gone.

We drove for what seemed like an age but was probably no more than ten minutes. The back doors of the van opened, two more policemen appeared and hustled me inside a modest white building, down a corridor and into a bare room containing nothing but a table and four wooden chairs.

Still handcuffed, one of the officers went through my pockets, finding only my wallet, a handkerchief and the penknife which, together with my watch, he placed carefully in a polythene bag. He disappeared with them. I was directed to sit in one of the chairs on the opposite side of the table.

'Water?' I said. I mimed drinking. The policeman shook his head.

'Handcuffs?' I said, holding my wrists out. He shook his head again.

I sat down, and he left me, closing the door behind him. I heard the snick of a key in a lock.

I was alone.

I sat back in the chair and breathed out. The room was airless and stiflingly hot. There was a dry, musty smell. I was aching from a couple of bruises that I had somehow acquired, and the handcuffs were abrading my wrists. Otherwise, I was unhurt.

I suppose I should have counted myself lucky. But sitting in that bare room, locked in and handcuffed, shaken and bruised, I didn't feel lucky.

Without a watch, I had no idea of time passing. It seemed like I was left in there for several hours. Maybe they had forgotten me.

My mind wandered into dark thoughts; an image of Noy, blood spouting from his throat, his knees folding under him, Sarachi, his body flung backwards and twitching in death, or Bullen on that chair, or the guy who had attacked me when I was guarding the car, the one I had fought off with the stupid umbrella. Chanlina's face in front of me, smiling, her hair on my pillow – or flying at me, holding the knife dripping blood.

I had a recollection of the moment of falling, how her grip on my shoulders had suddenly released, the blade flashing across my vision, the sunlight glinting off the fresh blood.

Dark thoughts.

I was probably half-dozing when somebody finally unlocked the door and came in.

They were two Laotian men, one young and one old. The younger man was in full police uniform, while the elder wore a pale blue open-necked shirt. He had thinning hair combed straight back, so the pink of his scalp showed through, and there were liver spots on the back of his hands. He carried a plastic bottle of water and a notebook and pen.

The older man said something in Laotian to me. I shrugged my shoulders in incomprehension. The younger man translated:

'This is Major Nosavan,' he said.

'I see,' I said.

'What is your name?'

'Richard Powell,' I said. I thought it wiser to stick to the alias that Bullen had provided for me. 'Please may I have some water?'

'Water?'

'Yes, please. Water.'

There was an exchange between the two men. They looked at Major Nosavan's half-full bottle, as if debating whether to allow me some of that. He pushed the bottle across the table to me.

So much, I thought, for the local hospitality.

When they had gone, I sat and stared at the wall and sipped at the water.

Although there was no window in the little room, I somehow knew that the light outside had changed and it was nearing the evening.

I belatedly realised that I should have demanded to see the British Ambassador or the Consul, whoever. There was nobody in that police station who was actually on my side.

Considering it coldly, my situation was even worse than I had first thought.

It seemed like another couple of hours before anyone else came to see me. My stomach was rumbling with hunger by then. And I had no illusions about my next visitors; they were, without doubt, serious men.

The door opened without warning. A youngish Chinese man entered, followed by the leader of the Chinese group, Colonel Zhou. I recognised the younger man from earlier. He was the one who had translated for Zhou.

They sat down without preamble and stared at me across the table.

A uniformed policeman came in and removed my handcuffs, then left and closed the door behind him.

This, I thought as I rubbed at my wrists, is definitely irregular and probably illegal. These men were foreign nationals, nothing to do with the Laotian police and, as such, should not be interviewing suspects in a police station.

The younger man broke the silence:

'My name is Li; this is Colonel Zhou.'

'Yes,' I said.

'You are Richard Powell?'

'Yes. Are you the man I spoke to on the telephone?'

'Yes. Amongst my duties is to translate for Colonel Zhou.'

'Well, so, it's good to meet face-to-face.'

'Yes,' he said.

'Right,' I said, using my best irritated tone. 'So, I have some questions for you.'

'What?' said Li.

I had decided I had to go on the offensive – try to put *them* on the spot. Play the part of the offended innocent. Maybe it would work.

'Two questions. The first – do you have my *money?* The money we spoke about on the telephone, yes? The second – why did you not tell me that the man called Noy was working for you?'

There was another brief conversation between the two Chinese. I took the opportunity to look properly at Colonel Zhou. Mid-forties, at a guess, he had a wide forehead and a flat nose, suspicious eyes. There was a hard, narrow mouth above a pronounced jaw.

Li addressed me again:

'We did not tell you about Noy because we did not trust you. We knew nothing about you.'

'And I *might* have been killed. Or, I might have killed *him*. This was a mistake – if I had known, we could have worked together —'

'We did not trust Noy, either,' said Li.

'No? Well, you played a dangerous game. Which could have got me killed as well – so I repeat, do you have my money?'

There was another exchange of Chinese.

'Colonel Zhou says that you did not fulfil your side of the arrangement.'

'What? What crap are you saying?' I snapped, playing the outraged innocent for all I was worth. 'I did *exactly* what you wanted! I *delivered* the Cambodians to the Falls, all of them. Damn it! How can you even *suggest* that I didn't fulfil my side of the bargain? I persuaded them to come – and it was bloody difficult, let me tell you —'

'Please, Mr Powell, be careful with your tone. Colonel Zhou is not accustomed to such attitude. I suggest – *strongly* – that you remember where you are.'

'What? Are you trying to threaten me?' I demanded. 'After I did everything you asked ...?'

Li smiled back at me. It was not a pleasant smile.

'We have no need to threaten you. You are under arrest in a Laotian police station. The officer in charge, Nosavan, is a friend of ours. If we give the word – then, two reliable witnesses will testify that you killed Noy.'

'Don't be stupid!' I snapped. 'Chanlina killed him – and damn near killed me too, if she hadn't slipped and fallen. You saw it! All of you.'

'Who will say that we were even there, Mr Powell?'

'I will.'

'And who do you think will believe you? What were you doing there yourself? You are in a very awkward position, wouldn't you agree? And you would not want a conviction for murder, to serve out a sentence in a Laos prison? Think about it, Mr Powell.'

'But you *got* what you wanted,' I said. 'You got the woman! Where is she, by the way? Have you found her body yet?'

'We did *not* get what we wanted. We *wanted* to question Banh Chanlina —'

'Yes, yes, I know, about who approached her to assassinate a Cambodian Minister. But she fell – which isn't my fault, is it?'

'Bahn Chanlina is dead,' he said flatly.

'You know this?' I said. 'You found her body?'

'Now it is you who is being ridiculous, Mr Powell. She fell into the rushing water – we do not need to find a body. *Nobody* could survive in that torrent.'

'I didn't know that.'

'Of course you did!' said Li. There was a note of impatience in his voice. 'The question is this: did you betray us?'

'Betray you? How? By bringing the people you wanted to the place where you wanted them? How can that be a betrayal?'

'Mr Powell, we are not stupid men. We clearly saw that you all had weapons out when we approached your group. The Cambodians were expecting us.'

'Yes!' I snapped back at him. 'Yes! And who told them to take out their weapons? *Noy!* That's who! So, you explain that, Mr Li!'

The young Chinese looked at me for a moment, puzzlement clouding his expression. He spoke slowly as he replied:

'You say ... that Noy told them —?'

'Yes, exactly!'

Li sat back in his chair and sighed. I was aware that Zhou was watching me with his cold eyes. His mouth was turned down, in a look of distaste.

He spoke quickly to Li, and the younger man turned to me:

'We have one question for you, Mr Powell. You must answer very, very carefully. Do you understand?'

I nodded.

'Good. Because, depending on your answer, will be what happens to you next – whether we shall be talk to Major Nosavan about charging you, or whether it shall be something else ...'

'I understand.'

'Did the woman, Bahn Chanlina,' he said slowly, 'or anyone else, *ever* tell you – or tell Bullen – about exactly who had approached her about the assassination of the Cambodian Minister? Think very carefully about your answer.'

I was aware that Colonel Zhou was watching me more intently than ever.

'No, she did not.' I said, with an air of finality. 'I can't say if she told Bullen, of course, but if she did, he never mentioned it to me ...'

'Good. *Do* you, by any other means, know who approached her?'

'No.'

'Are you quite sure?'

'Yes.'

Li spoke to Colonel Zhou, who nodded thoughtfully. The two men stood up.

'We will talk further, Mr Powell.'

'I want to speak to the British Consul,' I said abruptly. 'I have a right to speak to the British Consul!'

'You think so?' said Li. He smiled. 'Maybe we will have some food sent in. We will talk again later.'

And then they were gone.

I was left on my own. My water was finished. I rubbed again at my chafed wrists. I got up and walked around the little room, stretching my back.

More to distract myself than anything else, I examined the cheap table. One leg was short by a few millimetres, so that it rocked. I crawled underneath to see if I could fix it. There was a loose bolt which, with great patience, I managed to tighten up.

The stupid things that you do to stop yourself thinking about your situation.

I was, nonetheless, thinking – and worrying – about a hundred things. Had I overplayed my hand with Colonel Zhou? Did they believe me? Was there a way out of this mess?

I tried not to think about Chanlina.

Despite myself, I thought about all the dead people.

I was sorry about Bullen; I had barely known him – and it was he who had dragged me into this whole fiasco. I ought to have been angry but, when all was said and done, I *could* have backed out any time I liked. And I had not done so. There was no one, I reminded myself, to blame but me. I had wanted the money, I wanted the adventure.

I could almost hear Bullen's voice in my ear: 'That's the thing about *adventures*, though – you never know what's gonna happen next.'

I thought about Sarachi. I wasn't sorry about him. I recalled him saying, looking at Bullen's ghastly corpse: 'If it was up to me, you would be joining him.' So, not much sympathy for Sarachi.

I wondered when I had become so cold-hearted.

I spent a little time examining the room. If I was Bullen, I thought, I would be planning an escape. But there were no windows to force, no means to dig my way through the wall. There was no fire alarm to set off, or anything clever like that. Perhaps, I might jump whoever came in and fight my way out – but that was absurd. I probably wouldn't make it out to the end of the corridor.

My darker thoughts wandered to the possibility that I might never get out of the little room. Would it not be more expedient for Colonel Zhou to simply dispose of me here? Would anyone care if he did? What was there to prove that I had even been there?

Then, an hour or so later, everything changed.

I must have been dozing, sitting at the table with my head resting on my arms, when a noise outside woke me. There was movement in the corridor, people hurrying, raised voices. Something was happening, but I couldn't make out what – I couldn't even understand what was being said or what the shouting was about.

After a while it went quiet, then the ruckus started up again. I heard footsteps outside the door, an angry conversation in Chinese, then the footsteps retreated. A moment or two later they returned, the sound of a key in the lock and the door was swung open. Li, the young Chinese man from previously, entered followed by another Chinese, a tall, smartly dressed man in his mid-thirties. There was a brief conversation between them, which I guessed was Li asking to remain in the room, a suggestion that the tall man dismissed. Li looked seriously unhappy.

Then Colonel Zhou appeared and spoke with the newcomer. He was agitated and also seemed to want to come in. Very politely, but with just a hint of steel in his tone, the man refused. Zhou started to protest, but was cut short. The newcomer said something with a tone of finality. Colonel Zhou looked angry and aggrieved, but retreated.

The newcomer closed the door, turned to me and smiled.

'Hello,' he said. 'My name is David Yi.'

'Hello,' I said automatically.

'Before we begin, do you need anything? Water? Tea?'

'I'm hungry,' I admitted. 'I haven't eaten since breakfast – and I could certainly do with something to drink.'

David Yi gave a wry smile.

'Not very good hosts, are they? Well, let's get that organised for a start.'

He leant out of the doorway and called out in Chinese. Someone came running, although I couldn't see who it was. David Yi rapped out a set of instructions – he had an ineffable air of command about him – and the unseen figure departed.

David Yi came back in and shut the door. He walked over to a chair on the opposite side of the table, hitched up the knees of his trousers and sat down.

'You, I understand, are Mr Richard Powell, and you British,' he said pleasantly. His English was perfect, almost accent-less. 'Please call me David. Now, we'll get all this sorted out, shall we? Firstly, I understand that you have been through quite an ordeal. A knife to your throat, guns pointed at you, a man killed in front of you – and then being arrested? Quite a day!'

'Yes,' I agreed. I was confused by this turn of events and was probably staring at him like a fool.

'So, let me assure you at once, Richard, you are no longer under any threat. May I call you Richard, by the way?'

'Oh, yes,' I mumbled. 'Of course.'

'Good. I understand that there has been some suggestion of having you charged with a crime that you didn't commit, yes? Well, we can also knock *that* nonsense on the head right away.'

'Oh,' I said.

'Excellent! So, we've got that straightened out. But I do need to ask you some questions, then we can get you to somewhere more comfortable than *this*,' he glanced casually around the room, 'rather ... disappointing accommodation.'

'I see,' I said. 'I'm sorry, but this is all a bit of a shock. Who exactly are you?'

'I'm David Yi.'

'So, are you with Chinese Intelligence then? Military Intelligence?'

'No, I'm not, Richard. I am with the ... *err*, Diplomatic Service of the People's Republic of China.'

'Do you outrank Colonel Zhou?' I asked.

David Yi smiled quietly.

'It's not a question of rank. Let's just say that the Colonel and I will work closely together. We will, of course, as servants of our Government, cooperate fully with one another.'

I could see why he was with the Diplomatic Service.

'Now tell me, Richard, how you came to be involved with this situation,' he said, and leant back in his chair. He spread his hands in a gesture of openness. 'In your own time and your own words, please.'

So I told him. I surprised myself as I began, almost without thinking, telling my story. Maybe it was just the arrival of a friendly face that disarmed me, but something made me trust this affable man with his impeccable suit and his polished manner – with just the hint of authority beneath.

He listened intently as I spoke, hardly interrupting except for an occasional question or exclamation of surprise.

The story that I told him was somewhat edited; while I struck as close to the truth as possible, I left out all the personal stuff between Chanlina and myself. I said that I already knew Bullen when I met him at Battambang Airport (which was pretty much true) but that it had been a chance meeting. I explained that I had needed the money (also true) and had gone along with him without really knowing what I was getting into. I talked about our stupid antics with the Russians, about going to meet Chanlina and Sarachi (something made me leave out any reference to her father) and how Bullen and I had argued about going to The House Above the Jungle.

Halfway through, one of the policemen came in with a tray of food, a bottle of water and some hot coffee. David Yi insisted I should eat at once, so I broke off to do so. He sat and watched me with a neutral expression on his face.

When the meal was finished, I told him about our little expedition to rescue the boy, about my absurd fight with the umbrella, about Chanlina saving me with her throwing knives. I related Bullen's explanation about the assassination of the Cambodian politician. I talked about how Bullen and I had been locked in the guest house, and Bullen's murder, and how I had persuaded Chanlina and Sarachi to go to the Falls (which was, of course, complete invention on my part). I also explained how jumpy Chanlina had been, almost as if she smelt a trap (which was true).

'And now, here we are,' I finished up. My confidence was returning to me, so I added: 'If I have survived to tell the tale, then it is no thanks to your Colonel Zhou.'

David Yi sat back in his chair and gazed at me ruefully.

'It's an extraordinary story, Richard. I'm not sure that I believe more than the half of it but ... it might *just* be true. In this shadowy business ... we become so accustomed to lies and fabrication, maybe we wouldn't recognise the truth if we fell over it.' He gave me another of his wry smiles. 'I take it that this isn't your usual line of work?'

'No, it isn't. I have a different occupation,' I conceded carefully.

'Well, that's your own business. You, Richard, strike me as a strange fellow to find amongst all this ... shall we say? ... dark dealing. An honest man, or maybe something close to it.'

'Shall I take that as a compliment?'

'Ha!' he laughed. 'If you *are* an honest man, then I think that the real compliment would be that you survived at all. The gods must look favourably upon you.'

I said nothing.

'But,' he went on, 'I have one final question for you. I know that you have been asked this already – but I shall ask you again. So, I want your truthful answer. While you were with the Cambodians ... did this woman, this Bahn Chanlina, ever tell you who had tried to hire her for the assassination of the Cambodian Minister? Consider your answer carefully.'

He paused. We looked at each other for a moment. I tried to keep my face impassive, but I was calculating furiously. Did I trust him with this one last thing, my trump card? Because I had one chance, just one, to get out of this with a whole skin.

Some instinct made me decide to trust him.

'Yes,' I said simply. I would tell him what I had kept from the previous interrogators.

'And? Did she give you a name?'

'Yes,' I said, and I hesitated for a moment before I dropped my bombshell. 'Colonel Zhou Jian.'

He stared at me in astonishment. '*What?* You mean ... *this* Colonel Zhou, the man who is here at the moment? Are you absolutely sure?'

'Yes, absolutely,' I said quietly. We stared at one another wordlessly for what seemed like a long minute.

'Just a moment, please – you are saying that Colonel Zhou went to Bahn Chanlina and asked her to kill the Cambodian Minister ... but she turned him down. She didn't take the contract.'

'That's right,' I said.

'And then,' he went on, 'Colonel Zhou hired Bullen to trick Bahn Chanlina, offering a fake contract, just to bring her to the Falls so that he could grab her ... so he could question her to find out who approached her to assassinate the Cambodian politician? But that doesn't make sense ...'

'The way that I see it,' I said, 'the reason why Colonel Zhou was so determined to arrest Bahn Chanlina was *not* because he needed her to tell him who wanted the Cambodian politician eliminated – of course, he knew that already. It was to cover up his own involvement. He didn't want her *arrested*. He wanted her *gone*, disappeared.'

'And you were keeping that up your sleeve, were you?' he said.

'Well, I wasn't going to tell Colonel Zhou, was I? That would have been pretty stupid.'

He nodded, then seemed to make a decision.

'You will excuse me,' he said, hurriedly getting up from his chair. 'I have some arrangements to make.'

I was left on my own again.

A moment later, the shouting started in the corridor again. I could hear people moving about, angry protests, more shouting, the bark of commands given, the pounding of boots on the cement floor.

And then, silence.

I sat staring at the wall and, for the first time that day, I found myself smiling.

To this day, I have no idea of how the man who called himself David Yi chanced to be there that day – and I was pretty sure that, had I asked him directly, he would have (very politely) deflected my question. Beneath the urbane exterior, I had no doubt that his loyalties were to his masters in Beijing, not to me.

Maybe our suspicions were correct; Zhou was operating something on his own behalf and the authorities in China were already wary of him and had David Yi keeping an eye on him. How much had he known already?

Or, maybe his appearance was simple lucky happenstance.

It was something that I would never find out.

Having no idea of time, I don't know how long I waited before the door opened again and David Yi leaned his head in, together with a uniformed Cambodian policeman.

'Right,' he said. 'We've been in touch with your embassy in Laos and told them that a British citizen has been involved in an unfortunate incident and is in need of their assistance. They are sending one of their consular officials over to collect you. He should be arriving here sometime tomorrow afternoon. We've given them the details of your hotel. Meanwhile, we have reserved a room for you at what, I am told, is the best place locally. This officer will take you there.'

'Thank you,' I said. I stood, my legs stiff, thrilled at the prospect of finally leaving the dingy little room. I hesitated, and then I asked: 'What about Colonel Zhou?'

David Yi paused – I could almost see the shift from amiable to diplomatic mode happening in his head.

'Colonel Zhou will be relocated back to Beijing, at least for the time being, to answer some questions that need to be resolved. I don't think that he need concern you.'

'So ... I'm free to go?'

'You are, indeed, free to go.'

Free to go! The words hit me like a squall of wind, making me feel both elated and bone-weary at the same instant. It was over, done with, the danger was past. And I, the least qualified to do so, had somehow survived when others had not – and I was *free to go*. I found myself leaning heavily on the back of one of the shabby wooden chairs – I was suddenly light-headed, relief flooding through me.

'Thank you,' I said. David Yi was watching me with his shrewd eyes again; if I had been a fanciful man I might have thought that he knew what was going through my mind. He said nothing.

When I could trust myself, I let go of the chair back and walked over to the door. I shook David Yi's hand and went out into the corridor.

The 'best place locally' turned out to be a pleasant hotel with an imposing carved timber frontage, at which nobody, or at least nobody that I could find, spoke English. The police officer dropped me off and talked briefly with the duty manager, a square, heavy-set man who looked like a demoralised sumo wrestler, and who stared at me with thinly disguised suspicion. Presumably he considered that anyone arriving with a police escort was some sort of criminal, so I was probably going to steal his statue of Buddha or the potted plants. It didn't help that I was only carrying cash, having removed anything with my real name on it from my wallet.

The police officer departed and I was left to my own devices.

I felt strangely disassociated from everything, as if I was looking at the world through glass – in hindsight, I think I was probably still in shock.

I found the dining room deserted; the kitchen staff were on the point of finishing for the night. I was lucky to get anything at all to eat, a plate of noodles and pork followed by sliced fruit. Afterwards, I walked out onto the empty terrace that overlooked the Mekong and drank a solitary beer. A waiter warily watched me from the doorway, presumably in case I pocketed the cutlery.

There was no phone in my room, and I had no mobile with me (still locked, I realised, in the metal box back at The House above the Jungle), so I went through to the front desk and asked if I could make a telephone call. This involved a deal of semi-comical miming and gesturing, during which the duty manager became fixated on the idea that I wanted to borrow a phone charger. It was with some reluctance (and only when I had laid out two twenty-dollar bills in advance payment) that he eventually let me use the phone on his desk.

I dialled the UK code and then the number for my ex-wife. I checked my watch and did the calculation – in England, it would be a quarter past five in the afternoon. She would be thinking about preparing dinner.

The line buzzed and crackled, then finally gave a ringing sound; I could picture the phone on the occasional table in the sitting room, her walking across to it, stepping between the sofa and the easy chairs. The mental image of that room, the wallpaper and furniture and the clock on the mantelpiece, the window overlooking the back garden surrounded by the trimmed hedges, suddenly made me yearn for England. I had been away in a foreign land for too long.

'Hello?' she said from thousands of miles away.

'Hello,' I replied. 'It's me.'

'Andrew?'

'Yes.'

There was a pause on the line, then she spoke again:

'Where on earth have you been? I've been trying to call you for days! You're not answering your mobile —'

'I got separated from it,' I said. 'Things have been a bit ... hectic here.'

'Hectic?' she said, in a tone of voice that didn't entirely believe me.

'Yes, hectic ... difficult.'

'What sort of things?' she demanded.

'Well, I can't go through it all now, I'll explain when I see you. I should be home in a couple of days. I just called to say that I'm alright. And I wanted to ask how you and Mattie are doing?'

'What sort of things?' she repeated, ignoring my question. 'A work thing?'

'Yes,' I said. 'A work thing.'

'Well, thank goodness for that, at least. When I couldn't get through to you, I had visions of you cavorting in a sleazy hotel with some Chinese floozy.'

'That's not very likely, is it?' I replied, and even as I said it I thought that, in one sense, she wasn't so far from the truth. 'Anyway, I'm not in China.'

'You know what I mean,' she said. To my ex-wife, everyone with the single-fold eyelid was Chinese. 'Anyway, what I need to know is: have you paid Mattie's school fees yet? I've had the office onto me, and they are getting a bit shirty about it.'

'No,' I admitted. 'I haven't. As I said, I've been busy here.'

'Too busy even to pay your own daughter's school fees?'

'Yes, too busy even for that.'

'For God's sake, Andrew!'

'I've been involved in some serious stuff, you know,' I said, weakly. 'Very serious.'

'Oh really?' she said and she made those two words speak volumes.

'Yes. You have no idea.' I was suddenly irritated with her and felt a need to prick her bubble of self-righteousness. 'People have *died*.'

That silenced her for a moment. I could imagine her searching for a response.

'Well,' she said at length, 'that has got nothing to do with me. What you get up to on your jaunts abroad is your business. Can you please do your duty as the girl's father and get them paid.'

I sighed heavily and wondered, not for the first time, how I had ever thought to marry this woman.

'I will,' I said. 'In a couple of days, I promise. Can you let the school know that, and explain, please?'

She made a dismissive noise.

'I just called to tell you that I'm okay,' I said.

'Well, I'm very glad to hear it,' she said in a voice that made it clear that she was nothing of the sort. There was a pause. 'Well, doubtless we'll speak when you get back.'

'Yes,' I said. 'Anyway, you two take care of yourselves.'

'Yes,' she said curtly. 'Goodbye, Andrew.'

The line went dead.

I stared at the handset, trying to recall the last time that I managed a civil conversation with my ex-wife. The duty manager was watching me with narrowed gaze. He slid the twenty-dollar bills into his pocket with the practised ease of a river crocodile pulling a young goat underwater.

I knew better than to ask for change.

I retreated to my bedroom, where I had a shower and cleaned my teeth with the toothbrush and paste provided in the little pack of complimentary toiletries. As I lay on my bed, gazing up at the ceiling fan, I made a mental note to find a market in the morning and buy a couple of travel essentials. I reflected that this was the first time I had ever stayed in a hotel room without having to unpack.

I found myself remembering, as I settled to sleep, that since I had last lain in a real bed (back in the guest house of The House above the Jungle) I'd been arrested, threatened at gunpoint, been interrogated several times, had knives held to my throat, and conspired to get a Chinese Colonel into serious trouble —

And lost Chanlina, the woman who had saved my life, into the rushing water of the Khone Phapheng Falls.

It seemed an awful lot to cram into two days.

I mulled it over, a violent and jagged film running in my mind; I was exhausted, but I doubted that I'd be able to sleep with all that filling my head.

Then I closed my eyes and slept like an innocent man.

In the morning, I received a phone call from the embassy in Cambodia, to let me know about arrangements. For logistics reasons, I was going to be met by someone from the Phnom Penh embassy, rather than from Vientiane. I took the opportunity to tell the woman, who had announced herself as Mrs Lockhart, that I had been separated from my personal possessions and my passport. I therefore needed to make a detour via The House above the Jungle. This caused Mrs Lockhart some concern, especially when she gathered that, having no passport with me, I would require an Emergency Travel Document to cross the border between Laos and Cambodia. The document would have to be prepared immediately – the embassy man would bring it.

At lunchtime, I strolled down to the local market and bought myself a change of clothes and two screwdrivers, together with an over-the-shoulder bag.

The embassy official, a man called Preston, turned up late that afternoon, with a long, printed document that included several important-looking stamps. He told me that this was both to get me into Cambodia and back into the UK. It was made out in the name of Richard Powell which, I thought, might yet turn out to be problematic, but I said nothing. I wasn't going to reveal my true identity until we were well away from here, preferably safely on a plane to London.

Although he avoided saying it directly, he made it clear that not only he, but also the Ambassador, the Foreign Office in London and (for all either of us knew) the Foreign Secretary himself, regarded me as a damn nuisance and possibly a serious embarrassment to Her Majesty's Government. I, for my part, took an instant dislike to him.

'Now look here,' he said. 'This detour you've been talking about in northern Cambodia, in ... what's the name of the place?'

I told him the name of the nearest village to The House above the Jungle.

'Yes, well,' he huffed, 'it's damned inconvenient.'

'But necessary.'

'And I understand that it's the home of this, err, *assassin* that you got entangled with, is that right?'

'Yes, it is,' I told him. 'It's also where most of my travel things are – my passport, for one, including a lot of visas. And my computer. I do need to go there.'

'This woman, this assassin, Bahn Chanlina, she's dead, isn't she?'

'Yes,' I said, 'and her associate, Edi Sarachi. He's dead too.'

'I've got to tell you that I'm not convinced of the wisdom of going back amongst such people – it's quite likely to be dangerous. I think, on balance, Mr Powell, I'm going to veto it.'

I had my own reasons for needing to go to The House above the Jungle, but not ones that I was willing to share with this annoying man. I was determined, and he wasn't going to stop me.

Persuading him, however, turned out to be a task in itself – he was obdurate. It was only when I assured him several times that there was no risk to us, and invoked the arrangements that I had already made with his superiors, that he relented.

We set off immediately; he had brought a car and a local driver, although he explained that we would not be able to drive straight through the border – we would have to change vehicles. His embassy driver would be waiting for us on the other side.

So it was off again across the roads of Indochina, navigating around the gaps and dips and flooded parts, until we got to the border late in the evening, presented our papers and walked the couple of hundred yards between the frontier posts, to be met on the Cambodian side by the embassy car and driver.

I can't say that I warmed to Deputy Chargé d'Affaires Preston (I never even discovered his first name); we did at one point start talking about the events of the past week (me mentally preparing to give him a sanitised version) but he cut me off pretty sharp; Her Majesty's Government were bound to render assistance to their citizens abroad, he said, but they were not prepared to condone, or be associated with, anything that crossed legal boundaries.

'You were not, I take it,' he said, sententiously, 'commissioned by any

UK Government agency to undertake activities on their behalf, were you?'

Well, the truthful answer was, of course, no, but he was annoying me so much that I decided to tweak his tail a little. I said, with great deliberation:

'That, I think, is probably above your security clearance, Mr Preston.'

That brought him up short.

'*What?* What are you telling me?'

I paused and let his question hang in the air. Finally I said:

'I am not telling you – *anything*. In fact, in security terms, the less that you know, the better it will be for both of us.'

Which was utter nonsense but, in my experience, one thing that really irritates most people is not being allowed in on secrets.

'But, I was not informed ...' he said, half-plaintively.

'Well,' I said – *God*, he was so easy to wind up! – 'that isn't really the issue.'

'But the Ambassador? He would have informed me ... surely?'

'That's assuming that he knew himself,' I said ingenuously. 'Listen, Mr Preston, I'm not trying to tell you anything, one way or another. Anything *at all*. I understand your instructions were simply to escort a UK citizen to Phnom Penh, making a short detour on the way. Just that. So let's focus on that, shall we?'

He stared at me.

'Right,' he said.

I tried very hard not to smile.

We didn't speak much thereafter, which was no great loss.

Some Greek philosopher once said that our lives are merely a series of malicious jokes played on us by the gods. The trick is not to be the butt of too many.

That was my own malicious joke for the day.

We travelled on through the night and the following morning, our driver showing no sign of tiring.

We arrived at The House Above the Jungle just after noon. I told Preston to pull up outside the gates; I would walk in on my own. He looked relieved not to be coming in himself.

I had my misgivings about this moment; when we had last all been together, we had been on friendly terms, but I was worried that their attitude might have changed after what had happened at the Falls.

The first person I spotted was Ak, walking across the garden. He set up a great fuss when he saw me. His shouts brought out the rest of them, Chanlina's father and Da and Sita the housekeeper.

I need not have worried. Chanlina's father was positively effusive to discover that I was safe and well. He poured out a torrent of incomprehensible Khmer and insisted on hugging me; Sita did the same, with tears in her eyes. We were united in our grief at losing Chanlina – Ak and Da, thankfully, confined themselves to handshakes.

They asked me a lot of questions, none of which I had a chance of understanding, and tried to explain things to me, which was hopeless. Sita insisted on preparing some food (that much, I could understand) and we climbed the stairs up onto the balcony overlooking the garden.

Chanlina's father went off and brought me back my phone and SIM card, which I slipped into my pocket.

I sign-languaged that they should perhaps send some food down to the men in the car outside their gates (it's amazing what you can communicate with sign-language when you really try). The one thing that I managed to convey to Ak, who was going to deliver the food (with the aid of fingers to lips, mimed zips across the mouth and stern shakes of the head) was to say nothing to them – *nothing at all*. Ak pantomimed it all back to me, to show he understood. I didn't want to confuse the situation by letting Deputy Chargé d'Affaires Preston know any more than he already did – and his driver would speak Khmer.

After I had eaten, I went back down the stairs and across the garden to the little guest house. Chanlina's father wanted to come with me, but I waved him away. I went first into Bullen's room. I stood for a few moments, remembering him; it seemed to be the respectful thing to do – I can't explain why. Maybe I should have said a prayer, because this was the nearest thing to a funeral he was going to get.

Then I went into my room. My suitcase was sitting on the floor; someone (Sita, I suspect) had packed all my things neatly into it.

I checked the window to make sure I wasn't being observed, then moved into the little bathroom, knelt down beside the shower and, using the screwdrivers I had bought in the market the previous day, unscrewed the side panel of the shower tray. Then I reached in underneath the floorboards and dragged out Bullen's flight bag that we had hidden there. I unzipped it and looked inside. My own original passport was still there, together with what Bullen had mysteriously referred to as his 'working capital'. I didn't want to carry out the bag – it was covered in wood shavings and dust from the floor void and might arouse suspicion – so I set about transferring the contents to my own bag, fat bundles of hundred-dollar notes. Now was not the time to count it, but it seemed to be a lot, a lot more than I had expected.

Then I carefully put the empty bag back into the floor void, replaced the side panel in position and put the screws back in. I used a wedge of toilet paper to wipe everything over, checked again and flushed the paper down the pan.

I went back out into the sunshine, hefting my suitcase in one hand and my shoulder bag in the other.

My parting from the four Cambodians was not easy. Maybe we had been through too much together – and Chanlina's painful absence was a real, but unspoken, thing between us. Sita hugged me again, and Chanlina's father wrapped his arms around me like a long-lost relative.

I only wish I had known what they were saying.

I waved over my shoulder as I walked back out the gates to the waiting car. We had a long journey ahead of us.

The drive was tedious and uneventful. I looked through the car window at the landscape rolling past; green fields and bullock carts and little temples beside the road, the occasional rolling hillside, scruffy villages, meandering rivers, boats, shabby stilt houses.

When I could, I snoozed.

It rained when we reached the outskirts of Phnom Penh, heavy rain that instantly flooded the highway. All around us were rusting factories and warehouses crowding right up to the edge of the highway and they all seemed to be disgorging their workers at the same time, so that the road – which, as far as I could tell, was one of the main arteries into the capital city – was jammed solid with cars, lorries, motor bikes and men on bicycles pedalling through four inches of muddy water. Cambodians drive on the right, but that seemed more guidance than a rule, so that the road became a circus of weaving vehicles, all trying to thread their way through in the bucketing rain, swerving round possible collisions while avoiding the alarmingly deep potholes.

I was reminded of what Chanlina had said to me: *don't judge us*. Watching through the window at the scene of utter chaos that presumably happened every evening here, I realised that Indochina may have access to mobile phones and computers but, fundamentally, it was at least fifty years behind the developed world. What I was seeing was like some drenched and dark scene out of Dickens.

Maybe a century behind.

The Sunway Hotel in Phnom Penh is a grand, almost palatial building on Daun Penh Avenue, opposite the Memorial Park and the Giant Clock. Looking out in the sunshine – the rain had stopped abruptly – from under its tall entrance arches, across the lush manicured grass and well-tended trees and bushes, and beyond, to the low skyline of the US Embassy, one might almost believe that Cambodia was a well-ordered, prosperous country.

Preston and his driver dropped me at the little turn-in. It was early evening.

'There's a room booked for you,' he said. 'You will have to settle the bill yourself. The Embassy budget doesn't run to hotel bills. You have money with you, haven't you?'

I agreed that I did, indeed, have sufficient money.

'Good,' he said. 'Do you need me to organise your flight back home, or can you do that for yourself?'

I said that I could manage that for myself.

'Okay,' he said. 'Then, Mr Powell, this is where we part company. I wish you a good trip back to the UK.'

'Thank you,' I said.

'And Mr Powell, one last thing. I don't know who you are, or what you've been doing here in Cambodia and Laos – or whether you have some ... *spook* ... position or not. But, from what I've heard about your adventures up north, I would strongly advise you against coming back here. You understand what I'm saying?'

'I do, Mr Preston,' I said. It was good advice; I wasn't intending to show my face in this part of the world for a long time to come. Some contrarian instinct made me hold out my hand to him, and we shook hands in farewell. Pompous prig though he was, he had at least got me here safely.

I took my bags from the Cambodian driver, thanked him and turned and made my way up the steps into the cavernous white hotel reception.

Having completed the formalities at the desk, I was shown up to my room by the porter and left alone. I was bone-weary and ready to shower and sleep but there was something that I wanted to do first. I upended the shoulder bag on the spare bed and the bundles of hundred-dollar bills fell out onto the counterpane. I carefully counted the number of notes in one bundle, then another and another. I satisfied myself that there were fifty bills in each bundle, $5,000 in each. Then I counted up the number of wads of bills in total, did the simple calculation and decided that Bullen's 'working capital' came to just over $280,000.

I counted again, just to be sure. I had never seen so much cash in one place in my life. Then I put it all back together into the bag, called down to Reception to ask them to start finding me the next flight back to UK – I would come down with my credit card when they were ready to complete the purchase.

I lay on the bed for about twenty minutes before I got the call from Reception; there were no flights tomorrow morning, not unless I wanted to wait eleven hours in Hanoi for a connection, but something would be available late afternoon. I said that was okay and that I would come down directly to complete the purchase. I picked up my real passport and my credit card, stowed the shoulder bag out of sight under the bed and went downstairs.

A very efficient young woman was waiting for me. She led me to a desk with a computer monitor and keyboard on it, and showed me how to fill in the onscreen booking form, which was in both Khmer and English.

In the space where it said FULL NAME, I carefully typed ANDREW FINCH. She raised a surprised eyebrow at me. I smiled back at her cheerfully.

I went back up to my room and dozed.

And that was when the Russians arrived.

'Bullen?' I said carefully.

'Yes, the fat American. You know? You were with him when we last saw you.'

'Of course,' I said. 'Well, Dmitry, I have some bad news about that …'

'Go on,' said the Russian. The geniality was gone from his face in an instant. 'Tell me.'

'Bullen is … dead.'

'Hmmm,' he said, pursing his lips and nodding. Nikolai frowned and said nothing. 'Bullen is dead? Well, it was … how do you say in English? … in-enviable.'

'Inevitable,' I said.

'Yes, yes … in-*evitable*. Well, *Gospod' upokoit yego dushu*. Now I must ask – *how* did he die?'

'Murdered.'

'Yes?'

'By a guy called Edi Sarachi.'

'Oh, yes, Sarachi. The Lithuanian or Latvian or …'

'Albanian.'

'And where is this man Sarachi now?' asked Dmitry.

'Dead also.'

'Oh,' said the Russian. He bit his lip, thinking. He glanced up at me and then down at the floor, as if he was going to make some deep pronouncement. At length he simply said: 'Good'.

He stared at the wall for a moment, contemplating something, mortality or whatever, and then he brightened.

'So, Andrei Simonovich, you will tell us all about it, your adventures, we will have dinner together and maybe one or two glasses of beer —'

'Dmitry, really, I can't. I'm exhausted and I have a flight tomorrow.' I recalled, all too clearly, the last time we'd had a drink together.

'When is your aeroplane?'

'Late afternoon —'

'Then there is no problem. You will get plenty time to lie in your bed in the morning. We can eat at Oskar Bistro — no, better, we will go to the FCC, the Foreign Correspondents' Club, on the waterfront. Any taxi driver can bring you there. It is the best … atmosphere in the city, and the food is not too bad. Where the American journalists used to meet and get drunk and make up their stories and lies about the Khmer Rouge time. Such history! Such bullshit! We see you there at nine-thirty, okay?'

I nodded reluctantly.

'*Khorosho!*' he cried happily. 'Until later, yes?' He turned on his heel and strode off down the corridor. Nikolai raised a polite hand to me as he followed on.

'*Dasvidaniya*,' he said over his shoulder. *Until I see you.*

The Foreign Correspondents' Club in Phnom Penh is situated on the Preah Sisowath Quay, overlooking the Tonle Sap River. By day, the river is brown and sluggish but by night it becomes everything that one might hope, a silver channel reflecting the glittering lights of the bustling city, carrying the waters down into the confluence with its big sister, the mighty Mekong.

I stepped out of the little *tuk-tuk*, into the hectic mass of humanity on the pavement, gave the driver a couple of dollars and looked upwards. The FCC itself is a three-storey building on a street corner, with open balustraded galleries looking out over the river. I walked up the entrance steps, across the ground floor bar area, and up the stairs to the first floor.

Dmitry and Nikolai were waiting for me at a table on the balcony. They rose to greet me and we shook hands warmly.

'You have been here before?' asked Nikolai, gesturing to the waiter for more beers.

'No,' I said. I paused. 'And no chasers tonight, please.'

'Exactly as you say, Andrei Simonovich, exactly as you say. Here you are within your friends, yes?'

I smiled. When the drinks came, Dmitry took a moment to stand, rather embarrassed I fancy, and proposed a toast:

'To Bullen, the old bastard! Wherever you are, I hope the fires are not so hot and the beer is very cold.' We clinked glasses.

'So, Andrew,' he said. 'Tonight, it is your big story that you must tell. You will be truthful, yes? Everything, please. Also, Nikolai will know if you try to deceive us.'

'I thought that Nikolai didn't speak English,' I said.

'You are right. He does not speak English, but he can understands it. Anything too difficult, I will translate for him. So, to start.'

Maybe I was unwise to tell them the truth – or, at least, most of the truth – but perhaps I was light-headed after all the tension and fear of the last few days. Maybe it was the drink.

I began as best I could, at the Classy Hotel in Battambang; I explained how I had thought that the stupid jump between the balconies was the 'adventure' that Bullen had hired me for, and went on to describe my reluctance to continue. As I told the tale, I found myself marvelling at it – how had all this happened to me?

The two Russians were a good audience; they reacted to the story, occasionally interjecting with a question. I told them about Chanlina ('the Green Mamba himself! A *woman!* We never knew!' they exclaimed) and the invitation to The House above the Jungle ('A *garden* deep in the jungle! Such a thing – a woman of taste, I think!') and about the mission to rescue the boy. They laughed about the fight with the umbrella, saying *'only an Englishman, eh?'* I spoke about Chanlina's clinic and the school, at which Nikolai nodded and muttered something. Dmitry translated for me: 'He says education for children is a fine thing; he thinks well of this.' But when I told them how I had slept with Chanlina, the big man shifted uneasily. 'He is the strong family man,' said Dmitry, 'this sort of thing, not for him! But for me, I say, good, and good again! The life is short and every day is the gift that you should take and hold.'

At some point we ordered food and more beer and I asked them if they wanted me to continue.

'Of course, of course. *Ah*, the Englishman is the dark dog, yes?'

'Horse,' I corrected, automatically.

'We say "horse", we say "dog" – what matters? You have wonderful story to tell to your grandchildren! Continue!'

I spoke about discovering, from Bullen, who his Client really was. Dmitry nodded sagely, saying he knew of this Colonel Zhou. ('And now,' he said, 'you do the first intelligent thing you tell us, apart from the bed with the Mamba. To find out what is *really* happening! First lesson in this business – never trust anyone!') Then I spoke about Bullen asking for the phone lead and arousing suspicion, about being imprisoned in the guest house, about swimming with Chanlina and my realising that she was the same woman I had seen in the pool in Battambang ('*Hah!*' said Dmitry). They became serious when I spoke about finding Bullen's body; (Nikolai mumbled something under his breath that I asked Dmitry to translate for me – 'He says: '*The Kingdom of Heaven to him,*' these are the words from the Russian Orthodox').

Then I told them about the awful evening and night that I had spent, almost sure that they were going to kill me too, and how I had received the phone call from Zhou's man. And about the threats from the Chinese, and how I had decided to tell Chanlina everything ('This was brave,' said Dmitry, 'or very foolish') and how we had talked about what Bullen had told me, that he was working for Zhou, and then she had told me that the man who had approached her about assassinating the Cambodian Minister was this same Colonel Zhou.

'*Yebat!*' said Dmitry. 'You say that ... the man Zhou who was paying Bullen to capture the Green Mamba to ask her a question – of which he *already* knew the answer!'

'Yes,' I said.

'Why would he do that ...? No, wait! It is obvious, no? He does not need the answer – he needs to silence her! So, it was *Zhou* who arranged the killing! And now he is ... covering the footsteps?'

'Covering his tracks,' I said. 'Yes, it's the only explanation. And when I thought about it, there was something else ... Bullen, when we went to The House above the Jungle, had planned to use his cell phone to call the Chinese to give them Chanlina's location, so they could maybe send in an assault team to capture her. But that didn't work because they took away our phones. So he had no way to communicate with them.'

Dmitry nodded.

'I reasoned that, perhaps, the killing of this Cambodian politician was not approved by his government – it was Zhou's operation and his alone. He had exceeded his authority; he had done something that he didn't want his superiors hearing about. Maybe he'd got a little private deal going, lining his own pocket.'

I sat back and took a healthy gulp of my beer.

'I understand this,' said Dmitry, leaning towards me. 'This happens. These people, the Colonel Zhous of the world, sometimes CIA, sometimes even KGB, they make operations in secret, then they forget what they are supposed to be doing and they see a way to make money themselves. The opportunity corrupts them.' He rubbed his fingers together in the *money* gesture. 'I have seen it happen.'

'Yes,' I said quietly, 'and there was more.'

'And you work this out yourself? Englishman, this is good! Maybe you think like a spy after all? And so, you went to the Falls. And there is more?'

'Sarachi had a man in Laos, a contact, a man called Noy. Nobody except Sarachi had ever met him. I'd had suspicions about Sarachi, but it was *Noy* who betrayed us.' The two Russians stared at me.

'*Details*,' I said. 'It's all in the details.'

I told them about my trick with the tree branches and the vines, and how that had given Chanlina an instant's opportunity when Noy was holding the gun to her head.

'But then she tried to kill *you?*'

'No ...' I said and I found myself hesitating. 'I don't know... I ... she was protecting herself, and maybe she thought that threatening me would make the Chinese back off. I don't believe that she really intended to kill me – there was a moment there ... I can't be sure ... but she had the knife at my throat and then, when she fell ... she moved her hand away, like she was trying *not* to cut me. It was so quick, all over in a second, but I really believe ... although maybe because I *want* to believe ... that she didn't intend to hurt me.'

I looked at the two Russians.

'But I'll never know for sure,' I said.

'You need to believe that she cared for you, yes? Maybe you were – a little bit – in love with her, and you want it to be the same from her?'

'Maybe,' I said.

Nikolai cleared his throat and said something in a low voice to Dmitry. Dmitry translated:

'Nikolai asks a question. He asks *why*, if you already know that there is a trap, why do you go to the Falls? It is the big risk, no?'

'Yes, we discussed that. Our thinking was that we *had to* go – if we didn't, we would have had this man Zhou pursuing Chanlina forever – and perhaps her people and maybe even me. They talked, Chanlina and her father, about falling under the gaze of the Dragon. At least, at the Falls, we would know he was coming. I think also that it was her pride, that she was the famous Green Mamba, that she would not run scared ... and, if she didn't go, she could never be sure again.'

I shrugged my shoulders and took a sip of beer.

'Anyway, that's my big story. That's all I have. What do you think?'

Dmitry leant back in his chair and grinned at me:

'We drink to your story and to your *adventure* you wanted so much, and we drink to you still being alive to tell us about it.'

He raised his glass to mine and Nikolai did the same and we clinked together and Dmitry cried '*Na Zdorovie!*' loud enough to attract looks from the other tables. Then, in a voice like low thunder below the horizon, Nikolai murmured something.

'Ha!' said Dmitry. 'Our friend here has something he wants to say you. He says, the *next* time you want excitement, you should come to us, your *Russian* friends, and we will take damn better care of you than – and *may God rest his soul* – the foolish fat American.'

I reached across and clinked glasses with Nikolai again.

'Thank you,' I said, '*Na Zdorovie!*'

Nikolai nodded politely to me, and rose to his feet. For a moment, I assumed that he was going to excuse himself to go to the toilet or something, but then he did someone much worse.

He filled his enormous chest with air and, without any introduction at all, sang:

'*Pad sasnoyu, pad zelenoyu,*
Spat palazhýtye vý minya.'

He had a fine rolling baritone, as good as anything I'd heard outside a professional theatre, and tremendous depth, so that the whole effect was like a small volcano rumbling under our feet. People stopped eating to watch him.

'Oh, Jesus,' I muttered to Dmitry, 'He's going to sing.'

'Already is singing,' he replied. 'He was one-time Red Army Choir, very good singers. This will go okay – just watch.'

Nikolai gathered himself and, still holding something back, sang:

'*Aida lyuli lyuli, aida lyuli,*
Spat' palazhýtye vý minya.'

The whole room went silent; even the bustling waiters had stopped moving.

The big man looked around himself and smiled, a huge, happy smile. He closed his eyes and went on:

'*Kalinka, kalinka, kalinka maya,*
F sadu yagoda malinka, malinka maya!'

Halfway through the second phrase, I realised that Dmitry was rising to his feet and joining in. He had a good voice – not as good as the big man, but deeper. Together, they sang again:

'*Kalinka, kalinka, kalinka maya,*

F sadu yagoda malinka, malinka maya!'

And this time, at the end of each phrase, they stamped down on the floor – *Crash!* – and clapped their hands in unison. They repeated the line three more times, by which point half the restaurant had begun to recognise the old Russian folk song and were stamping and clapping along with them. A few people were even singing with them when, suddenly, Nikolai raised his hands to stop them.

Dramatic silence, broken when the two Russians turned to each other and slowly sang the verse:

'Akh tý sasyenushka, akh tý zelenaya,
Nye shumi zhe nado mnoi,
Aida lyuli, aida lyuli,
Nye shumi zhe nado mnoi!'

Nikolai's eyes were positively shining. He gathered himself again and sang, very softly, the chorus:

'Kalinka, kalinka, kalinka maya,'

A pause.

'F sadu yagoda malinka, malinka maya!'

He repeated the chorus, Dmitry joining in, picking up the beat, and then the entire restaurant seemed to be joining in:

'Kalinka, kalinka, kalinka maya, [*CRASH!*]
F sadu yagoda malinka, malinka maya! [*CRASH!*]

A couple were up on the floor, arms around shoulders, doing an approximation of a Russian dance, then another and another. The room was shuddering and people were coming up the stairs to see what was happening as the beat grew faster and faster.

Well, I can recognise an exit as well as the next man. I got to my feet, caught Dmitry's eye and reached across to shake his hand in goodbye. He caught me by the shoulder and pulled me into a bear-hug followed by a kiss on each cheek, while the whole restaurant seemed to be shaking. Nikolai saw that I was leaving, whereupon I was wrapped in an embrace that might have displaced several vertebrae, followed by a pair of resounding kisses from him as well. I broke free and retreated, raising a hand in farewell.

'Kalinka, kalinka, kalinka maya, [*CRASH!*]
F sadu yagoda malinka, malinka maya!' [*CRASH!*]

I pushed my way down the stairs, through the stream of customers coming up to join the party. The noise was terrific, and I wondered if the famous old building would withstand the beating it was getting from a hundred feet stamping in unison.

I made it to the street and paused for a moment. The warm soup of Phnom Penh night air hit me. I stood there, surrounded by the thronging mass of humanity on the pavement, the taste of the fumes from the traffic, the incessant honks of the motorbikes streaming past, the river glistening in the darkness, the smell of cooking, the chatter of the crowd.

I looked around for a *tuk-tuk* to take me back to my hotel.

When I think back to that evening, those are the things that I like to remember, always accompanied by the noise, drifting out from the balcony above, of those two Russians and the crowd in the Foreign Correspondents' Club roaring out '*Kalinka Malinka*'.

And, in my glowing memory of that moment, they are probably singing it yet.

Chanlina

The shop on the Parkway 800 block was wedged between an Italian Restaurant, displaying bold signs in the window: ('Daily Specials!', 'Pizza by the slice' and 'We deliver!') and a store simply announcing itself as '*Liquor*', showing big posters of Coors Light and Heineken and something called 'Landshark'.

I pulled my rental car into the kerbside and parked up.

For the tenth time, the twentieth time, I asked myself what I was doing here in Florida. Why, I wondered, having established that the shop was real and trading, hadn't I simply telephoned ahead? Why fly five thousand miles to the States at all? There was nothing here that I couldn't have established by phone.

Except that some sixth sense told me that I was *supposed* to come.

The fifteen months since I had left Cambodia had been good to me. Bullen's 'working capital' had been put to work in Andrew Finch Consulting, clearing debt and allowing me to cautiously expand the business. I now had a full-time designer on the books, with a graduate trainee starting next month and a woman doing administration three mornings a week. Things were looking up.

I killed the engine and stepped out of the car. The heavy Florida air hit me at once, so I paused for a moment on the sidewalk, breathing and collecting my thoughts. This is crazy, someone's idea of a joke, I thought – but I'd come too far to turn back now.

I crossed the sidewalk and walked through the door marked 'Monroe's of Palm Coast'.

Inside the shop, the smell of the dry-cleaning chemicals was strong, despite the two big extraction units at the back. There was also the underlying plastic scent of the hundreds of polythene slip bags over the garments hanging on a rotary rail behind the divider.

The sole occupant of the shop was behind the counter, her head bent over a ledger of some sort, so that only her long straight black hair was visible. She was wearing a white polo shirt beneath a blue tabard with the words 'Monroe's of Palm Coast' above her left breast. I slowly walked the length of the shop and took out the dry-cleaning ticket, the ticket that I had received last week in an otherwise empty envelope. I had studied that ticket so often and so carefully that I could have redrawn it from memory:

Monroe's of Palm Coast, FL
Ticket no: 65872592
(Please retain for your records)

'Be with you in a moment,' said the woman, without looking up.

'Okay,' I said.

I slid the ticket, face up, across the counter.

'I'd like to collect that, when you're ready,' I said quietly.

'Ju-s-s-s give me ... two ... seconds,' she drawled, then stopped.

She looked up. Her face went from surprise to comprehension to slow delight.

Chanlina. It was Chanlina.

'Hi,' she said, very softly.

'Hi,' I said.

'You got here,' she said. Her American accent was more pronounced now.

'I figured that's what you wanted me to do.'

'Yeah, that's exactly what I wanted you to do.'

'I have a thousand questions,' I said. 'But only one truly important one. Is it really you?'

'Oh, yes, it's really me. Aren't you going to ask me about ...?'

'How you made it through the Falls?'

'There are two answers for that. The first is: *I swam*. The second is: not without a deal of difficulty and a few knocks and bruises.'

'Nothing serious?'

'Nothing serious.'

We stared at each other.

'I thought you were dead,' I said.

She shrugged and gave me a shy smile: 'But, as you can see ...'

'Chanlina,' I said.

'Hello, Englishman,' she smiled. 'So, you made it?'

'Yes,' I said. I felt something break itself free inside me, something that had been tight and locked up so long I barely noticed it anymore, and I found myself smiling so broadly that suddenly I was laughing, laughing out loud without being able to stop myself and then she was laughing too and I reached across the wide counter for her hand and she took it.

'God, it's wonderful to see you,' I said when I could catch my breath.

'Yes,' she said. 'And you, to see you as well. My father, he told me you had been to The House above the Jungle; he said that he told you I had survived but, of course, you couldn't understand.'

'Google Translate,' I said automatically.

'Oh, sure, Google Translate,' she repeated. '*My* father? Are you kidding?'

We started laughing again.

'There's someone I need you to meet, in back,' she said, and her eyes were shining. 'Come on. You can slide over the counter.'

I did so and an awful idea occurred to me. Who did she want me to meet? Her boyfriend? Her husband? It wasn't impossible.

I followed her through a door at the rear of the shop and into a small break-out room.

There was nobody there. She turned to me and there, standing in that dull little room, dressed in the cheap nylon uniform of a shop employee, I had never seen her look as beautiful as she did at that very moment, like a queen, blazing with confidence and pride.

'Andrew Finch – meet your son,' she said and she bent down to a little carry-cot that I hadn't noticed and lifted up a bundle of white blankets. In the midst was a tiny face, a shock of black hair, an elfin face with bright blue eyes. She offered him to me, to hold.

'Support his head,' she said.

'My ... son?'

'Uh-huh,' she said, nodding.

I was stunned. *This* was beyond all expectation. *This* was extraordinary.

'I called him Richard, after you,' she said.

'But ...' I said, words seeming so inadequate for what I was feeling. 'I had no idea ... I mean ... how? You could have — you did this all on your own? I had no idea ... why didn't you write ... or call me, I could have been here ...'

'I didn't want you to come here for him. I can take care of him – I will *always* take care of him. If you came here, you had to come here for me, for *us*, you and me.'

'I did,' I said. 'I came here for *you*. This ... our son ... I am so delighted, happy, I can't tell you —'

'You are pleased?'

'I am far beyond pleased.'

'Good.' Her expression changed, became serious. 'This, today, you must understand, is not a happy ending. I do not allow myself to believe in such simplicities. Life is complicated, challenging, hard. There will be many difficult problems ahead of us, Andrew Finch, for you and me and this child.'

'Then we'll get through all of them together, you and me ... and our son,' I promised her.

'Then, we shall simply call this — a happy beginning,' she said.

Author's Notes

The Green Mamba is, of course, a work of fiction but it is none-the-less worth noting that many of the events and places mentioned in the novel are real.

The Khmer Rouge regime seized power in Cambodia (renaming the country *Democratic Kampuchea*) and held it from 1975 to 1979. They were eventually ousted by an invasion from neighbouring Vietnam. Their leader was Pol Pot who, as a young man, had studied in the early 1950s in Paris – Cambodia being in those days a French colony. He and his fellow leaders had been influenced by the writing of the philosopher Jean-Jacques Rousseau and the belief that Mankind was born fundamentally good but became corrupted by the world; perhaps this explains the Khmer Rouge's rejection of modernity and their brutal insistence on purification through a forced return to rural life. Whatever their underlying ideology, they are estimated to have killed between 1.5 and 2 million people, about a quarter of the population – an ocean of blood.

After their ejection, the Khmer Rouge continued fighting and disrupting Cambodia until 1999; Pol Pot himself died in 1998 whilst under house arrest, either by a heart attack or suicide by poison.

Anyone wanting to learn more of the extraordinary history of the country could do worse than to read Joel Brinkley's excellent *Cambodia's Curse: A Modern History of a Troubled Land (2011)*.

On a lighter note, the Classy Hotel is a real place, with its rooftop bar, fine swimming pool and ornate reception. The balconies are exactly as I have described them – but the jump between should be avoided at all costs. The Bamboo train is also an actual thing. I have been a little harsh on Battambang airport, which is basic but not so basic as drawn here; in any case, at the time of writing, it is closed.

Similarly, the Mekong Riverside Resort is real and it is truly a small piece of paradise; I confess, however, that I have moved it for narrative purposes across the border from Laos into Cambodia. The Khone Phapheng Falls are frighteningly real and well worth a visit. I am told that people have survived falling into the racing torrents, but not many.

The Foreign Correspondent's Club in Phnom Penh is real, the food and drink and atmosphere is good, although I cannot promise any singing.

Finally, I must express my enormous gratitude to those for helped in the writing of this novel: Jane Read for her scrupulous editing and ruthless hunting down of my errors; my Agent, Barbara Levy, for her belief and encouragement across many years; the wonderful WordWatchers for their input on the early manuscript; my brother Mark for his studious reading and comment and, finally, my darling wife Harriet, without whom none of this, or much anything else for that matter, would have been possible.

About the Author

Rowan MacNeill was born on Teeside, in north-east England, into a family with roots in England, Ireland and Scotland. He did most of his growing up in Liverpool.

He worked at an assortment of jobs, barman, dishwasher, labourer, electrician, interpreter, technical draftsman, before studying Civil Engineering at King's College, London after which he had a long career in construction, starting as a site dogsbody (also referred to as a 'Junior Engineer') and ending as a company Director.

Rowan MacNeill lives on the Hampshire/Berkshire border, with his wife and an English Shepherd with too much personality.

See more at: https://rowanmacneillstoryteller.com/

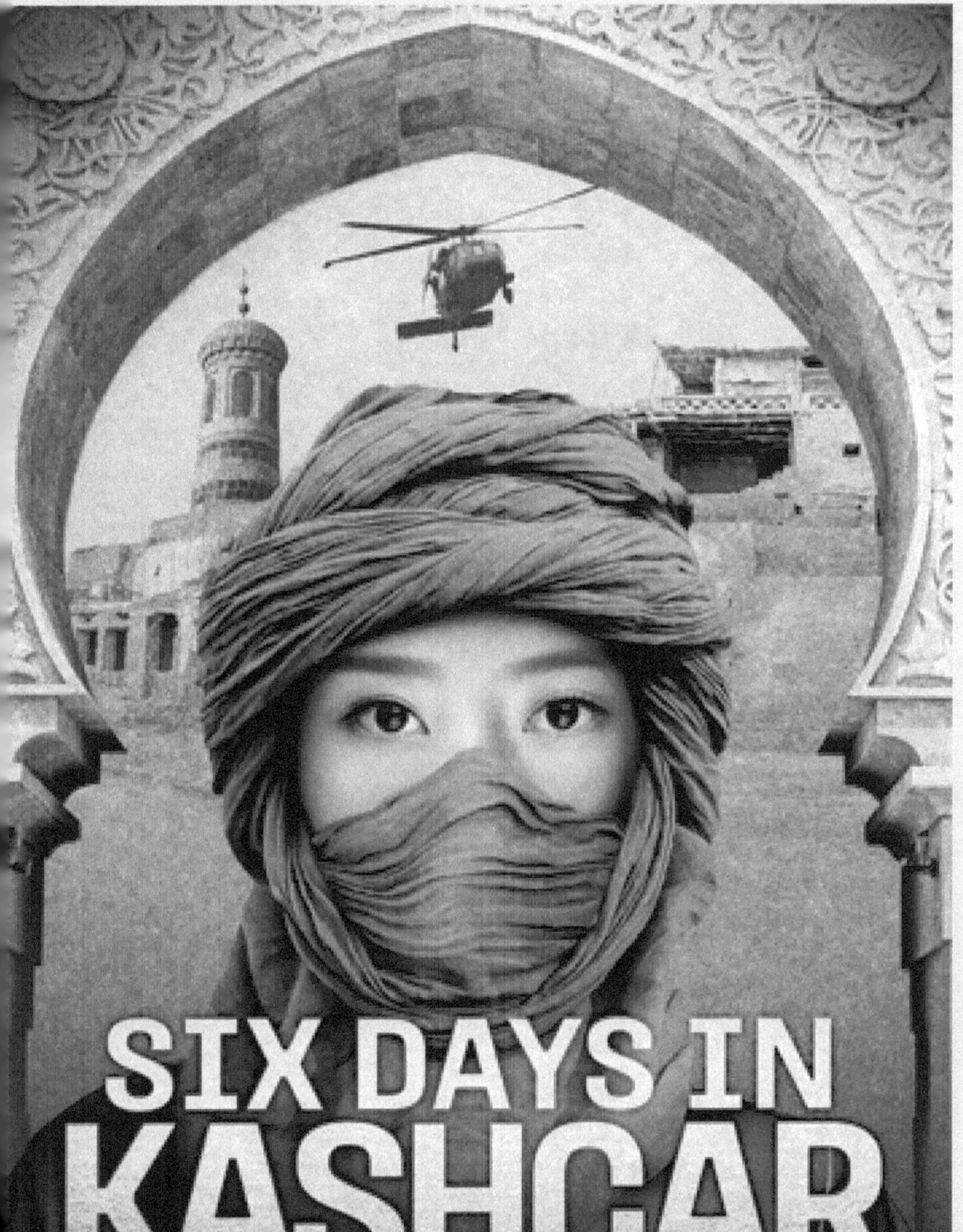

Also by Rowan MacNeill
SIX DAYS IN KASHGAR
Rowan MacNeill

An extract from "Six Days in Kashgar"

If the General had not got up that morning in such a filthy mood, he might still be alive today.

This is not mentioned to evoke your sympathy. The General was largely the author of his own misfortune - and his death, although regrettable, was not central to what happened in those six days in Kashgar. The point is made simply to illustrate that trivial events sometimes lead to tragic consequences.

Big things can happen for very small reasons.

When the official accounts are written of what happened in those six days – better, perhaps, to say if they are written, and that's a big "if" because none of the Governments and great statesmen involved emerged with much credit – the General's demise will probably not be recorded at all. The official history will be brief and simple and anodyne and will lack detail. It will not contain the truth, the essence of what happened.

Because the truth, as that playwright said, is rarely pure and never simple. And to tell the story of those six days in 2006 properly, to tell the absolute truth, any account would have to include the many things that pass beneath official notice.

It would have to include, for example, the fading light as dusk falls over the old city in Kashgar, dusty orange and pink and some indefinable colour, and the sound of the muezzin calling the faithful to prayer.

And it would need to talk about the sun over the Taklimakan desert at midday, like a blazing diamond in the sky that feels like it would slice your retina to pieces just by looking at it. Or the scent of the new mown grass in a

Washington park on a summer's afternoon.

It should also include that Tech guy from State snorting and snapping the tension in the room: "Of course there's a radio transmitter in the damn thing, for Christ's sake" he said, "it's a cell-phone!"

And later, that same group of people, watching in horror as the orange and red blots grew on the screen showing the feed from the satellite.

It should mention the almost solid vibration that passes through your feet from the deck of an aircraft carrier at sea when it turns its enormous tonnage into the wind to launch planes, or the overpowering smell of aviation fuel as the jets engage afterburners for take-off.

And, of course, it would have to talk about the extraordinary old Yankee who seemed to be made out of grit and sinew and willpower. Not forgetting the part, the very important part, played by that tiny and wizened Chinese woman, her ancient body too far-gone in years to even sleep at night any more, though there was nothing wrong with her eyes. Or her brains, for that matter.

Then there was the girl, the exquisite girl with the perfect oval face. And her eyes, as innocent as a child one moment, that could change in a single blink to reflect all the mystery and tragedy and utter strangeness of China. My God, but you could lose yourself in those eyes.

Above all, it would absolutely need to include that sprint, that unbelievable helter-skelter lung-bursting run that might have brought an Olympic stadium to its feet, when only the sand lizards and scorpions were there to see it -

But we're getting ahead of ourselves already.

So, the truth, rarely pure, never simple.

Let's start at the beginning.

1992

Her first thought was for her children.

The three thunderous knocks on the front door woke her, and she was starting to rise from her sleeping mat when she heard the splintering crash of the door being broken in.

"*Mahmut*," she hissed at her husband, shaking his shoulder (he was always slow to rouse). "*Mahmut!* Wake up!"

"What? What's happening?" he mumbled, fogged by sleep.

There was the heavy pounding of boots on the floorboards of their little hall. Instinctively, she slid off the mat and lifted little Yusuf out of his cot, gathering him into her arms. Ismail, their four year old, was already sitting up. She beckoned him to her. Powerful torch-beams skittered across the wall opposite

"*Police!*" shouted a voice from the hall, "Get your hands in view!"

Suddenly there was a figure looming in the doorway, then another and another, spilling into the sleeping room. The torches were shone directly at her, at Mahmut, at her children, stabbing into their eyes.

"Get your hands where we can see them!" bellowed the voice. It spoke in Mandarin. "You! Woman! I need to see your hands!"

Reluctantly, she released her sons, lifting her hands.

"Get the light," said the voice and someone found the switch and clicked it on. She blinked painfully, still holding her hands up. There were now four men crowded into the small sleeping room. She could make out their black uniforms, the *Han* Chinese faces beneath their helmets, the heavy weapons aimed at her and her little family.

"You are Mahmut Torre?" snapped the voice, evidently the officer in charge.

"Yes," said her husband. She glanced across at him. He had pulled himself into a kneeling position, hands raised above his head like a supplicant.

"Who are you?" demanded the officer, turning to her.

"I am his wife," she said. Her eyes flicked down to her children, cowering beside her. The toddler started to whimper.

"Your name?"

"Meryem Torre," she said quietly. She gestured towards little Yusuf. "May I comfort my child?"

The officer regarded her for a moment, as if assessing the threat she might pose. He nodded. She reached out and wrapped both boys in her arms.

The man turned to one of the other black-clad figures. "Meryem Torre?" he said. "Have we anything —?"

"She's not on the list, no," said the second man.

"Very well," said the officer briskly. "She stays here". He addressed her husband again. "*You* – Mahmut Torre. You will come with us."

"Why?" she gasped, her anger getting the better of her terror. "What has he done?"

"Your husband is under arrest for consorting with known terrorists. We have witnesses who saw him, in a café in the Old City, three days ago."

"What!" she blurted out. "What are you *talking* about? *He* isn't a terrorist!"

"That remains to be seen," said the officer.

"I had no idea —" said Mahmut. "I didn't know *who* they were. We were simply chatting."

"About what?" said the officer.

"Sport . . . the price of animal feed. *Nothing*. Small-talk. I had never seen them before in my life. That can't be a crime, can it?"

"What you have - or have not - done, will be established under questioning. Get up, *Turki*, and don't do anything foolish if you value your family's safety."

Mahmut rose to his feet, holding his hands up.

"Where will you take him?" she demanded. "We have the right to know!"

"You have no right," said the officer flatly. "He will be taken for questioning. There, it will be assessed if he is to be charged; or, possibly, if he requires re-education."

Re-education! The word sent a shiver through her. Everyone knew what *re-education* might mean, detention in some dreadful, distant prison camp. Men - especially Uyghur men like her husband - could disappear into those camps for ten, twenty, thirty years. Some were never heard of again.

"*No!*" she cried, throwing aside her caution. "You *cannot* take him! He has done *nothing*. Do you hear, *nothing!* He is a husband and a father and —"

"Be quiet, woman! We can arrest women as easily as males. Who then would care for your children, huh?"

"*Hush*, Meryem," said her husband softly. "Do not make this worse than it has to be."

"*Way Khodayim*," breathed Meryem - *Oh God* - gasping at the terrible realisation. What could she do? There were guns pointed at her, at her little boys – but for one wild moment she imagined launching herself at the *Han* officer, clinging onto him, furiously sinking her teeth into his neck, biting through some artery before they shot her dead.

Were not for the children . . .

No, *impossible.*

They had started to bundle Mahmut outside. She got up, lifting little Yusuf onto her hip, grasping Ismail by the hand, and followed out through the tiny hallway, across the courtyard, into the alley outside.

The night was cool, late April in Kashgar, still hours before dawn. Some instinct made her tell herself: *you must remember this moment. This is the moment when your life changed forever,* and she saw it as an outsider might see it, the narrow alleyway, the anonymous black-clad Security men, the dark police van standing waiting, her husband being led away in his nightshirt...

...and herself, a woman barely out of her twenties, a mother, still pretty, an infant in her arms - and the small figure of Ismail standing beside her, his face implacable as if he somehow understood what was happening and was determined be strong, not to show fear or make a fuss.

There was a pause while the van was unlocked and Mahmut turned, still held by his escort:

"Meryem," he called out.

"Yes," she said, edging forward.

"Wait for me – I will come back to you."

"Of course," she said.

"Now you must take care of my boys. Keep them safe."

"Yes," she said. *They are all I have left,* she thought, but didn't say.

"And Ismail?" he said, addressing the solemn little figure beside her.

"Yes, father?"

"Take care of your mother and Yusuf. Be a good boy."

"Yes, father."

"That's enough," snapped the officer in charge as the back door of the van swung open. In the dim interior light, Meryem could see seated figures inside, all men, all Uyghurs. Mahmut stepped up to join them. He turned to gaze at her as the door slammed shut.

The Security men were milling around, getting into another vehicle. One of them slapped the side of the van twice, the signal to leave.

A minute later the alleyway was empty except for Meryem and her two sons.

Yusuf, who had only started to speak a few words in the last months, was whimpering in her arms. He looked up at her and mumbled:

"Daddy gone?"

"Yes, Daddy's gone," she said.

"Back tomorrow?" he said softly.

"No," said Ismail, staring forward into the darkness. "Daddy's gone."

2004

Malone had got to know Kashgar City during his first stint to the Archae-ological Dig, and he was already acquainted with Beijing from the time he had spent there as a student, nine years before. But he didn't know much about the vast tract of the China interior, almost three thousand miles of it, that lay between the two cities. His first trip out to the Dig had been by plane. You learn nothing about a place by flying over it, obviously. This time, he wanted a closer look.

The possibility of making the journey by train was too daunting, even for him; Chinese railways had improved from the old 'hard-seat' days, but the thought of spending 60 or 70 hours cooped up in a basic carriage was too disheartening to consider. Instead, on his return from leave, he decided to hitch a ride on a lorry travelling west.

He spent a day hunting around the factories and transport hubs on the outskirts of Beijing, asking around in his efficient Mandarin Chinese, for a vehicle bound for Kashgar. He finally found what he was looking for and approached the driver.

Mr Wang was a broad and stolid individual and not much given to conversation. He had difficulty, at first, understanding what Malone was looking for. Why would anyone make such a journey, if he didn't need to? Malone explained that he wanted to see the country close up; he couldn't do from a plane. Mr Wang consulted with his co-driver, Mr Li. Mr Li looked sceptical. Only when Malone started to talk about the money did the two Chinese become interested.

Their truck was an old Isuzu 10-tonne with pale blue paintwork so faded that some panels were almost white with red rust spots showing through. The piston rings were blown; the exhaust trickled oily black smoke at tick-over. The cab was littered with stuff, open packets of cigarettes and two broken lighters and sweet packets and torn maps and a pile of music cassettes without cases. There was no air conditioning, the steering wheel had a crack through it, and one of the plastic seats was split.

Malone gathered that Mr Li, who was missing several teeth, was probably more of a mechanic than a co-driver, and was distantly related to Mr Wang on his wife's side.

Money changed hands, Malone tossed his bag into the back, perched himself on the split seat and they set off through the vast sprawl of Beijing.

He stared out of the window as they passed the endless narrow little shops, modern precincts, car showrooms, pagodas, grand new hotels, temples, faceless office buildings, sweat-shops and workshops and hideous blocks of flats with washing hanging out the windows, mean little homes and luxury modern houses. Tower cranes grew overhead like mechanical trees, hanging perilously over hundreds of building sites. Mr Wang drove through it all without any expression on his wide, flat face.

When they finally left Beijing behind, Malone started to see things he had not expected; there were hillsides like Surrey, soft rolling slopes with a forest of low bushes rising up them. Further on, the landscape became dramatic where the rivers had cut their courses through rocky outcrops, leaving majestic hanging valleys in their wake.

Occasionally, Mr Li would attempt conversation:

"So, Mr Malone, why do you go to Kashgar?" he asked. It was the first time the subject had been mentioned.

"I work there," replied Malone simply. "For the University of London."

"For a University," repeated Li, in surprise. "A University? You are a teacher, yes?"

"No. I'm an Interpreter. On an Archaeological Dig in the desert."

"An interpreter? What languages do you speak?" pressed Mr Li.

"Mandarin Chinese. English, of course; some Arabic, a little Spanish, bits of French."

"So many!" said Mr Li, clearly impressed. "Tell me, is it very difficult to speak the English?"

Malone smiled despite himself. "Not," he said, "if you are born there."

At dusk, when they had finally had enough for the day, they pulled over and unrolled their sleeping bags. One man slept in the cab, spread across the seats, while the others bedded down beneath the chassis, carefully avoiding the oil leaks.

Days passed. When Mr Wang tired, Mr Li took over and Mr Wang snoozed. Mr Li hummed slightly as he drove, battling the decrepit gear box on the inclines.

On the third morning, some sixth sense alerted Malone that *something* was wrong. A warning antenna was twitching. He wondered if it was simply nerves - he was, after all, far from home and alone, travelling with two strangers.

But no, *something* was in the air. He couldn't put his finger on it, but it was there. He needed to stay alert.

That evening they stayed at a cheap hostel. Malone and Mr Wang showered and shaved in the communal bathroom and the three men made their way down to the local night market, where they ate fried noodles and drank several bottles of *Tsingtao* beer.

"For a Westerner," said Mr Li, "someone like you, this is a hard journey. You must be used to a softer travelling."

Mr Wang was staring at him narrowly.

"Not really," said Malone. He felt he was being assessed in some way. He took a swallow of his beer. "You see, where I grew up, there are no *soft* men."

"Where *you* come from? You are a British, no?"

"I'm from a part of Britain they call Ulster."

"Ulster," said Mr Wang, rolling the strange word on his tongue. "Tell me, is your country like this?" He gestured with his bottle to encompass the night market, the steaming cauldrons of noodles beneath the strung cables of bulbs, the crowds of chattering Chinese, the chickens on spits, the smoke rising up into the warm night air.

Malone was momentarily nonplussed by the question. A picture came to his mind of the countryside around his native Londonderry; the dry stone walls, the dripping hedges, the dank grey sky, the endless green fields, and he felt a sudden pang of unexpected melancholy.

"No," he said carefully. "My country is nothing like this."

The conversation lapsed, and Malone glanced at the two Chinese. He didn't trust them – but then, he reflected ruefully, he didn't really trust anyone. What if, perhaps, they were planning to rob him – and his uneasy feeling wasn't just foolish imagining? If it came to it, he reckoned that he could handle either of them. Mr Wang looked strong, but slow. Mr Li was probably quicker, younger, maybe more dangerous. But no, he thought, should it come to it, he could deal with Mr Li.

But, on the other hand, what if they came at him together – then, well, who could say? He guessed they would not be so co-ordinated. If they *did* try anything, it would be opportunistic. They would have to get their courage up first. *Stay sharp*, he reminded himself, *don't turn your back on them*.

Coming into Dunhuang on the fourth day, China surprised him again. Stretching out wide across the horizon were rolling red sand dunes. There were camels wandering across the road. Apart from the lettering on the road-signs, he might have thought himself on the edge of the Sahara.

"Like Africa, yes?" said Mr Wang, indicating the dunes around of them.

"Uh-huh," said Malone. There was a pause, then he added: "This is why I wanted to travel like this; I wouldn't have seen *that* from a plane."

He was musing on his situation, and wondered what his Masters in London would say. Actually, he had no need to speculate – he knew *exactly* what they would say. If there was any doubt at all, they would say, he should abandon his companions immediately and find alternative transport to Kashgar. *It isn't your job to have adventures*, they would tell him; *stay as safe and inconspicuous as possible.* Maintain a low profile. This is *not* your mission.

Malone smiled inwardly. He followed his instructions *almost* all of the time.

He also knew that, if anything were to happen, he could not go to the police. The last thing that London wanted was for him to get tied up with Chinese officialdom.

And, in a curious way, he even had some sympathy for Mr Wang and Mr Li – *if* they were planning to rob him. For them, a Westerner was like a millionaire, with a living standard they could only dream of. Westerners were fair game. His suspicions were hardening; there were unmistakable signs, little whispers out of his earshot, glances and barely concealed smirks when they thought he wasn't looking.

Ten hours of bone-jarring driving further on, they arrived on the surface of the moon, a vast undulating landscape of small black stones, with wild wind-sculpted rock outcrops. There wasn't a blade of grass or a tree in sight, and no birds in the sky. This was the fearsome Gobi Desert. At six o'clock in the morning, Malone's shirt was soaked through with sweat. He felt a nagging sense of unease. He began to wonder if, perhaps, he had come *too far*.

And now there was something else to notice. The faces of the people sweltering in their little settlements under the cloudless sky, had changed.

They were no longer *Han* Chinese. The women wore headscarves and brightly coloured clothes, with zigzag designs reminiscent of the Uzbeks and the men wore dull blue shirts. These were the Uyghurs (pronounced *Wee-Ghurrs*), a Muslim Turkic people, They had entered the province of Xinjiang. For Malone, it was another of the enigmas of this extraordinary country; you travel deep enough into China, and it wasn't even Chinese anymore.

Now the hardest part of the journey began. Mr. Wang turned for Korla, and so along the northern road beside the great Taklamakan Desert, a 600 mile long burning basin of sandy nothing, bounded at the northern edge by the Tian Shan, the Heavenly Mountains, to the south by the peaks of Kunlun Shan range.

Now, more than ever, Malone needed to be on his guard. Here, all they had to do was to abandon him, without water, somewhere off the road – in this heat, no-one would survive for more than a day or so. He was starting to feel vulnerable.

That night, Mr Li and Mr Wang seemed even less talkative than usual, as if they had come to a decision. They barely spoke or looked at him as they ate and prepared for sleep. *Right*, thought Malone, no longer doubting his instincts, so *this* is it.

Malone carried no weapons. For a foreigner to be arrested in China with such things was suicidal. He would have to rely on his wits.

He bedded down beneath the truck, lying on his sleeping bag, the hard sandy earth beneath him. He positioned himself close to the prop shaft, using it as a barrier from one side, so that anyone coming at him would have to approach from the outer edge of the truck.

People talk about *sleeping with one eye open* but this was nonsense. Animals, however, can sleep and listen, alert to sound – *with one ear open -* and Malone had trained himself to do the same. He had also collected five big steel bolts, which he built into an unstable little pile and covered with a spare shirt, hoping that anyone crawling under the truck would disturb them, giving him a moment's warning.

He slept.

Something woke him just after two a.m. He kept his eyes closed, senses stretching into the darkness, trying to imagine what was happening. He had heard a footstep, the creaking of a knee, someone breathing nearby.

There! The tiny '*clink*' of his little pyramid of bolts collapsing. A change in the air, the unmistakable smell of sweat, another human being close by. He opened his eyes. A shadowy figure was reaching out towards him.

He shot out a hand and grasped Mr Li's wrist in a grip like a steel trap. Mr Li cried out in pain – and Malone took advantage of the moment to lash out with his boot, taking the Chinese on the side of his skull.

Malone jack-knifed his body and slithered out into the open, still grasping Mr Li's wrist. He pulled sharply, hauling the Chinese out from under the truck. In the moonlight, he could see the knife that was still in Mr Li's other hand - he stamped hard on the fingers and reached down to grab the weapon. The Chinese rolled onto his back, so Malone planted a well-aimed kick into his groin. Mr Li doubled up, moaning in pain. He was out of the fight.

Panting, Malone turned around to square up to Mr Wang. The heavy-set Chinese was watching from ten yards away, his expression one of horrified uncertainty. In his hand he held a tyre iron, but loosely, without conviction. Malone glared at him, then spun the knife into the air and caught it one-handed.

"Come *on*," he said.

Mr Wang didn't move.

"Well?" demanded Malone, shifting his weight from foot to foot. His blood was up. Part of him *wanted* the big Chinese to attack.

Mr Wang looked from Malone to his companion, writhing on the floor, then back to Malone. He shook his head. *No.*

"I warned you," said Malone, grinning mirthlessly, "There are no *soft men* where I come from."

Mr Wang dropped the tyre iron. It fell to the sand with an audible crunch.

"Then, this is finished," said Malone. "You had better attend to your friend. I imagine that he'll live."

Mr Wang nodded.

"I'll keep the knife, I think," said Malone. "And this never happened, right?"

"No, it never happened," said Mr Wang, shaking his head sadly.

In the morning, they resumed their journey westwards. Mr Li had a livid bruise on the side of his head and his left hand was purple. He moved carefully and avoided Malone's eye.

Getting into the cab of the truck, Malone had to assist him up the step.

When they were seated, he reached across and examined the Chinese's damaged hand. Mr Li winced but did not protest. Malone felt the joints carefully, nodded and commented: "Nothing broken. You'll be okay." Then he sat back and watched the landscape roll out ahead of them.

The only way to get from the east end of the Taklamakan to the west (and so to the mountain passes that lead to Tajikistan and Kyrgyzstan and the outside world) is to choose one of two roads, one to the northern edge of the desert, one on the southern, at the foot of the mountains. For millennia, these roads had been travelled by merchants with their mules and their donkeys and their caravan trains and the roads existed for one reason; at the foot of the mountains, fed by the rainfall off the upper slopes, there was occasional water to be found.

In the Taklamakan, water is more precious than gold.

And, at the spot where these two ancient roads converged, at the very western end of the desert, stood Kashgar, the great teeming Oasis city, the gateway to China for over two thousand years. If this is not the end of the Earth, one could certainly see it from there.

They stopped the truck near the train station, and Malone alighted, hefting his bag across his shoulder. He politely handed the knife back to Mr Li, nodded a farewell to Mr Wang.

He had arrived.